STRANGERS
in the LAND of
EGYPT

STRANGERS
in the LAND of
EGYPT

Stephen March

THE PERMANENT PRESS
Sag Harbor, NY 11963

For information, address:
   The Permanent Press
   4170 Noyac Road
   Sag Harbor, NY 11963
   www.thepermanentpress.com

Library of Congress Cataloging-in-Publication Data

   March, Stephen
      Strangers in the land of Egypt / Stephen March.
         p. cm.
      ISBN-13: 978-1-57962-185-8 (alk. paper)
      ISBN-10: 1-57962-185-6 (alk. paper)
         1. Juvenile delinquents—Fiction. 2. Holocaust survivors—Fiction..
      3. Loss (Psychology)—Fiction. 4. Revenge—Fiction. 5. Faith—Fiction.
      6. Spirituality—Fiction. 7. Psychological fiction. I. Title.

   PS3613.A733S77 2009
   813'.6—dc22   2008050366

Printed in the United States of America.

For Julian and Leland

ACKNOWLEDGEMENTS

Thanks to Rabbi John Friedman, Mary March, and Marty and Judith Shepard for perceptive and helpful editorial comments; and to Susan Ahlquist and Rania Haditirto for patient and conscientious copy editing.

Now there is at Jerusalem by the sheep market a pool, which is called in the Hebrew tongue Bethesda, having five porches. In these lay a great multitude of impotent folk, of blind, halt, withered, waiting for the moving of the water. For an angel went down at a certain season into the pool, and troubled the water: whosoever then first after the troubling of the water stepped in was made whole of whatsoever disease he had.

—John: 5:2-5

~ PART I ~

CHAPTER 1

The old goblin moon was perched on an oak limb outside my window, wearing a wig of Spanish moss. I walked the floor, my blood on fire. When G.T.'s alarm clock went off by mistake in his room, I jumped straight up like a man trying to escape his skin. I sat on my bed, aimed my rifle at the pockmarked moon. *Click, click, click.* It was one of those nights when you want to tear something up.

I was catching a breeze on the front steps when these Pottstown boys, Mick, Bone, and Skeeter, came over with a blunt and a bottle of Mad Dog wine. We sat on the edge of the porch and passed the joint around. Mick claimed it was pure Colombian but I could tell after one hit it was the same old homegrown. Still worked, though—slowed time down, made me feel like I was floating up there with the stars and that bad ass moon.

After we finished the wine we slipped on down to the B'nai Shalom Synagogue on East Harnett Street. Using a can of red paint he stole from K-Mart, Bone sprayed a swastika on the back wall, then Mick and I kicked in the back door. We went through a hallway, Mick shining his flashlight around, and turned left into the sanctuary, a big room with a cathedral ceiling. There were no pews and no altar, just rows of chairs and a platform near the back wall. A flame burned in a lamp high on the back wall above a cabinet. Brass light fixtures hung from the ceiling, with branches holding slim, unlit bulbs.

I said, "They don't let men and women sit together."

"Got something to do with their periods maybe," Mick said.

"Kikes," Bone said. "Ought to go back where they come from."

"They don't come from any one place," Skeeter said. "They wander the world like gypsies."

"Israel is their home now." A part of my bad self was already standing back from this situation, frowning at what we were doing. *They never did anything to me,* I thought.

Mick shined his light at the table on the platform—at a bottle of dark red liquid and two glasses on a tray. "That's blood!"

"They sacrifice animals," Bone said, "Cut their throats and drink the blood."

I took out the glass plug, sniffed what was inside, and told them it was just wine. I took a swallow—it had a light, sweet taste. I passed the bottle to Mick. He took a drink, too, passed the bottle to Bone, who took a swig, then spit it out. "Ahhh! What if they put blood in there?"

"Won't hurt you, Bone," I said. "Build up your iron."

"I ain't no vampire."

Snatching the white cloth off the table, Mick threw it over his shoulders, then shook it out like he was a matador. Skeeter went after him, fingers pressed to his temples like a bull's horns, Mick pivoting with the tablecloth. After they got tired of playing matador and bull, Bone slashed the tablecloth into strips with his hawk bill knife. Skeeter picked up the tray and sailed it, spinning like a Frisbee, toward the cabinet. It bounced off the wall and hit the floor with a clatter. We passed the bottle around again. Mick chugged what was left, then hurled the empty bottle against the wall. I heard it shatter. I shined the light on the floor. The broken pieces sparkled like slivers of ice.

We went back to the cabinet. A metal plate above the lamp had strange letters on it, an inscription. Mick asked what kind of writing it was.

"Looks like chicken scratches," Bone said. "Wonder what's in the cabinet?"

"Jewels maybe," said Skeeter. "Or gold. Let's break it open."

"No need to do that," I said, pointing to the key in the lock.

Skeeter turned the key and pulled the door open by the handle. Inside there were some fancy scrolls on wooden rollers, each one tied with ribbon and covered with a velvet cloth. A strip of bronze-colored metal was attached to the scrolls with string. Bone picked up one of the scrolls, pulled off the cloth, the shield, and the ribbon, then unrolled the scroll. It was thick, heavy paper. Something from another time. "This ain't English either." He unrolled more of the scroll, then threw the whole thing on the floor.

Skeeter and I threw the wine glasses at the light fixtures, trying to knock one of the candles out. The glasses broke against the ceiling. I ducked to keep from getting hit by the falling pieces.

"Where do they kill the animals?" Mick asked.

We were looking around for their sacrificial altar when I saw a circle of light moving over the wall behind us. I looked out the front window, saw a cop car parked out front. "Five-O!"

We were out the back door, scattering like buckshot.

I heard a shout, saw a light off to my right. I plunged through the hedges in back, jumped a low wood fence, and hit the alley. I was flying but whoever was after me stayed right on my ass, close enough for me to hear him breathing.

A cop car turned into the end of the alley, blue light flashing. Damn, I was cut off!

I swerved to the right and climbed over the wooden privacy fence around the coin man's yard, knowing his Rottweiler was in there on a fifteen-foot chain. Dropping to the ground, I stayed close to the back fence, just out of its reach. I heard it growling, heard its jaws snap shut. Cop followed me over the fence, only he didn't know about the dog or have any sense of its limitations due to the chain. I heard him cry out as the dog got him. I leaped over the side fence, tumbled, rolled, and then I was on my feet, running, thinking I'd pulled a Houdini. But somebody slammed into me from behind, taking me down. He had me on my face, arms twisted around behind my back. He pounded the back of my head. A flash bulb went off in my brain and I had the sensation of falling backwards into black empty space.

Then voices, as if from a distance.

"Looks like he's out cold."

"Read 'em to him anyway. I'm a witness."

"You have the right to remain silent . . ." The voice floated in and out of my mind, like a will-o-the-wisp. Cuffs on too tight for me to move my arms.

They got on either side of me and yanked me to my feet. My whole head felt like I had been beat with a ball peen hammer.

I was quiet as I stumbled to the squad car, a cop holding me by the back of my belt.

Lieutenant Dopodja, moon-faced with a big Arabian nose, wore these tinted glasses that get dark in sunlight. They were dark now due to the bright light in the interrogation room. He sat across from me at the table. Sergeant Rizzo, his ace assistant, sat to his left, taking notes on a pad while Dopodja told me what I was charged with—breaking and entering, destruction of property, resisting arrest, and assault on an officer. "You're looking at three to five in Sheridan, Terrill. You're what—sixteen? That means you could be locked up 'til you're twenty-one. Want to make it easy on yourself? Tell us who was with you. Testify against them, and we'll ask the D.A. to go easy on you—might even get you probation. What do you say?"

"Told you I was alone."

"Don't give me that bullshit. At least three other boys came out of that synagogue with you. Hoffler and Jenkins ran them down to Cedar Street but they got away. You had the misfortune to get Nolan, a state champion in track."

Looks to me like he had some bad luck, too, I thought, remembering the way the dog got him. Man who lived there owned the coin shop on Griffin Street. Took that Rottweiler on a chain to work every morning as protection against robbers. Dog stayed behind a high counter, topped with bullet-proof glass. Coin man did his business through a slat in the glass.

As if he was a mind reader, Dopodja said, "By the way, that was a cute trick you pulled running through the yard with the dog. Nolan is in the ER right now. He's going to need a tetanus shot. Know who's going to pay his bill?"

I shrugged. Like I really gave a shit.

"The taxpayers. That have any meaning to you?"

I looked down at the red marks the cuffs left on my wrists. My head ached from front to back. I wished I was home in bed.

"They are the decent, law-abiding citizens. Not the vermin—drug dealers, freaks, thugs, whores, gangbangers, bikers, and thieves. The tax-payers are responsible for the streets you drive on, the schools you go to. They make a positive contribution to society. But you wouldn't know about that, would you?"

Dopodja's voice had a high whine in it, like a dentist's drill. If I had it I would have given him twenty dollars just to shut up.

Rizzo put down his pen and got up so close in my face I could smell his garlicky breath.

"Terrill, if you give us the names of those other perps, it's going to make the rest of your pathetic life a whole lot easier."

"Didn't see anybody else. Too dark."

"Bullshit."

Rizzo and Dopodja were the precinct's juvenile cops. They cruised the streets in a navy blue Crown Victoria. A month earlier Skeeter and I had stuck an ice pick in their back tires when their car was parked down the street from Nick's Café. Rizzo and Dopodja were in there sucking down pie and coffee and coming on to Mimi, the waitress, all on the tax-payers' dime.

Dopodja said, "You want to play hardball? Straight up, Terrill. You don't give us those names I'm going to talk to the DA and the judge about you. I'm going to make sure you get sent to Sheridan 'til you're twenty-one. Know what those gangbangers are going to do with you? Going to make you into their sweetheart."

"You'll be some stud's bitch," Rizzo said.

"Ain't nobody going to mess with me that way."

"You'll be hollering for your mama."

"You're dreaming, too."

"Punk." Rizzo smelled blood. "Mama's boy."

My mama's long gone, fool. My heart was knocking around in my chest like an engine that's thrown a rod.

Dopodja jabbed his finger in my face. "Terrill, you know how many bad-ass wannabes like you I've seen? I couldn't even count them all. Know where most of them end up? In the morgue with a bullet in the brainpan or up in Sheridan where the days run together like gutted chickens on a conveyor belt."

"I've got nothing else to say."

"Officer Rizzo, take this perp over to the jail."

Rizzo stood up. "Let's go, Terrill."

"Put him in with the drunk."

Rizzo cuffed us together, then took me through the side door of the police station, down the walkway to the jail next door. It was a two-story building, bricks the color of dried blood. Walk by the back section during the day and the inmates call to you from the cells on the second floor.

We went up the concrete steps. At the top Rizzo rang a buzzer. A slat in the metal door slid open and two blue eyeballs peered out. Then the door opened, and Rizzo and I stepped in to a hallway that led back to a room. Jailer was a fat, bald man wearing Army pants and a T-shirt spotted with grease stains. "Evening, Sergeant," he said, in this high, sweet voice. "Who've you brought me now?"

"Jesse Terrill," Rizzo said. "Lieutenant Dopodja said put him with the wino they brought in earlier."

"Come on in," he sang out. "Plenty of room at this inn."

Rizzo unlocked the cuffs, and the fat man led me through a door into a room off to the left, where there was a desk with a computer on it, a chair, and TV on a stand. On the desk was a paper plate piled high with chicken bones and a cigarette in an ashtray. Jailer told me to empty out my pockets on the desk and take off my belt. Dopodja had already poked through my things. I lay down my wallet, key ring, good luck charm, comb, and coins on the desk, along with my belt. Jailer put them in a plastic bag, wrote my name on a tag, attached it to the bag, and put it in a drawer. Then him and Rizzo took me back to that front room. There was another door at the far end—opposite the hallway—a barred door beyond that. The jailer unlocked the barred door and we entered a corridor lit by a bare bulb hanging from the ceiling. A wall with barred windows to the right, cells to the left. We passed two empty cells. Jailer unlocked the third cell, and Rizzo pushed me inside, slammed the barred door shut. As they walked back toward the front, I heard Rizzo telling the jailer about how the man who lived next to the synagogue had called to report there were "gangsters and hooligans loose in the . . ."—the steel door at the end of the hall clanged shut before I could hear the rest of the sentence.

I leaned against the bars, my bones heavy with the weight of my own evil, and thought about my phone call to my uncle G.T., the way he kept asking me questions I didn't know how to answer, like why I had left the house without telling him where I was going.

All I could think to say was, "I'm sorry, G.T."

Like that really helped.

The old man's breath came rasping from the bottom bunk. He had snow-white hair and whiskers, scrawny, wasted arms. His eyes were closed, his mouth open. The single tooth in his bottom gum was the color of a banana gone bad. Besides the bunk there was a sink, a stained toilet with no lid. Place smelled nasty—a mixture of piss, sweat, vomit, mildew, and whatever rotgut wine the old man had been drinking, coming out of his breath and skin. An unlit bulb dangled from the ceiling by an electric cord.

I put my foot in the bars, climbed up to the top bunk, lay down on the raggedy mattress, looked at the writing on the walls and ceiling, mostly crude black lettering done with the carbon from matches. Prisoners holding them in their fingers long enough to trace out a letter, then lighting another one, writing their messages with smoke. Names. Dates. Right above me on the ceiling I read, Hell is just a state of mind.

The wino moaned in his sleep. "Lila. Lila, baby."

I wondered who Lila was, if she would even care about this wreck of a man with his lonesome brown tooth.

A dream woman, maybe. Someone who lived only in his head.

Putting me in with the wino was Dopodja's way of punishing me for not giving up the names of my boys. Word on the street was he wanted to be chief. That's why he was so gung-ho to clean up the precinct. He was on a campaign to rid the city of all the undesirables, rejects, and misfits. So far that year he'd already busted Wink Sanders and Trey Blivins, sent them to the state reformatory at Sheridan. I heard all about that place. They shave your head and throw you in solitary if you break the rules. You can scream till your voice is gone but nobody hears you. Guards are Dobermans, too. They held Trey down and stomped on his hand because he wouldn't work, then claimed "unknown" inmates did it to him. Trey has never been right since. Can't make a fist. I didn't want to get sent there but there was no way I was going to drop a dime on my boys.

They will be passing out crucifixes in hell first.

Dopodja made me nervous. I had this idea he might shoot me, then throw a gun with a missing serial number down by my dead self and claim self-defense. Wouldn't be any way I could tell what happened. If you could testify from the other side, courtrooms would be packed from here to Tibet.

I looked at the ceiling and thought of the prisoners who had written their names and messages up there with fire. I remembered reading this article once about a cave with paintings on the walls from more than thirty thousand years ago—images of saber-toothed tigers, bison, deer, birds, a sorcerer. Those cave artists had to crawl down through a tunnel just to get to the cave, and they worked down there by firelight, using paint made from materials they got from the earth. I tried to picture people living that long ago, with no cars, no electricity, no shopping malls. Just trees, rivers, sky, caves, and animals. I wondered what their lives were like, what they dreamed about. What were they were thinking when they painted those mysterious pictures on the earth's rocky heart?

My uncle G.T. bailed me out of jail next day, just before noon.

As we walked out of the jail, he was silent and scowling. We climbed into his truck, which had *Terrill's Roofing Co.* painted on the doors. A laminated picture of a blonde in a bikini dangled from the rearview mirror. Rosalita, his girlfriend, said it gave his truck "a trashy look." Picture came with the truck, G.T. told her. He can be hardheaded sometimes.

We passed a hamburger joint. Smelling those burgers reminded me of how hungry I was. At first light a trustee had slid two bowls of cold, lumpy oatmeal through a slat in the cell. No milk or sugar, plus snaggletooth had puked on the floor. Who could eat in a place like that?

"Jesse," G.T. said. "What in the hell are you doing vandalizing a Jewish temple?"

"I'm sorry, G.T."

"That means about as much as the wind that blows out of a rat's ass."

I sighed, rubbed my temples, wondered if some food in my belly would ease my aching head. I had a big knot back there from where the cop hit me. I wondered what he used. A blackjack maybe.

"Who else was with you?"

"Just some Pottstown kids."

"Yeah, who?"

"You don't know them."

"How come you're the only one to get caught?"

"Cop chasing me used to run track."

"Not only an ignoramus but unlucky, too."

Touching the good luck charm in my pocket, I remembered Dopodja's threat to send me to Sheridan until I was twenty-one. Which would mean I might never get to see Angela Salazar again. She'd go away to college, get married, and I would lose touch with her for good. I pictured her oval face, her brown eyes, her shiny black hair, her red lips that looked like they were just made for kissing, and I wished I'd turned the light out when my boys came over, pretended I wasn't home.

Now look at the mess I am in.

I saw a yellow arch just ahead. "Hey, G.T., you think maybe we could stop and get some lunch somewhere? I'm kind of hungry."

"I'll bet you are. Hell-raiser such as yourself ought have to have worked up a bodacious appetite."

I couldn't really blame G.T. for being pissed. I figured I would open a can of soup and make a sandwich when we got home. Maybe by then my headache would be gone.

G.T.'s given name was Galen Thomas, but most everybody called him G.T. I used to think that was because he didn't like his name, but my daddy told me G.T. couldn't pronounce his name when he was a little kid so he just abbreviated it. Anyway, the nickname stuck. G.T. had a deep tan, with crow's feet around his eyes, which were smoky gray like mine. He worked on roofs all day in sun, wind, and rain. Ran his business out of a shop downtown on East Market. He had a part-time bookkeeper and two Mexicans to help him, cousins named Carlos and Ricardo. They lived in a three-room apartment with four other men to save expenses. Sent most of their money back home to their families in Guadalajara.

I used to work for him during the school year, too, but that job ended last year after I flunked algebra. G.T. said I needed to spend more time studying. Now I just help him out in the summer.

I'd been living with G.T. since my daddy went to stay at St. Aubin Hospital, three years earlier. We lived in G.T.'s white frame house on Rose of Sharon Road, across from the pet casket factory, in a section of the city called Pottstown. G.T. had bought the house and land two years earlier, after his divorce went through. House had a one-way ticket to ruination when he bought it, floorboards rotting through on the front porch, a leaking roof, bugs and mice running around like they owned the house. G.T. and I cleaned it out, replaced the roof, painted all the rooms, replaced the bathroom and kitchen fixtures, and bought all new appliances and furniture. By the time we got finished improving the place it was right good and decent. I often dreamed of having a place of my own like that someday.

Pottstown got its nickname from old John Potts, who founded the cotton mill on Asbury Street, three blocks east of Oleander, back in 1920. At one time the mill had over three hundred employees, but it had less than a hundred now. John Potts built most of the houses in the neighborhood around the mill as rental units for his employees—two or three bedroom one-bath houses all constructed on the same basic design. At one time Pottstown was outside the city limits but the city had grown out this way over the years and now Oleander was cluttered with gas stations, 7-Elevens, pizzerias, pawn shops, bars, tattoo parlors, and strip malls. The road we lived on, Rose of Sharon, was one of the few remaining gravel roads left in the city. It was also the shortest, being only a block long. A block east of Oleander, it ran from Jessup on the south of us to Sheffield. When you drove down our road, it was almost like you were back in the country again. If you came from Jessup there were woods on either side of the road, pines and hardwoods, then on the right you would see a field owned by our neighbor on the right, Hoagie Ambrose, who was retired from Norfolk Southern Railway. His place was on the left, a single story, white frame house like ours. In the spring and early summer, Hoagie planted corn, tomatoes, squash, beans, and watermelons in front of his house and in his lot across the road. Gladstone and Son, Pet Casket, Inc. owned the land directly across from us. Past the pet casket factory there were more woods on either side of the road, a few houses, then Sheffield, which went up to Oleander.

Although you'd never know it to hear him talk, G.T. raised seven different kinds of hell when he was growing up. At nineteen he had a black, turbocharged Trans Am that could outrun any cop car in three counties. One summer he flipped it three times in a field while trying to outrun a state trooper. Cost him his license for two years but he walked away

- 19 -

from the wreck with some bruises, sprains, and a cracked collarbone. That winter he broke a bouncer's jaw after the guy kicked his friend Buddy McBane in the balls. Bouncer was supposed to be some kind of champion kick boxer, but his feet weren't fast enough for G.T. One of the cops who came to arrest G.T. thumped his head with a flashlight, for no good reason that my uncle could see. G.T. KO'd the cop with a right cross and spent six months in the county jail for assault. Cop had to get his jaw wired shut. After G.T. got out of jail it took him almost two years to pay off all the money he owed for lawyers, fines, and medical bills. But he didn't stay down, because, as he will tell you himself, this is the U.S. of A., land of hope and opportunity. He enlisted in the Army on his twenty-second birthday, which gave him the opportunity to get out of Pottstown, see the world, and save up enough money to start his roofing business when he came back home three years later. Roofing work was good to G.T. He worked hard and eventually became a successful businessman. He owned his roofing business, his house plus two and a quarter acres, a retirement account, and a bag of twenty-dollar gold pieces in a metal security box he had buried behind the shed. He had the gold pieces in case the America haters were ever able to set off an A-bomb in Washington DC, which he said would make paper money "worth less than a wheelbarrow full of ashes." My mama used to claim G.T. was unlucky, but compared to Daddy and my aunt Lynette, G.T. was not doing so bad in the luck department that I could see. Lynette lived in Bat Forks, a little town in the mountains. Taught her two kids at home. They had no TV, CD player, or radio—she claimed they are controlled by "Satan's minions." She and her husband and their two kids attended a church that uses copperheads and rattlers in the service. Lynette tried to get me to go to that church one time, but I was like, "No way." Last preacher they had got bit in the lip. Watermelon head spent three days dying. Refused medical help the whole time. Claimed his faith in Jesus would cure him.

Lot of good his faith did him. Trouble with Jesus is he never seems to be around when you need Him. Maybe He did do all those miracles—raise the dead, walk on water, multiply the loaves and fishes, come back from the other side. I wasn't there so I couldn't say. But I did know one thing: if I had to kiss a copperhead to get saved, I'd take my chances with the Devil.

I woke up to the aroma of Rosalita's tortillas. I put on my pants and shirt and went down the hall to the bathroom, where I brushed my teeth and combed my hair.

Rosalita was sitting at the kitchen table, sipping coffee from a mug. She has chestnut-colored eyes and hair, big strong teeth, skin the color of honey. She was wearing one of G.T.'s white T-shirts.

"Morning, Jesse. You have good dreams?

"Sure. Dreamed I was *muy rico.*"

"You can make that dream come true with hard work."

"Right, hard work will really get you somewhere. Hard worker moves at the speed of light."

"You might try giving it a chance."

There was a stack of freshly made tortillas on a plate beside the coffee pot on the counter, along with a bowl of batter and the tortilla press she used to make them fresh. Chicken strips cooking slow in the iron skillet.

I poured some coffee into a mug and sat down across from her. She leaned back in the chair, and I could see her nipples outlined under the thin cotton. "Oooo, I'm so sore," she said. "That G.T."

"What you all do together is your business."

"FYI, he took me dancing last night."

"Didn't know G.T. could dance."

"G.T. is a wild man on the dance floor. Rock and roll, baby."

"That's a side of G.T. I've never seen."

"You look at an apple, you only see one side. Got to turn it all around to see every part of it."

"That what you do with G.T?"

"What do you think?"

"I can't see into a woman's mind, Rosalita. Be like trying to see all the little fishes way down on the bottom of the sea."

"You're not too old to learn. When you going to get a steady girl, Jesse?"

"I'm too young for a ball and chain."

"Oh, horse dookey. If you had a girlfriend you wouldn't be getting in so much trouble, mister walking stick of dynamite."

"You smell something burning?"

Rosalita got up and went to the stove. I stole a look at her ass in her tight denim shorts. Curved and firm as an apple.

"G.T. hates it when his food is burnt," I said.

"It's just right, FYI." With a fork she took the chicken strips out of the skillet, put them on paper plates on the counter. "How many eggs you want?"

"Two."

"Hand me the carton out of the fridge."

I got them for her. She began cracking them into the skillet.

I sat down at the table and thought about how nice it would be to have a woman come over and spend the night with me. Someone I could hold close and talk to, the way G.T. did to her. Rosalita left her two kids at her aunt's house when she came to see G.T. She had two little ones, a boy and a girl. Their daddy, Estaban, died three years earlier in a construction accident. He was working down in a pit and the earth caved in on him. Rosalita didn't date at all until she met G.T. She met him when he was putting a roof on the carpet and tile store she worked at over on Tull Street. At first they only saw each other once in a while, but it wasn't long before she began spending most every Saturday night at our house. They only got together on weekends. G.T. said he liked it that way. When he and his wife Michelle split up five years earlier she got custody of their daughters, Dawn and Saxon. Michelle married a football coach and they moved to Phoenix. G.T. sent his ex-wife child support checks every month, but he hardly ever saw his daughters. I knew for a fact that this grieved him even though he only talked about it when he had been putting down Coronas. G.T. isn't one to let you see a hurt place.

Watching Rosalita, I pictured Angela Salazar in my bed. Her black eyes and shiny hair. Her red lips. I imagined her wearing my shirt, what she might look like underneath. My heart kicked into overdrive.

"Go tell your uncle that breakfast is ready."

I went back through the living room, took a left down the hall to G.T.'s room. Pounding on the door I called out, "Hey, G.T., boss lady says it's time to eat." It bugged him when I called Rosalita his boss, which is why I liked to do it, even though I know any man would be lucky to have her in his life.

By the time G.T. got into the kitchen Rosalita and I had the table set—eggs on one plate, tortillas stuffed with chicken strips, salsa, black beans, and grated cheese on a bigger one. Using a food processor she pureed the salsa from tomatoes, herbs, and spices. There was coffee and a pitcher of orange juice, too. I sat across from Rosalita. G.T. sat at the head of the table. Red-eyed, hair messed up, hands nicked, scabbed and scarred from working on roofs.

I reached for a tortilla but Rosalita stopped me. "Jesse, could you please wait until I ask the blessing?"

Sometimes she prayed in Spanish, a musical language that poured over me like warm honey even though I could only understand a little of it. Today, however, she prayed in English, asked God to bless her two children and all her relatives. She called each one by name—brothers, sisters, uncles, parents, grandparents, second and third cousins. I usually tried to put my mind in neutral during these sessions, but being really hungry this morning, I couldn't help but get impatient. I looked out the window, at two hummingbirds hovering in the air by the feeder Rosalita had hung out there. Hurry up, girl, I thought. Damn, you must be related to half the people in Mexico.

Rosalita ended her prayer by asking the Holy Virgin to watch over me so I would stay out of trouble. For whatever that was worth.

As I chewed my tortilla I wondered if all that whoop-dee-doo about the virgin birth was just a story somebody dreamed up a long time ago, a story that got told so often people started believing it was true. How could you ever know for sure? Only person who could answer that question would be Mary herself and her phone number wasn't listed.

After we ate and got the dishes washed, Rosalita and G.T. went back to his bedroom, where I could soon hear her giggling. When they got going good back there she really cut loose, screamed and talked dirty. Guess she figured the Virgin Mary wasn't listening then. Under the hair dryer maybe.

Time for me to give the lovebirds some space. I got my .22 Magnum rifle and a box of shells from my closet and went outside to see if I could crank up G.T.'s '63 Dodge truck. He only let me drive it on weekends, during daylight hours. Which was fine with me because it would be no good for dating anyway. The Dodge was parked in front of the shed, Amos the peacock sitting on the hood. Spiderweb cracks in the windshield, the bed eaten up with rust. Rings and bearings about to give up the ghost. Burned a quart of oil every hundred miles. I rubbed Amos's head, then got into the truck, turned the key in the ignition. It started on the third try, but Amos just sat there as I revved up the engine.

"Amos," I said, "You ain't going for ride. Get off of there."

He stood up, fanning his iridescent green and blue tail like a magician spreading a hand of cards.

"You're real pretty, dude. But I got to go. Now get down off of there."

He hopped down to the ground and strutted around the yard, pecking at the ground like he was trying to tell me he was hungry, although I had given him a big meal just last night. A mixture of cracked corn and dry cat food. We kept a bag of it in the shed.

I eased the Dodge onto Rose of Sharon and turned left onto Jessup. It was a block up to Oleander. My destination was the old city dump on Cotton Gin Road, south of the city. I took Oleander all the way out to the bypass, took the Herring Road exit. Past the city limit sign, I turned right onto Bethea Church, then took the right fork onto Cotton Gin Road, a two-lane blacktop that ran through a country of red clay fields and swamp, pines and cypress trees growing in pools of gunmetal-colored water. I passed tin roofed shanties with junk cars outside, the Assembly of God Church, where my mama used to take my brother Lee and me on Sundays, a graveyard, a warehouse, and an abandoned oil refinery. G.T. said lead and arsenic had seeped into the ground water from the oil refinery. I wondered what kind of effect this would have on the people who live out here, especially the little kids. Maybe make their heads turn green and glow in the dark.

Our old house was six miles out this road but I didn't want to go there. Didn't even know who lived there now. A half-mile or so past the railroad tracks, I turned off onto the gravel road leading back to the old dump. A few years earlier the county had closed it down and opened up a landfill north of the city, but people still brought their trash here. There was a chain link fence around the dump and a locked gate, but they threw their junk and trash over it. As I pulled up to the fence, I saw a shiny new lock on the gate. The really serious dumpers, the ones with industrial waste in fifty-gallon drums, came at night and cut the locks with bolt cutters, but some fool kept replacing them—about like putting a paper mache chastity belt on a streetwalker.

A twisted metal sign, shot full of holes, was attached to the fence: *No trespassing. Violators will be prosecuted.*

I parked the truck by the front gate. Hooking the rifle's sling on my shoulder, I climbed the fence and dropped down between a commode and two black trash bags. Plastic cups and spoons spilled out from holes in the sides. I wondered how long it takes plastic to decompose. Some of that junk was liable to be here long after the people who threw it away had been eaten by worms.

The dump was a wasteland of bottles, cans, mattresses, sofas, chairs, stoves, refrigerators, and rusted fifty-gallon drums. Somebody had bulldozed big mounds of the trash into piles, then covered them with dirt. Clouds of fat green flies buzzed everywhere. I walked between the mounds, looking at the junk. A wheelchair, its rims sunk into the red clay. A naked GI Joe leaning back in the chair, his right fist raised in a black power salute. A TV with the tube broke out so you could see the transistors and wires inside. A pair of plastic glasses with springs attached to fake eyeballs on top. I remembered coming out here with my brother Lee, back before the fence was put up. We found bicycles, lawnmowers, TVs, toasters, even a Civil War musket. It's amazing what people will throw away. Once Lee and I found a moldy canvas bag full of silver dollars. I still had some of them in a cardboard box under my bed, along with the postcards and letters Lee wrote me from Parris Island, Quantico, and Italy, a locket my mama owned, my daddy's sharpshooter's badge and dog tags from when he was in the Marines, a photo of all of us at Disney World, and a pencil that Angela Salazar had given me last spring in health class. I had borrowed it for a test, and when I tried to give it back to her she smiled and told me to keep it. Big true heart in that girl. Face of an angel. At night I held my pillow, whispered her name.

I picked up a busted rocking chair and carried it on into the dump, set it down beside a weed-covered mound. From there, I had a clear view of a couple of acres of trash and weeds. I sat on the chair, slipped seven shiny rounds into the magazine. I inserted it into the bottom of the rifle, jacked a round into the chamber, and flipped off the safety.

My finger resting on the trigger guard, I studied the scene: the mounds of dirt, the cans and bottles, the piles of junk surrounded by weeds. Off to the right was a black 1950 Ford with empty headlight sockets, its bumper a chrome grin. A field of chest-high green corn beyond the chain link fence. A buzzard sailed against the clouds. I came out here to get away from my troubles, but they hung around like stray cats. I couldn't stop thinking about the possibility of getting sent to Sheridan, about how everyone at Washington High would react to the news about me getting busted for trashing a synagogue. Probably knock me down to the bottom of the social misfit scale, only a notch or two above Luther Bozeman, who got busted for molesting his little sister. The public revelation of my crime was a burdensome thing, but what could I do about it now? Give those Highland Park kids something to talk about.

Highland Park was a gated neighborhood northwest of Pottstown that G.T. called 'millionaire row.' Highland Park kids walked through the halls like they owned the whole school. Pass a Pottstown boy like me, their faces turned to stone.

I was distracted from thinking about them by the sight of a brown wharf rat slinking across the open space. Sleek and fat, he was about fifty yards away—a challenging target since he was in motion.

I led him just a little with the front sight, holding my breath, then squeezed the trigger as I exhaled. The rifle cracked, my shot was true. The rat jumped up in the air, then rolled over on his back, kicking his feet like he was trying to push off an invisible weight. His tail twitched a few times, then he lay still. I smelled the ammonium nitrate, saw a thin trail of smoke curlicue out the barrel. Sweat trickled down my face. I jacked another round into the chamber, waited for more rats to crawl out to see what all the excitement was all about.

High above the dump Mister Buzzard flew in a wide, lazy circle. Spirit-graceful, at home in the air.

CHAPTER 2

"You must like trouble, son," Mr. Jake Quittlebaum said. "Either that or it likes you."

G.T. and I were sitting across from Mr. Quittlebaum's desk, in his law office on East Market Street. He reminded me of a basset hound, with his sorrowful brown eyes and heavy jowls.

"How much is it going to cost me to keep his sorry ass out of Sheridan?" G.T. asked.

"You might have to mortgage the farm, Galen."

"Damn," G.T. said, shaking his head.

"This young man's nocturnal shenanigans have been featured on Channel Five and the front page of all the newspapers. Not only that, the wire services have picked up the story. That's the kind of world we live in now. A two-headed monkey is born down in Zimbabwe, and next day everybody knows about it. It's the age of information."

"This ain't the kind of information I want spread around."

"Bad news and strange occurrences are generally what folks are interested in, Galen. People are funny that way."

"What kind of chance has he got?"

"Hard to say. One thing he does have going for him is his age. We should be able to get his case tried in juvenile court, but even there it's all up to the judge." Mr. Quittlebaum focused his hound dog eyes on me. "Jesse, according to the police report you refused to reveal the names of the boys who were with you in that synagogue."

"That's right."

"As your attorney I strongly recommend that you consider changing your mind."

"Can't do that, sir."

Jake Quittlebaum heaved a big sigh, like he was carrying the weight of a sorrow too grand for words. "Son, the law as it is actually practiced is a pliable thing. Know what 'pliable' means?"

"Not exactly."

"To put it in relevant terms, it means you can work a deal. But if you're going to deal you got to have something to offer. And if you refuse to reveal the names of your confederates, you're a card shy of a straight."

I looked up at the law school diploma hanging in a frame behind his desk and wondered how long he had to go to college to earn that thing. Seems like I heard once a lawyer had to go to college seven years. I can't imagine someone staying in college that long. Who would pay their bills?

"Jesse, how many of your so-called friends would protect you if they were in the stewpot, with the fire stoked up below?"

I shrugged, patted my foot on the floor. A crow landed on the ledge outside his office and peered through the window. It cocked its head as if it was studying us.

"You know the DA is up for re-election soon," Mr. Quittlebaum said, drumming his fingers on the desk. "He's going to look at a boy like you and see a big golden egg of opportunity. That's bad timing for you. Good for him, though, if he can win the case."

"You think he can win?" I asked.

"We're going to do everything we can to see that he doesn't, son. Long as your uncle here has got the money, I got the time."

There was a rapping sound against the window. We all turned to look at the crow. It pecked the glass again.

"Jesus Christ," G.T. said, shaking his head. "Jesus H. Christ."

Rolling and tossing in bed, I listened to a hoot owl calling back in the trees. He was somewhere close by, probably in one of those oaks behind the shed. G.T. had more than an acre of woods. I wondered what an owl was doing this far from the country. Lost his way maybe, took a wrong turn somewhere. I remembered how Lee and I used to lie in bed and listen to the owls and peacocks calling. We had two peacocks and three peahens. At twilight, the peacocks would fly up into the trees and the males would holler to each other and to birds, too. "Ahhhhhh!" Sometimes it sounded like they were crying for help. "Hellllp." The peahens would holler "hell-oooo, hellooo." The males would talk to the owls, too, back and forth, sometimes for what seemed like half the night. On full moon nights the peacocks would set all the dogs to howling. During the day the peacocks wandered the yard and woods in back. We gathered their tail feathers and kept them in a vase by the door. When the peachicks hatched out, we kept them in a wire pen, to protect them from predators—hawks, foxes, and snakes, even dogs.

We used to go fishing in the creek behind our house, or in one of the nearby farm ponds. We would catch bream, bass, bluegill, shellcracker.

We would take them home, clean them, roll them in batter, and fry them in an iron skillet. On weekends, my daddy would barbecue steaks or chicken breasts on the grill and we would eat on the deck out back. After supper Mama would get out her guitar and she and my daddy would sing songs like "Darkness on the Delta," "Yellow Rose of Texas," "In The Sweet By and By," and "When The Roll Is Called Up Yonder."

Every year we planted a garden with squash, tomatoes, butter beans, corn, okra, onions, and watermelons. The land we lived on had a grape arbor and peach trees and a creek at the back. Each spring the air was fragrant with the scent of peach blossoms. One year my daddy built a tree house for us in a live oak in the woods behind the house. The tree house was about ten feet off the ground, with wooden slats on either side so we couldn't roll out. We could only get up there by climbing up this thick rope and after we got up we could pull the rope up after us, so nobody else could come up. We'd sit up there at night, eating peanut butter sandwiches, grapes, and peaches. Lee would point out the constellations—like the Big Dipper, Leo the Lion, the Archer, and Pegasus, the winged horse. He had learned about them from a book of stars. Sometimes he would tell me stories. He liked to talk about different girls he knew, all the things they had done together or were planning to do, but I knew those stories were generally either exaggerated or imagined. In truth, my brother Lee was always shy around girls. He didn't even have a regular girlfriend until his senior year in high school.

My mama wanted Lee to go to college, but he decided to be a Marine like our daddy, even though Daddy tried to talk him out of it. Lee finished boot camp and went to school in Quantico, Virginia. He ended up in Italy, guarding an American embassy. He sent us letters, postcards, and a snapshot of him standing in front of this fountain with an Italian girl he had met over there. In the photo Lee was wearing his dress uniform and the girl was wearing a white dress. One day while Lee was standing guard a man drove a car full of dynamite through the front gate. My brother never even had a chance to get a shot off before the driver set off the dynamite and blew up his own evil self and the car too. The explosion killed my brother, another Marine, three members of the embassy staff, and a mom and her two children, a boy and a girl. They were on the sidewalk in front of the embassy.

Everything changed after Lee got killed. We all curled up into ourselves, holding on to our grief. We didn't know how to talk about it, didn't know how to let it go. I would try to talk to my mama but her mind would be somewhere else. Mama and Daddy started arguing, both of them using the kind of words that leave wounds you can't see. Daddy started spending more and more time away at night. I'd wake up mornings and find him asleep on the couch. Looking back on that time, I wish I could have done something to bring them back together. It was like being in a boat that keeps springing leaks, but instead of trying to plug them, you just look off at the shore and pretend that nothing is wrong, that you aren't really in a sinking boat.

A year after Lee's funeral my mom took off for parts unknown with a car salesman named Curt Mosely. She left a note on the kitchen table:

> Glenn, I am leaving now don't try to follow me cause the love is gone and you know it in your heart. Jesse you be a good boy and stay out of trouble. I will contact you when I get settled. Love, Mama.

Someone told my daddy they were staying in a motel in Lurie, a town twenty miles south of here. Daddy went to Lurie and broke down the door of their motel room, but they had already gone. All he found was some empty beer bottles and KFC bags. He could smell my mama's perfume on the sheets.

For the first few months after she left, Mama used to call me, usually late at night. As time passed her calls got less frequent. If I asked her where she was, she would just say something like, "I'm job hunting in Florida," or "I'm on the road right now." The last couple of years before she left she worked as a cook and a waitress at Nick's Café in Pottstown. I've heard her say more than once if you can cook or wait tables you can find a job anywhere you go. I figured she was doing that kind of work now. I often thought about trying to find her, but I had no idea where to begin looking. She could have been anywhere. Sometimes at night when I was drifting off to sleep I would picture her waiting on a customer in a restaurant in some distant city. I would imagine her coming back to her room after her shift, taking off her shoes and rubbing her feet, the way she used to do when she worked at Nick's. In my reveries there would be photographs of Lee and me on her dresser.

The owl had stopped calling.

I was too wired to sleep. I kept thinking about Lee.

The driver was in a black Fiat. I didn't know all of the details but this is the way I pictured it. The man was driving toward Lee, and he was standing there in his neatly pressed Marine uniform and his white gloves, holding his rifle with the barrel pointed skyward, staring at the guy driving towards him while I was screaming a warning, "Lee, Lee, look out!" But he could never hear me, because I was in dream time and space, and he still can't hear me now.

The judge at my trial, a black lady named Ms. Myrtle Simms, sat high above the courtroom at a bench with sunburst designs on either side. Mr. Quittlebaum and I sat at a table to the judge's right. G.T. sat in the first row of the courtroom behind our table, along with Ms. Ermenta Rawls, the counselor from Washington High. The DA and his assistant were at a table to the judge's left, across from us. Rizzo and Dopodja and some other cops were in the row behind him. Directly behind them, filling up the second, third, and fourth rows were the Jews. Some of the men wore those funny little hats that just cover the backs of their heads. I wondered if they really did sacrifice animals, and, if so, how they got them, since they didn't look like people who would steal your pet. They were too well dressed. Maybe they hire it out, I thought. Pay some beamer ten bucks for each dog or cat he can steal. People's cats and dogs disappeared all the time in the city. You would see the fliers advertising rewards for lost pets on telephone poles, in store windows, and on bulletin boards in Food Lion and the Piggly Wiggly.

Two deputies stood on either side of the judge's bench. There were two more on either side of the doors to the courtroom, which was in a three-story granite courthouse on Main Street, one block east of the jail. A bailiff stood down front. The court recorder sat at a small table to the right of the judge's bench, near the witness stand.

The district attorney, Sidney Knapp, had blow-dried hair and a jaw that my mama would have called "chiseled." Although he looked like he just stepped out of a soap opera, he sounded like a man talking with a clothespin clamped over his nose. When my trial began, he started off by telling the judge how I had desecrated the B'nai Shalom Temple "with malice and forethought," by painting a Nazi symbol on the back wall, by breaking the Jews' sacred cups, and by damaging their holy writing. He said I refused to reveal "the names of the other gang members who aided and abetted my crimes." Pacing back and forth in the center of the courtroom, he called me "a walking powder keg" who should be locked up where I could do no more harm. The judge listened to him with a calm, almost sleepy expression—no way to tell what she was thinking. But I noticed Dopodja and Rizzo nodding their heads with gusto.

After the district attorney finished with his opening statement, Mr. Quittlebaum presented his argument. His style was different from

Mr. Sidney Knapp's. Whereas Mr. Knapp waved his arms, paced, and punctuated his comments with dramatic facial expressions, Mr. Quittlebam stood in one place and spoke in a firm, confident voice. Calling me "a troubled teenager with a great deal of grief and tragedy in his past," he said he would present evidence about the special circumstances in my family background that would help shed light on my mental state that night the temple was vandalized. He pointed out that the police had no evidence that I had spray painted the swastika on the back wall. He said I was an above average student with the potential to become "a useful and productive member of society," a phrase which made me think of an ant or a honeybee.

Judge Simms listened to Jake Quittlebaum with the same sleepy-eyed expression she used with the DA. Observing this, I decided I would hate to be in a poker game with her and try to figure out her cards based on her expression. She was a pretty shade of brown, like mahogany.

Following Mr. Quittlebaum's opening statement, the district attorney called Frank Nolan to the witness stand, and the bailiff swore him in. Officer Nolan testified how he saw me running out of the synagogue and how he chased me through the back yard of the temple, down the alley and over the fence, only to get attacked by the Rottweiler. He described the injury to his leg, which didn't sound that bad to me, and said he had missed a day of work. He also described the damage done to the B'nai Shalom Temple, emphasizing the swastika Bone painted on the back wall.

When it was Mr. Quittlebaum's turn to question the witness, my lawyer asked Officer Nolan if he had seen me paint the swastika on the back wall. He also asked him if I had paint on my hands or a can in my possession when I was arrested. The policeman said, "No, sir" to these questions. Then Mr. Quittlebaum asked him if he would be able to tell the Rottweiler was in the yard just from looking at the wooden fence, and Nolan said no, he could not. Mr Q. asked Nolan if he heard the Rottweiler bark before he jumped the fence or saw any 'beware of dog' signs and Nolan admitted that he did not. My lawyer said, "No further questions."

The DA's next witness was Sandor Rutherford, the cop who tackled me, twisted my arm behind my back, and slammed his fist or a blackjack into the back of my head. A lightskinned black man, Sandor Rutherford had the thick neck and chest of a weightlifter. He said he saw me running when he turned down the alley in his squad car. He chased me and "subdued" me, he said. That's a funny way to put it, I thought, considering how he slammed me in the back of the head and knocked me senseless.

I was already down. What did he need to hit me for? Must have been having a bad day.

When Mr. Quittlebaum asked Sandor Rutherford if he had struck me in the head, the cop said, "No sir, I most assuredly did not. I only used the minimal force necessary to subdue the defendant and no blows were struck."

So much for his promise to God to tell the truth. Mr. Quittlebaum had already said he couldn't raise the police brutality issue because I had never gone to the ER. I didn't even think to tell G.T. about the knot on my head right away. He was too pissed.

Lieutenant Dopodja, the DA's next witness, said that I was "sullen and uncooperative during questioning," and that I refused to reveal the names of the other "gang members." Mr. Quittlebaum objected to this phrase. "The witness has no proof the defendant is a gang member," he said. Judge Simms agreed and asked Dopodja to "just report the facts, please." Dopodja scowled, squirmed in the seat, looked like he had recently eaten something sour. He cheered up, though, when the DA gave him the opportunity to discuss his "prior experience with the defendant." Reading out of a folder, he began listing the times he and Rizzo had questioned me about various crimes that had been committed in Pottstown, mostly burglaries and vandalism.

Mr. Q. objected again, calling this information "irrelevant and prejudicial," pointing out that my being questioned did not indicate I was guilty of any crimes. Judge Simms asked Dopodja to comment on my record of arrests. His face flushing, the lieutenant testified I had only been arrested twice—once for disorderly conduct and another time for assault with a deadly weapon. This was when my buddy Skeeter got jumped by two guys in front of Lucky's Billiards. Skeeter was supposed to be hitting on one of the thug's girlfriends, but that was a crock. All Skeeter had done was ask her out on a date. Anyway, one of them was beating him with a pool stick. I got the pool stick away from him and in the process happened to knock out one of his teeth. Only the juvenile cop didn't say anything about that, just that I was arrested for "assault with a deadly weapon," when all I was doing was helping my friend out. I sure wasn't going to stand there and watch them beat Skeeter to a pulp.

Mr. Q. asked if the charge was later reduced, and Dopodja, once again, had to back-pedal. "Reduced to simple assault," he said.

Next the district attorney called Rabbi Ari Zimmerman, the rabbi for B'nai Shalom Temple to the stand. The rabbi was a slender man with horn-rimmed glasses. Mr. Knapp questioned him about the congregation's reactions to the "attack on their place of worship." Although my lawyer objected to this, too, the judge overruled him. Mr. Zimmerman testified that both he and his congregation were deeply hurt, angry, and fearful to have seen their house of worship violated. They were especially devastated about the mishandling of the Torah, the sacred scroll we unrolled.

What the hell, I thought, it was just paper. Looks to me like they'd be madder about the spray paint and broken glass. But I couldn't help but feel bad about the way I had hurt these people, who had never done a thing to harm me. It was one more sin I would have to answer for when I crossed over to the other side.

My lawyer asked if the damage was covered by insurance. The rabbi said that insurance would cover most of the physical damage, but added, "Insurance will not cover the injury to our hearts." The Jews all nodded in support. Right then I wanted to shrink down into a ball of lint and roll into the nearest crack in the floor. Why couldn't I just have stayed home that night?

After all the prosecution witnesses had testified and the prosecutor had badmouthed me some more, my lawyer called Ms. Rawls, the counselor from my high school, to the stand. Ms. Rawls, who was a few shades darker than the judge, was the only person my lawyer had contacted at Washington High who would agree to testify on my behalf. I'm not sure how many others he asked, and to be honest I didn't really want to know. Mr. Quittlebaum started off by asking her if she was "acquainted with the defendant," and under what circumstances she had come to know me. She said she had talked to me several times in her office, including two times last year after I was suspended from school for fighting, and that she had always found me to be polite and respectful. Declaring that I had a high IQ and "a strong potential for achievement," she hoped I would be able to continue attending school. Her last statement caused Dopodja to scowl and shake his head. Rizzo looked like he smelled something nasty in the air.

Mr. Knapp surprised me by declining to question Ms. Rawls. I guess he couldn't think of any hateful questions to ask her.

My lawyer called G.T. to the stand. As G.T. sat down in the chair, his navy pinstripe suit jacket was pulled so tight across his shoulders and chest it looked like it might bust apart at the seams. He had bought that suit thirty pounds ago, but then G.T. didn't have much call to wear a suit. Mr. Quittlebaum asked him about my study habits, my attitude and disposition, the work I did for him in the summer. G.T. put a positive spin on all of his answers, saying I was an obedient, respectful boy and a hard worker. The lawyer asked G.T. a lot of questions about my family—how I behaved after my brother Lee was killed, the way my mom left us, how long she had been gone, and how my daddy had gotten hurt. I was much aggrieved by all of this personal information about me coming out in the courtroom, and glad when the DA objected on the issue of relevance. He and Mr. Q. got into a big fuss about this, and the judge asked them both to approach the bench. After a conference up there, Mr. Quittlebaum appeared to have won out, since he asked G.T. a few more questions about my personal life, while Mr. Sidney Knapp frowned down at the notebook he was writing in.

Mr. Sidney Knapp then lit into G.T. like a little feist dog, the kind that yaps and snarls with so much frenzy that you realize it might be dangerous if it had some size to it. Waving his arms and pacing up and down, he asked G.T. if I had ever received any hate literature at the house in the mail or if he had ever heard me mention the names of any skinhead gangs, especially the "Aryan Knights." G.T. said no. The DA made a big show of rolling his eyes. He asked G.T. if he had ever caught me using drugs or found any illegal substances in my possession. Again, G.T. said no. The DA asked G.T. a lot of questions about the hours he worked—intending to show that G.T. really didn't supervise me much. G.T. answered the questions in a calm and respectful manner, which seemed to make the DA more agitated. I kept waiting for Mr. Quittlebaum to object, but he seemed to be enjoying this part of the trial. It wasn't until Mr. Knapp began discussing G.T.'s prior arrest record himself that Mr. Q. stood up and objected. He accused the DA of "badgering the witness, who is not on trial here." This time the judge called them both up to her bench. After another mini-conference up there, Mr. Knapp announced he would have no further questions.

Next came the time I dreaded the most, had been dreading for days: my lawyer called me up to testify. I walked up to the witness chair, feeling everyone's eyes on me; the Jews were looking at me as if I was a demon out of their worst nightmares. Mr. Quittlebaum started off by asking me how often I saw my daddy. When the DA objected, my lawyer said, "Your honor, since the defendant is a juvenile, I think his family circumstances should have a clear bearing on the case."

Judge Simms nodded and said, "Proceed."

Mr. Quittlebaum asked me more questions about my brother, my mom, and my daddy, focusing on the hurtful events that had taken place and how I felt about them. Although I understood his strategy, I had trouble talking about these subjects in front of all the people in the court-room and I found myself struggling to give him even brief answers. I was relieved when he moved on to a new subject. He asked me if I hated Jews, and I told him the truth, that I had never known any Jews and there-fore had no reason to hate them, being that they had never harmed me personally.

He asked me what my mental state was the night I "visited" the temple, if I was upset about anything, and although he had already advised me that I should try to elaborate on any feelings I had about my brother, Lee, and the injury to my daddy, any thoughts I might have had about these subjects slipped away from me before I could have put them into words; and I found myself saying I wasn't feeling mad about any one thing, just edgy about the way the moon was shining in the window. I told him I was feeling restless and that I wasn't thinking too straight, because I had a strong desire to break something.

G.T. was staring down at his hands. I felt like I was letting him down and wished I could have said more of what the lawyer wanted me to say, but it was one of those situations where my discomfort with lying took over my good sense, and once I started talking I couldn't seem to stop myself.

I figured all hope was gone after Mr. Quittlebaum sat down and then Mr. Sidney Knapp stood up and began asking me questions. He looked like a man with lockjaw. Referring to my earlier statement that I had nothing against Jews in general, Mr. Sidney Knapp asked me if I had ever received any literature in the mail from groups that hate Jews and I told him no. He asked me if I knew who Adolf Hitler was, and I told him yes. He asked me how I felt about Hitler and I told him the truth, that from what I knew about him, which wasn't much, he was an evil man who had murdered a lot of innocent people. I added that if there was a hell I fig-ured he was in the hottest room available—a comment that caused the prosecutor to raise his eyebrows and ask me if I believed in God.

My lawyer objected, and the DA withdrew the question before the judge could chime in. The DA asked me why I did not tell the police the names of "other vandals" who were with me that night, and I told him a pop-eyed lie—that I did not know who they were, that they were just some kids I met on the street, and I figured they might have been vis-iting from somewhere else. Mr. Knapp asked me if I had ever seen them around since, and I told him no, which of course was another lie, but not one that really bothered me much, since I sure wasn't going to drop a dime on my boys. The DA rolled his eyes and asked me whose idea it was to vandalize the synagogue, and I told him I didn't remember, that it just kind of happened on the spur of the moment, which was the truth. He asked me lot of questions about the vandalism itself, like who had painted the swastika on the back wall, and I told him I didn't know for sure, even though I knew it was Bone that had done it, with his damn fool self. I did tell them it wasn't me.

By then I was sweating and I had a nervous tic in my left eye. I never have been good at lying, mostly because I don't like to do it. Most really good liars I have known have a deep, abiding love for a lie and would much rather tell you one than the plain unvarnished truth.

The prosecutor finally finished grilling me. Judge Simms excused me from the witness stand and I returned to the table, where I listened to his final statement to the judge. It was a replay of points he had made earlier, about how I was a menace to society and not fit to be living among civilized people. He finished by asking the judge to send me to Sheridan until I was twenty-one years old.

Mr. Quittlebaum then discussed the "mitigating circumstances" of my family background, my "confused, impulsive emotional state" the night of the damage, and my youth. Pointing out that Ms. Rawls had testified about my potential, and G.T.'s statements that I was obedient and a hard worker, he asked the judge to temper justice with mercy and let me continue going to school. It was a sincere and impressive effort, but I noticed the judge listened to him with the same poker face she had worn during most of the trial. I had already decided I was on my way to Sheridan, even though it looked like Mr. Jake Quittlebaum had given it his best shot.

After my lawyer finished delivering his fine speech on my behalf, the judge said she would like to ask me some questions. So I returned to the witness stand, where the bailiff reminded me I was still under oath.

"Jesse Terrill, I've heard quite a bit of information and discussion about you. But I don't feel yet like I have a clear sense of how you really feel about all this. Do you have anything to tell me?"

When I turned in the chair to look up at her, her glasses were at the right angle to catch a beam of sunlight from a window and throw it straight into my eyes, so that her voice seemed to be coming from the light. While I tried to think of something to say, Dopodja, Rizzo, the D.A., and the Jews stared at me like I was some black goo on a space rock that had dropped out of the sky.

All I could think of to say was, "No, ma'am."

"What do you think about the people who worship in B'nai Shalom Temple?" Judge Simms asked. "What ideas do you have about them?"

Once again, I tried to focus on some of Mr. Q's earlier suggestions, that I could stress how sorry I was and how I just wanted to see what the place looked like, but when I opened my mouth to speak these words came out instead:

"I heard they sacrifice animals."

There was a murmur in the courtroom.

"And who told you that?"

"I forget."

"Do you believe it?"

I shrugged, looked at my lawyer for help, but he was just sitting at the table, his eyes rolled skyward like he had done all he could do.

"What else have you heard about Jewish people?"

"They killed Jesus." These words jumped out of my mouth so fast they caught my own weird self by surprise. I heard a loud "amen" in the back of the courtroom. The Jews down front were talking and whispering among themselves.

Judge Simms hit the bench with her gavel, a cracking sound so loud that it made me jump in my chair.

"The individual at the back who just disturbed the tranquility of this court needs to listen very carefully to what I have to say." Her voice was like one of those high-tech knives you see advertised on late night TV, the kind that will cut through anything, including steel bolts. "If I hear another word out of you, I will hold you in contempt."

Silence in the courtroom. Judge Simms stared at the back row a while longer as if she was daring somebody to say one more thing and then she looked back at me.

"Now Mr. Terrill, according to Ms. Rawls you are an intelligent young man. Do you really believe the people who attend the B'nai Shalom Temple could have had any responsibility for an event that took place two thousand years ago?"

"No, ma'am."

"So how can you use that as justification for vandalizing their place of worship?"

"Wish I hadn't have done it." It killed me to say this, with Dopodja and Rizzo there.

"Why did you do it?"

I looked up at her, squinting. Her glasses were still reflecting the light from the window.

"I wasn't thinking too straight, ma'am. I was wrong, and I'm truly sorry for what I did. I'm not making any excuses for it. I was feeling crazy that night and I wanted to break something. I had—all this anger built up inside. I don't have anything against those people or their synagogue. I'm sorry I hurt them. And I'm truly sorry I damaged their place of worship. I was wrong, and I wish I never would have done it. I didn't paint that swastika back there—never even touched the paint can. But I broke in the place and I threw the glasses up against the wall and I put that scroll on the floor. That's all I've got to say except that I'm guilty and I'm ready to take my punishment."

Judge Simms took off her glasses and rubbed her eyes. I could hear rustling in the courtroom, the hum of the fluorescent lights on the ceiling, the tapping of the DA's pen against the table. Judge Simms acted like she had all the time in the world, like there was no hurry to do anything. Although I could see I had convicted myself, and let G.T. down, I felt as if a weight had been lifted from my heart because I knew I had spoken straight and true.

The judge put her glasses back on and looked at me.

"Jesse Terrill, the state has presented a solid argument for you serving out an active sentence for your crime. And make no mistake about it, what you did was a crime. When you vandalized the B'nai Shalom Temple, you were attacking not just the people who worship there but also a whole way of life, including a religion that has existed on this earth long before you arrived, and will be here long after you are gone. Taking into account your age, your family background, and your contrition, which I believe is genuine, I'm not convinced that a state facility is the best place for you. In fact, I have another idea. Let me tell you the conditions first. You are to clean that hateful image off the back of the temple. I don't care how you do it, but I want it done and I want it done right. You are also to pay for the damage—every single cent. The temple officials will send the statement to your attorney, with a copy to your probation officer, and you are to make monthly payments to the rabbi until the bill is paid in full. And finally I want you to spend one year attending to a Jewish resident of a nursing facility in this city. Mr. Mendel Ebban. The specific days of service can be worked out among Mr. Ebban, the supervisors of the nursing home, and your probation officer, but I want you to visit him twice a week. You will spend a minimum of six hours a week with him, providing whatever assistance he needs or requests. I expect your legal guardian to cooperate in this arrangement, making sure that you attend these sessions on a regular basis and providing transportation, if necessary." She looked at G.T. "Mr. Terrill, are you in agreement with this?"

"Yes, I am, your honor."

"What about you, young man?"

"Yes ma—your honor."

"Good. I understand Mr. Ebban's eyesight is failing, and he is confined to a wheelchair. I believe he would appreciate a young person to help him get around, read to him, and generally tend to his needs. During that time you will report to your probation officer in a timely manner, keep the curfew, attend school regularly, maintain at least a C average, and obey all the terms of your probation. Your probation officer will also be responsible for monitoring your performance. If, for some reason, your relationship with Mr. Ebban becomes untenable, that will reframe the way I view your case. I want to make that very clear. Do you understand?"

"Yes, your honor."

The judge placed me on probation for two years and released me into the custody of my uncle, Galen T. Terrill, who was looking at me as if I had just come back from the dead.

Later, in Jake Quittlebaum's office, he fixed me with a hound dog stare and said, "Son, you flat pulled a rabbit out of what sure looked to be an empty hat."

"Does that mean I get a break on your bill?" G.T. asked.

"It means I'm going to treat you both to lunch," Jake said. "We'll talk about my fee later."

CHAPTER 3

"Judge Simms sure surprised me, Terrill," said Clarence White, my new probation officer, as he was driving me out to Havenwood Guardian Care, the nursing home on Greenwich Avenue where the old Jew lived. Clarence had dark brown skin, a skinny mustache, and a half-inch gap between his two front teeth. He was wearing a green polyester sports coat with a miniature American flag pin in the lapel. "I figured you was going to do some time."

"Why is that?"

"She usually throws the book at hate crimers. Last month she gave two skinheads ten years for beating and robbing a gay dude."

"I didn't hurt anyone."

"That depends on your point of view. Folk who worship in that synagogue might see it differently."

I remembered the way the Jews had looked at me in the courtroom. I wondered if the old man would be the same way, angry and fearful. If he is, I thought, I will have to put up with whatever shit he throws at me if I want to stay out of Sheridan.

Havenwood was about four miles northwest of Pottstown, across from the Northside Medical Complex, a whole little city of doctors' and dentists' offices, laboratories, opticians, and pharmacies. I figured I could take the bus there on days I had to visit but I would have to learn the schedule.

The nursing home was a one-story brick building with two wings. It had a public park behind it, with a pond, benches, swings for kids to play on. As we entered the driveway, Clarence said they kept the real bad off ones in the east wing, the ones who could still take care of themselves in the west wing. I wondered which one the old Jew lived in and how bad of shape he was in.

The lobby was furnished with a lime green sofa, chairs, a piano, and a pitiful looking ornamental with piss-colored leaves. A TV was fixed to the far wall but no one was watching it. Clarence and I talked to the director, Ms. Katrina Lynch, in her office, behind the front desk in the lobby. She was a stocky woman, with frog-belly white skin and straw-colored hair pulled back in a bun.

"Mendel Ebban is an unusual resident," Ms. Lynch told us. "A complex and challenging patient. He was in the Warsaw ghetto and Treblinka, too. Lost all the members of his immediate family there."

"How did he survive?" Clarence asked.

"You'll have to ask him." Ms. Lynch looked at me—frost in her eyes now. "I read about what you did, young man. You know you're lucky you're not behind bars."

I looked at her collection of fuzzy-haired trolls. They were arranged in a semicircle on the desk, with several larger ones on a table behind. Some were smiling, others were scowling, still others had these maniacal grins, like they had just kicked a man in the balls and were excited by his suffering.

"We've worked with the courts successfully in the past," Ms. Lynch said. "But I want to make it clear we also will not tolerate stealing, rude behavior, foul language, or violations of any rules. Our overriding concern here is for the safety and well-being of our residents."

"I believe Jesse understands he is fortunate to have the opportunity to be of service here, Ms. Lynch. I'm counting on him to do a great job and mind all the rules."

Grateful for Clarence's willingness to speak up for me, I listened to Ms. Lynch's sermon on the details of my "service." My schedule was a minimum of two days a week, two to three hours a visit, Tuesday and Thursday. If I came on weekdays, I should arrive between 6:30 and 7:00 p.m., after Mr. Ebban had eaten dinner. I could come on Sundays, but only after 1:00 p.m. I should always sign in and out at the front desk. Ms. Lynch told me I must attend to Mr. Ebban, doing whatever he asked. His vision was failing and he needed someone to read aloud to him. If he requested it, I could take him in the park behind the nursing home, but I must sign him out first at the front desk and "remain with him at all times." He suffered from arthritis and had difficulty pushing his wheelchair, although he could do it for short distances. I should always push his chair for him, so as not to place any unnecessary strain on his arms and shoulders. Most days, Varden Story, the attendant assigned to that wing, would be my immediate supervisor, and I should clear all trips to the park with either him or Ms. Lynch.

"The first time you go to the park, Mr. Story will accompany you," she added. "Most of the other residents on Mr. Ebban's side of the building take their meals in the cafeteria, in the back section of the building, but due to his special diet, he generally eats his meals in his room. If you arrive while he is still eating, you are to let him eat in private unless he specifically asks for your company."

After Ms. Lynch finished telling me the rules, she asked me if I had any questions.

"No ma'am."

She picked up a phone and called a number, asked the person on the other end to report to her office. After she hung up she gave Clarence a chilly smile.

He stood up, said he guessed he'd be going. He thanked her again, aimed his finger at me, and left me alone with Ms. Katrina Lynch and her menagerie of trolls.

She put on some small rectangular glasses and began shuffling through papers on her desk. She was the kind of person who makes you feel sized up and then dismissed as being generally worthless. She would tolerate you out of a sense of duty, but she let you know she did not find the obligation pleasant.

There was a knock on the door and a black guy came in. He had copper-toned skin and broad shoulders tapering down to a narrow waist. A picture ID pinned to his white shirt. Cell phone clipped to his belt. He carried himself with such confidence—shoulders back, head erect—that I couldn't help but wonder why he was wasting his time in a nursing home.

Ms. Lynch introduced him as Varden Story, my supervisor. She told him I was "the individual" they had discussed earlier and she asked him to take me down to meet Mendel Ebban.

I followed Varden Story outside, past the front desk, into the lobby. He asked me my name and I told him who I was.

"Judge sent you here, huh?"

"That's right."

"Look like you'd rather be somewhere else."

"Wouldn't you?"

"Not really. Place keeps me cool in the summer, warm in the winter, and dry in the rain. Gives me a decent paycheck and the opportunity to help folks in need."

"Where's the old man?"

"Come on. I'll introduce you to *Mr. Ebban*."

Just past the desk there was a row of white-haired, milky-eyed ancients sitting in wheelchairs, their bodies shriveled up like mummies. They called to Varden as he went by. Some of them babbled, others spoke his name. One old lady grabbed his sleeve. He bent over her, listening to her say something. Patting her shoulder he said, "Don't you worry about that, Miss Lucy."

We walked down the hall, turned left into the west wing. Place smelled of old peoples' poop and stale pee, mixed in with some kind of pine disinfectant. I wondered how the folks who worked there could stand this odor. They must take it home in their clothes.

Maybe they have got so used to it they are not aware of it anymore, I thought.

The old man's room, number 142, was about halfway down the hall, on the left. The door was slightly ajar. Varden peeped in, then held his palm up. "He's saying his afternoon prayers. We have to wait until he's finished."

"How long will that take?"

"Who knows? Only a fool be looking at the clock when he's talking to God."

Varden went on down the hall, knocked on a door, then went inside.

I peeked through the doorway and saw an old man with a white beard, sitting in a wheelchair. He had a shawl wrapped around his shoulders, a pitiful excuse for a hat on the back of his head, a black leather box tied to his wrist with a black band, and another one around his forehead. His eyes were closed and his lips were moving, but I couldn't hear what he was saying.

Someone was moaning in one of the rooms. This nursing home was already giving me the heebie-jeebies. Reminded me of St. Aubin Hospital, where my daddy lived. Crazies sitting around in wheelchairs up there, too. And shuffling around zombie-eyed. Whole place was full of the walking dead.

Varden Story came out of the first room, then went to another one across the hall, where the moaning was coming from. While he was doing this I heard some weird orchestra music begin playing in the old man's room. Sounded like something you'd hear in a horror flick on late night TV. I shut my eyes, rubbed my temples, wondered how anyone could stand working in a creepy place like this.

"You ready?" Varden asked. He had slipped up on me in those rubber soled shoes. I made a mental note of the quiet way he moves.

"Yes. I'm ready."

He knocked once and we went in.

The old man had on a white shirt, gray slacks, slippers on his feet. Deep lines in his face reminded me of rain gullies in the earth. He was nearly bald, although he had some white hair on the side of his head, a few tufts on top. More white hairs sprouted out of his satellite dish ears. He had big-jointed, gnarly fingers. He had taken off the shawl and the black leather boxes and put them on his bed. The shawl had a blue stripe running through it.

The ghost music was coming from an antique record player on a stand in the corner. The room smelled of oranges and old books.

"Mr. Ebban, this is Jesse Terrill. He's going to be visiting you a few hours each week to help you with anything you need. If you want to go out to the park, he'll take you and bring you back when you are ready to come back. He can also read to you and help you any way he can."

The old man aimed his crooked pointer finger skyward. "Listen."

Varden stood with his head slightly bowed and leaning to the side, listening to this scratchy ruckus. "That's mighty fine, Mr. Ebban. I'm going to leave you now, give you a chance to get to know your young assistant here. You need anything, just give me a holler."

After Varden left, the old man sat in the wheelchair, eyes half-closed like he was deep in thought about an important matter. I could tell he was listening to his creepy music. He had a faded number—751332—tattooed on the inside of his left arm. I wondered if this was some old girlfriend's phone number. If it was, it looked like he'd have sense enough to remember it instead of getting it tattooed on his arm. Where the hell was she now?

A six-pointed yellow star, which looked like it had been cut out of some material, was hanging in a picture frame on the wall above his bed. A curved horn from some animal, maybe a bull or a ram, hung by a leather strap from his bedpost. On a stand by the bed there was a pitcher of water and a glass, a bowl of oranges and some orange peels in a dish. Shelves on either side of the window. The eye level shelf on the right had some faded photographs in stand-up picture frames. Both bottom rows were lined with books. There were more books on the other shelves.

The record went off, and the old man looked at me like he knew something I didn't. His deep-set eyes were black as seeds. Wild gray eyebrows looked like tangled fish line.

"Know who that was?" he asked.

"Not really."

"Alexander Weprik, the great Jewish composer. It's from 'Songs of the Dead.' A copy of an original recording made in Berlin in 1928."

I wondered how often I would have to be tortured by this screech-owl music.

"Stalin threw him in the gulag in 1950. A brilliant musician, doing hard labor in the gulag."

"What's a 'gulag'?"

"A diabolical place designed to break the human spirit. But Stalin's gangsters couldn't do it. Weprik organized an orchestra among the prisoners."

He put his head back in the wheelchair, hands in his lap. I waited for him to say something else, but he was silent. I figured his mind had taken off lickety-split for parts unknown. Which was fine with me. I already liked him better when he was like this. But before I could get relaxed he sat up so fast he made me flinch. "Do you go to school?"

"When I feel like it."

"And when you don't?"

"I stay home."

"And what do you do there, when you stay home?"

"Watch TV. Throw darts. Sometimes I take my rifle out to the dump and shoot rats."

"You like to kill rats?"

"Sure. Who wouldn't?"

"I wouldn't. What's a rat done to me?"

"He could do something though."

"Like what?"

"Bite you."

"If he was about to bite me, then I would kill him," he said, moving his gnarly finger back and forth like a pendulum in a grandfather clock. "Not before."

"Look, you want me to read to you or something?"

His disorderly eyebrows shot up in this exaggerated expression of amazement. "Can you read?"

"Sure I can read. What do you think I am—a dummy?"

"Dummies are made of wood. Are you made of wood?"

"Do I look like I'm made of wood?"

"Can we always trust our eyes? There's a species of moth whose wings have a design that resembles the face of an owl. Now why do you suppose that would be?"

"I've got like—no idea. Look, what do you want me to read?"

"We could start with Genesis. Have you ever read the Torah?"

"What's that?"

"First five chapters of the Old Testament. Words straight from God to Moses."

"Oh, that. Yeah, a few passages."

"So—what do we have here? A *forbissima* young man who only goes to school when he feels like it, who shoots rats and throws darts in his spare time, and who has only read a few passages in the Bible."

"For-biss-i-ma. What kind of word is that?"

"It's Yiddish."

"What does it mean?"

"In English? It means—let's see—'bitter.'"

"So you think I'm a bad person, huh?"

"No, not *shlekht*, just a mass of clay without a proper shape."

"Clay? You think I'm dirt?"

"What's the earth made of?"

"Dirt."

"That's an oversimplification. There's nickel, iron, silicates, volcanic ash, water, most of the elements in the periodic table. And where did all of that come from?"

"You got me."

"Stars. Everything in the earth came from stars that exploded long before you were born. And where did the stars come from?"

"I guess they were always here."

"No. They've only been here since time began."

I shook my head, thinking he was out there with the astronauts. I had a powerful urge to leave, just turn around and walk out. But I was stopped by the memory of Judge Simms staring at me through her fiery glasses.

"And when did time begin?"

"You tell me."

"No. You will tell me." The old man pointed to the middle row of the bookshelf to the right of the window. "Get one of my Torahs, please. Choose the brown book, third from the right there, next to the Bible."

I got the book like he asked.

"Now begin reading on page twelve. Aloud."

"Where do you want me to sit?"

"Wherever you are comfortable."

My only choices were the windowsill, the bed, and the chair at the desk. I sat on the ledge in the window, as far away from him as I could get. I opened the book and began reading. *In the beginning Elohim created the cosmos, including the planet Earth. The earth was empty and without shape, with darkness covering the waters. Elohim's life-giving winds blew over the surface of the water. Elohim said, 'Let there be light,' and there was light."*

As I read I glanced back at him every so often, hoping he would fall asleep so I could leave. Finally, after what seemed like a solid hour of reading, I saw that his head was slumped to the side and his eyes were closed, the only sign he was alive the slow rise and fall of his chest.

I returned the book to the shelf and eased out of the room, heading up to the front desk to sign out. Judge Simms said I had to spend at least six hours a week with him. I didn't know how long I had been there but I had already had more than enough of the place, especially for a first visit.

Coming around the corner to the main hall, I ran into Varden Story.

"Heard you reading to him, how'd it go?"

"How'd you like to be shut up in a room with a crazy person?"

"You know something, slick? You need to get yourself a cane and a seeing eye dog."

He went on down the hall before I could think of a comeback for this diss. Smart ass fool, was all I can think of to say, but that didn't seem even half good enough, cocky as he was.

I continued toward the front desk, passing a resident rattling along on an aluminum walker. I saw the pink skin of her scalp under the thin white hair. She was all stooped over, gripping the walker with her bony hands. I wondered who came to see her, what her life was like before she got here, how she must feel about being a relic in a country that believes in throwing things away when they get old.

The pine disinfectant they used on these floors could not begin to cover up the smell of old people's poop that lingered in the halls. It was enough to gag a whole colony of maggots.

The ancients were still in their wheelchairs by the front desk, lined up like roosting pigeons. Some of them held little cups of juice in their hands. Heads dangled to the side or forward, chins against chests. A few of them were drooling.

Their dead eyes took no interest in me as I passed by.

Early Sunday morning, G.T. dropped me off in front of the B'nai Shalom Temple, along with a lunchbox and a bucket full of cleaning supplies, including turpentine, rags, and a brush. I asked him when he would be back. "Sometime before dark," he said and he pulled off without saying goodbye. He could be like that sometimes. G.T. had had more of his share of worries himself, and I had dragged him down even more with my bad behavior. This pained me more than a little. But it was no use to wish I could turn the clock back because I knew that wasn't possible; and if I could do it I'd turn it back a whole lot farther than to that night we broke into the synagogue. I would go all the way back to when Lee first started talking about joining the Marines, and I'd try to talk him out of it, even if I had to hog-tie him until he saw things my way.

I could see where someone had replaced the back door and fixed the doorjambs. I wondered how much all of this damage was going to cost. I hadn't heard from the lawyer yet about what I owed. I knew G.T. would have to pay them, since I didn't have any money of my own. I would pay him back by working for him over the Christmas break and summers, too.

I got out the turpentine and rags and brush and went to work on the wall. While I worked I could hear people's voices, floating over from nearby yards. For awhile I fretted that some of the Jews would show up. The thought of actually facing them was enough to make me break out in a sweat. Then a bigger worry hit me—that the rabbi would discover something missing after I left and claim I stole it. Who would believe me? Not a single one of them. The Jews would have their vengeance and I would be in the jailhouse, struck down by my own evil. Wouldn't be anything anybody could do to help me then, not even Jesus.

My nose full of turpentine, I prayed they wouldn't find anything missing.

The longer I scrubbed the wall, the more I began to resent Mick, Bone, and Skeeter for getting away scot-free, even though they were just as guilty as I was. I cussed Bone, too, for being such a damned fool as to paint a Nazi symbol on the back wall. What the hell was he thinking? I'd like to see him out here breathing turpentine and cleaning up the mess he made instead of me. Although I figured I deserved my punishment, I couldn't help thinking about how cockeyed the world was, the way some no-count people just seemed to have all the luck and decent ones would end up in quicksand, often through no fault of their own. My daddy was a good-hearted man who worked hard, loved his family, served his country, and paid his bills on time. But his luck ran out one winter night in an alley down from the Flamingo Bar and now he was unable to care for himself or even tell you what day it is. What did he do to deserve that kind of suffering? Not a damn thing that I could see. My brother Lee was young and smart and full of promise but he got killed because he joined the Marines and was in the wrong place at the wrong time. Which all went to show you what a crapshoot a person's life was. Rosalita had faith in her prayers, her statues, and her prayer beads, but to me those things were like the teddy bear I used to sleep with at night. I was afraid a one-eyed swamp monster would crawl through the window and kill me and my family, and I felt better having Fuzzy to hold. Lot of help Fuzzy would have been. If a monster had actually come through my window, I'd a whole lot rather have had a Louisville Slugger than Fuzzy the teddy bear.

Took me what seemed like half the morning to get the wall clean. After I was finished I sat in the grass, eating one of Rosalita's tortillas and listening to a mockingbird sing in a nearby magnolia tree. I couldn't shake this feeling that I was being watched. Suddenly, I looked up and saw a man at the window of the house next door. Looking at me like I was some kind of strange bug. Must be the neighbor who called the cops.

I put the tortilla back in the bag and went around to the front of the synagogue to wait for G.T. Later in the afternoon, after I got cleaned up, I planned to visit Havenwood to continue doing my community service.

Evil was bubbling like a witch's black cauldron in my heart.

Even though we were going along at a good pace, the old man leaned forward in his wheelchair, as if he was trying to make the thing go faster. His tufts of snowy hair were stirred up by the wind generated by our motion. We had only been out there a few minutes and I was already sweating in the Indian summer heat. My hands still smelled of turpentine. There was no breeze, just the hot, still air and the faint squeaking of the wheelchair. Earlier Varden had taken us through the park to show me the route the old man liked to take: follow the sidewalk in back of the nursing home to the path that led down to the pond at the center of the park; circle the pond once—twice, if the old man wanted to go again—then up to the children's play area. From there the walkway led to a fountain surrounded by a basin, then up an incline through some hardwoods to a cleared area. A walkway took you back to the nursing home. There wasn't much to see, but I figured he got some enjoyment out of it. Sure must beat being shut up in his room all day listening to spooky music and mumbling useless prayers.

We had not gone very far before he held up his hand, his signal to stop.

"Listen," he said. "Did you hear that?"

"What?"

"That bird."

"Yes."

"Do you know what it is?"

"No."

"A chickadee."

"So?"

"It's telling the other birds something."

"What?"

"That there's a snake nearby."

"A snake, huh?"

"You can tell by the number of notes at the end of the call. They have different calls for different predators. They change their call according to the degree of danger. That was their warning for a snake."

"How do you know that?"

"I lived in a forest once."

I pushed him on, shaking my head. Lived in a forest, right. Tell me another one.

Ahead was the pond. Gray-green and sun-dappled, it had a cluster of lily pads in the center. It was surrounded by water oaks and weeping willows. Some green-headed ducks were swimming around in the water. Mr. Ebban held up his hand to stop. The ducks emerged from the water and waddled up the hill towards us, quacking. From under his shirt he took out a plastic bread bag, with some muffins and rolls inside. He broke off pieces of the muffin and threw them to the ducks. They surrounded us like a gang of muggers.

A duck pulled at my pants cuff. Another one pecked my shoe.

The old man fed them until he ran out of food. He held up the empty bag. "All gone, no more today."

I pushed him on around the pond and up the hill. A whirligig of purple butterflies passed us by. The branches of the oaks beside the walkway formed a green canopy overhead. A bird was singing somewhere up in the leaves.

Just over the hill was the playground, which had swings, a slide, benches, and a sandbox. A woman sat on a bench by the sandbox, watching two boys throw a red ball back and forth.

One boy missed the catch and the ball rolled toward the old man's wheelchair. He tried to pick it up, but he couldn't bend down that far. Seeing that he was having trouble, I got it for him. I was going to throw the ball to the kids but Mr. Ebban held out his hand for it. I gave the ball to him and he tossed it to the taller boy, a towhead.

"Hey mister, how come your chair has wheels?" the boy asked.

"So I can get around."

"What's wrong with your legs?"

"Joints wore out."

"What happened to your hair?"

"Big wind blew it away. It went like this—wheeeeeeee! I put my hand on my head, and most of my hair was all gone."

The boys laughed.

"My grandpa's hair is all gone," the smaller one said. "His head is smooth like an egg."

"Lucky for him."

"Why."

"He doesn't have to worry about haircuts."

"That's right!" the older boy said. "I don't like haircuts."

"We saw a snake today," the little one said.

"Where did you see it?"

"Just over yonder," he said, pointing back to the way from which we had come.

The old man cut his eyes at me, giving me this "what did I tell you?" look.

The woman on the bench was calling now to the kids. "Come on over here, you two, and leave those folks alone."

"They aren't bothering us," Mr. Ebban called out.

The boys asked the old man if he was coming back tomorrow.

"I hope so."

I pushed his wheelchair on down the path, thinking he had a good way with these kids. I wondered if he had children of his own somewhere.

I still didn't believe he could understand what the birds were saying, though. The fact that those kids saw a snake had to have been a coincidence, even though the sly old Jew was sure quick to jump on it.

He is trying to mess with my mind, I thought, but it won't work.

We came to the fountain. It was a big, concrete basin, maybe ten feet across, with a spinning metal obelisk in the center that threw out water. The bottom of the basin was lined with coins—pennies, nickels, dimes, quarters. Mr. Ebban threw a penny into the water. He closed his eyes, like he was making a wish, then held another penny out to me, asked me if I wanted to make a wish.

"I'm all out of wishes today."

He put the penny back into his pocket. I wondered what he was wishing for. To be young again, maybe. To have his legs and eyesight back, to be somewhere else besides this nursing home, drinking a cold beer or a glass of wine with some of his Jewish friends.

I leaned against the concrete basin, listening to the sound of falling water, and pondered what I might wish for if a genie offered me three wishes. I'd wish for my daddy's mind to be all healed, and for him and my mama to still love each other. I'd wish for Lee to come back from the dead, too. I looked at the old man's hands resting on the concrete rim of the basin and thought what a waste of time it is to wish for anything.

As we were going back down the hill to the pond I saw a man come out of a stand of pines to our right. He had on a green Army shirt over a dirty T-shirt. Sooty face, pine needles in his hair. Shoes missing the laces.

"How are you doing, sir?" he called out.

"Good day to you, sir," Mr. Ebban said.

"Could you help a hungry man out today?"

I kept going, ignoring the old man's signal to stop. He seized the wheels, though, forcing me to either stop or risk hurting his arms.

He asked Mr. Army Jacket what he needed.

The man's eyes were full of red, spiderweb veins. He smelled like he had been sleeping in a wine bottle. You could look at him and tell what he wanted—another bottle of wine.

"Just something to eat, sir. I haven't eaten since day before yesterday."

"What is your name?"

"Tom Dolan, sir."

Mr. Ebban held his hand out, and the beggar clasped it in both of his.

"Mr. Dolan, this is for you."

The man looked at what the old man had given him—a ten-dollar bill. "Thank you. And God bless you!"

"And may God bless you. Today and all days."

"You come here often?"

"We've got to go," I said, and I pushed the wheelchair on.

The beggar was walking fast down the hill.

"He's going to use that money to buy wine."

The old man raised his bushy eyebrows. "So you think he's a *shiker*?"

"What's that?"

"A drunkard."

"That's right. And he just ripped you off."

He kept looking at me like he knew something I didn't. Fool, I thought. Why not just throw your money down an open manhole?

We were silent on the way back to his room, where he had me read this passage from the book of Devarim in his Torah: "*Do not harden your heart to the poor. Open your heart and your hand, giving them what they need.*"

Then he had me get down one of his Bibles and read these lines, which was more of the same: "*You must give freely from the heart, and in return the Lord will bless you in all that you do. There will always be poor and hungry ones in your land."*

When I finished he directed me to another section to read aloud, from Isaiah.

"Look, can't I just read this to myself?"

"Aloud," he said.

"*Always offer your compassion to the hungry creature. If you do this your light will shine in the darkness, and your gloom will be as noon. The hand of the Lord will be upon you. The Lord will give you water when you thirst and strength in your bones. You shall be like a garden watered from a spring that does not fail.*"

I finished reading and sat there fuming—waiting for my next order. I felt like I had had about all I could stand of this hardheaded old man and his lunatic ideas.

Just then Varden came in with a tray containing a slice of chocolate cake, a knife and fork, and a glass of orange juice. "Snack time." He set the tray on the old man's lap. "How's your young assistant doing? I see he's reading the good book."

"He reads very well. He's smarter than he looks."

Varden's raised eyebrows conveyed his personal doubt about Mr. Ebban's statement. The smartass.

"By the way, where is his cake?"

"They didn't give me any for him." Flashing a crooked smile, Varden glided out on his rubber soled shoes.

Mr. Ebban took a plastic knife and fork and paper plate out of his desk drawer. He cut the cake in two and offered one half to me.

"No thanks. I'm not hungry."

He set the paper plate on his desk, began eating his half of the cake.

But I was hungry. I looked at the cake awhile, and when I saw for sure the old man was not going to eat it, I eased down out of my seat in the windowsill and picked up the paper plate. Returning to the window, I began eating the other half of the cake.

"I know about the Nazis," I said, after a while. "I know what they did."

He didn't answer, although I noticed he had stopped chewing. He just sat there still as a stone angel in a cemetery.

"I don't understand why they did it," I said.

When he spoke his voice was so low it was almost a whisper: "Why don't you ask God?"

This comment caught me by surprise because I had expected him to speechify. I had asked God a lot of things—like why my brother Lee had to get killed, how come my daddy was in the state asylum, why my mama left me. God still had not answered those questions yet, so I figured I'd be wasting my time to ask Him why the Nazis murdered six million Jews. If He had really wanted to, it looked to me like He'd have done something to save them when He had the chance.

After I left the nursing home I caught the bus in front of the medical complex and rode it all the way to the corner of Oleander and Jessup. When I reached our driveway I saw G.T. sitting on the front steps, sipping a beer.

"How'd it go?" he asked.

"O.K." I sat down beside him on the steps.

"There's lemonade in the fridge."

"I can't have a brew, too?"

"When you're legal you can have one. I expect you've had plenty already, when I wasn't around."

We sat there awhile, watching Amos peck for bugs in the yard. I looked across the road at the buildings of Gladstone and Son. They made the plastic hulls of the caskets in back, in a metal building painted bright yellow. I had toured that place once. They had a showroom with their caskets on display. Their caskets came in a variety of sizes, for everything from a parrot to a Great Dane. The front section had a chapel for pet funerals, with candles and flowers and a minister to preach a sermon. I wondered what you could say in a sermon about a pet dog.

I asked him where Rosalita was. He said she had taken her kids to mass.

"She ever try to get you to go with her?"

"She knows better."

About the only time G.T. went to church was for a funeral. I guessed he was like me, in that religion never took with him, although his mama, Eunice, was a serious Baptist. My grandma Eunice raised Daddy, Lynette, and G.T. mostly by herself, since her husband, Brent, was killed in a logging accident when Daddy was twelve. Like Rosalita, she would pray for her whole family, too—even folks she hadn't seen in years and strangers she had just heard about. I recalled the leather boxes the old man tied to his arm and forehead when he prayed. Varden told me they contained pieces of paper with passages from the Old Testament written on them. He said the old man wore them because to him they represented "the connection of his arm and mind to God."

"G.T., you ever pray?"

"Sometimes, why?"

"I never hear you."

"You don't hear a lot of things."

"How come you don't pray out loud?"

"Because I don't feel like it, that's why. You know you might want to try it yourself sometime instead of tearing up other people's places of worship."

I didn't know G.T. prayed. This was a whole new side of him I never considered. Made me think I didn't know him as well as I had thought.

"That old man I got to visit—he prays three times a day. Starves himself all day Saturday. Won't eat a bite of food."

"Saturday is a holy day for Jews. It's like Sunday for Christians. I knew some of those guys in the Army. The serious ones don't eat from sunup to sundown on Saturday."

"What's the point of that?"

"Like I told you, it's just their way of doing things. You should try to respect a person's faith when it's different from yours."

I knew I didn't have much faith. But at least I was honest enough to admit it. I wondered how many of the people in the church pews on Sunday were true believers and how many were there for other reasons—to make business connections, check out the women, show off their new outfits, find out the latest dirt on their neighbors. I scuffed my feet in the yard, digging a hole with my toe. Amos ambled over to me and I rubbed him behind the neck, the way he liked. He rested his head on my knee, closed his eyes.

"That old man is missing a couple of gears, G.T. Half the time he doesn't even make sense. Claims he understands what the birds are saying to each other. I asked him how he knows that and he said he used to live in a forest."

"You know he might be able to teach you something. I think that's what the judge had in mind."

"Like what? Today he gave ten bucks to a wino in the park. Man claims he's hungry so Mr. Ebban hands him the money. That ought to be an important clue right there about how much sense he's got."

"It was his money, wasn't it?"

"He sure wouldn't have been giving mine away."

"You don't have any damn money."

"If I did I wouldn't be giving it to some deadbeat wino."

"Everybody's got their own way of looking at things."

You said that right, I thought. Him and me, we got real different ways of seeing things. I got better things to do with my time than to starve myself, give my money to hustlers, and pray to a God who's put me on call waiting.

As for all that religious hocus pocus, I wondered again how the Jews could still believe God was looking out for them when He let the Nazis kill so many of them. This seemed to be one more example of the way people will get a death grip on an idea, even when all of the available evidence proved it questionable, if not downright false.

A mosquito landed on my arm. I slapped it with my palm and saw it leave a red smear of blood on my skin. I wondered whose blood it was. Could be G.T.'s, could be Rosalita's, could belong to Amos, a horse, a bird, a rabbit, or someone who worked in the pet casket company. I thought about how blood was the same color, regardless of who it comes from, how black people could give blood to white people and a Jew could give blood to an Arab. This struck me as somewhat amazing, all things considered.

Chapter 4

"Excuse me, ma'am," I said to the cafeteria lady. "Could I have a little more macaroni, please?"

"Too much starch is bad for you," she said, scowling. A leaf-colored booger dangled from her nose.

"Let's go, man," Mick said, giving me a nudge from behind.

I went on through the line and paid the woman at the register. She was so fat her ass hung over the stool. Ric Farina and Andre Grier had a ten-dollar bet that she would break it by Halloween.

Mick and I sat at the table with Andre, Bone, and Skeeter, all kids that Clarence, my probation officer, would have called "undesirables." If you looked around the lunchroom, you'd see the way the "birds of a feather" rule applied at Washington High. The jocks were at their tables, the black kids and Latinos at theirs. The Highland Park kids sat together, as did the freaks and loners, the jumbos, the anorexics, Rambo wannabes in their camouflage clothes, and the geeks and nerds. Even most of the disabled kids sat together. Where else would I have fitted in except here, with the Pottstown rats?

I took a bite of my hamburger, listened to Mick and Bone complain about the cafeteria lady.

"Woman is a booger factory," Mick said. "You know some of her bodily products got to be ending up in your food."

"Looks like you got one right there," Andre said.

"Where?" Bone poked at his macaroni with a fork. "Damn, I'm going to throw this shit away."

"You hear what she told Terrill?" Mick asked. "Starch is unhealthy. She's got some room to talk with her big-assed self."

"She's got a beard, too," Andre said. "Probably taking male hormones."

"Cafeteria lady might be changing into a man," Bone said. "Other day I saw a TV show about men who want to be women and vice versa. The show was about the ones who take female hormones and got operations to make them women. Had a woman on there whose husband turned into a woman and they were still married. She said she wanted to try to work the marriage out. Now is that weird or what?"

"No way," Skeeter said.

"It was all right there on TV. Channel Three documentary."

"Sounds like the sci-fi channel," Skeeter said.

"I saw that freaky couple," Mick said. "Both of them in makeup and dresses. TV showed a picture of them together when he was a he. Dude looked a whole lot better as a man. He was one ugly woman, even though he claimed he was a lot happier as a 'she.'"

"That ain't natural." Skeeter was blinking his eyes faster now, the way he did when he was excited. That was how he got his nickname. Somebody said it looked like he had mosquitoes in his eyes and the name stuck.

I looked up and saw Angela Salazar moving through the lunch line. The way she walked made me think of tall grass swaying in the wind. I pictured myself stepping out of an alley and jumping on the back of an alligator that was about to attack her—tying its jaws shut with my belt. Angela smiling her gratitude, her arms around my neck. *Jesse, thanks so much for saving my life. How can I ever repay you?*

Terra, LaFay, and Snookie, three Pottstown girls, came up with their trays and sat down at our table.

"Same old shit," said Terra, looking at her food. "Looks like they could surprise us once in a while." Terra had on a denim skirt, black blouse, and silver bracelets on both wrists. Long purple fingernails, her black hair teased up on top of her head, pale purple lipstick. That had been her look all week. Miss Halloween.

"Yo, Snookie, let me hold some of that cake," Bone said.

"You got cake," Snookie said. She was wearing one of those push-up bras that made her boobs look bigger than they really were.

"Your cake is sweeter than mine."

"You can look at it, baby, but you ain't ever going to taste it."

"Terra," Mick said. "You check out the beard on that cafeteria lady?"

"She got a beard?"

"That's right. We think she might be changing over."

"What you talking about, Mick?"

"Talking about trannies." He winked at me. He and Terra used to go out last summer, but she broke up with him, claimed he gave her the clap. Mick swore she must have got it from someone else, claimed she gave it to him

"Sounds like freaky business to me. But if you talking about it you must be thinking bout trying it—that is, if you ain't tried it already."

"I'm talking about sex change operations, Terra. Ain't you ever heard of them?"

"What, you thinking about getting one?"

"Are you deaf? I said the cafeteria lady might be thinking about it."

"Ain't nobody's business but her own if she is," Terra said. "Some people might not be happy with the way they're built, but I don't happen to be one of them."

"I ain't heard no complaints," Mick said.

"Hit dog will holler," Terra said.

Snookie and LaFay laughed. Color rising in his cheeks, Mick looked down at his food.

I could see I needed to change the energy flow at the table, so I told the girls about the show Mick and Bone had seen on TV, about men changing into women.

"That's right," Andre said. "You can't tell who's got the real thing these days and who ain't. My cousin was in Savannah last month. Met this person in a nightclub, said she had a body like a goddess. She sat on his lap and sucked his fingers like they was lollipops. But when he gets her up to his room, guess what he finds at third base?"

"What?" Skeeter asked. He was blinking like a flash bulb just went off in front of his face.

"She is a *he*."

"Damn," said Skeeter. "Ain't never going to that club."

"He got himself a he-she," LaFay said.

"He go ahead and get a little action?" Snookie asked.

"Hell, no, my cousin ain't gone mess with no fairy!"

"How do you know what he did?" Terra asked.

"'Cause I know my cousin. He ain't messed with no he-she, dammit!"

"I wasn't there, so I can't say what he did."

"This is for you, Terra," Mick said, giving her the finger.

"You made it you ride it."

Mick got up, kicking his chair against the table. He picked up his tray and headed toward the tray return slot that led back to the kitchen.

Terra cut her eyes at me. "What are you looking at, Jesse?"

"Still trying to figure that out."

"How's the community service going?"

"OK."

"What do you do?"

"Mostly I read to this old Jewish man. Push his wheelchair through the park so he can get some fresh air and feed the ducks."

"That's good," LaFay said. "We're all going to be old some day."

"Some of us, maybe," Terra said.

We all looked at her.

"Who the fuck wants to get old?" she said.

No one said anything else. We ate our food silently, like prison inmates, avoiding each other's eyes. I appreciated LaFay saying something nice about my job with the old man. Her last name was "Roux," which was supposed to be Cajun but she looked like she could have some Latina or maybe even some Indian blood. She had dark brown eyes, shiny black hair, and olive-toned skin. She and her mama moved here last summer from South Louisiana.

On the way back from taking my tray up to empty it, I stopped by the table where Angela was sitting with her friends, Margot and Desiree. Margot had both hands fanned out, admiring her nails.

"Hey Angela," I said.

"Hi, Jesse."

"I—uh—just stopped by to see if you got the English homework."

"Sure. Got it right here." She opened up her book bag, took out her notebook. Desiree rolled her eyes at Margot.

"Read the second act of *Othello*. And answer questions two, four, and seven at the end of the play. Want me to write it down?"

"I can remember that." I tried to think of something else to say, to keep the conversation flowing, but my thoughts were all jumbled up, and I was scared to speak for fear something foolish would come out.

I thanked her and went back to my table, wondering why I get so tongue-tied and knock-kneed around Angela Salazar. I'd like to ask her out some day, but what kind of chance would I have with a girl like her? She lived in Highland Park, in a three-story brick colonial. Her mama drove her to school every day in a white Cadillac. What would her parents say if they heard a misfit like me was out with their daughter?

I remembered Rosalita saying I needed a regular girlfriend. Snookie was my girl for a while last summer—until I found out she spent the night at Ric Farina's house when his parents were out of town. She tried to make up with me after that, said she was drunk at the time and she was sorry it happened. I told her I wasn't mad at her. I just didn't want her to be my girl any more. What really got to me was she had just told me two days before she spent the night at Ric's house that she was in love with me and wanted us to be together forever. She was stone sober, too. I might have tried to forget her night with Ric Farina if not for that. I never have had much patience with people who say one thing and do another. This goes back to my daddy, I guess—at least when he was in his right mind. Daddy believed a person's word should be his bond. "That's the kind of simple thing that holds the whole world together, Jesse," he said once. I remember he sold a truck to a man once. They shook on the deal and agreed to meet the next morning to transfer the title. The man offered to pay my daddy some money down to hold the truck for him, but Daddy said that wasn't necessary. Later that day another man offered Daddy a much higher price for the truck, said he'd pay him in cash, but Daddy refused to sell it. He said he had given his word and it was already sold. The man tried to talk him into it, but Daddy wouldn't change his mind. He told me later that as far as he was concerned his handshake and his word were just as good as a legal contract. That experience stayed with me. I figured I didn't have much going for me, but I wanted to try to at least live up to my daddy's standards, which was probably one reason why I hated to lie. I'm not claiming I wouldn't tell one, I've told my share, sure, but it almost always disgusted me to do it. Terra said Snookie spent the night with Ric because she was afraid she was getting too involved with me, but I figured that was her problem, not mine; I didn't lie to Snookie and I didn't cheat on her, either. I played it straight and honest, and I expected her to treat me the same way.

I don't have room in my life for a girlfriend anyway, I thought, as I left the lunchroom for my fifth period class. Girls cost money, and I had a major shortage of revenue, not to mention the lack of a decent set of wheels. Even if I could afford to date someone, I just had too many demands and limitations on my time—homework, my curfew, and my "community service," which was another way of saying being a vassal for the old Jew. Who had time for romance?

Working on an algebra problem in my bedroom, I heard voices on the front porch. Then a knock on the door.

I got up to see who it was. On the way to the front door I noticed G.T. snoozing in his recliner.

I opened the door. It was Mick and Bone.

"Yo, Jesse," Mick said. "What's up."

"Algebra. What's up with you?"

"Ain't algebra."

"We was going to the skating rink," Bone said. "Thought you'd like to come."

"Jesse, you finished your homework?" G.T. called from the living room.

"Not all of it."

"You don't need company then."

I stepped out on the front porch. "G.T. says I got to study."

"Got you on a ball and chain, huh?" Mick said.

"I'm on probation, dammit!" I lowered my voice and added, "Unlike some people who are slicker than me at getting away from the cops."

"No offense, Jesse," Mick said. "Just thought we'd ask."

"Maybe next time."

"Catch you later, homeboy," said Bone.

"Come back when you can stay longer," I called after them. I wasn't feeling too friendly.

I went back to my room, where my books were spread out on the bed. I had fifteen algebra problems to do and a dozen sentences to diagram. I would like to forget about this work and just throw darts at the target on the back of my door, but I couldn't afford to, due to the terms of my probation. I had to maintain at least a C average in all my courses. I worked a few problems, and when I took a break I found myself thinking about the passages I had been reading to the old man. I was amazed at the amount of lying and backstabbing that went on back during Bible days. Cain murdered Abel, Jacob cheated his brother out of his land and father's blessing, Joseph's brothers sold him into slavery. Jacob had to work for Laban for seven years in order to get the wife he wanted, Rachel; and at the end of that time, her father brought his older daughter, Leah, to the marriage ceremony under the cover of darkness and fooled Jacob into marrying her instead, since she was wearing a veil. When Jacob found out he had married the wrong woman, he complained about being cheated. Laban told him it was customary to marry off his older daughter first. Jacob did get to marry Rachel a while later but only after agreeing to provide seven more years of servitude to Laban. It was plain to see people were about as slippery and two-faced back then as they are today. That story made me feel sorry for Jacob and Leah. Imagine getting hustled by your own daddy like that.

I wished I could have gone with Mick and Bone to the skating rink. It was up on Tull Street, north of the Pottstown mill. Once Angela Salazar came down to the skating rink—only time I ever heard of her visiting Pottstown. She was with her older sister and another girl. It would be just my luck for that to be the night she would show up again, when I had to sit around in my bedroom, trying to solve all these algebra problems. I wondered what I would say if Angela's daddy told me he was adding seven more years of servitude onto the original agreement. I could see I probably would have done just what Jacob did. Which just goes to show a fool in love hadn't changed all that much in the past five thousand years.

CHAPTER 5

I heard the racket when I opened the front door of Havenwood. It was a series of blasts, long and smooth, then a whimpering sound of broken notes, then long and smooth again, all of it getting louder as I went down the hall towards the old man's room. It was a weird, primitive sound that made you think of deserts, camels, women in flowing robes, with veils covering their faces.

Ray Thorne, who had the room three doors down from Mr. Ebban, came up the hall, shaking his head and frowning. A scrawny man with thick-lensed glasses, he had the tattoo of a cowboy riding an alligator on his right forearm. The gator's jaws were gapped open, displaying bloody, jagged teeth.

"You seen the Devil go by?" he asked.

"What?"

"The Devil should be skedaddleling about now if you believe all that Jewish mess. Mendel is blowing that ram's horn he keeps by his bed."

"What's he doing that for?"

"Today's some kind of holy day for Jews. Damn nuisance if you ask me. Keep thinking I'll get out my boom box, set it by his door, and let Al Green sing 'Amazing Grace,' just to give us Christians equal time."

I went past him toward the old man's room.

"Ain't no use to go in there," Ray Thorne called after me. "He's going to be praying and fasting today. He ain't going to want to be around no gentiles."

"Is that right?" I looked around for Varden, wanting him to clear up the mystery of the weird-sounding horn.

"Hell yeah," Ray said. "Watch out for the Devil, too. Horn's supposed to drive his warty ass on out of here."

He went on down the hall, cackling and mumbling.

The old man's door was open. I stood in the doorway and watched him blow the horn. He was sitting in his wheelchair, his cheeks puffed out, his face flushed red.

At last he lowered the horn, put his head back, and closed his eyes. His chest was heaving.

"Mr. Ebban," I said softly. "It's me—Jesse."

"Man is like clay," he said, keeping his eyes closed. "Easily broken, like the grass that withers, like the shadow swiftly passing, like the cloud floating by, like the wind rushing along, like the dust blown away and like a dream that vanishes. But Thou art King, the Living, Everlasting God."

"You want me to read to you today? Want to go for a ride in the park?"

"Not today. Come back tomorrow." He began praying in Hebrew.

I walked back to the front desk to sign myself out. Ms. Katrina Lynch was standing by the secretary, Rhonda. Ms. Lynch asked her where Varden was.

"He hasn't gotten back from his break, Ms. Lynch," Rhonda said.

"I'm going to call him on his cell phone. I want that racket to cease. That's way too much noise for our patients."

"He's already stopped, ma'am," the woman at the desk pointed out.

"Tell Varden I want to see him when he comes back."

Ms. Lynch's eyes focused on me, and her scowl immediately intensified, as if I was somehow responsible for the disturbance. She went back into her office.

Beside my name, I wrote, *Mr. Ebban did not need my help today. He asked me to come back tomorrow.*

As I went out the front door I met Varden coming in. "Going the wrong way, ain't you?"

"Mr. Ebban sent me on. He's been blowing on that horn."

"That's right. It's Rosh Hashanah."

"What's that?"

"The Jewish New Year. He blows his shofar to announce it—you know, get himself in the spirit."

"Mr. Ebban's neighbor in one forty-eight wasn't too happy about it."

"Ray Thorne? Last time he was happy was when Truman dropped the A-bomb on Japan."

"Ms. Lynch is looking for you. She wants you to tell him to hush."

"He don't blow it long. No need for her to get her glasses fogged up."

I walked outside, happy to get a day off from my service. I got a kick out of Mr. Ebban blowing that horn, too, especially the way he rattled Ms. Lynch. Whole place needed a little excitement anyway.

Remembering what Ray said, I thought that it would really be something if you could get rid of all the evil around you just by blowing an old ram's horn.

Lee and me, driving down a mountain road in a car. Just ahead of us a big boulder blocks the road. I get out and try to push it out of the way, but it won't budge.

My brother is still sitting in the car. I turn to look at him and the car starts to go backwards, running down the mountain. I run after him, heading blind into the curves, shouting his name, over and over.

I woke up with G.T. shaking me, calling my name.

I sat up in bed, my heart pounding. Rosalita stood in the doorway to my room, holding a rosary in her fist.

"Get ahold of yourself, Jesse," G.T. said. "You're going to wake up all the pets in the cemetery."

"I'm sorry."

Rosalita said something in Spanish, made the sign of the cross with her fingers against her forehead and chest.

G.T. said, "Are you all right?"

"Yeah, I'm OK. Go back to bed."

"Want me to leave the light on?"

"No. You can turn it off."

G.T. turned out the light and they left, leaving the door open behind him.

I lay there in the dark, embarrassed that Rosalita had heard me crying out like that. I tried to pray, but all I could think of was "Now I Lay Me Down to Sleep." I said it twice, but it didn't do much good. I lay there thinking about Lee, remembering the last time I had seen him. He was getting on the airplane to fly to Washington, D.C. for his connecting flight to Italy. I shook his hand, and then we hugged each other. He said, "You look after yourself, Jesse, you hear?" The sun was so bright that day I could see every pore of his skin, the faint shadow of his beard, beads of sweat on his forehead. He kissed Mama, hugged Daddy, and then he walked out to the plane and walked up the ramp, turning back to look at us, to wave at us one last time before he stepped into the plane. It was a 747, sitting all alone on the tarmac beneath the clear blue sky. Mama, Daddy, and I stood there, trying to catch a glimpse of Lee's face through the window but he must have gotten a seat on the other side. We waited until the plane taxied down the runway; the whole time I was hoping I might see his face again before the plane was airborne. I stood there and watched it until it faded into a speck and then disappeared altogether in the vast emptiness of the sky. I have recalled this experience many times since then, searching for a clue that might have warned me it was the last time I would ever see my brother, but I just can't find one. What

I remembered was how strong and alive he looked and how I felt like someone was pressing a fist against my heart. It wasn't just that he was leaving, but also because I was remembering him as someone who already existed only in my memory: a boy in a tree house, in air fragrant with the scent of peach blossoms, pointing out the shapes that stars formed in the night sky. Every shape told a story. Pegasus, Orion the Hunter, Perseus, Ursa Major and Ursa Minor. They had been discovered and named by humans who lived long before our time but even then the earth was much older than either one of us could ever imagine.

"He did it with magic," Ray Thorne said. He was standing in front of Mr. Ebban's wheelchair. I was in my spot in the windowsill, Mr. Ebban's leather-bound Bible in my lap.

"What kind of magic?" asked Mr. Ebban. He was peeling an orange.

"How should I know?"

"How do you know it was magic?"

"Because he's God. He can do anything."

"Look, you were married, right?"

"Three times." Ray grinned, showing a mouthful of crooked teeth, all the color of tree bark.

"What would you say if a virgin told you that God had made her pregnant? Would you believe her?"

"No, but this is now. All kinds of wondrous things happened back in Bible times. Those were the days of miracles."

"Do you think Joseph believed her?"

"Sure."

"Why would he believe such a thing?"

"You're blaspheming the spirit!"

"I'm questioning your line of reasoning."

Ray aimed a finger at me. "Talk some sense into him, will you?"

"You've got to be kidding."

"I can't talk to you, Mendel. Drives up my blood pressure. I'm going out to the lobby and wait for the clowns." Ray looked at his wristwatch, then he shuffled to the door. "They're due here in ten minutes. I sure need something to cheer me up after being in this Godless room."

"Please continue reading, Jesse."

I started reading to him again. I was in the second book of his Torah, Shemot, although the old man wasn't following any real chronological order—he seemed to want to hear different sections at random. He had four or five different Bibles and a collection of other books too on different subjects, including astronomy, science, and history. In this section I was reading, Moses was trying to convince the Pharaoh to let him take the Jewish people out of bondage in Egypt. God had already sent plagues of frogs, lice and flies on the land, but the hard-headed Pharaoh wouldn't keep his promise to let the Jews leave. I guess signs and wonders don't work for some people.

Soon the old woman at the end of the hall began hollering. "I want a cigarette! Help me. Help me. Somebody help me!"

Sometimes she would carry on like this a good twenty minutes before someone took her outside for a smoke. She was making so much racket I stopped reading. "What's wrong with her, anyway?"

"Acts like she's been possessed by a dybbuk."

"What's that?"

"Spirit of a dead person, usually someone who was evil during his life. Angels chase them around and punish them. To find some peace a dybbuk tries to enter your body—at least that was what I was told as a child. If somebody was acting crazy, we blamed it on a dybbuk." He spelled it out for me: "d-y-b-b-u-k."

"So how do you get rid of them?"

"The rabbi would perform an exorcism, with incense and prayers. Dybbuks can't stand the prayers and smoke. They leave through the little finger or one of the toes." The old man studied me slyly. "Know how to tell the dybbuk is gone?"

"How?"

"It leaves a little drop of blood on the victim's little finger—the exit point."

I looked at my little finger. "You expect me to believe this?"

"Believe what you want. I'm just telling you what I heard."

I began reading again but I was soon interrupted by a group of clowns sashaying into the room. They had yarn wigs on—red, green, yellow; white faces, white gloves, and oversized mouths that were red as blood against their white face paint. The hobo clown switched on a boom box that played this psychedelic circus music—a bass drum, calliope, penny whistle, xylophone. Swaying to the beat, the clowns lined up in front of the old man's bed. A clown with green hair gave us each a balloon. Then they performed a little skit. A short clown with a turned-down mouth walked around with her head down, and another clown tried to cheer her up by making faces, sticking her tongue out, wagging her head from side to side. A clown with big floppy feet tried a little tap dance but that didn't work either. Still another clown offered the depressed clown balloons, but the sad-faced clown just shook her head and looked away, her arms folded together.

Finally, the floppy-footed clown took out a Bible. She made a big deal of showing it to the other clowns, who began prancing all around and acting excited. Then she pretended to read it to the sad-faced clown. The sad clown brightened up and began waltzing with the clown who had given us the balloons. All of the clowns did a little do-si-do together, changing partners in a square dance routine, before they headed out to the next room to entertain someone else.

I looked at the old man to see if the clowns had cheered him up, but he was looking out the window. His half-eaten orange was on the stand beside the bed. The old woman had stopped crying. I guessed somebody had taken her outside, or else maybe the clowns had distracted her.

"There were clowns in the Warsaw ghetto," Mr. Ebban said. "They visited the orphanages and the nursing homes to entertain the children and old people. They traveled around in a green bus. I used to wave at them from my window when they went by. In the winter of 1942, the SS men stopped the bus and ordered the clowns out into the street. They cursed them and beat them with their rifles and machineguns."

"Why'd they do that?"

"They were looking for someone, a leader of the Jewish resistance."

"They find him?"

"No. But the SS men lined the clowns up against a building and shot them, anyway."

"They killed the clowns? Why?"

"Perhaps because they made people laugh. Eased their misery for a little while."

I asked Mr. Ebban who the "SS men" were, but his eyes were distant now, his mind far away. "They set the bus on fire."

I wanted to distract him from this nightmarish and hurtful memory, so I began reading—about how the plague of locusts ate up all the crops in Egypt, leaving nothing green, not even a blade of grass. This made the Pharaoh call for Moses and his sidekick Aaron and tell them he had sinned against their God and ask for forgiveness. But after the Pharaoh promised Moses he could lead the Jews out of bondage, God hardened the old Pharaoh's heart again and he still refused to let the children of Israel go. God's declared purpose in hardening the Pharaoh's heart, was to "multiply my signs and wonders" to the Egyptians—turning the Nile to blood, for instance, and setting numerous plagues and pestilence upon the land. From reading some of these passages I had already figured out that the old man's God had a cruel side of his own. I even considered suggesting this to Mr. Ebban once, but observing the way he argued circles around Ray Thorne I decided to keep my comment to myself. Mr. Ebban always seemed to stay one step ahead of you in an argument. Also you never quite knew when he was telling you the truth or just trying to hoodoo you, like his story about the dybbuks.

Sometimes, I wondered if he even knew himself.

CHAPTER 6

The hummingbirds that visited Rosalita's feeder by the kitchen window were gone. There was frost on my windowpane some mornings, and the air was chilled when I walked to the bus stop. The leaves on the sweetgum, maple, and hickory trees were red, yellow, and orange. Three days in a row when I took the bus to school, the fog was so heavy I could only see the faint outline of buildings. Even after the fog cleared the light seemed different somehow. Cooler and bluer, with a tinge of purple.

My days had settled into a monotonous routine—school, homework, chores, tending to Mr. Ebban at Havenwood Guardian Care, with its smells of Lysol, urine, and soiled diapers. I wanted to break bad, get drunk, and raise some hell with the Pottstown boys, but I couldn't risk getting in trouble or arrested for a curfew violation. I was so bored I volunteered to help Lamont Atwater and Jared Ramsey, two students in my English class, do a rap version of Samuel Coleridge's "Rime of the Ancient Mariner." We were doing this, in part, to improve our averages, since the teacher had said she would count it as an exam grade if we could give an oral presentation of the works we had been studying. We practiced in the gym after school, with music provided by Jared's boom box. Jared and Lamont had their own rap group, and they coached me on phrasing, delivery, and rhythm.

First time I had read this poem I was caught up in its spell. I could picture the scrawny ancient mariner with his wild eyes, all out of place at the wedding where he tells his story, the sea as green as an emerald at first and then turning to ice that cracked and growled like a monster, then the albatross flying through the snow-fog and the ice breaking up after that, the wind blowing clean and strong while the good luck bird sat on the mast—until the ancient mariner killed it with an arrow from his crossbow. He had to pay a hellacious price for his act of mindless cruelty—his tongue shriveling up from thirst, being forced to walk amidst all of the dead crew members and gaze into their sightless eyeballs, with the dead bird hanging around his neck.

Jared, Lamont, and I had been working hard on this rap interpretation of the poem. We studied the lines carefully and had corresponding moves to help the audience picture key scenes. For instance, Jared acted out the shooting of the albatross, and Lamont and I wiggled our bodies like water snakes. I had a high B average in English. I hoped my participation in this performance would not only bring my grade up to an A but also help Angela Salazar see me in a positive new light.

First Saturday in October, G.T. and I rode to the state capital, to visit my dad at St. Aubin Hospital, his home for the past two and a half years. On the way G.T. played his Cajun tapes—bands like Happy Fats and Jivin' Gene and the Hackberry Ramblers. They played some of the songs we all used to listen to when we lived out on Cotton Gin Road, tunes like "Jolie Blonde" and "The Cypress Island Swamp." This music gave me a pain in my heart. I looked out the window, at the fields rolling by, and thought of my mama. I wondered where she was, who she was with, if she was doing OK. After a while, I turned off the tape, spun the dial on the radio to a station that played black gospel music. I leaned back in the seat, closed my eyes, listening to a choir sing "God is Real." According to the Bible a mustard seed of faith will move a mountain. If that's true then I doubted if I could move a dead mosquito out of the road. But I still liked to listen to gospel music. It wasn't so much the lyrics. There was something in the feeling of the gospel music, like the sound of Rosalita's words when she was praying in Spanish, that let my dark thoughts and fears take a siesta.

G.T. and I made this drive about once a month. It was about three hours one way, not counting meal stops. I hated the idea of my daddy being up there in that mental hospital. At first we had tried to look after him ourselves, but he just got to be too much for us to handle. He was a completely different person after he got hurt. He was coming home late one night from the Flamingo Bar with his cashed paycheck still in his wallet, and somebody slipped up behind him and hit him in the head with what the cops called "a blunt object." The mugger stole his wallet and left my daddy unconscious and bleeding in the alley. Daddy might have frozen to death if the man driving the early morning garbage truck hadn't seen him and called the rescue squad. It was six weeks before he could sit up in the hospital bed. He had brain damage from the injury and the swelling afterward—part of it resulting from the hours he lay there in the freezing cold without medical help. After he came home he got confused about times and dates and places he was supposed to be. Although he went to rehab, he didn't ever seem to improve much. He couldn't work at the lumberyard anymore, and he went out on disability. I worried about leaving him alone because he would leave the house and wander around the streets. I would come home from school and find him gone, with no idea where he was. I'd walk the streets, looking for him. I worried so much about him I almost flunked my grade that year. Lynette and G.T. finally decided to have him put in the hospital where people could take care of him. And I moved in with G.T.

St. Aubin Hospital was founded back in 1850 by Althea St. Aubin, a Northern woman who was able to convince our state legislature that mentally disabled people shouldn't be put in jails. Up until that time, most mentally ill people in our state were kept in poorhouses, private homes, or jails, according to G.T. The hospital grounds covered fifty-five acres. There were a dozen or more buildings on the grounds, for administration, different types of patients, warehouses, and supplies. My daddy stayed in a four-story brick building near the front entrance of the hospital. It was a section for long-term care, but the people who stayed there weren't locked up like they were in some other sections.

As G.T. took the exit to the hospital, Doc McKenzie & the Gospel Hi-lites were belting out "I'm Trying So Hard." I looked out the window at the city landscape. We passed a shopping center, a church, a warehouse, a car dealership. Brightly colored balloons tied to the new cars lining the road bobbed in the wind.

By the time we got to the main entrance of the hospital, about two miles off the bypass, the Saints were singing "Don't Leave Me, Jesus." G.T. turned the radio down so he could talk to the uniformed attendant in the security booth at the front gate. G.T. showed him his driver's license, told him who he was, who we were there to see, and the building we would be visiting. The guard put a visitor's pass in the windshield, then waved us through.

G.T drove his truck down the oak-lined driveway and turned into the parking lot at the right. There were only a few cars here today, but on Christmas the lot was usually full. We walked up to the main building where my daddy stayed and told the attendant at the front desk we were there to visit Glenn Terrill. While she arranged for someone to bring him out from his section of the building, we waited in the lobby to the right of the front door, as we entered. It was a wide, spacious room, with a fireplace. An oil painting of Ms. Althea St. Aubin hung over the fireplace. In the painting she had a narrow, aristocratic nose, and pretty, hazel eyes, but her jaw was set at an angle that let you know she could kick ass if she didn't get what she wanted. I liked this painting because it reminded me that there were strong women who made a difference in the world even back then. Ms. Althea hated the idea of mentally disabled folks being put in jails with common criminals, and it was due to her dedication and hard work that people like my daddy now had a decent place to stay.

When the attendant brought my daddy out to the lobby he was stoop-shouldered and dazed looking, like he was still waking up from a dream. His arms, which had once rippled with muscle, were skinny now. He wore a white shirt with a plastic holder in the vest pocket, with two pens inside. A plastic ID bracelet encircled his wrist.

I hugged and kissed him. "Hi, Daddy. What's the pens for?"

"Letters," he said. "Been writing letters to my friends."

Daddy's 'friends' were guys he used to know in the Marines. He always said he wrote them, but as near as I could tell, he didn't have any of their addresses.

G.T. and I took him out to the truck, Daddy sitting between us as G.T. drove to the Italian restaurant where we usually went for lunch. It was in a shopping mall a couple of miles from the hospital. On the way there I asked Daddy how he had been. He said he had been fine, that Lynette and her family had been to see him "a few days ago," but I knew for a fact they hadn't been there for a month or more. Then he asked the question I always dreaded hearing: "How come Lee didn't come this trip?"

Since his injury Daddy lived in some other time, back before my brother died.

I didn't answer. When Daddy repeated his question, his voice agitated, G.T. said, "Lee had to work today. Said he'd see you next time."

Daddy was silent, like he was trying to absorb this information. "You tell Lee to come see me next time."

"OK," G.T. nodded too fast, like a film speeded up. He didn't like this part, either.

"You tell him, you hear me?" Daddy said. I could see the white, jagged scars under his thinning hair.

"No problem, Glenn. We'll sure tell him."

I took one of his hands in mine, tried to remember the last time I held hands with someone. I remembered the time he took me to my first day of school. I was pretty sure he held my hand then.

When we got to the restaurant a stocky man with a shaved head and a red goatee was standing by the door, like he was waiting for someone inside. He glared at us. My daddy and I were still holding hands. The skinhead sneered at us as we passed by. "Faggots."

I felt a hot wave move through my body. I turned loose of Daddy's hand and moved towards Mr. Goatee, but I was too late: G.T. already had him up against the wall. His fists, gripping the man's black leather jacket, were pressed into his throat.

"G.T., let me have that son-of-a-bitch!"

"Take your daddy inside!"

Daddy and I went on into the restaurant. I looked back and saw the skinhead's face was turning purple. His mouth was moving like he was trying to talk, only I didn't think that would be easy with G.T.'s sledge-hammer fists pressed against his voice box.

Daddy and I sat in a booth against the wall. He had the same vacant look in his eyes, as if he was still back in time. I realized I was lucky G.T. had taken care of that skinhead instead of me. I couldn't afford to get busted for fighting or assault and battery. Especially not if Dopodja found out about it.

G.T. came in the restaurant, looking around for us. He sat down in the booth across from us and began cracking the knuckles on his big, scarred hands. I wondered what he had done to the skinhead—probably just roughed him up a little. Man was lucky G.T. didn't break his damn fool neck.

Daddy said, "It's great to see you, G.T. How come you don't come more often?"

"Jobs keep me jumping. Everybody needs a new roof."

"Hard for me to jump, can't get very high." He looked at me. "Durned if you haven't grown big, Jesse. You were a little bitty thing when we brought you home from the hospital. How old are you now?"

"Almost seventeen, Daddy."

"Seem to have lost some time there." He frowned and rubbed his eyes.

The server came with the menus. Daddy didn't open his. "Ma'am, are you getting enough sunshine?"

"Can't get no sunshine. Got to work all the time. What you all want to drink?"

I asked for iced tea, G.T. wanted a Coke. Daddy kept staring at the waitress like he was trying to place her.

"God's light is shining all the time," he said.

She cut her eyes at G.T., pursed her lips, tapped her foot on the floor, looked back at my daddy. "What you want to drink?"

"Drink?"

"Bring him some tea," G.T. said.

"Be right back with your drinks."

Daddy took a notebook out of his pocket and looked at it. "Got to get some letters written today."

"They got a jukebox since we were last here," G.T. said. It was by the door. G.T. walked over to it, made some selections, put in some coins. Hank Senior began singing "Your Cheatin' Heart."

"Who's he singing about?" Daddy asked.

"Somebody he knew a long time ago, Daddy." I was thinking maybe that wasn't such a good song for G.T. to play.

"I might have known her, too. But I can't . . . recall her name. Memory isn't so good these days."

My daddy was still holding my hand. He kept holding it after the waitress brought the tea. He picked up his glass with his other hand, still holding my right hand. He held it tightly, like I was a balloon that might slip away from him and float up into the sky.

Before my daddy got hurt he stood with his shoulders straight, and he would look you in the eye when he spoke. He could fix anything that was broken around the house, do plumbing and electrical work, and solve just about any math problem I asked him to help me with, usually without even consulting the textbook. He liked to read, too, especially books about the Civil War. He could tell you about the major battles that took place, the strengths and weaknesses of the commanding officers, their military strategies, and how effective each one was. This made me see how a person's life can change from good to bad in a few heartbeats. I remembered Mr. Berry, my daddy's boss at the lumberyard where he worked, visiting Daddy in the hospital after he got hurt. A short, heavyset man with three chins, Mr. Berry kept wiping the sweat off his forehead with a handkerchief, even though it wasn't hot at all in the room. "Tell Glenn not to worry about the medical bills," he told G.T. "I've told him that but I'm not sure it registered. Insurance should take care of most of it. He just needs to focus on getting well." My daddy was on a ventilator then, his head wrapped in bandages, his eyes closed. You could tell by looking at him we would be wasting our breath to tell him not to worry about hospital bills.

Strange thing about that night—the night he got hurt—I woke up out of a deep sleep, with a sharp pain in the back of my head. I called out for him. When he didn't answer, I got up and looked in his bedroom. His bed was empty. It was 3:30 A.M., way past time for him to be home. Sometimes he went out to the bars on Friday night, to watch TV, shoot pool, socialize, and unwind from the work week, but he was always home by midnight. When I couldn't find him, I looked to see if his truck was in the driveway. In a panic I called the Flamingo where he usually went, but no one answered. I brewed some coffee and sat in the kitchen, waiting for him. Wasn't any way I could sleep.

G.T. called just after daylight to say Daddy was in the hospital. He was on the way to pick me up. I didn't go to school that day or the next one either. I spent both days at the hospital, sleeping in a chair or on a couch in the lobby.

The money in my daddy's wallet was probably gone in no time, pissed away on crack or booze. But the damage that thug did to him will last a human lifetime. The detectives still had not found out who did it—I didn't know how hard they tried. About a year and a half after it happened I thought I overheard G.T. say he knew who it was. He was drinking whiskey on the front porch one night with his friend, Buddy McBane. G.T. and Buddy were talking in low voices, and the only thing I heard after that was *". . . in prison now but he won't be in there forever."* G.T. later denied he had ever said any of this, claimed I must have imagined it, but I had a vivid and clear recollection of him saying it. I remembered thinking about it a long time afterwards, too. I remember thinking I would kill whoever hurt my daddy if I could find out who it was.

Even if my soul burns forever in the fiery pit.

CHAPTER 7

"Look at this!" Ray Thorne said, shaking a newspaper in my face. "They caught another truckload of illegal aliens trying to sneak into Texas. Border Patrol busted twenty-one wetbacks. I'm sick of it. Whole country is being taken over by foreigners.'"

I was sitting on the windowsill, the old man's Bible in my lap, waiting for him to come back from one of his trips to dreamland. I figured Ray's outburst would rouse him, and sure enough it did. His eyelids flew open, his fishline eyebrows raised high, giving him a fierce and startled look. "What do you mean by 'foreigners?'"

"Illegal aliens, rice eaters, Q-tip heads. They're swarming all over the place. Hell, go into a gas station now in this city, who is going to pump your gas? Likely as not it will be somebody who believes Mohammed is the engineer driving the whole damned universe—or else some wetback who swam across the Rio Grande one night when the moon was behind a cloud."

"Ray, you're a Christian, right?

"Damn right."

"You ever read the Bible?"

"Of course I read the Bible."

"Jesse, get that Old Testament off the shelf, the one with the dark red cover."

I did what he said.

"Turn to Leviticus, chapter nineteen, and read verses seventeen through nineteen."

I found the place and began reading:

"*When a stranger resides with you in your land, you shall not wrong him. The stranger who resides with you shall be to you as one of your citizens; you shall love him as yourself, for you were strangers in the land of Egypt: I am the Lord your God . . .*"

"There you have it," Mr. Ebban said. "The word of God for the believers in God. Those are words from your King James Bible. As a Christian, how can you speak of any other human being as an alien?"

"A passage like this has got to be put in perspective, Mendel. First of all, I don't think it covers infidels and heathens. And second, I'm all for lending someone a helping hand, but not if he's going to be stealing my property, taking over my neighborhood, trying to have sex with my wife—"

"Your wife? Did someone try to have sex with your wife?"

"I'm talking about possibilities."

"What kind of possibilities?"

"Here's what I'm talking about. What's to stop these rice-eaters, Q-tip heads, and illegal aliens—in short, all your swarthy, sweaty hordes—from taking over the whole country?"

"Let's get back to your wife. Somebody is trying to pinch her *tuchis*? Are you keeping her in a safe place?"

"She passed, Mendel! Dammit, you know that."

"Then you don't have anything to worry about."

"I'm not talking about my wife per se, but the values and the beliefs of our beloved nation."

"I see. Tell me exactly how these people you fear are going to take over the country."

"Hell, I don't know. They'll figure out a way. They're probably already working on a plan. Even if they're not, sooner or later, they're going to outnumber all of the white people, and then they can do whatever the hell they want. Wake up and smell the tacos, Mendel. The white birthrate is plummeting. But these river rats and desert runners are baby factories. They're not only streaming across the border, they're multiplying like coyotes and fire ants."

"Ray, what do the words say at the bottom of the statue in New York Harbor, that greets people coming to America from all over the world?"

"How the hell should I know what's written on a *French* statue?"

"I'll tell you what it says," Mr. Ebban said. "It says, '*Give me your poor, your downtrodden, your huddled masses, yearning to breathe free air, all those who are heavily laden, and I will give them refuge.*'"

"That's just a bunch of fancy words. You can't take in every damn boat person with a jones for a Big Mac and a wide-screen TV. If you do, sooner or later, the whole country's going to be out to sea in a leaky bucket. We might not live to see the worst of it, but this young fellow here will." Ray fixed his beady eyes on me. "What do you think about all these foreigners?"

I shrugged, thinking of Rosalita and her kids, of Carlos and Ricardo. "America is a big country. It's got plenty of room to grow."

"Ain't no hope for either one of you. Excuse me, I got to go get some air."

After Ray left I asked the old man if he wanted me to read some more.

"No, let's get some fresh air, too."

I signed us out at the front desk, then wheeled him out the front door and around the walkway to the park in back. Ms. Lynch wanted us to enter and leave this way, instead of out the back, so she could keep track of who was coming and going. I kept thinking about Ray's fear of "foreigners and aliens" taking over the country. He was talking about people like Carlos and Ricardo, along with the migrants who worked on the potato and cabbage farms out in the county. It seemed to me that they were mostly hard-working people who lived in two-room apartments or trailers and ate cheap food so they could send money back home to their families in Mexico. I tried to imagine Ray Thorne doing something like that but couldn't picture it. I'd heard him say he had a daughter who was married to a minister in Las Vegas. He was complaining about having to send her money. Apparently his son-in-law wasn't earning enough to pay their bills. It's no wonder he's not doing so well out there, I thought. Most people who go to Las Vegas probably aren't looking for a preacher.

It had rained earlier, and the air still smelled wet and clean. The wind was blowing the clouds off to the west. The sun was shining again, and there was a rainbow above the clouds.

As I pushed the old man through the park, I thought how Ray was too slow to realize Mr. Ebban was mocking him. The old man thinks he's smart, I thought, but there's plenty of unnatural behavior in his sacred Torah. Those Jews in the Torah were very uptight about sex. In the book of Davarim it says if a man discovers his wife wasn't a virgin when they got married, the whole town should stone her to death. And in the Book of Vayikra, if a woman is having her period both the poor woman and anything she sits on is considered "unclean" for seven days. I read all of this on my own. Sure makes you feel sorry for any woman or girl having her period back then.

When we came to the fountain Mr. Ebban held up his hand for me to stop, then bowed his head. The wrinkles in his neck reminded me of the rings around the insides of trees, that tell how old the tree is. "Blessed are you, our Lord, our God," he said, "for setting this rainbow in the sky." He did the same thing last week when he heard thunder—made me stop so he could say a prayer of thanks. Everything reminded this old man of God.

If I had to live like that I'd get flat out weary, I thought. Seeing God Almighty in a rainbow, hearing Him in thunder. No wonder Mr. Ebban was so crazy. Must feel like he's walking a tightrope every minute of the day. Somebody ought to tell him a human being has got to break bad once in a while, just to stay sane. But how can you do that when God is watching you from every cloud and bush?

CHAPTER 8

Our rap performance of "The Rime of the Ancient Mariner" was a big hit with the class. All the black students were on their feet, clapping and keeping time on the desk. Jared, Lamont, and I got a big round of applause afterwards. Angela Salazar's warm smile of approval gave me a moon-glow all over.

The ancient mariner made a mistake when he shot the albatross, sure, but he paid for his sin with his suffering. And he learned a lesson, too. I figured I was paying for my sins too, by cleaning off the swastika Bone painted at the back of the synagogue, and by tending to old Mendel Ebban. Maybe now some good luck would finally come my way.

I wanted to ask Angela out on a date, but every time I thought about calling her I got the shakes and lost my nerve. It would be easier to talk to her face to face, but she was usually accompanied by one or both of those frost queens, Margot and Desiree. If you smiled at them and said, "hey," they would either look like you had just asked them if they needed a rectal exam or else pretend they couldn't hear you at all. Each time this happened I swore I wouldn't try again, but I kept trying. Because they were Angela's friends, I wanted them to like me, too.

As I walked down the hall towards the old man's room, I heard him shouting. A wild hurtful cry, like he was in mortal pain.

When I got to his room, he was just sitting up in his bed, trembling. His face twisted and purple. Veins raised in his neck like thick blue cords. "The babies!" he cried. "They're killing the . . . babies!"

He began bucking and rolling on the bed, holding his hands over his ears, his eyes closed, like he was hearing some loud noise. He was moving around so violently that he rolled off onto the floor. His body struck the stand by the bed and knocked over the pitcher of ice water, the glass, and his bowl of oranges, too.

"Mr. Ebban, what's wrong?" I bent over him, but he was thrashing around so wildly that I couldn't do anything with him. He rolled over into the broken glass.

"Come from the four winds, O breath, and breathe upon these slain, that they may live!" he cried. Shards of glass were imbedded in his cheek.

"Mr. Ebban, it's me—Jesse. What's wrong? Tell me what's wrong. I want to help!"

I felt a hand on my shoulder—Varden. "Get the nurse!" he said.

I ran out the door and down the hall, looking for the nurse. I bumped into her as I went around the corner toward the front desk. She was holding a syringe.

"Mr. Ebban—" I said, but she rushed by me before I could complete the sentence.

I followed her down the hall. When I got to the room I saw Varden and Mr. Ebban on the floor. The old man had his face in Varden's chest, and Varden was struggling to hold him still.

The nurse took the plastic top off the needle. She knelt down and plunged it into the old man's hip, right through his clothes.

"It's all right now," Varden said, still holding Mr. Ebban. "Everything gone be all right. Old world is rocking along, birds singing in the trees, sun shining down on us. We all gone be here when the morning comes."

I went down the hall to the front desk, past the line of drooling ancients. My hand trembled as I signed myself out. I went out the door, into the sunlight, glad to be out of there, away from that crazy old man.

I had his blood on my fingers. I had to ride home like that on the bus. With his blood on my hands.

I went back to Havenwood Guardian Care on Sunday afternoon.

I saw Varden standing by the front door, drinking coffee from a Styrofoam cup.

"How is he?" I asked.

"Doing OK now."

"Sure glad to hear that. I don't want to be around him when he throws another one of those fits."

"You don't know shit, Terrill."

"What are you talking about?"

"You ever notice those numbers tattooed on his arm?"

"Yeah, I've seen them."

"Do you know where he was?"

"No."

"Treblinka."

"Where's that?"

"Nazi death camp in Poland. Mr. Ebban wasn't a whole lot older than you when he got sent there. He used to talk to me about it a lot, when he first came here. Especially when he couldn't sleep. I was working third shift then. Anyway, the Nazis rounded him and his family up from the ghetto in Warsaw at gunpoint one day, put them in cattle cars attached to a train. Crammed that cattle car full of people—men, women, and children—in every car, with only one little bucket in the center to do they business in. So many people wasn't no room to lay down. Jews thought they was going to a work camp, because that's what the Nazis told them, see. They spent two days in that cattle car without any food or water. When Mr. Ebban's daddy got the runs, he had to watch his daddy squat over that bucket in front of all those other folks. When they finally got to the camps, the guards took his mama off to one part of the camp and his daddy to another part, and they separated him from his little brother and little sister, too. He never saw them again. Know why?"

I shook my head, but I could already see where he was going with this nightmarish story.

"Here's what the Nazis did with Mr. Ebban's family, along with the other Jews they'd herded onto the train that day. Lined them up—men, women, and children—stripped them naked, shaved all of the hair off they bodies so they looked like skinned rabbits, then made them walk single file to the gas chambers. Packed them in there tight as they could, then locked the door and turned on the poison gas. These folks, these human beings, was all in the dark, coughing and choking, knowing they was dying, knowing there wasn't no hope. Nazis killed Mr. Ebban's mama, his daddy, his brother and his sister that way. But Mr. Ebban was young and strong so they kept him alive. They had a job for him to do, see. He was a stoker. Know what that was?"

"No."

"He separated the bodies out according to how they would burn. The Nazis was very scientific. They studied the way the corpses burned, took notes. They burned the well-fed bodies with the scrawny ones to get the most efficient combinations. Figured out the most economical way to do it was to burn a well-fed person with a bony, starved body. Sometimes they'd put a child or a couple of babies in there, too. They be burning so many thousands of people every day the ovens couldn't take it. Bricks crumbled. When the ovens broke down, they dug pits and burned the dead people there. They had a ditch at one end of the pit where they drained the fat off, and they poured that boiling fat over the bodies to help them burn. That was to save fuel. Now Mr. Ebban he's sorting the clothes off the ones waiting to be gassed. That's his job. All day long. The smell of the burnt dead folks got in his hair, his clothes, on his skin. That smell stayed there at night, when he slept in a barracks, with lice and bugs crawling all over him. Think about what his life must have been like. His whole family burned up and gone. All those dead bodies. Nazis kicking him and beating him every day. Nothing to eat to keep up his strength but a few pieces of bread and cabbage soup. It was a living hell.

"Here's something else to think about. The whole time the SS men and their Ukrainian flunkies was burning the Jews in their death camps, those good Christian citizens who lived nearby be sniffing the air. They be like, "I smell something burning. Smells like—*meat*." You think any of those people complained? Hell no. Whole countryside stinking with those burning bodies, but the good citizens just like those three monkeys that see no evil, hear no evil, and speak no evil. That's the problem with the whole world, Terrill. When bad shit be coming down, most everybody acts just like the see-no-evil monkeys.

"Before the Nazis started gassing the Jews, they took their property, beat them, shot them, made them wear a yellow star wherever they went. Jews be leaving towns and cities all over Europe—Poland, Hungary, Lithuania, places they'd lived for centuries. They was looking for some place to stay, somebody to take them in. What was America doing? America was like, 'Yo, man, we sorry about this Jewish refugee problem but we already met our immigrant quotas so we can't take no more Jews.'

"Same kind of shit went down in Dixie when all the original people was trying to vote. Some of the meaner white folks just declared open season on all the black folk—and any white folks who wanted to protect us, too. Dudes in sheets burning down houses, shooting us, and stringing us up from trees. But the problem wasn't just the Ku Kluxers and nightriders. It was all those upstanding Christian folks who looked the other way and acted like the three monkeys. And check this out, Terrill. When the stories about the camps and the dead Jews started coming out of Germany, whole world didn't want to believe it. They was like the three monkeys, too. Folks said, 'Na, they ain't doing that shit. That's just some propaganda, is all. Oh, maybe they just put a few Jews in them ovens and gas chambers, but it was probably just the criminals. Not the law-abiding citizens, and certainly not the women and children.'"

I had a sick feeling from hearing all this. I asked Varden how Mr. Ebban had gotten away from the death camp, why he didn't get killed, too. He said Mr. Ebban quit working one day, just couldn't take it any more. Sat down like a mule in the middle of a row and no matter how hard they beat and kicked him, he wouldn't work. The guards took him and some other Jews, all of them walking skeletons by now, to a field at the edge of the camp and made them dig a hole in the ground. Then they lined them up and shot them. Mr. Ebban was one of the first ones to fall, but the bullet only grazed his skull, and the others fell on top of him. It was late in the afternoon and the guards were half drunk so they decided to come back and fill up the grave with dirt in the morning. After they left, Mr. Ebban crawled out from under the dead men down in that hole. He dug under the barbed wire fence and escaped into the forest, trying to put as much distance as he could between himself and that death camp. He lived on what he could find in the forest—berries, mushrooms, seeds, nuts, and bird's eggs. He traveled for days and days, heading west, and somehow escaped the German patrols. A widow woman who owned a farm found him out by her chicken coup one day when she went to gather the eggs. He was near about dead by then. This woman, who had lost a son about his same age in the war, took him into her house and nursed him back to health. After he got his strength back she helped him get to the Baltic Sea, where he caught a ride on a freighter to Sweden.

"One more thing about Mr. Ebban, Terrill. Every day of his life, he's got to live with guilt because he survived and all those other people didn't. Now you think about what I told you. You think about that the next time you be putting that old man down cause he has slipped a gear or two or has a devil chasing him through his dreams."

Varden crunched up his Styrofoam coffee cup and went on into the building. I stood there looking at the reflection of the sky in the glass windows and door. I felt as worthless as a piece of scum floating on a cesspool. I'd had no idea Mr. Ebban had survived this kind of hellacious experience. I could see how I had misjudged him—from the very first day I had met him. He had even been telling me the truth about being able to identify the kind of warning calls a bird might make when it sees a snake.

I slunk back to his room, feeling lowdown and miserable. Mr. Ebban was sitting in his chair, a Band-Aid on his forehead, cuts on his cheek and over his eye. That ghost music playing on the record player in the corner. I picked up his Bible, took my seat in the windowsill, waited for the record to finish playing, then asked him what he wanted me to read to him. He just shook his head and wouldn't speak. We sat there for I don't know how long, me waiting for him to talk. I could have left, but I didn't. I just sat there with him, thinking I could just keep him company for a while.

When he finally fell asleep, I thought about going up to the front desk to sign out, but I couldn't leave; I kept trying to get my mind around the horror he had experienced in that death camp. I thought about him seeing his daddy shit in a bucket in the middle of a train car, about him seeing his mama and daddy and brother and sister taken away and killed, about sorting out the bodies of the dead to get them ready to burn in a brick oven. I thought about what he must have thought and felt at night after looking at dead people all day. And having to see them burn. I could get pieces of it all right; I just couldn't get my mind around the whole experience. It was like trying to pour the ocean into a gallon jug. I thought of the way he prayed at least three times a day, about the way he saw God in thunder, rainbows, and clouds. I wondered how he could even believe in God after all the death and suffering he had seen. This was one more thing about Mendel Ebban that was beyond my mental reach, no matter how much I thought about it. He was without a doubt the most mysterious person I had ever met on the whole godforsaken planet.

After I left Havenwood, I got off the bus at my stop on Oleander, but I didn't want to go home, so I started running. I headed out to the bypass. I ran along the shoulder of the by-pass, then all the way to the railroad tracks out on Cotton Gin Road. By then my lungs ached and my heart was pounding in my ears. Just past the tracks I went off the road through a cornfield and into the woods. I wanted to run away from the memory of Mr. Ebban sitting on the side of the bed staring at the wall, but the image had burned itself into my mind and I knew I would never be able to get away from it, no matter how far I ran.

"Look like you got caught in the middle of a cat fight," Clarence said. "What happened to your face?"

"Ran into some briars."

"Briars, huh?"

"That's right."

"What you doing out in the briar patch, Jesse?"

"Went for a little run."

"Running in the briar patch." Clarence leaned back in his chair, his hands folded behind his head. "Do you remember what the judge said?"

"I remember, yeah."

"Good. You know I had to haul in a probation violator last month. He's in Sheridan right now, cleaning toilets. Somebody make you mad, I want you to picture that dude, you hear? Toilets get stopped up, it's his job to clean them." Clarence pretended he was plunging a toilet. "Some of them cons can let loose some powerful big stinkies, too."

"I'll try to keep that in mind."

"You be sure and do that. Judge Simms put her butt on the line for you, Jesse. One day you might want to thank her. And in the meantime you might want to think about getting down on your knees and thanking the good Lord for giving you a second chance."

My eyeballs ached. My temples throbbed. I leaned forward in the chair and rubbed them. I was tired of hearing about the good Lord and God Almighty. Where was God when that terrorist drove a car full of dynamite into the embassy and killed my brother? Where was God when that mugger slithered out of the shadows and cracked my daddy's skull? Where was God when the Nazis were gassing all those innocent Jews?

CHAPTER 9

The bell over the door to Nick's Café jingled as I walked in. Nick's was on Oleander Avenue, about six blocks from my house—a rectangular metal building with a big neon sign out front announcing its name, although it was more of a diner than a café. Inside there was a counter on one end, with a grill behind it. A row of booths lined the other side. A juke box in the far corner played old songs from the fifties and sixties, by singers like Elvis Presley, Billie Holiday, Jerry Lee Lewis, Etta James, Brenda Lee, Sam Cooke, and Fats Domino. Nick Pappas, who owned the place, loved that old music, I guess because he had grown up with it. Pottstown kids complained about it, told him he needed to get some more modern songs on there. "This is roots music," he would say, with a big grin. "Can't have a tree without roots."

Nick, wearing his white chef's hat and a greasy apron, was frying two burgers on the grill. Two men in hardhats were sitting on stools at the counter. Nick's "Greek Burgers" were a big hit with the local men. They were about twice as big as a regular burger you'd get at a fast-food joint. Nick smothered them with spices and garlic, and some kind of original sauce he called "Cajun love juice." You could get them with onions, cheese, tomatoes, jalapeno peppers, and horseradish, too. Nick's burgers were about the best burgers you could find anywhere in the city.

LaFay and Snookie were in a booth down at the end. They saw me and waved.

"Hi, Jesse," LaFay said. "What's up?"

"Ain't making much noise," I said, as I slid in beside Snookie.

"Looking kind of scratched up today, Jesse," she said. "Somebody reject your advances?"

"Got into some thorns and briars."

"What you doing in thorns and briars?"

"I ran into them."

"Who was chasing you?"

"I just felt like running, is all."

Snookie rolled her eyes. There was still some tension between us, ever since I had broken up with her over Ric Farina.

"They got a special today on the blueberry pie," LaFay said. She was wearing a short-sleeved blouse that revealed a tattoo of a black cat high on her left arm. Its eyes were the color of blood.

I looked in my wallet for some money. I counted out the change on the table. Eighty-nine cents. "How much is the pie?"

"Ninety-nine cents plus tax."

"Looks like I am a little short."

LaFay took a change purse out of the pocket of her jeans, a little rubber thing, looked like something a kid would carry. Opening it up she gave me a dime, nickel, and some pennies.

"Thanks, LaFay." I went over to the counter and asked Mimi, the waitress, for a piece of blueberry pie. I figured if I took it back to the booth myself maybe she wouldn't feel like I had stiffed her on the tip.

Mimi, who used to work with my mama, was about her same age, forty-three. She had dark blue eye shadow, dyed blonde hair, and acne scars that she tried to cover up with make-up. She put the plate of pie on the counter, along with a fork. "Here you go, hon." She gave me a look and I knew what question she was going to ask before she asked it. "Heard from Loretta?"

"Not lately."

"I still can't understand her leaving like that." Every few months or so Mimi would say something like that. "Just don't add up."

I went back to the booth, sat there looking at the pie. I'd lost my appetite since Mimi mentioned my mom.

Snookie elbowed me in the ribs. "You going to eat it or watch it like a TV show?"

"Guess I really wasn't that hungry."

"If you ain't going to eat it, give it to me."

Sliding the pie over to her, I glanced at LaFay. I figured she would be irritated with me since she had loaned me the money to buy this pie, but she was gazing out the window. I wondered if she knew about my mom leaving with Curt Mosely.

"Mmmm, Jesse," Snookie said. "This is some bodacious good pie. You just don't know what you're missing."

I watched her eat the pie. Snookie lived with her mom and sister in a mill house over on McAlester Street, two blocks east of Oleander. Back when I used to go with her, we would cut school and meet there in the afternoon while her mom was working. Like a lot of kids in Pottstown, Snookie's dad was missing from the picture. Her parents had split up when Snookie was ten years old. Her father moved up North somewhere and she hardly ever heard from him now. One time she showed me a photograph of him holding her in his lap. Snookie looked to be about four years old in the picture. She had pigtails, and she was holding on to her daddy real tight.

She finished the pie, licked the fork clean, then looked at her watch. "I got to go. Got a date coming over at seven. You coming, LaFay?"

"Not now," LaFay said.

"Catch you all later then."

"Have fun on your date."

"I plan to," Snookie said, cutting her eyes at me.

After Snookie left, LaFay and I sat there listening to Fats Domino sing "Blueberry Hill." She had long, thick eyelashes and full lips. I looked at her boobs under her blouse and thought of how nice it would be to kiss her there.

She was in a relationship with Tony Moran—he owned the video game parlor on Tull Street. I thought how lucky he was, to have a girl like her.

"Fats is from New Orleans," she said.

"Is that where you're from?"

"Delacroix. We used to live there, though."

"You ever see him?"

"He was before my time, but my mama saw him once. She said he had a diamond ring on every finger."

I was staring at the tattoo on her arm.

"You want to know why I got it, huh?"

"Figure you just like black cats."

She drummed her fingers on the table, looked out the window. Her fingers were slim and rounded at the ends, the nails chewed down to the quick.

"When my mama was young she got a little down on her luck," she said. "She was turning tricks in the Quarter. She was supposed to be using birth control, but she messed up one night, and one of those little devils got through. I used to ask her if she remembered anything at all about the man that was my daddy. All she could remember about him was he had a tattoo of a black cat with red eyes on his left arm, high up near the shoulder. Hell, he could have come from anywhere—Pascagoula, Dallas, Memphis, Chicago, maybe even another country. People visit New Orleans from all over the world. When I was little, I used to look at men I saw on the street, wonder if one of them could have been my daddy. I knew there was no way I could ever check all the men in the world to see if they had the tattoo of a black cat up near their shoulder, so I got one on my arm. I figured that way if my daddy ever sees it, maybe he'll claim me."

She had a strand of hair hanging in her eyes. I had this urge to brush it away from her forehead, but I didn't. I was afraid she would take it wrong. "I hope you find him, LaFay."

She pushed out her lower lip and blew the hair out of her eyes, gave me a little smile.

"It's a long shot. But it's the only one I've got."

Lying in bed that night I thought about the way LaFay's dark eyes sometimes seemed to catch and hold the light. I thought about the way she held herself in reserve, like she was watching the world and not going to show you much on the surface, leaving you to try to figure out what was going on underneath. I thought about her lean, toned arms and her shiny hair, her high cheekbones, her pretty lips.

I pictured a man and woman on a bed in a dimly lit room, the motion of their sweating bodies reflected in a mirror on the dresser, where, on the man's bicep, was the tattoo of the black cat. And superimposed upon this reflection was the image of LaFay's face with her dark sad eyes.

Chapter 10

While reading to Mr. Ebban about the purification of the Levites, I was distracted by a cricket raising a ruckus somewhere in the room. Sounded like the Devil's personal fiddler, the one he would send you at your lowest point to ratchet up your misery.

I finally spotted him by the nightstand and crushed him with my foot.

"What did you step on?" Mr. Ebban asked. He had an orange in his hands.

"I killed that cricket."

"Why?"

"He was making a hellacious racket."

"Couldn't you have caught it instead and put it outside?"

"Why should I? It's just a cricket."

"Just a cricket." He began peeling his orange. I waited to see if he was going to try to hassle me about the cricket. He remained mercifully silent, however, eating his orange, the juice staining his beard.

I continued reading, hoping to put him to sleep, but he soon told me he wanted to go down the hall to see Gertrude Zahorski, the old woman who drove everyone crazy hollering for a cigarette.

"I'll wait here," I said.

"No," he said. "You come, too."

I didn't comment, but I was irritated that I would have to visit this old woman, whose bell tower had a major infestation of bats. I wondered what she was even doing on this wing, where the residents were supposed to be independent. Why wasn't she on the east wing with the ones Ray Thorne called "the veggies and babblers?"

When we got to her room, she was sitting up on pillows, drool trickling from the corner of her mouth. She had splotchy, discolored skin, purple bags under her eyes, bony little hands like claws. Her room smelled of stale piss and air freshener.

"Hello, Gertrude," the old man said. "It's Mendel and Jesse, here to pay you a visit."

"No one ever comes to see me," she said, working her face into a mummified pout.

"We came to see you."

She puckered up her gash of a mouth and puffed air out, like our presence was of no importance. "My husband is dead. We were married forty-eight years. He wasn't a bad husband. Every morning he brought the paper in for me to read. He never forgot my birthday or our anniversary. Always put the lid down on the toilet."

"Sounds like a *mentsh*."

I wondered why he used these Yiddish words when people didn't understand them, but Ms. Zahorski appeared not to have heard him.

"We had two children. They're gone, too."

"Do you have grandchildren?"

"Yes. They never come and see me."

"I see." Mr. Ebban was nodding, looking like he was pondering this deeply.

"How about you—why don't your children come to see you? Did you do something mean to them?"

"Never had children."

"Lucky man. They're nothing but trouble."

"Gertrude, your room gets a lot of sun."

"It does?"

"Yes. The sunlight comes through your window and strikes that sun catcher up there."

She turned to look at the glass prism hanging in the window. "So it does."

"Where did you get it?"

"I got it—somewhere. I don't remember."

"It must be a joy to look at every day."

"It's all right, but you know these attendants are a pain in the ass."

Mr. Ebban moved his wheelchair closer to her bed, looked around as if checking to see if anyone was listening. "Gertrude, did you know your eyes are an unusual shade of blue?"

"They are?"

"Yes. They are the color of robins' eggs."

She looked at me, color rising in her downy cheeks. "He's full of shit, isn't he?"

I shrugged, turned my palms up.

"Go ahead, stick up for him. He's just like all the other men. Only wants one thing."

"All I want is to see you smile."

"Well, you should come to see me more often, then."

"We can come see her again, can't we, Jesse?"

I was silent, hoping he knew I had zero interest in visiting her anytime in the next century.

Mrs. Zahorski looked at Mr. Ebban. "You're all right, I guess, but he looks shifty." She jerked her head at me. "Do you keep an eye on your valuables when he's around?"

"Are you kidding? Jesse has to keep an eye on his wallet."

"I wouldn't trust him if I was you. He has a slippery look. My husband had a bad dog once with that same look in its eyes. He'd bite you when your back was turned."

Mr. Ebban asked her what kind of dog she'd had, and she launched into a rambling description of three different dogs, all long gone from the world, the old man listening and nodding like it was the most fascinating story he had ever heard. I eased out of the room and leaned against the wall outside, waiting for him to finish his cockeyed errand of mercy.

By the fountain in the park, the old man took something out of his pocket and held it up for me to see. It was a small carpenter's level, looked like it was made of brass.

"Jesse, do you know what this is?"

"Sure, it's a carpenter's level."

"Yes, otherwise known as a spirit level. Now, notice what happens when I tilt it this way."

"Bubble moves to the left."

"That's right. Now what happens if I tilt it this way?"

"Bubble flows to the right."

"What happens if I put it here?" He placed it on the rim of the fountain.

"It's centered between the two lines—I know how to use a level, Mr. Ebban."

"Imagine that the whole world is like this level—poised in perfect balance between good and evil, between love and hate. One side is the world when it has a heart of stone and the other side is the heart of mercy, the eyes open to the light of God. Imagine that what you do or say every moment of your life influences this delicate balance. You commit a sin, even one of omission, you push the whole world to this side—" he tilted the level to his left. "Show mercy and forgiveness—you tilt the balance in this direction." He tilted the level to the right. "We must keep this awareness in mind at all times, that we hold the power to tilt the balance in one direction or the other, every moment of our lives."

He put the spirit level into my palm, closing both his hands around mine. "You say you are an *apikoros*, a non-believer. But I want you to keep this."

"I'm not a carpenter." I tried to pull away from him but at that moment I could have no more opened my hand than I could have touched the moon. It was as if the old man's hands had some kind of magic power.

When he turned me loose, I put the level in my pocket. I didn't want the thing, but I didn't want to hurt his feelings, either. "Most people never get the chance to influence the whole world. I'm not going to make a difference one way or the other."

"What if everything in the world were connected, like a spider's web? Jiggle the web in one place, the whole web vibrates. Touch the web in one place, every strand feels the effect of your influence, no matter how small."

"What if pigs could fly? We'd all have to carry umbrellas even when the sun was shining."

"Perhaps they can fly."

"Tell me another one."

"Can you prove to me that they can't fly?"

"I've never seen one fly."

"Ever seen a sperm fertilize an egg?"

"No, and I don't want to either."

"Have you ever seen photosynthesis?"

"Not lately."

"Then how do you know those things could happen?"

"Everybody with any sense knows about that stuff, Mr. Ebban."

"That's a flimsy test for truth, whether everybody 'knows' it or not. People used to 'know' the earth was flat."

I was getting frustrated with him now, the way he could talk circles around a subject. "If pigs can fly, where are their wings?"

"Would you believe it if you saw it?"

"I guess."

"I saw a pig fly once."

"Sure you did."

"A big wind picked it up and sailed it right by my window. I saw it go by. There was a rooster right behind it."

I was all out of words. This old man could talk the Devil into giving up his pitchfork, I thought, as I pushed him on up the path.

That night I lay in bed, looking at the moonlit bubble in the vial of the carpenter's level on my dresser. I wished he wouldn't have given it to me, because I knew I would have to keep it now. I would put it with all my other keepsakes, most of them in the box under my bed—the photos, the locket that used to belong to my mama, the letters from my brother, my mama's blouse, that pencil Angela Salazar gave me. I wondered how long Mr. Ebban had owned this level. I thought of his hands, his swollen joints, his crooked fingers, and his wrinkled, age-spotted skin. That was the last thing I remembered thinking about before I drifted off to sleep, Mr. Ebban's hands holding up that spirit level by the fountain in the park.

On Friday afternoon I got a phone call from Ms. Lynch. She told me that instead of my regular hours on Sunday afternoon, I was to report to the nursing home on Saturday at 7:30 A.M., to "assist Mr. Ebban." I asked her what for.

"I didn't ask him, but that's your assignment," she said, in a frosty tone. "We'll expect to see you bright and early tomorrow morning. On time, please."

I wondered what the old man wanted with me on the morning he attended his worship service. Maybe he's sick, I thought. Could be he wanted me to read to him in his bed.

When I arrived at his room, however, he was all dressed up in a blue suit, a white shirt, and navy tie with his prayer shawl around his shoulders. He had his brown beanie on his head.

"You ready, mate?" Varden asked. He had slipped up on me in those rubber-soled shoes.

"For what?"

"You're going to accompany Mr. Ebban to temple today."

"Me? I thought that was your job."

"Got to be in a wedding this morning. I'm best man. You the stand-in today."

"You got to be joking." I only knew one synagogue in the city, and that was a place I had no interest in visiting.

"Ain't fooling, Terrill." Varden looked at his wristwatch. "Let's get him out to the van, or we're going to be late."

On Maupin Avenue, Varden slowed down to avoid hitting a mud-covered snapping turtle. Maupin ran along the edge of Indian Lake, which was where the snapper must have come from. After we passed the turtle Mr. Ebban asked Varden to stop the van.

Varden glanced in the rearview mirror, slowed down, then pulled off onto the side of the road. There was a guardrail, and then the land sloped down to the lake. A truck went right over the turtle, the tires missing him.

"Jesse," Mr. Ebban said, from the back seat. "I want you to get that turtle off the road."

"What?"

"You know that's a snapper, sir," Varden said. "They like pits bulls when they mad."

"Jesse," Mr. Ebban said.

"What you want me to get him for?"

"Because he does not know the danger he is in. He thinks his shell will protect him. But his shell wasn't designed for three thousand pounds of steel hurtling down the highway. Now go quickly—and watch out for cars!"

I got out of the van and walked along the edge of the road to where the snapper was sitting, his claws trailing green slime. He was a hoss, looked like he would weigh twenty pounds. Smelled like old, wet mud. I got a stick from the roadside and used it to try to turn him around and get him off the road. Snapper didn't like that at all. He grabbed the end of the stick in his jaws and crushed it. I pushed the stick against his shell, but he seized it again. I pulled him forward with the stick—until another piece came off in his jaws.

Varden was hollering something out the window, but I couldn't hear what he was saying. Cars swerved into the next lane to avoid hitting us. I pushed the snapper again with the stick, but he bit it in two. He opened his jaws wide to let me know what he would do if he could get hold of me.

I finally heard what Varden was saying: "Get that sucker by the tail! Pick him up that way and he can't bite you!"

Considering this advice, I remembered my daddy telling me about a man who was trying to get a king snake off his back porch. He picked it up by the tail and tried to throw it into the field behind his house. King snake bit him on the thigh.

A semi was bearing down on us. The driver gave a warning blast with his air-horn. It seemed like a good time to jump out of the road and let Mr. Snapper take his chances with the semi. But like a fool, I moved behind the turtle, grabbed him by his gristly tail and hoisted him up. I got him off the road just before the semi thundered by, blowing diesel fumes in my face.

The snapper was not only heavy, his bony tail was so slippery it was all I could do to hold him. To make matters worse, he was doing his best to bite me. But Varden was right—he couldn't reach me with his powerful jaws, although he was so mad he was hissing and coughing like a cat. I hoisted him up to show the old man I had got him and then I stepped over the railing and slid down the slope to the lake. Heaving him into the water, I turned around and scrambled back up the slope.

When I got back into the van, Varden was whooping and laughing. "Wooooeeee! Wish I had a video camera." He put the van into gear and pulled back onto the highway. "Lord, that's the most fun I've had all week, watching you wrestle that snapper."

"I don't see what's so damned funny, Varden. Sure didn't see you risking your ass to save an old snapper."

"Mr. Ebban didn't direct his request to me."

I wondered why I was so quick to do a foolish thing like that, just because the old man had asked me to do it. When I agreed to community service, wasn't anything said about getting a snapping turtle off the highway.

I sat there fuming over Varden's laughter and also the fact that the old man hadn't even bothered to thank me for my trouble, as if I was some kind of slave. Varden got into the right lane and turned onto Willow Street, which led to Oleander and the B'nai Shalom Temple.

By the time Varden had pulled up to the front of the temple, I had a funny feeling in the pit of my stomach, like I was on an elevator descending too fast. I looked out the window at the synagogue and wished to God I could just disappear and reappear at any other place on the whole planet.

"Let's get that wheelchair out of the back," Varden said.

While we were getting the wheelchair out I asked Varden when he was coming back.

"Ain't no telling, dude. This is a spiritual occasion. Now you just go on in there and enjoy them nice folks. I imagine you all will have a lot to talk about."

I wanted to hit him, I really did. But all I could do was stand there watching him push the wheelchair around to the side door to help Mr. Ebban out of the back of the van.

People were going into the synagogue, most of the men wearing those funny little hats. I saw a young woman carrying a baby in her arms, and I remembered how Mr. Ebban had woken up screaming from that bad dream. He was dreaming they were killing babies. Looking at this woman holding her infant, I wondered how anyone, even Nazis, could hurt a baby. And I wondered how the old man could even take time out to worship God after having seen so many of his people murdered, their ashes floating over the Polish countryside like little gray butterflies.

As I pushed him up the walkway toward the B'nai Shalom Temple I was seized with a sudden fear—that these Jews planned to murder me and cover up the crime somehow, maybe by claiming I had fallen down and broken my neck. I broke out in a cold sweat.

The doors were propped open. A tall man with a grey beard stood just inside the synagogue. I wondered if he had been at my trial. As I pushed Mr. Ebban into the hall or lobby, he and the bearded man shook hands, greeted each other with "Shalom." Mr. Ebban introduced us. The man's name was Aaron Mintz.

"I know who you are," Aaron Mintz said, scowling. He gave the old man a prayer book.

"Let me have another one. I want one for Jesse."

"You want one for *him?*"

"That's right."

Mr. Mintz's body stiffened, like somebody had jammed a gun in his back.

"He will need one, too." The old man's bushy eyebrows were raised high, his jaw lifted in a determined way.

It was a Mexican standoff, both of them staring at each other, neither one willing to give an inch. I did not want to witness this conflict. Also, I wanted to get the smell of turtle off my hands before I entered their sanctuary.

"Uh, excuse me, sir," I said. "Is there a place where I can wash my hands?"

The bearded man directed me to a bathroom, down a hall to the left of the foyer. I went into their john and washed my hands. I looked at my face in the mirror on the wall. I had a splotch of mud on my forehead. I imagined it taking the form of the numbers 666. The mark of the beast. My heart fluttering, I scrubbed off the mud with a hand towel.

When I got back to the hallway, Mr. Mintz and Mr. Ebban were having an intense conversation, with hand gestures. They stopped talking as I approached. I noticed the old man had two prayer books in his hand.

People were walking by them, picking up prayer books from the stand by the door as they entered the sanctuary. Most of them stopped to greet the old man with "Shalom." They touched his shoulder, a few shook his hand.

One man looked at me, scowled, and shook his head.

"Ready to go in?" Mr. Ebban asked.

"Don't you want me to wait out here?"

"No. I want you to come in."

"I'm not welcome in—"

"Put this on," he said, holding up one of their strange caps. He had been concealing it under his prayer shawl.

I shouldn't have come here, I thought. I should have told Ms. Lynch I was sick. He didn't really need me, anyway, he could roll his own fool self up the walkway. He just wants to punish me in some way.

I put the beanie on my head and pushed his wheelchair on into the sanctuary.

Morning sunlight streamed down through the tall rectangular windows. There were about forty people in the room, some sitting in chairs, some standing. I noticed that men and women were together, not separate as I had previously thought. The Jews were speaking in unison, in a language I didn't understand but which I knew to be Hebrew, since I had heard Mr. Ebban pray in Hebrew before. The men had taken off their wristwatches. I could see white circles on their suntanned arms, where the watches had been. I guessed they didn't believe in keeping track of time on a holy day, or else watches weren't allowed in the sanctuary.

I looked at the prayer book, trying to make sense out of it. The prayers were printed in English on one side, in Hebrew on the other. Some of the people sitting in the chairs were reading the prayer book aloud; others were just whispering quietly together. Suddenly a man standing down at the front began chanting words in Hebrew—the same language in the prayer book, the same language as in the Torah. The language of Moses and the prophets. As if on some cue, the people all stood and chanted together; then they sat down. I stood there like a dummy, not knowing what to do. Thinking they were following the prayer book, I looked at the words in English on the side to find out where they were. I was thinking I could at least follow along in the book to keep up, but I was totally lost. A woman standing to my left turned the pages of the book to the back, all the while reciting in Hebrew in my ear, and pointed to the text at the right. She immediately returned to her place, and I wondered if she would get in trouble for helping me out like that, showing me this small kindness. I looked at what they were reading and recognized the words in English. I had read them before for Mr. Ebban: "*O earth, hear the words I speak. My truths shall fall like rain. My commandments like water on the green plants. I will speak the name of Adonai. I give Him glory.*"

The people's voices flowed together in a musical rhythm, as they sang, chanted, and recited prayers. Now and then I could hear the old man's voice among them. It would rise and fall, like an instrument, sometimes standing out, other times blending in with the other voices. Although he was holding the prayer book, I knew he could not read print that size. I was amazed that he could recite all of these words from memory.

The prayer book began at the back and moved toward the front, opposite from the way a regular book would be. I scanned some of the words on the right side of the page. *Keep these words of mine in your heart and in your soul. Bind them on your arm and let them be a sign on your forehead. Teach them to your children and speak them during the day and when you lie down to sleep. Write them on parchment and attach them to the doorposts of your houses.*

I saw in this passage where the Jews had gotten some of their practices—like the boxes Mr. Ebban wore around his arm and head when he prayed.

Although I was touched by this woman's generous willingness to help me find the place in the service, I didn't feel any holy presence. I was conscious only of the sounds, the lilting, chanting voices, the clear gold light falling through the windows, people swaying to the rhythm of their chants, my sweating palms on the back of the old man's wheelchair. He was swaying, too, in his wheelchair. I shifted my weight from one foot to the other, wishing I could have waited for him outside, but he had ordered me to stay here with him, wearing this ridiculous hat—his way of humiliating me for my sins.

While a young man with a high clear voice sang and chanted on the elevated platform down front, a little Bambi-eyed girl in a white dress watched me from the side of the platform, her thumb in her mouth. Thinking of the children in those concentration camps I felt a sudden pain in my chest, and I looked away. The swaying and chanting people all created a kind of spell around me. My mind drifted away to times my daddy, Lee, and I had fished in the county's ponds and rivers. I was distracted from my reverie by a lull in the service, like the pause when you are shifting gears in a car or truck. Two men were approaching the cabinet at the front while the congregation sang. As one man opened the door the seated worshipers stood up. The reader was singing in Hebrew. He paused and the congregation sang in response. The first man picked up one of the scrolls and slowly and carefully handed it to the reader. Resting it on his right shoulder, he draped his arm over it and supported it with his left hand. The other man closed the cabinet and stood behind the reader, who faced the congregation. He chanted something in Hebrew, and the congregation responded with another chant. With one of his assistants walking in front of him and the other walking behind, the reader carried the scroll through the assembled people, all of them standing for this part of the service, except Mr. Ebban. They touched it with their prayer books or their shawls, kissing their fringes afterwards. The Torah passed by us, and the old man reached out and touched the scroll with his prayer shawl, and after it passed, he kissed the fringes. I remembered the rough way Mick, Bone, and I had torn the ribbon off the scroll and thrown it on the floor. I pictured the mantle on top taking the shape of a snake, which uncoiled itself in the air above the scroll, fangs bared, and struck down at me with lightning speed. I drew back so fast the old man turned in his chair to see what was going on.

"So what did you think of the service?" Varden asked, on the way back to the nursing home.

"It was really something," I said. "You ought to try it some time."

"Might just do that. I like to see how different people worship the Lord."

The old man was silent in the back seat.

I realized that the Jews were much kinder to me than I deserved. Even the rabbi, who had testified at my trial had said, "Shalom" as Mr. Ebban and I were leaving. I thought of him, the little Bambi-eyed girl, the woman who helped me find the place in the prayer book, and the half dozen others who either smiled at me or wished me "Shalom" at the end of the service. Why couldn't they have spat on me and cursed me? That would have made a lot more sense. But if they were trying to punish me they did a damn fine job of it. I left there feeling lower than a lizard's ass and twice as foul.

— PART II —

CHAPTER 11

Snookie, LaFay, Terra, and I were in a back booth in Nick's Café when Tony Moran came in. He had a muscular chest and arms and a handsome face—olive-toned skin, curly black hair. Walked with a swagger like he thought he was God's gift to the world.

LaFay smiled and waved. "Hi, Tony. Come join us."

He just stood by our booth, though. Clenching and unclenching his jaw.

"Called your house three times last night. You weren't there."

"That's right, Snookie and me went bowling."

"You didn't tell me."

"Thought you were working."

"Still like to know where you are."

LaFay frowned and looked down at her hands.

Tony's shirt was open at the front, a shiny gold cross nestled against his chest hair. He rapped his hairy knuckles on the table. "So why didn't you call me?"

"Let's talk about this later, Tony."

"I'd like to talk about it *now*."

LaFay just sat there, like she was trying to make up her mind what to do. I was hoping she would tell him to get lost, but she finally said, "Not here." She slid out of the booth and walked to the door. He followed her out.

"What the hell she got to tell him she's going bowling for?" Snookie asks. "Is he her parole officer?"

"Fool thinks he owns any girl he goes out with," Terra said. "I warned LaFay about him, but she wouldn't listen."

"Check out Prince Charming's chariot." Snookie was looking out the window at Tony's shiny black Lexus, which was parked in front of Nick's. "He's got some fine wheels. You know that man has got money. His daddy owns the Shanghai, nightclub on Decatur Street."

"Tony Moran is a Neanderthal," Terra said. "Men carry cell phones and wear designer clothes but their minds are back in the Stone Age. Take off the designer clothes and put on the animal skins—they'd be right at home in the caves, rubbing sticks together to start a fire."

"Some of them are all right," Snookie said.

"Not Moran," Terra said. "He's got the brain of a gorilla."

Through the window I saw LaFay and Tony standing by his car. He looked like he was fussing at her. She had her arms folded, her head down. This really rubbed my fur all wrong. I realize how much I didn't like Tony Moran, and, even more, how much I hated the fact that LaFay was going out with him.

"How old is he anyway?" I asked.

"Too damn old to act like a fool," Terra said.

I was hoping LaFay would come back in, but she got into his car. Moran got in, too, and peeled off, leaving a strip of smoking rubber on the street.

Snookie and Terra sat there awhile, trash-talking Tony, wondering what LaFay saw in him. Terra said she heard he had beat up a girl he used to go out with—broke her nose and cracked some ribs. Snookie asked how come he didn't go to jail and Terra said she heard Tony's father had got him out of it.

"Tony Moran better not lay a hand on LaFay," Snookie said.

"That's right," said Terra. "She's got that wild Cajun blood."

I was thinking he'd better not hurt her, too, but I didn't know what I would do about it if he did. It wasn't like she was my girl or my sister. I wished she would break up with him and find somebody who would treat her the way I would treat Angela Salazar if she was my girl.

Terra and Snookie had to leave for their jobs. Terra had a waitress shift at Roma's, the Italian restaurant, and Snookie had to work at the 7-Eleven. But after they left I stayed there in the booth. I didn't want to go home. G.T. would be at Rosalita's and there wasn't anything to do there except study. I got out my English book, figuring I would just study at Nick's. Halfway through the second act of *Othello* I looked up and saw Dopodja and Rizzo, both of them chewing toothpicks.

"What are you doing, Terrill?" Dopodja asked, pointing his big nose at me like a weapon.

"Reading a play." I held it up for him to see. "It's by Shakespeare."

"Who you waiting for, Shakespeare?"

"Nobody. Told you, I'm just reading."

"Funny how you got to read here," Rizzo said. "Where you can see be seen in the window."

"Stand up," Dopodja said.

"What for?"

"I want to see what you have in your pockets."

"You want to search me right here?"

"Here's where I'm asking you, isn't it?"

I just stared up at him.

Dopodja said, "You want to go back to jail? We can do it that way."

I stood up, wishing I'd left with Terra and Snookie.

"Turn around and put your hands on the table."

I did what he said. Rizzo frisked me, then told me to put everything in my pockets on the table. While I was doing this I glanced at Nick and Mimi behind the counter. Nick was scowling. Mimi looked like she had just ate something that had turned sour on her stomach. There were a half dozen customers in Nick's. They were all looking at me.

"You conned that judge, Terrill," Rizzo said. "But you can't con us. We're watching you."

"I'll be sure and pull down my shades tonight."

"It's just a matter of time," Dopodja said, rolling the toothpick around in his mouth.

I put my things back in my pocket, picked up my books and notebook from the table.

"What are you leaving for?" Dopodja asked. "Party's just started."

"Stinks in here."

"Going to stink a whole lot worse where you're going," Rizzo called after me.

I walked down the sidewalk, past the strip of rubber Tony Moran left on the street. Dopodja and Rizzo made me feel small and worthless. There was crime and criminals all over this city—drug dealers, killers, armed robbers, muggers, pimps, burglars, and child molesters. Looks to me like those apes should be out catching criminals, like the thug that hurt my daddy, instead of hassling me when I am just trying to study.

Ahead I saw their Crown Victoria, parked just out of sight of the window.

Taking the house key out of my pocket, I dug it into the metal and raked it from front to back, leaving a deep scratch all the way down to the metal.

World is a web, assholes, I thought. Here's a little sign of my love.

I sat in the windowsill, holding the Torah in my hands, waiting for Mr. Ebban to come out of the bathroom. I heard the toilet flush and a moment later he rolled out in his wheelchair.

"So, Jesse, what do you want to read today?"

"It doesn't matter. What do you want me to read?"

"I thought I'd let you pick something."

"That's all right."

"You don't have any favorite chapters yet, a special verse?"

"Not really."

"Why is that, do you suppose?"

"Look, Mr. Ebban, your God isn't exactly a role model for kids today. He has a man stoned to death for gathering sticks on the Sabbath. People sacrifice animals to him, cut their throats, and burn them on an altar. What kind of message is that to send out to young people today?

"A message they badly need to hear—that God is all powerful and that He must be obeyed. '*I am the first and the last*,' he tells us, in Isaiah. "*And there is no God but me*.' We don't have to take everything in the Bible literally. We can read it as poetry, metaphor, history."

"I already took history. Wasn't anything in our book about the sea parting or a voice coming from a burning bush."

He leaned back in his wheelchair and closed his eyes. He'd done this before, used silence as a tactic. Trying to rattle my nerves.

"What do you want me to read?"

"Your choice."

I got down one of his Bibles, opened the book, and read to him from the Book of Ruth. It was one of the few chapters I really liked in the Old Testament. It was just a simple story about a woman following her heart into a strange country, with no guarantee she would even end up with food to eat or a roof over her head. I read the chapter to Mr. Ebban, and when I was finished, I looked up and saw Ray Thorne, standing in the doorway.

"Jesus is coming again," he said, pointing his finger at me. "Are you ready?"

I didn't answer him.

"This time he'll be in a chariot of fire. He's going to melt the faces of all the infidels. He'll point his finger at them and their flesh will dissolve from their bones. They'll attack him with tanks, airplanes, and missiles— from trucks, cars, tractors, and motorcycles. He'll clap his hands and the earth will break open. The infidels, perverts, devil-worshipers, idolaters, heathens—all of them emblazoned with the mark of the beast—will tumble to the fires below. Let me tell you, there will be much wailing and gnashing of teeth."

I glanced at the old man in his wheelchair. He wasn't paying Ray any attention. Mr. Ebban might as well have been in a rocker on the front porch of his house, listening to the wind go by.

Ray shuffled into the room. "What do you have to say for yourself, young fellow?"

"Nothing."

"You a Christian?"

"Not so you could tell it."

"You believe Jesus Christ is the only hope for man's salvation?"

I shrugged, looked away.

"Either you're on the path to heaven or the highway to hell. Ain't no middle ground, young fellow."

"I don't believe in much of anything if you want to know the truth."

"Here you have it, Mendel," Ray said. "A picture of the whole sorry generation. Don't want to do anything with their lives. Too lazy to commit to Christ. They remind me of the servant who only got one talent and buried it. You know that story, don't you? Master gives one servant five talents, another two and another one. First two use their money wisely and return them to the master with interest. Third servant is foolish. Takes his talent out and buries it. What happened to him? We have it from the word of God for the people of God. Jesus said the master scolded him, then took his talent and gave it to the servant who had ten talents. And Jesus said, 'He who has given much will be given more and he who has nothing will be given less.'"

"The man who buried his talent was afraid of his master," Mr. Ebban said.

"So?"

"Jesus was a merciful man, wasn't he?"

"Of course."

"Why isn't he telling us to show mercy on the man who was afraid? Plenty of people are paralyzed by fear. The story tells us the master was harsh and that the servant was afraid."

"He was stupid," Ray said. "That's the whole point of the story."

"You can read it in different ways. You could read it as a story for investment bankers, how the rich will get richer and the poor get nothing. You could read it as a story about favoritism and fear. Why did the servant only get one talent and the other two get more—twice as many in one case, five times as many in the other?"

"I don't care how you read it. It's a story for the me generation that only wants to smoke pot and play video games. They're like the servant that buried his talent."

"Ray, you ever have a dog?"

"Sure."

"Ever see your dog bury a bone?"

"A time or two."

"Did you get rid of him for it?"

"Of course not. He was just doing what comes natural."

"And so was the servant who was afraid to do something with his talent. Wouldn't it be better to help him overcome his fear rather than condemn him to hell?"

"Jesus had no use for him. That's enough for me. His problem was laziness."

"How do you know that for sure?"

"I read it in the good book, which is the word of God. The *whole* Bible—Old and New Testament."

"Many people read the words but fail to understand them, because they are literal and unimaginative thinkers."

"I got plenty of sense, Mendel, FYI. I know a turd when I smell one."

"Do you now? You can smell a *fortz 'n zouver?*"

"Speak English, please."

"The foul air out of your fanny."

"Yes, and that reminds me—it's time for me to clean out my pipes."

Mr. Ebban's bathroom was to the left of the door as you left, on the right coming in. Ray put his hand on the door. Mr. Ebban said, "Use your own bathroom, please."

Ray shuffled out the door, muttering about investment bankers and shaking his head.

"The mouth of the fool is an imminent ruin," Mr. Ebban said, quoting a line I remembered reading in Proverbs. He closed his eyes, took one of his catnaps.

I thought of how dumb Ray was to go up against him. Even if Ray was right about Jesus, Mr. Ebban was just too smart for him. I remembered how my grandma used to make me say my prayers at night, which made me see how far down I had tumbled since then—a jailbird with sinful thoughts, who didn't even take the time to worship Jesus. Leaning back against the window, I pictured a highway in the desert, some small figures in the distance. The figures got bigger, and I heard the sounds of motorcycles. It was a bunch of guys on Harleys, only I could tell these weren't regular bikers when I saw the man out front: it was Jesus, his long hair and beard flying in the wind, and behind him a whole army of biker angels. They were armed with bazookas, broad swords, flame-throwers, bows, and axes. There were tornadoes on either side of them, too. Lightning flashing in the bruise-colored sky.

In this dream movie I was hightailing it across the desert, trying to find a place to hide.

Coming around the corner from the west wing to the lobby, I saw three members of the city Rescue Squad pushing a gurney out from the east wing. Person on the gurney was all covered up with a sheet. The men started to wheel the gurney around to the front lobby, but Ms. Lynch and an attendant stopped them.

"Excuse me," Ms. Lynch said, "we ask that the deceased be taken out the back door."

"Why is that, ma'am?" the man in front asked. He had dark circles under his eyes. "This is the quickest way to our ambulance."

"It upsets the residents," Ms. Lynch said. "We have quite a few in the lobby right now."

The man's expression soured a little, but he turned the gurney around and they pushed it back by the rec room, the kitchen, toward the back door.

"Who was it?" Ray Thorne asked in a loud voice. "Who was it that croaked down there on the east wing?"

Mrs. Lynch said, "I'm not at liberty to release that information to you, Mr. Thorne. Now if you'll excuse me, I have work to do."

I went up to the front desk to sign out, glad to be through with my community service for the day.

CHAPTER 12

Saturday morning I got up early so I could talk to Rosalita without G.T. being there. She was in the kitchen, drinking coffee.

"Rosalita, I need some advice."

"OK."

"I want to ask this girl out."

"So ask her out."

"It's not that simple. She's a nice girl."

"So?"

"I don't have a very good name around school. Got in a couple of fights last year. Plus I'm on probation. Can't stay out past ten o'clock."

"That's exactly what you need, Jesse! A good Christian girl to calm you down. Is she Catholic?"

"I think so."

"Do you have a class with her?"

"Yes, English."

"Why don't you try to spend some time around her in a relaxed situation? Ask her if she wants to get together to study."

"Good idea, Rosalita."

"That way she can see the real you. You have a good heart, Jesse. Let her see it."

I went back to my room and sat on my bed, pondering Rosalita's advice. Angela sat three seats ahead of me in English class. I could ask her if she wanted to study for the exam on *Othello* we were having on Friday. I had been reading the play and maybe we could talk about it, compare notes. I could tell her my thoughts on *Othello*—that even though he was a man of strength in war, his fatal weakness was his inability to understand people, to see their true natures. He was so much more easily deceived than Hamlet, who we had studied earlier in the semester. Hamlet would have seen right through Iago's evil web of lies. I got up and threw my darts at the target on the back of my door, hoping Rosalita's advice would turn out to be the lucky break I had been dreaming about for almost two years, ever since I first saw Angela's face.

Monday morning, I put on a white shirt and khaki pants, took special care with shaving, slicked down my hair with water, and splashed on some of G.T.'s aftershave. I was feeling fairly confident until I got to English class, but as soon as I saw Angela come in, my nervousness came back. The teacher, Ms. Mizelle, was discussing the character of Desdemona. Although I tried to focus on what she was saying, all I could think about was Angela, how I was going to ask her to study with me at the end of class. She was wearing a blue dress and her hair shone like coal in sunlight.

The bell finally rang. *It's now or never,* I thought.

I rushed to catch up with her. She was walking out with Margot.

"Hi, Angela. Ready for the test on Friday?"

She shrugged, smiled, her chocolate-brown eyes already putting me under a spell. "I've been working on it. How about you?"

"I'm not sure." And then, rushing the words, I added, "I was wondering if you'd like to get together with me, maybe after school, to study together."

Margot pushed herself between us.

"I'm pretty busy this week," Angela said, bending around Margot so she could see me. "But thanks for asking."

"Sure," I said. "No problem. Maybe some other time."

Angela's tight-lipped smile told me there wouldn't be another time. I saw this in a flash and it was like a snakebite to my heart.

We had reached the end of the hall, where I turned left to go to gym. She went right to algebra. As they went around the corner Margot threw a cold, pleased look at me over her shoulder.

My face felt like it had been covered with ice.

"Hear you got shot down by Angela Salazar," Snookie said, at lunch.

"What are you talking about?"

"Talking about a girl who said, 'no way Jose.'"

"I just asked her if she wanted to study with me for the English test on Friday."

"What were you planning to study—her boobs?"

"You got a one-track mind."

"She ain't going to go out with you, Jesse."

"Who said I wanted to go out with her?"

"You don't need to say it. I've seen the way you look at her."

"You're dreaming."

"Know who she dates?"

"Who?"

"Brad Tillett."

"The football player?"

"That's right. Lives in Highland Park. Parents bought him a new BMW for his birthday. You think she's going to want to ride around in that rustbucket your uncle lets you drive? Miss Priss wouldn't be seen in that junky thing."

"You got a nasty attitude."

"Stick with your own kind, Jesse."

I couldn't eat the rest of my lunch. I pushed my chair back from the table. Leaving my tray there I walked out of the cafeteria onto the school grounds. I walked back to the baseball field, cussing Brad Tillett, Margot, Snookie, the school, myself, the whole stinking world.

After school that afternoon, I was walking up the road to our driveway when a navy blue Crown Victoria pulled off the road ahead of me. Rizzo and Dopodja got out.

"Hands on the car, Terrill," Dopodja said.

"What for? I haven't done anything wrong."

"Up against the car! I'm not going to ask you again."

I leaned forward against the car and they patted me down, taking my wallet, my house key, my comb, and my four-leaf clover charm.

"I think we got a probation violator here." Dopodja said. He was holding my house key in his hand.

I looked him in the eye, ignoring the key. I already knew what he had in mind.

"I'm taking this to the lab to see if it has any paint in it."

"Go ahead," I said, knowing they wouldn't find any evidence on that key. The one I had used on their car was hanging on a nail in the tool shed. I exchanged it for this one the night I had keyed their car.

"If there's a single flake of blue paint under here, you're on your way to Sheridan."

"Only way there'd be paint under there is if you put it there."

Rizzo's eyes glittered. I was quiet, wishing I had kept my damn fool mouth shut. No need to give them ideas.

I watched Dopodja put the key in a plastic bag, then slip it in his pocket.

Rizzo dropped my other things onto the ground; then he and Dopodja got back into the car, pulled off.

I picked up my things and walked home. I opened the door to the shed and got the spare house key off the nail on the wall. While I was there I got out the bag of cracked corn and cat food for Amos. I sprinkled it along the ground, wishing I'd had enough sense to keep my mouth shut. Now I had one more thing to worry about.

Some days it doesn't even pay to get out of bed in the morning, I thought, as I watched Amos eat. Better to just pull the covers over your head and let the whole raggedy-ass day pass right on by.

CHAPTER 13

The second week in December, I began checking the mailbox for a Christmas card from my mama. The first one I had gotten from her had a Dallas, Texas postmark, the second one was from Seattle, Washington, and the third from Joliet, Illinois. The first two cards had contained brief notes, telling me she was thinking about me and that she hoped I was doing OK. The last one was just signed, "Love, Mama."

Friday night I lay on my bed, studying the map of the USA I kept on my closet shelf. I had put a gold star sticker on the three locations. The arrangement of gold stars suggested she was traveling in a circle. Maybe by next Christmas she would be close enough by to pay me a visit.

I locked my door, turned out the light, and got her blouse from the box under my bed. I put it on my pillow next to my face. My mama had this special scent, a mixture of soap and sweat and perfume. I imagined I could still smell her on it, although the scent had faded so much by now it was mostly only in my memory. I drifted off to sleep this way, pretending she has just come in to kiss me goodnight and that she was still somewhere in the house, watching TV or fixing daddy's lunch for the next day at his job.

After school let out for the Christmas vacation G.T. gave me a job helping Carlos and Ricardo put a new roof on a house on a street behind the Catholic hospital, in the northern section of the city. I was glad for the opportunity to work because I wanted to earn some money for Christmas, although I knew G.T. would keep most of it to cover the damage to the synagogue. Also, I got bored just sitting around the house. If I sat around at home I'd worry about things too much, like Dopodja and Rizzo showing up to take me to jail.

Roofing work is hard on the body. The first few days I did it I was always sore—especially my knees, arms, and back. Even though I wore gloves, my hands still ended up getting cut and blistered from pulling up nails, handling the shingles, or working with the sheet metal "flashing," which we used at junctions of different planes to prevent leaks. A roofer has to be able to spend time in cramped positions, pounding nails, reaching for shingles and nails, as well as inching along the slope of the roof. There's irritating substances you have to breathe, too, like the tar we had to sometimes use on flat roofs, the roof coatings, the cement and caulking for nail heads. We didn't talk much while we were working. Carlos knew basic English but Ricardo, his cousin, only knew a few English words. They both treated me with respect because I was their boss' nephew. They acted like they didn't expect me to work hard, but I tried to work even harder than they did, just to show them I wasn't a lazy gringo. In fact, I just about ran myself ragged trying to keep up with them.

They still worked like machines, nailing down two shingles for every one of mine.

When we took a lunch break, I ate two peanut butter and jelly sandwiches, and some carrots and raisins. Ricardo and Carlos had Slim Jims, cupcakes, cans of potted meat on crackers, and potato chips. I wondered how these guys could work so hard on food like that. During our lunch break, Carlos, a stocky, powerfully built man with a gold front tooth, talked about his family in Mexico. He said he had a wife and three children, and he sent them money every two weeks when he got his paycheck. Carlos said Ricardo had a wife and two boys back in Mexico, too. When he heard what we were talking about, Ricardo took out his wallet and showed me a photo of his children, two boys and a girl. Carlos had to help translate what Ricardo told me, using a combination of English and Spanish. He hoped to one day bring his family to America to live with him, but until then he would have to work hard and send money home, because there was no work in the village they were from.

I tried to keep them talking, so I would have a little more time to rest my aching back and arms, but they grabbed packs of shingles and went back up the ladder. I got some shingles too and followed them up to the roof. I was amazed by how hard Carlos and Ricardo worked. Day after day, on poor diets, just so their wives and kids could have food to eat back home. It was enough to revive your faith in the whole miserable human race.

After school was out for Christmas, I shifted one of my community service days with Mr. Ebban to Sunday, so as not to interfere with my job.

The first Sunday I went to Havenwood, a Christmas tree in the front window of the lobby sparkled with lights. When I entered the lobby a children's choir was singing "Jingle Bells," while a woman played the out-of-tune piano. A group of residents sat nearby, listening to the carolers. Some of the old folks were in their wheelchairs; others were on the sofa and chairs. A few sat in folding chairs.

I had brought a big sack of oranges for the old man, because I knew how much he liked them. I set them down to sign in at the front desk.

"What's you got there?" Ray Thorne asked.

"Bag of oranges for Mr. Ebban."

"Mendel might eat them oranges, but he ain't going to understand the spirit behind them."

"He understands a lot more than you think."

"He's a Jew, boy."

"So?"

"Wake up and smell the bagels. Surely your brain cells ain't been so fried by smoking dope and playing video games that you can't grasp the simple fact that Jews don't celebrate Christmas."

"I don't play video games."

"You didn't say nothing about marijuana. Last I heard that was against the law, too. Not a good idea for a boy on probation to be breaking the law now, is it?"

Flashing me a nasty smile, Ray Thorne went over to listen to the singers. I went on toward Mr. Ebban's room. But Ray had got me so riled up I had to lean against the wall and take some deep breaths to calm down before I could get ready to go into the old man's room. While I was doing this, Varden came around the corner from the main lobby and walked down the hall, whistling.

"I don't want to hear one word about these oranges," I told him. "I've heard enough already."

"Don't let Ray Thorne get to you, Terrill. It's the season of love and light."

Not with him around, I thought.

I knocked once on the door and then went into Mr. Ebban's room. He was sitting in his wheelchair by the window, looking down at one of his Bibles, squinting as he tried to make out the words.

"I brought you some oranges, Mr. Ebban."

"Thank you, Jesse."

"Where do you want me to put them?"

"On the floor by the bed. Were the children in the lobby when you came by?"

I nodded.

"Were they singing?"

"Yes, sir."

"I'd like to hear them."

"They're singing Christmas songs."

He set his Bible on the shelf. "Let's go listen."

This caught me by surprise, being that he didn't celebrate Christmas, didn't even believe in the whole reason behind it.

As I pushed him down the hall to hear the kids sing, I was reminded once again how full of surprises this old man was. There was absolutely no telling what he was going to do from one minute to the next.

Maybe he just likes kids, I thought. Or could be he just wants to get out of that stuffy old room for a while. Sure couldn't blame him for that.

When I got back home from Havenwood, I found a note from G.T. on the kitchen table, telling me he had gone to see Rosalita. I went outside to crank up the Dodge. On the seat beside me I had the holly wreath I had bought with the money G.T. had given me for helping Carlos and Ricardo. I had just enough money left over to buy G.T. and my daddy some presents, plus a couple of toys for Lynette's kids. I eased the truck down the driveway, keeping an eye out for Amos. He stayed away from the road, but sometimes he'd sleep in the driveway. I went out to Oleander, followed it out to the bypass, and headed west a few miles before I took the exit to Memorial Gardens Cemetery. The sun was just about down when I got there, the sky streaked with red and pink light. The cemetery was laid out in sections, each one with a different name. Lee was buried in the third section on the right, the one for military veterans. It was called "The Garden of Honor." If you came here in the spring and summer, when the grounds were green and the azaleas and crape myrtle were in bloom, it wasn't so bad, but it was barren and desolate in winter, the grass yellow and brown, the trees stripped and black against this darkening sky.

I parked the truck on the road and walked back to Lee's grave. His stone had an image of an angel carved in it, with his full name, *Daniel Lee Terrill*, and dates of his birth and death. Below that were the words, *In Loving Memory*. Lynette had wanted the tombstone company to add, *He died a hero*, but Daddy, G.T., and I vetoed that idea, even though he would always be a hero to me. It just didn't sound honest somehow, under the circumstances. He was a young man standing in front of a building. Dreaming about his girlfriend, thinking about what he was going to eat for supper that night, maybe, or just wishing he was somewhere else when Death came rolling through the front gate. One second he was alive, his heart pumping blood through his veins, and the next second he was blown apart in the air. One of the news stories about his death reported that his rifle hadn't even been loaded, but we never could confirm the truth of that statement. Daddy called and wrote some officials in Washington about the issue, and they all answered him with pat phrases like "our embassies are well-protected."

I knelt beside his grave and put the holly wreath on it, by the headstone. I remembered how at Lee's funeral a girl had sung "Just A Closer Walk With Thee." I had felt a chill down my spine when she hit the high notes. Her throat turned scarlet with her effort. She had been a friend of Lee's, one of his classmates. She looked so full of life. Lee was directly below her, in a closed casket. Not much they could do to fix up a man hit by a carload of dynamite.

The sun went all the way down and the stars came out. A cold wind blew from the north. The trees creaked and moaned in the wind gusts. The city's lights cast an eerie yellow glow against the sky. Looking at the angel on the tombstone, I began talking to Lee. I told him about how I was working for G.T. and doing community service for Mr. Mendel Ebban. I told him about how Daddy always asked about him, and how hard it was for me when that happened. I told him that I loved him and missed him and wished he was still alive. "I'd give anything to see you again, just for a few minutes," I said. I prayed he could somehow hear my words, but I couldn't get past a feeling that they were just words spoken and gone, like dead leaves blown away in the wind.

Chapter 14

The signs of Christmas were everywhere in the city, but it was hard for me to get into the spirit of the season. Everything I saw—the decorations, the shoppers with their arms full of packages, the Salvation Army workers ringing their bells, the lights and the nativity scenes—always reminded me of better times, back when Lee was still alive and my daddy and mama still loved each other.

G.T. wasn't any help, either. He had gotten into a black funk after both his sorry daughters told him they were too busy to come see him, even though he had mailed them airplane tickets. He moped around the house, drinking beer, not saying much. Swore he wasn't even going to put up a tree. Rosalita kept bugging him about it, however, and a week before Christmas he finally came in with a runty tree that looked like something somebody had thrown out. Rosalita and I put it in a stand, and decorated it with ornaments, strings of popcorn, and angel hair. The whole time we worked on the tree, she complained about G.T.'s daughters. She called them "spoiled brats" and said they should show their father more love and respect. I couldn't say I missed Dawn and Saxon much. They had visited us last Christmas for a few days. Spent most of their time sleeping, watching TV, eating junk food, talking on the telephone, or complaining about their accommodations. They didn't like having to share a double bed or that G.T. didn't have cable TV. Dawn had bragged about the size of her house in Phoenix, which had a swimming pool and a Jacuzzi. She also commented on how small G.T.'s house was, how she couldn't believe we only had one john, and how she couldn't wait to get back home to see her friends and sleep in her own queen-sized bed. G.T. took them out to eat all the time and bought them hundreds of dollars worth of clothes. He even took days off from work to spend time with them. But nothing he did seemed to please them. After they left, he sat in his recliner staring at the TV set without even turning it on, drinking Coronas and tequila. When he finally got up to go to bed, he only made it to the hall before he passed out. I just about put my back out trying to get him back to bed. G.T. weighed over two twenty and most of it solid muscle. I finally put a pillow under his head, covered him up with a blanket, and let him sleep on the floor.

Another obstacle to G.T. and me getting into the spirit of the season was we both knew where we were going to be on Christmas day: at the hospital with my daddy. Lynette would drive there from Bat Forks with her husband and two kids. We all opened presents in the lobby around the Christmas tree there. I would have liked to have brought daddy home for Christmas, but G.T. didn't want to try that again. The last time we brought Daddy here—the first year he was in the hospital—he didn't want to go back. Locked himself in the bathroom and G.T. had to take the doorknob off and practically drag him to the car, Daddy hollering for Lee the whole time. This shook me up so bad I went into my room and cried.

Then when G.T. came to get me to ride back with my daddy, Daddy jumped out of the truck and ran off into the woods. We looked for him half a day before we found him at a laundromat way down on McAlester Street. He was sitting on the bench out front, drinking a Coke.

Daddy's doctor called in a prescription for some pills. Once we got them down him, the medicine made Daddy quiet and easier to manage. I hated the idea of doping him up like a zombie but it was about the only way we could get him back to the hospital, without wrestling him down and hog-tying him, which I wasn't willing to do.

I didn't hear from Mama. No card, no phone call. Nothing.

I still checked the mailbox every day.

The day before Christmas I was standing by the mailbox, waiting for the mail truck. When the postman handed me the mail, he asked me if I was waiting for a letter from Santa. I could see he was trying to be friendly but I couldn't summon up much of the same spirit for him, so I just shrugged and didn't answer. Checking the mail I saw we had gotten Christmas cards from Dawn and Saxon and two advertisements—a postcard addressed to "resident" trying to sell burial insurance, and another one promoting an after-Christmas sale at a car dealership. I tore the advertisements into small pieces and threw them into the air, watching them blow away like confetti.

Across the street the cars were pulling away from Gladstone and Son in a procession to the pet cemetery outside of town. The bereaved was riding in the long black limousine in front. I caught a glimpse of a woman with a black veil over her face, a man's hand on her shoulder. The chaplain usually rode up there, too. I had met him when we took the tour: a rab-bity little man with a hump in his back.

Some people might say he had an easy job, I thought, as I walked back to the house. But I figured it must be a tricky thing to dream up something to say at a funeral service for a dead cat.

When G.T. drove into the hospital parking lot, Lynette was waiting for us in her minivan, along with her kids, Wayne Jr. and Bobbie Rae. They all got out to meet us. Wayne Jr. was wearing a hunter's camouflage coat and pants. Bobbie Rae had on a pink coat, with fur around the collar.

I got out of the truck, holding the box of presents we had for them under my left arm. I gave little Wayne a high five and kissed Bobbie Rae on the top of her head.

"Uncle Jesse, I had a birthday!" She held up four fingers. "I'm four years old."

"That's great, Bobbie Rae," I said. "Where's your daddy?"

"He's out West," Bobbie Rae said, making a sad face.

"Snowbound in Colorado," Lynette said. She had put on weight since I had last seen her. In her bulky down jacket, she looked as big as Wayne, who was five nine and weighed over two hundred. Her brown hair was pulled back in a ponytail. Her face was pale and swollen-looking—she didn't wear makeup. Lynette had my grandmother's eyes, blue and deep-set, but they didn't light up the way my grandmother's did. Lynette didn't smile much. Life was serious business for her, all about making sure you lived right and were saved for the next world. That was a major philo-sophical difference between us, being that my main concern was to just survive this one.

As she got the presents out of the back of the van, Lynette was com-plaining about the high price of gas. Said Wayne couldn't make a living and that she had half a notion to move back to Pottstown, where he might be able to find better work.

"Doing what?" G.T. asked. "Can't anybody get on at the mill or any of the other factories. They're laying people off—jobs all going to India and China."

"Anything's better than being on the road all the time, away from the kids," Lynette said. "And having to pay all that money for gas. Meanwhile, we got Santa to worry about."

Wayne, who used to work in a paper mill, got laid off not long after my daddy got hurt. I remembered Lynette had a real hard time back then.

Not only was Wayne out of work, she was also worried about my daddy. Wayne Jr. needed an ear operation and they were without health insurance. She called it "a time when my faith was tested," but she believed her prayers had gotten Wayne that trucking job. I couldn't see where they were so divinely blessed, though. They had a brick ranch house and two acres out back for the kids' pony, but Wayne and Bobbie Rae didn't see their dad that much because he was on the road all of the time, trying to earn a living. Since Lynette taught them at home, they didn't have much of a social life or get to listen to any music other than hymns. Lynette's social life centered on that backwoods church where they fooled around with snakes. I asked Lynette once if she had ever touched one. She said she hadn't been called to test her faith that way yet, but she was willing to do it if she was ever called.

"I was thinking you could give him a job, G.T.," Lynette said.

G.T. flinched a little, like somebody had just swung a hand a little too close to his face. I could see him calculating all of this real quick in his profit and loss column; taking on a snake-handling brother-in-law was sure to be over in the loss column.

We were silent as we walked up to the building, carrying the presents.

Wayne Jr. and Bobbie Rae both looked like their dad, stocky and ruddy-faced, with small blue eyes set a little too close together. I pictured them sitting in church, watching the adults dancing around with copperheads and rattlers, and I got a chill down my spine. I knew Lynette believed she was going to heaven, but to me she took a wrong turn somewhere, and it worried me, not just for her and her kids, but for me, too, because it made me wonder if there was some kind of curse on my family, like the one on the ancient mariner.

The lobby was decorated with plastic reindeer and a sleigh driven by an oversized teddy bear with an angel hair beard. There was a Christmas tree in the center of the lobby. A man wearing a tuxedo jacket and blue pajama bottoms sat in a chair by the tree, looking at the lights. He was bobbing and weaving like a shadow boxer.

We all sat by this Christmas tree, waiting for the nurse to bring my daddy out. I had our box of presents on the floor beside my feet.

"How's school, Jesse?" Lynette asked. She held Bobbie Rae on her lap.

"Doing better this semester," I said. "I'm hoping for some A's this time."

"You can't pray in your school, can you?" Wayne Jr. asked.

"Could if I wanted to."

"They don't have organized prayer," Lynette said, smacking Bobbie Rae's thumb out of her mouth. "Federal government took God right out of the schools."

G.T. asked Wayne Jr. if he had been hunting lately. He didn't like to talk to Lynette about religion.

"I got a six point buck," he said. "It's at the taxidermist right now. Daddy's having him mounted."

Behind him, Lynette mouthed the words, *Waste of money*.

"Your daddy take you hunting?" I asked.

"Daddy was on the road. Uncle Mac took me."

"Wayne was supposed to go, too, but he was late getting in," Lynette said, frowning. She didn't have much use for Wayne's brother, Mac, who lived with a stripper. I was a little surprised she'd even let him take Wayne hunting.

"Six pointer, huh," I said. "What did you use?"

"Daddy's two seventy. Shot broke his back leg but he made it down to a holler about a quarter of a mile from my stand. Uncle Mac had to finish him off with his twenty-two pistol. Shot him in the heart so he wouldn't mess up the head."

"At least we have plenty of venison in the freezer," Lynette said. "That sure helps, with all the pressures on truckers these days."

I studied my Aunt Lynette, taking in the tightness in her mouth and look of frustration and defeat in her eyes. Remembering the way she had looked at her wedding, slim and glowing and happy, I contrasted that image with this sad, overweight woman who was worried about the price of diesel fuel and how her brother-in-law was living in sin with a stripper; and it occurred to me that Wayne might not be all that concerned about being snowbound in Colorado, that lonesome as the road was he might not be in that much of a hurry to get back to her. Lynette's ways might be wearing him down. I had heard my daddy say more than once that over time a little stream of falling water can eat a hole clean through stone.

When the attendant brought Daddy out, he was smiling a little. He had shaving cream on both ears.

"Merry Christmas, Daddy." I hugged him and wiped the shaving cream off his ears with my fingers.

"Who's that there?" he asked, nodding at Wayne Jr. and Bobbie Rae.

"That's your niece and nephew." I took his hand and led him over to the sofa. His hands hung limp at his sides as Lynette kissed him. G.T. hugged him too and told him, "Merry Christmas."

"Lots of people here," Daddy said, looking around the lobby. He looked even more dazed than usual, which made me wonder if they had increased his medicine. I guessed the medicine would keep him from getting too agitated, but it seemed to be one more barrier placed between us.

"We brought you some presents," I said.

Daddy sat down on the sofa and looked at the kids like he was trying to place them. Bobbie Rae worked on her thumb. Wayne Jr. scuffed his foot on the floor, avoiding my daddy's eyes.

"Ain't you all going to tell your Uncle Glenn Merry Christmas?" Lynette said.

"I shot a buck," Wayne Jr. said. "Six pointer."

Daddy looked at Wayne Jr. "Lee," he says. "Lee?"

Tears sprang to my eyes. I wiped them away with my fists.

"Let's open some Goddamn presents," G.T. said.

G.T. took Christmas Day off but he was back at work December 26th. I helped him finish up a flat roof on a dry cleaner's down on East Oleander Street. It was the kind of roof where you have to put everything down in layers—insulation, roofing felt, and then hot tar over the felt. We repeated these steps, sealing the seams each time to make layers. We heated the tar in a vat on a trailer G.T. hauled behind his truck. I came home nights with that smell in my clothes, hair, and skin. The smell seemed to linger on your skin no matter how hard you washed.

When he finished that job, we started working on another roof, in a neighborhood near Havenwood. G.T. had jobs all over the city.

The last day of the year, New Year's Eve, G.T. stopped working a couple of hours early, having promised Rosalita they could go out dancing. But after he got home Rosalita called to say both her kids had come down with a stomach virus, so she was going to have to cancel their date and stay home with them. G.T. asked her if there was anything he could do to help, but she told him no, that she would try to come over on New Year's Day if the kids were feeling better by then.

He told her not to feel bad, that he would stay home, too, and watch the ball drop at Times Square on TV. He talked to her in a low, reassuring voice, reminding her to be sure and call him if she needed any help with her kids.

G.T.'s decision to stay home on New Year's Eve put a crimp in my secret plan to go to the party Snookie was throwing at her house. I had planned to slip out to her house, drink a few beers, listen to music, have a little fun for a change, and get back home before G.T. did. But that would be a violation of my curfew, and now that G.T. was staying home I would have to stay home, too.

G.T. and I watched TV in the living room. My back and arms were sore from working on roofs all week, and I had blisters the size of quarters on my hands. It was a warm night for December. Around ten o'clock I went outside and sat down on the porch. Although I was beat from working so hard, I had a restless feeling, too. I paced the yard awhile, then stretched out in the back of G.T.'s truck and looked up at the stars. If you looked up at the sky in the middle of the city, you couldn't see many stars, but we got a good view of them out on Rose of Sharon. They were glittering like fragments of ice in the black dome of sky above our house. I rested my head on a pack of shingles and tried to see how many of the constellations I could identify from the times my brother Lee had pointed them out. I saw the Big and Little Dippers—they were easy—Orion the Hunter, and then Ursa Major, but after that I started getting sleepy, and I closed my eyes.

Sometime later, I heard a motorcycle engine revving up in the yard. I knew without looking who it was: G.T.'s friend, Buddy McBane, on his Harley. I heard G.T. open the door and go outside. I heard Buddy cut the engine and the two of them sat there talking. I was drifting off to sleep when their conversation took a turn that drew my full attention. Fragments of what they were saying drifted in and out of my hearing: "*. . . out of prison now . . . seen him on the street just last week. Sposed to be working . . .*"

I listened carefully for a name and finally heard one, "Steigner." They both fell silent then, and when they spoke again their voices were too low for me to make out what they were saying. G.T. must have silenced Buddy somehow, perhaps thinking I might have been somewhere around. Soon afterwards, Buddy and G.T. went into the house.

I waited a while and went in, too. G.T. was in the recliner, Buddy was on the couch. They were drinking beers and watching TV. Buddy, who was six foot three, had broad shoulders and thick, muscular arms. He wore jeans and a denim vest over a white T-shirt. A long, jagged scar ran from his left eye to his ear.

"What do you say, little G.T?" he said. He often called me that.

"Hell of a place to be on New Year's Eve."

"Beats some places I been," Buddy said.

"You got a point there," I said. Buddy had spent five years in prison after he killed a man in a fight. According to G.T. his friend had acted in self-defense, but "the cops had it in for him because he was a biker." G.T. said a biker attacked Buddy with a knife, and in the ensuing fight, Buddy managed to get the knife away from him and kill him with it. The fight left Buddy with that scar on the side of his face.

Buddy said, "G.T. promised his little senorita he won't go out. Never thought I'd see the day he'd be that whipped."

"That's all right," G.T. said. "You'd like to get one to whip you but no one will have you."

"That little Mexican girl done put some voodoo on you," Buddy said, winking at me. "Used to be the baddest man in Pottstown and look at you now. Ain't nothing but a fart on a skillet. How come you won't let this boy here drink a beer on New Year's Eve?"

"Don't want to teach him bad habits."

I wanted to somehow get Buddy alone and ask him some questions, but I knew I wouldn't get any information out of him. There was no way he would have told me something that G.T. wouldn't want me to know.

I went back to my room. No sense in trying to get any information from G.T. either. I shut the door and threw darts at the target on the back. My aim was terrible, I didn't get one bull's eye. But I had thrown two of the darts so hard the metal shafts were completely imbedded in the wooden door.

They were talking about the man who hurt my daddy, I thought. Steigner, Steigner . . . was that his name or just someone he worked for? Another thought was like someone in my brain pounding away on a piece of metal with a ball peen hammer: *G.T. knows who he is. G.T. knows who he is.*

CHAPTER 15

The second day of the New Year, G.T. came into my room to wake me up for work. I told him I had a stomachache and that I wanted to stay home, so I would be close to the john.

"You must have got what Rosalita's kids had," he said. "I'll bring you back some Pepto."

After he left I got dressed, ate breakfast, and took the bus downtown to the city library. I logged on to one of their computers and started looking through the archives of the city newspaper. I paid special attention to the arrest reports. I figured Steigner must have gotten put in prison after the date my dad got hurt, December second. So I began looking there, three years back. It was slow going, and I only got through February. I found two Steigners, one who had gotten arrested for DUI, but that couldn't have been him because according to Buddy this guy had gone to prison. I came across another one who had been arrested for bad checks, but that Steigner was a woman. I was getting a headache from looking at the computer screen and was about to give up when I found a report that a Steigner was arrested March third for assault and arson. He had set a woman's car on fire. No photo, just a name, Marc K. Steigner, of 1612 South Rhodes Street.

A chill ran up and down my spine. I had already looked in the phone book but there were no Steigners listed. I wondered how G.T. had found out the information, how Buddy knew about it. No use to ask them about it; I knew before I even tried that neither one of them would tell me anything.

South Rhodes ran through the edge of "Little Haiti," an area east of the Pottstown Mill, where most of the city's poor black people lived. The sixteen hundred block was a neighborhood of dilapidated wooden houses, built so close together you could probably hear your next-door neighbor fart or blow his nose. I found number 1612 and knocked on the door. A brown-skinned woman with a blue bandana around her head opened it part way. She was holding a baby in her arms.

"Looking for Marc Steigner, ma'am."

"Don't know him. Don't nobody live here by that name."

"He used to live here. Three or four years ago."

"We just renting this place."

"How long you been here?"

"That don't matter. I'm telling you I don't know him."

"I believe you, ma'am. I just need to find him."

"Well I can't help you."

"Is there somebody who would know, somebody else who lives around here?"

"Don't know no one else. They be moving in and out of these houses all the time."

"Wait, please," I said, as she was closing the door. "Can you tell me where you pay your rent?"

"Wolf Creek Properties." She closed the door.

Returning home, I found the number to Wolf Creek Properties in the phone book. I called and asked for the rental agent. I told her I was looking for my cousin, Marc Steigner, whose last known address was 1612 South Rhodes Street. I said I knew he had lived there about three years ago.

The rental agent said she had just started working there and didn't know the location of the records that far back. She told me to call back in thirty minutes and ask for Ruth.

When I called back Ruth put me on hold for five minutes. She finally came back on the line and said the house at Rhodes Street had been rented to Wallace Rankin. She spelled the name for me. I asked her how I could find him.

"We'd like to know the same thing," she said. "He left owing us three months rent."

The Flamingo Bar was just off East Market Street, in a neighborhood of old hotels, pawn shops, tattoo parlors, warehouses, muffler and car repair shops, pool halls and abandoned buildings. The bar was in the middle of the block, between Hampton Street on the north and Isley on the south. There was a blood-red neon sign over the front, but the *l* and *a* were burned out, so the sign read *F mingo*. It was the bar my daddy had been in the night he died. It was a long shot, but I thought the thug who attacked him might still go here.

I pushed the doors open and went inside. A Talking Heads song was playing on the bar's stereo system, "Burning Down the House." A couple of men in dusty jeans, flannel shirts, and brogans were sitting at a table to the right, drinking beer. Two other guys were throwing darts at a target on the wall. There was a pool table at the back.

The bartender had his back to me when I sat at the bar.

He turned around and saw me. He was a heavyset man with a receding hairline.

"You got to be kidding," he said.

"I don't want anything to drink. I just need some information."

"Yeah, what kind of information?"

"About a guy who comes in here."

"A lot of guys come here."

"His name is Marc Steigner."

The bartender shook his head—too fast. "Never heard of him," he said. But I had already noticed the way his face changed when I said the name. It was a definite hardening of purpose, an unwillingness to get involved in something that might backfire on him or have a significant imbalance in the reward-risk ratio.

"Look, I just have a message for him."

"I can't help you. Now you better ease on out of here. State man might come by and pull my license."

I left the bar, thinking that the bartender's eyes had given him away. He knows who he is, I thought.

I retraced the steps my daddy took that night. Down the sidewalk toward Isley Street. I passed a pawnshop, a pool hall, an apartment building, a store that sold wigs. I saw my image in the glass, superimposed on a mannequin. Several other mannequins were scattered around the display window on their backs. Ahead was the alley where they found him. I tried to picture it: my daddy, walking in his gray down coat, not expecting anybody to be behind him. A man, a shadow without a face, coming out of the alley, striking my daddy with a hammer or iron bar, my daddy crumpling, the shadow man dragging him back into the alley. I came to the alley and looked at the pavement where my daddy had lain. I felt a tingling along my scalp, a hammering at the base of my skull. My chest felt so hot and tight I had trouble getting my breath.

I came around the corner of the house and saw G.T. feeding Amos by the shed. He was wearing a red plaid shirt, his Army jacket, boots. He set the bag of feed down, then squatted to pet Amos, the peacock nuzzling in his pocket where G.T. sometimes kept special treats like peanuts and cashews. I walked lightly up behind him, to see if I could catch him by surprise, but G.T., who had sharp ears and good instincts, whirled around fast to see who it was.

"Cold winter nights are coming," he said. "Got to get some more straw in here for Amos."

"He sleeps up on his perch, doesn't he?"

"Yeah, except when it's real cold."

"Reckon he needs a lady friend. Maybe we could get him one."

"We get a peahen, first thing you know there'd be peachicks running all around. They'd get out and dogs would kill them, or else they'd get run over by cars."

"Be nice to have some chicks, though." Talk like this brought back good memories. My daddy and mama singing on the back porch. The peacocks' cries in the night. Lee and me on our backs in the tree house, looking up at the stars.

"Too much trouble."

Amos nuzzled my leg with his beak. I rubbed the back of his neck while G.T. petted him on the back. His tail feathers were dull-looking and short now, but they would grow long and colorful in the spring.

"I heard you and Buddy talking about Marc Steigner."

G.T. looked up at me, his eyes flat and metallic in this hard winter light. "Jesse, don't even go there."

"He ain't getting away with it, G.T. Not as long as I got breath in my body."

"You got no evidence. Nothing to go on. Just drunks talking. A bunch of mess."

I walked back up to the house, went into my room, slammed the door. I lay down on the bed, put my face into the pillow. I had known it was no use—why the hell did I ever bother to try?

G.T. opened the door, came in, and sat down in the chair by my bed.

"Let it go, Jesse. Let the police take care of it."

"The police? Dopodja and Rizzo? You think I'd trust those jerks?"

"There's detectives who work these kinds of cases. I've talked to them."

"What the hell good has that done?"

"They haven't caught him yet. Doesn't mean they won't."

"Talking ain't going to bring my daddy back like he was."

"Ain't nothing going to bring him back. You know that."

I clenched my fists, digging the nails into the palm, thinking of my daddy in the hospital, his head wrapped in bandages, his eyes closed—that scar on his head. The way he wrote those imaginary letters.

"Look Jesse, if I find out anything solid, something to really go on, I'll talk to the detective again. Now you stay far from this, you hear me?"

I didn't answer.

"I mean it, dammit."

G.T. got up and left, closing the door behind him.

I am not going to lie to him, I thought. I am not going to make a promise I can't keep.

Lying on a plastic sheet I drew a bead on a wharf rat at the county dump. Just then I flashed on the rain-gullied face of the old man: *What's a rat ever done to me?* I squeezed off a shot. The rat tumbled over and over, twitched a minute, then lay still.

"Nothing," I said. "He hasn't done nothing at all to me. Nothing at all."

I woke straight up out of a sound sleep, shaking and shivering, my stomach churning. I had just enough time to make it down the hall to the bathroom to throw up. After I finished I rinsed my mouth with mouthwash and went back to bed. The window was open and I could see the orange moon over the shed. An old memory came back to me. I was a little boy, maybe five or six, and I woke up with a stomachache. I called out for Mama but she didn't come. Finally, the door opened and Daddy came into my room. He sat beside my bed and wiped my face and forehead with a cold cloth. "I'm scared, Daddy," I said. "Nothing to be scared of, Jesse," he said. He picked me up, and that was when I threw up, all over his shirt and the floor, too. I thought he was going to be mad, but he wasn't. He just said, "Don't worry, I'll clean it up." He took me into the bathroom and set me on the sink and started cleaning me off with a washcloth, although he had more of the vomit on him. When he got me all washed, he put clean clothes on me and put me back in the bedroom. Then he left and came back with a bucket. He said, "If you need to throw up again, you can use that." I was afraid he was going to leave. I had never thrown up before and I was scared I was going to die. I told him this, and he laughed and he said, "You're not going to die, Jesse. You're going to be fine, although your mama might be a little upset if she sees that floor before I can clean it up." I guessed Mama was still asleep.

When I woke up next morning, Daddy was sleeping beside me in the bed, and the floor beside my bed was clean. This memory came back to me so strong it seemed as if it had just happened yesterday instead of more than ten years earlier.

I remembered the way my daddy's hands felt on my face, the soothing sound of his voice, and the sound of his beating heart as I drifted off to sleep with my head against his chest.

I pushed Mr. Ebban up the path and we stopped by the fountain. I tossed a nickel into the water, saw it spin to the bottom. Mr. Ebban was looking at me.

"Making a wish?"

"Yes." I wondered what he would think if he knew what I was wishing for—that I could find Marc Steigner and prove that he was the one who hurt my daddy. I pictured a man with his wrists tied to a tree limb, me standing in front of him, a knife in one hand, and an hourglass in the other. "Confession is good for the soul, Mr. Steigner. You got three minutes to talk before I go to work . . ."

But even as I was picturing this scene, I realized it was just a fantasy. I had no idea how I could find this man; and even if I did, how would I know for sure he was the one who had hurt my daddy? G.T. was right. I had no evidence, just a name spoken during a conversation by a drunk.

Still, I recalled the way that bartender's expression had changed when I mentioned Steigner's name. He knows who he is, I thought. That must mean he either goes into the bar sometimes, or he has been there in the past.

Maybe I could put the word out with some of the people I know, to see if any of them could find out where he was. Ric Farina's dad owned a body shop down on Market Street. Snookie worked sometimes in the 7-Eleven to pick up extra money. Terra's mom was a beautician. It wouldn't hurt to try. That's one thing I could do, something to make me feel like I was moving forward instead of stuck in a mudhole, my wheels throwing up wet dirt.

At school I talked to Mick, Andre, and Terra, told them I was looking for a man named Marc Steigner, and that I would pay a fifty-dollar reward to anyone who could find him for me. They wanted to know why I was looking for him and I told them I couldn't say. I told them they needed to keep the whole issue quiet, too.

A couple of days later Snookie brought up the subject again, while we were eating lunch. "Hey, Jesse, this man you trying to locate—what's he look like?"

"I don't know."

"How we going to find him if we don't know what he looks like?"

"You got a name."

"Could be an alias."

"That's all I got to go on now."

Skeeter said, "You going to pay fifty to whoever finds him, right?"

"That's right."

"Hell," Snookie said. "I'll pay you fifty bucks to tell me why you want to find him so bad."

They were all looking at me. I figured I had to say something.

"Could be he owes me some money, all right?"

Terra said, "Dude owes you money but you don't even know what he looks like? What kind of shit is that?"

"I'm just asking for a little help is all. If you can't do it, fine."

"We want to help," Snookie said. "We just want to know why."

"Can't tell you right now."

"Why not?" Terra asked. "Inquiring minds want to know."

"Everybody's got secrets, Terra," LaFay said.

"Not me," Terra said. "My life is an open book, baby."

"A closed book, you mean," said LaFay, "and a mystery at that."

"I'll put the word out on this Steigner guy, Jesse," Snookie said. "Mister Public Enemy Number One. I'll tell everybody there's a fifty-dollar bounty on his ass, how's that?"

"Just keep it on the down low, OK?"

I was relieved when the conversation at the table moved to another topic. I thought maybe I had played the wrong hand, but it was too late now. I felt like I had gotten on a train without knowing for sure where it was going, but it was moving too fast now for me to get off.

Chapter 16

A winter storm hit the city the third week in January, closing down schools and businesses and knocking out power to residential areas. The buses weren't running. G.T. brought some wood in and got a fire going in the fireplace. After breakfast he put some chains on his truck and went over to Rosalita's house. I put on my coat and went out to the shed to check on Amos and feed him some corn. He acted glad to see me, prancing around in the snow, bleeping and cooing. I gave him an extra cup of feed, figuring he would need some additional calories, as cold as it was. It hardly ever snowed in this part of the South. I didn't even know if Amos had ever seen snow before, let alone an ice storm.

While I was feeding him I heard the *chug-chug* of a tractor. I looked up and saw our neighbor Hoagie Ambrose coming over from his place on his John Deere. He had a blade attached to it. He used it to clean the snow off our driveway. I waved at him on the return trip and he waved back. A tall, brown-skinned man with deep-set eyes and gray hair. When his wife died a year earlier, G.T. and I had taken him over a bucket of fried chicken and a case of beer. We sat with him in his kitchen for a while. G.T., who used to hang out with Hoagie's son, Rufus, said he spent a lot of hours at Hoagie's house when they were kids. Hoagie taught him how to pitch horseshoes. He said Hoagie was the one who called him to let him know this house was coming up for sale. "This was a good deal," he said. "Hoagie could have called plenty of black folks, but he called me instead. That right there shows you how fair the man is when it comes to race."

G.T. came back at lunchtime with Rosalita and her kids, Carmen and Miguel. He wanted to know if Hoagie had cleaned the snow off the driveway and I told him yes. G.T. said he would like to pay Hoagie for that but he knew Hoagie would never take it from him.

"Hoagie is the best neighbor I've ever had," G.T. told Rosalita. "But he sure does make you feel beholden to him." Hoagie also gave us vegetables from his garden every summer—corn, tomatoes, okra, and beans.

"He likes to give, G.T.," Rosalita says. "So do you. Givers are God's angels on earth."

Leave it to Rosalita to work God into the conversation. I figured we owed a debt to Hoagie for a clean driveway, not God, but I held that thought to myself. I didn't want to get her started.

G.T. set up his propane stove on the kitchen counter, and Rosalita fixed everyone fried tortillas. After lunch we went into the living room where she and her kids sang songs in Spanish. Carmen was six, and her little brother, Miguel, was four. The little girl had big brown eyes, like Rosalita, and the same honey-colored skin. The boy was darker, with a slimmer face; I guessed he must resemble his father, Esteban. G.T. told me the job Rosalita's husband had been doing was hazardous, but that the crew bosses at the construction company always sent the Mexicans down to do the most dangerous jobs. And the Mexicans were willing to do them because they were glad for the work. The unfairness of this was one more example of how cockeyed and mean the world can be. I doubted if the company bosses ever spent any time worrying about the wives and children of the Mexicans who worked for them.

After a while, Miguel crawled up into G.T.'s lap on the sofa and went to sleep, sucking his thumb. I wondered what G.T. was thinking while he was holding a dead man's child in his arms.

Outside, the sky was mirror-bright, the tree limbs bent nearly to the ground with the weight of ice.

Even after the snow and ice melted, Washington High was closed down for another day, due to some broken water pipes in the gym, so I took the bus out to Havenwood to put some time in with Mr. Ebban. He asked me if we had lost power and I told him yes. He said power was out in his section of the city, too, but Havenwood had a back-up generator so they still had heat and lights. He asked me why I was not in school, and I told him about the broken pipes. He asked if I had water at home, and I told him yes, that I was even able to take a cold shower this morning. I wondered if he had missed me, since I usually come on either Mondays or Tuesdays. I pictured him sitting by the window, looking out at the parking lot, waiting for me to come. Maybe I should have called him, I thought. Left word that I wasn't coming.

I read to him from Joshua, which was mostly about a bloody series of battles between the Hebrews and the Canaanites. They were fighting for possession of the same land. Joshua and his men killed everybody in one city, setting it on fire afterwards. Later, God helped the Jews by raining down hailstones on their enemies. And he made the sun and moon stand still, prolonging a day so the Jews could go after their enemies and put them to the sword.

I couldn't resist pointing out to the old man that these ancient Hebrews seemed to take a lot of pleasure in killing their enemies. "They don't seem that religious to me."

"They were surrounded by enemies. Pagans who killed children and worshiped idols. This warfare was a part of that struggle. If the Jews had not been willing to fight, neither they nor their faith in one God would have survived. They would have been destroyed by their enemies."

"But they showed no mercy to anyone. Joshua personally slaughtered those five kings he finds hiding in a cave. Doesn't that go against one of the Ten Commandments Moses got when he went up on the mountain?"

"The Hebrew word in the commandments is 'murder.' There is a difference between killing and murdering."

I told him it was a fine line he was walking there, and it seemed pretty clear to me that the Hebrews had done plenty of murdering themselves.

He shrugged and said something in Yiddish. When I asked him to translate, he said, "We're all stained with the blood of Cain."

I thought maybe he was agreeing with me, but then again, who could tell for sure? Mr. Ebban kept you off balance from one minute to the next so you never knew what he was thinking or exactly what he meant. His comment did set me to thinking about the nature of murder, especially as it related to my prime suspect, Marc Steigner. If I could find him and make sure he was actually the one who had hurt my daddy, would I be a murderer in the Biblical sense if I put him on a night train to the other side? It would be murder from a legal standpoint, but what if I looked at it from the point of view of fairness? Why should he be able to live free and clear after he left my daddy brain-damaged for life? Why were thugs like him—along with serial killers, pedophiles, and Nazis—able to get away with causing so much suffering in the world? Why didn't God use his power to stop them? I puzzled over this question a long time, but no matter how much I thought about it I couldn't come up with an answer.

Although I wouldn't tell Mr. Ebban this, I could understand the anger the Jews felt toward their enemies. When Samson pulled the pillars of the stadium down on the Philistines, for example, he was getting his revenge on the people who had blinded him, not to mention the ones who tried to make him dance for them like some kind of trained monkey. Who could blame him for that?

I walked down Pendleton Street, my head down against the cold wind. Halfway down the block, I turned into the alley that ran back to the old Magnolia Hotel, a four-story brick building that G.T. said was so old Teddy Roosevelt had stayed in it once when he visited this city. It was abandoned now, closed down with *no trespassing* signs posted in the front windows. The hotel's ground floor windows were covered with bars. Some of the glass was broken out, and sheets of black plastic had been put up from inside. Around back, there was a metal fire escape coming down from the apartment building next door. I climbed up the fire escape, swung over to the ledge, which extended about four inches out from the building, and inched along it, my face against the bricks. In this way I was able to reach a second story window of the old hotel. I slipped my knife blade under the sash and tried to raise it, but it was locked from the inside. With the back handle of the knife I tapped out the glass, unlocked it, and then raised the window, hoping no one would pass by the alley and see me back here. I bent down and crawled through. The room smelled moldy and sour. In the murky light I saw an antique single bed, a dresser, a lamp and nightstand, a shoe on the floor. I took out my flashlight and went through the room, into a hallway. I went down the hall, past more rooms of this old hotel, and came to the stairs. I eased up the stairs to the third floor, shining the light ahead of me. The place smelled of dust and mold and damp wood.

On the third floor I went down the hallway, looking in the rooms. Strips of wallpaper were peeling off the walls, and everything was covered with a layer of dust. I went into one of the rooms that was furnished with a double bed, a dresser, a lamp, just like the others. I went to the window and looked down at the street. Directly below me was the front of the Flamingo Bar. I could see who entered and left. I dusted off the chair and sat in it, looked down at the bar. I looked at my watch. It was four o'clock. Soon people could be getting off work and going there for happy hour.

Over the next hour, I studied each customer who entered and left. Most of the bar's patrons were men, but I saw a few women. I paid special attention to the men, noting the clothes they wore, the way they walked. I was thinking maybe I would know him when I saw him, that I would know him just as if I had second sight, that something about him, maybe the way he walked or the way he carried himself would tell me this was the man whose hands were stained with my daddy's blood.

At dusk, the bar's red neon sign came on out front. The letters *l* and *a* still missing.

No one ever looked up and saw me in the window.

After it got dark, I eased back down the stairs to the second floor, climbed out the window, closed it behind me, and hung and dropped from the ledge to the alley. I had stayed in the hotel longer than I intended, which meant G.T. would ask me where I had been.

I can tell him I missed the bus and walked home, I thought. I'll add that I stopped on the way to play basketball with some guys I know.

Even though I didn't like to lie to anyone, it was especially hard for me to lie to G.T., who had taken me in and given me a roof over my head and who worried about me more than my own mother did.

On the way home I mulled over the men I'd seen enter the Flamingo. I had identified three suspects: a slim man with a face like a weasel; a broad-shouldered man who walked with his jaw thrust out, as if he were expecting someone to challenge him; and a man in a cowboy hat who had stood out in front of the bar awhile, looking around like he was waiting for someone, before he went inside. What was it about these three? Something about the way they looked made me think they might be the type to hit someone when he wasn't looking and leave him to freeze to death in an alley.

When I got home I was relieved to see G.T.'s truck was not in the driveway, just Rosalita's green Ford. This surprised me, since she didn't usually come over during the week.

Rosalita was in the kitchen, rolling chicken strips in flour. There was water boiling on the stove and some red balloons tied to G.T.'s chair. I asked her where G.T was and she said he was still at work, finishing up a job with Carlos, and that she had come over to surprise him with a special meal.

"How'd you get in?"

"The spare key!"

"So you know about that, huh?"

"It's a woman's job to know things."

I was surprised G.T. had told her about the house key that hung on a nail in the back of the shed. I had gotten another one made at the hardware store on Tull Street, after Dopodja took my house key from me. "What's with the balloons?"

"It's Valentine's Day."

I poured myself a glass of tea from the pitcher in the refrigerator, then sat down at the table to drink it. I had forgotten all about it being Valentine's Day.

"Did you get your favorite girl some chocolate?"

"I don't have a girlfriend—don't want one either."

"You need some love in your life."

"Did you know you had flour on your nose?"

She brushed her nose with her forearm and went back to rolling the chicken strips. I watched her put them in the skillet. When she finished she washed her hands in the sink, then sat across from me at the table.

"Jesse, what's wrong?"

"Nothing."

"You seem *muy trieste*. Do you want to talk?"

"Nothing to say."

"You know I'm here if you need me. You know that, right?"

"Sure, Rosalita. But I'm OK."

I wished I could talk to her, tell her about the way I couldn't stop thinking about this Marc Steigner, but there was no way I could. Sooner or later she would tell G.T. anything I told her.

Rosalita began singing in Spanish. She filled a pot with water, then put it on the stove. She opened a box of rice and poured it into the pot. Watching her I was touched by the way she had come over here to bring G.T. balloons and cook him a surprise dinner. He would sure be tired and hungry when he got home from work.

I wondered if he realized how lucky he was.

Like a boxer who had been studying his opponent for a weak point, I finally launched my attack on the old man's faith. My launching point was the Book of Job, which I had just finished reading to him. I was purely disgusted about the way God had just basically turned Job over to Satan, to torment him by killing his children, stripping him of his land, his servants, his property, afflicting his body with painful sores.

"The God that did that to Job is not worthy of being worshiped," I told Mr. Ebban. "All he demonstrated is that he could beat the Devil."

"The Book of Job is a parable, Jesse. The Talmud tells us this. Job never really existed. It is a parable about the way our faith and love of God are tested."

"Even as a parable, it wasn't fair for God to let Job suffer like that. He didn't do anything to deserve it. Surely you can see that."

"Yes, I can see that," the old man said. Always catching me by surprise. "And although I see it purely as a parable that enables one to study its ideas, I have no answer for the painful issue the story raises—the suffering of the innocent. No answer. No answer at all." Mr. Ebban sat with his shoulders slumped forward in the wheelchair. "All this has come upon us, yet we have not forgotten You," he said, quoting some verse from somewhere, his eyes closed. He looked old and lonesome and beat down.

I felt I had finally scored a crippling blow to his grand vision of God. But later, riding home on the bus, the image of the old man looking so sad came back to me like a thorny bush wind-whipped against my heart.

From my perch in the hotel window I watched one of my prime suspects come down the sidewalk, the one with the skinny, sharp-featured face that put me in mind of a weasel. He walked with a bouncy strut, like some of these gangbanger wannabes you saw over in Little Haiti. I pressed my face against the glass, studying him carefully, noting his khaki jacket, the black boots, and the cigarette he was smoking. He flipped the butt into the gutter and went on into the Flamingo. In my notebook I made a notation that he was a smoker.

Thick, blue-black clouds rolled in from the west. The light was fading fast. I knew I should leave, but I stayed, hoping I would see the weasel-faced man again. I thought I might follow him to see where he lived, even though I didn't know his name, didn't even know if he was Marc Steigner. He might not even be a criminal at all, I thought. I recalled the pictures I had seen of the Nazis in a book in the school library, how, except for Hitler, you couldn't have told they were evil just by looking at them. One of them, Hitler's minister of information, was a dead ringer for Mr. Osterhaus, the principal of my high school. This made me realize the man who hurt my daddy might not look evil at all. He might just look like an ordinary person, someone wearing jeans and a flannel shirt, a denim jacket, a toboggan pulled low over his eyes, like that man who had just left the Flamingo and was standing out front, looking up at the sky.

Rain pounded the street in wind-blown sheets. In a flash of lightning I saw my image in the grimy glass. My reflection was ghost-like, a face seen in a dream.

I drive out to the dump to look for some treasure I have heard is hidden there. I climb over the fence and walk back into the dump, only to find I am surrounded by grinning skulls—a mountain of them. I try to turn around and go back, but I can't find the way out—the skulls are piled halfway up to the clouds. I come to the edge of the fence and try to climb over it, but there is barbed wire on top and I can't get out. The sky is as red as it must have been on the first day of creation. At first I think it is the sunset; then I realize it is red from burning bodies, so many of them they have turned the sky red.

I woke up shaking all over. Sitting up on the side of the bed, I tried to get the memory of the dream out of my head. But I couldn't forget it.

I lay back down and waited for morning to come.

CHAPTER 17

March brought more cold, drizzling rain. The workers at Gladstone and Son walked from the parking lot to the warehouse in yellow raincoats, the only splash of color in the gray landscape. At school I sat in the back of my classrooms, thinking about suspects I had seen entering and leaving the Flamingo. After the bell rang to change classes I zombie-walked through the halls, my eyes turned inward. I was so quiet and withdrawn Snookie accused me of being stoned, claimed I had been smoking pot in the john.

Nearly every afternoon after school I was up in the Magnolia Hotel, taking notes on the men who entered and left the Flamingo. I identified the bar's male patrons with codes, using letters and numbers, and recorded observations about them—what time they arrived and left, the cars they drove, the way they were dressed. I left the notebook under the moldy mattress in the hotel room. Like the room itself, the notebook was part of my quest for revenge.

The rain finally stopped and the sun came out. Daisies, honeysuckle, and dandelions bloomed at the edge of the woods behind the house. Pale green flowers appeared in the silver-gray leaves of the Spanish moss in the oak outside my bedroom window. At night I lay in my bed, listening to the wind-whispers in the trees, the lilting voices of the bobwhites and whippoorwills. When the weather turned hot, Amos cranked up his mating call. Kept it up all day and half the night. "*Eeeeeou! Eeeeeou!*" Rosalita said he sounded like he was in pain. But I knew what his problem was: he was just lonesome.

I would like to have gotten a peahen and raised some chicks, but I knew there wasn't any use to even ask G.T. about it. He didn't want the hassle of raising them—and I think he also hated it when the chicks got killed by dogs and hawks. When they were small, we could keep them fairly safe in their wire-enclosed pens, but sooner or later they would get out and be at risk for predators.

At Havenwood more and more residents were sitting outside in their wheelchairs when I arrived. Their veins were blue as bottles beneath their parchment skin. As I pushed Mr. Ebban in his wheelchair through the park, crocuses, daffodils, tulips, and yellow jasmine bloomed beside the walkway, and the air was drenched with their fragrances. When we reached the pond, the ducks swam toward us, quacking, the old man directing me to take him close to the water's edge to meet them. He had a plastic bag full of muffins under his shirt. Someone—Varden most likely—was sneaking them to him from the kitchen. He fed the ducks beneath the oaks, the Spanish moss rippling like ribbons in the wind.

One afternoon by the fountain I saw a dust devil moving through the park, picking up dust and scraps of paper. Right after that Mr. Ebban began shivering like he had caught a chill. I stopped the wheelchair and stepped around to the side to see what was wrong. His hands were trembling and his face was drained of color.

"Are you OK?" I asked him. "What's wrong?"

"I am *faklempt*." He was shaking all over, his hands over his ears. "I can't speak."

I looked around to see if anything might explain his behavior. I saw nothing unusual. A woman pushing a stroller. Two men standing by the fountain, talking in a foreign language. A man and a boy tossing a Frisbee back and forth.

"Nooooooo!" he cried.

"Mr. Ebban, what is it?"

He put one hand over his heart. He was opening and closing his mouth, as if he was trying to speak.

"Where does it hurt?"

But he could only shake his head and point to a spot off to the right. As I wheeled him up the path toward the nursing home, he sat with his head bent forward on his chest, his body shaking. I wondered if he was having a heart attack.

I pulled open the door to the nursing home and pushed him into the lobby, shouting for Varden as I entered.

"What's wrong?" asked the attendant at the front desk.

"Call Varden Story," I told her. "Quick!"

She picked up the phone on her desk to call Varden on his cell phone.

Mr. Ebban was breathing in short little gasps, his eyes half closed. "It's going to be all right," I told him.

But I was afraid that the old man was dying. Once this idea took root in my mind, I couldn't shake it. I felt like I was on the tilt-a-whirl ride at the carnival. I knelt beside Mr. Ebban, my hand on his trembling shoulders. Where in the hell was Varden? Why didn't he come?

"They were talking German," Varden said. We were by the front desk. We had gotten Mr. Ebban into his bed, and the nurse had given him a shot to calm him down. "Seen him go off like that once before when he heard that Kraut talk. It tears up his nerves. And who can blame him?"

"It wasn't his heart, then."

"No."

"I thought he was leaving the world."

"Believe you starting to care for Mr. Ebban."

"I just didn't want him to die on me, OK?"

"Getting kind of attached to him, I see." Varden nodding and grinning now. Always has to be a wise-ass.

I signed myself out and walked out to the bus stop by the front of the nursing home.

I am not attached to him, I thought. I just don't want him to die.

Not on my watch.

Amos's tail feathers filled out in their iridescent splendor. When he spread them out, they made a swishing sound, like a woman's silk dress. One afternoon I found a feather that had dropped from his tail in the back yard. The feather had a big green and purple eye swirling in the center. I put it in my vase by the window, with my other peacock feathers. I told myself he had left it there for me as a gift, as a way of saying thanks for all of the times I had fed and watered him.

The next time G.T. and I drove up to St. Aubin Hospital to see Daddy, I took Amos's feather with me and gave it to him.

"What's this?" he asked.

"It's a peacock feather. From Amos. You remember Amos, don't you?"

Daddy had raised Amos from a chick and given him his name. Now he just sat there, holding the feather, looking confused. I wondered what he was thinking, what strange country he had gone to in his mind.

"Amos," he said slowly. "I don't believe I remember Amos."

One Sunday afternoon when I got home from Havenwood, I saw G.T. and Hoagie Ambrose sitting on the front porch, drinking Coronas.

Hoagie smiled and waved at me. The beer bottle looked small in his big brown hand.

"Hey, Mr. Hoagie. Saw you out plowing your garden the other day."

"We had a lot of rain there and I couldn't do much. When the sun come out and dried the ground, I knew that was my chance. I had a plan but it didn't work out. Farmer's got to work around the master's plan."

"Mr. Gladstone wants you to work on his plan, too," G.T. said.

"Lord, G.T., what am I going to do about that?"

"I don't know, Hoagie. If you need a lawyer you can call mine. Name's Jake Quittlebaum."

"It's a sad day when a man has to consult a lawyer just so he can grow some corn and watermelons."

I sat on the porch and asked Hoagie why he needed a lawyer.

"Hoagie got a letter from Gladstone's lawyer," G.T. said. "Seems they want him to coordinate his plowing with their pet funerals. They say his tractor is too loud. They also don't feel he should be plowing while a service is going on. Claims it upsets the bereaved."

"G.T., you know I've always tried to get along with my neighbors. But there's lines a reasonable person knows not to step across. That's one of the things that facilitates us all living in harmony—when we are able to, that is. For example, I wouldn't tell Mr. Gladstone how to make his pet caskets. And by the same rule, I don't appreciate him trying to tell me when I can plow my land."

"Makes sense to me, Hoagie."

"What should I do? I'm no writer. I want to respond, but I don't know how to put the words down on paper so they'll sound right."

"Jesse here is right good in English. Get him to write the letter for you."

"I don't want to trouble this young man with something like that. I'll figure something out."

"I'll be glad to write the letter for you, Mr. Hoagie."

"You would?"

"Yes, sir. Tell me what you want me to say, and I'll do my best to write it."

"I sure would appreciate that, Jesse."

I went into my room and got my notebook. Returning to the porch I took notes while Hoagie told me the points he wanted to make—that he could only plow certain times due to the limitations of the weather and his arthritis, which made it too hard to sit on the tractor some days, and that he never plowed on Sunday. He hoped they would understand he needed the food he raised in his garden, and would therefore not be able to comply with their request. He promised to get his muffler fixed so the tractor wouldn't make so much noise, however.

I wrote all of this down on two sheets of paper and handed them to him. He put on his glasses and read what I had written, his lips shaping the words.

"This is perfect, Jesse. I'm going to sign my name to this and mail it on to them. And I'm much obliged to you for your generous help."

"Don't you want me to type it up first? I can use G.T.'s typewriter."

"What do you think, G.T.?"

"It would look more business-like."

"Fine, then. You go ahead and type it up, Jesse. And I'll sign it."

"I'll type it up after supper and bring it over to your house."

Hoagie took his glasses off, folded them up, and put them in his pocket. "You know I wouldn't give you a nickel for a whole roomful of pet caskets."

"Some people must like them. I hear Mr. Gladstone is getting rich off those caskets."

"Folks get rich off all kinds of projects these days. We always put the dogs and the cats in the ground. No caskets. Dog goes back to the earth, where he come from. Where we all come from. That's all Adam was at the beginning. Big handful of dirt in the master's hands."

"You want another beer, Hoagie?" G.T. asked.

"One is my limit, G.T. I drink any more than that I'm liable to start thinking too much."

G.T. smiled. "We don't want that to happen."

"No, sir," said Hoagie, "we surely don't."

After supper that evening, I typed Hoagie's letter to the Gladstone Pet Casket Company on G.T.'s old Royal typewriter, which he had used to type up bills before he got a part-time bookkeeper, and I took it over to Hoagie's house. I knocked on the door but he didn't answer. I looked in through the window and saw that he was asleep in a rocking chair, a Bible open in his lap. There was a reading lamp beside his chair, the light directed on the Bible. I folded up the letter and left it behind the screen door, figuring he would find it in the morning. As I returned to our house I remembered the way Hoagie had cleared the snow off our driveway back in the winter, and the way he was always giving us vegetables out of his garden. It gave me a good feeling to know I had done something to help him for a change.

I couldn't help comparing him to Mr. Ebban, even though they had different ways of believing. I wondered if getting old just made people get stronger in their faith. Maybe they want to feel more secure about what comes afterwards, I thought, since they generally are closer to the end of their lives. The trouble is, how can they know for sure there's anything afterwards? Could be just a big nothing. No harps or golden streets, no fiery pits either, just a big long empty nothingness for all eternity. Considering this possibility gave me a cold, hopeless feeling, because it meant I would never see Lee again, or my daddy made whole and sanctified, the way he was when we lived on Cotton Gin Road. Even though it might turn out to be true, it was the kind of thought that makes you want to get blind drunk, just to keep the blues from pecking away at your heart like an old baldheaded buzzard.

Chapter 18

I climbed up the ledge, raised the window, and slipped into the back of the Magnolia Hotel. I eased down over the radiator and went into the hallway, conscious of the strong stench of a dead thing. A rat maybe, I thought, as I eased up the stairs to the third floor. Passing by the room next to the one I always used, I shined a flashlight inside. The room had an empty brass bed, a chair, a dresser. My light picked up a shriveled pair of shoes on the floor, a metal washbowl, a lamp, a pitcher on a stand. I was turning to leave when my light moved over to a figure sitting in the chair: a man, his hands folded in his lap. His face, or what had once been a human face, was partially eaten away, so I could see the bone underneath, the strips of flesh hanging down. The eye sockets swarmed with maggots. I ran down the hallway, down the stairs to the window, but when I opened the window and looked down I didn't see the alley, only a scarred and shadowy landscape, like the surface of the moon.

"This man you're looking for—does he have a bat tattooed on his neck?" Snookie asked. I was drinking coffee with her, LaFay, and Terra in Nick's Café.

"I don't know. Why?"

"I ran across somebody who knows a Steigner used to live down on South Rhodes."

"That might be him. Where is he now?"

"Dude didn't know. I got him to give me a description, though. Said he was about six feet tall, two hundred pounds, kind of bald, with a tattoo of a bat on his neck."

"Where is this guy? What's his name?"

"Name's Earl. He works construction. I met him at the bowling alley the other night. Old enough to be my daddy and he was hitting on me. We got to talking and on a whim I just asked him if he knew anybody named Marc Steigner. He said he used to know the guy a couple of years ago, doesn't know what happened to him."

"What's this Earl's last name? Where does he live?"

"Don't know. A motel probably."

My mind raced through the list of suspects in my notebook, still up in the old hotel room. I was trying to match Snookie's description with one of them. It occurred to me that I might not be able to see a tattoo from the window; I would need binoculars or a telescope.

"Maybe he's at the bowling alley now. If we go over there, you can point him out to me."

"I doubt if he's there now. Man seemed like a rolling stone to me."

"Maybe we ought to get more than fifty," Terra said. "All this time and trouble it's taking."

"Can't afford but fifty."

"You still helping your uncle on the roofs?"

"Only on vacations since my grades went down. He says I got to study."

"You going to be a roofer, too, after you get out of school?"

"I don't know. I guess it's something I could do."

"What about you, Terra?" Snookie said. "What do you want to do when you get out of school?"

"I want to own laundromats. And rubber machines, the kind they have in gas station johns."

"I figured it would be something like that, something where you wouldn't have to work too hard."

"Don't knock it, baby. You got a string of laundromats and rubber machines, all you got to do is ride around all day, picking up your money. Plus you got all your clothes washed free, not to mention free rubbers."

We laughed. I remembered I had once heard Terra say she wanted to be a child psychologist. That was Terra. Never wanted to let you know how she really felt.

I asked LaFay what kind of work she wanted to do.

"I want to be a physical therapist," she said. The bruises on her face had faded to a dull yellow. "Work with people with disabilities."

"Plenty of people in the world with disabilities, only they aren't always the kind you can see," Terra said. "Hey, who wants to go bowling?"

"I've been too broke to do much of anything, since G.T. took my part-time job away," I said.

"You need to get a job at Gladstone's," Snookie said. "Making caskets for Fido."

"They only hire full-time. Plus you got to be at least eighteen."

"Let's get the check from Mimi," Terra said.

When we went to pay the bill, I was short twenty cents for my coffee. Terra tossed in two dimes to cover for me. I thanked her, and she said, "No problem, Jesse."

After we paid the bill we went outside. It was dusk and the street-lights had come on as we walked along the sidewalk. There was a faint trace of blood-colored light in the sky.

The bowling alley was about seven blocks from Nick's, on Tull Street. It was a block up Oleander, then right on Hudson. We had only gone a little way up from Nick's before a black Lexus pulled up to the curb and Tony Moran jumped out. "LaFay," he said. "I want to talk you."

LaFay kept walking, though, Terra on one side, Snookie on the other, me trailing a little behind. I felt a tightening in the pit of my stomach. the kind of feeling you get when you can tell some major trouble is heading your way.

"Dammit! Did you hear what I said? Said I want to talk to you."

We all kept walking. Moran got back into the car and pulled off, following us. "Don't pay that jerk any mind, LaFay," Snookie said, taking her arm. "Ignore him and maybe he will go away."

We turned the corner onto Hudson and Moran turned, too, the car going slowly along the edge of the curb. He sped up suddenly, then slammed on the brakes and turned into an alley ahead of us, forcing us to walk into the street. He got out and leaned against the car, arms folded across his chest. He was wearing a purple shirt, the top buttons unbuttoned, that gold cross hanging around his neck.

"LaFay!" he shouted.

The girls went around the car. Moran moved to follow them but I stepped in front of him, blocking his path.

"Why don't you leave her alone, Tony? She doesn't want to see you."

"Get the fuck out of my way."

I smiled at him now, seeing any chance I might have had to talk him out of making a fool out of himself was gone. I could hear LaFay and Snookie calling for me to come on, but their voices seemed to be coming from a distance. "I'm not going anywhere," I said.

He tried to kick me in the balls, but I turned aside so that he only got the muscle in my left thigh. Still, it was a solid blow, and if I hadn't been so mad it would have hurt more than it did. I was on him fast, swinging at his face. My fists connected—good solid punches that snapped his head back. He tried to box me awhile but I was all over him, slamming some hard jabs into his face. He landed a few blows, but they were mostly glancing and I didn't feel them much. Then, seeing that he couldn't win on his feet, he headed-butted me back against the wall of the building and caught me around the waist. We went down onto the pavement, rolling and punching.

I could see it was a mistake to have let him get me down. I should have moved away from him, onto the sidewalk, where I would have had the advantage with speed and wind. He had weight and power on me on the ground. He kept trying to get on top of me and pin me with his knees.

Moran was out of shape—he was already panting—and I figured I would wear him down, then get him in a sleeper hold or an arm lock. But I misjudged his strength. He seized my left arm with his right and twisted it behind my back; then he threw one leg over me and, holding me down with his thigh, he got the other arm down with his right arm, and climbed on top of me, pinning both of my arms with his knees. He was too heavy for me to throw him off. I bucked and arched my back, trying to reach his shoulders with my feet to pull him backwards that way, but he was bent forward too far for me to reach him. He punched me in the side of the face, a hard blow that made my ears ring.

Before he could hit me again, an arm with shiny bracelets appeared from off to my right, the hand holding a cylinder. A stream of something shot out of the cylinder. Tony grabbed both eyes. "Ahhhhhh!"

Terra hit him in the face with another blast of her hairspray.

Tony tried to keep me pinned with his weight and the force of his knees, but he was unable to keep me down without his hands, which he had plastered to his eyes. I flipped him off, slid out from under him, rolled away, and scrambled to my feet.

An easy target now, he was just kneeling there, holding his eyes. When I hit him I felt the shock of the blow all the way up to the shoulder joint. Tony went down on his back. He groaned and put his hands to his face.

Terra was pulling me away. "Let's go, Jesse. You can't afford getting busted."

I let her pull me away, but as we walked toward Moran's car Snookie shouted a warning, and I turned around and saw him coming toward me with a knife in his hand, blood streaming out of his nose.

"Jesse!" Terra said. "Catch!"

I turned around and she tossed me the can of hair spray. I sprayed it in Tony's face. He put a bloody hand over his eyes and I kicked him in the knee. He backed up and somehow lost his footing on the pavement. He went down by his car, his arm holding the knife between the seat and the open car door. I slammed the car door against his forearm, crushing it between the door and the car. I heard him scream. I opened the door and the knife fell to the alley. As I picked up the knife I heard Moran moaning and cursing. I leaned over him, still holding the knife.

"Keep your damn hands off LaFay, Moran. Don't you ever touch her again."

The girls pulled me away, pushed me down the sidewalk. Snookie had me by one arm, LaFay had me by the other. Terra came along behind, walking backwards, her finger on her can of hairspray.

Three blocks up Hudson, we stopped at a sandwich shop, and the girls cleaned me up with little towelettes from their purses, wiping the grease and dirt off my face and clothes. While they did this they talked about the fight with Tony Moran. Snookie and Terra were laughing, but LaFay was quiet and subdued.

I thanked Terra more than once for saving my ass with that can of hairspray.

"He had me so I couldn't move. He was fixing to rain on my good looks."

"LaFay and Snookie were going to jump on his back. I figured I had to do something before they got into it. I didn't want him to hurt LaFay again."

"Girl, you are the fastest can in the west." Snookie gave Terra a high five.

LaFay said we needed to forget about the bowling alley, go home and give Tony time to cool down. "I don't know what he'll do."

"That sucker ain't going to do nothing tonight, the shape he's in," Terra said. "Got forty pounds on Jessie and he's still got to pull a knife."

"Where is that thing?" Snookie asked

"I got it right here." I took the knife out, opened the long, curved blade. It locked into place with a clicking sound.

"Guy that carries a knife like that has got to be trying to compensate for something," Terra said. "He's probably kind of small down in the male equipment department."

"I wouldn't know about that," Snookie said. "But he sure is small in the brain department. You'd better give me that knife, Jessie. Dopodja catch you carrying that thing you'll be gone from here."

I closed the blade and gave the knife to Snookie. "What are you going to do with it?"

"Use it to clean fish. Mama's fish knife is so dull you could ride it to Texas and back."

Snookie and LaFay wanted to buy me something to eat, but I didn't feel like eating. I just let them buy me a cup of coffee. My head and face hurt, and I had a pulled muscle in my back. I had the feeling the fight with Tony Moran was going to lead to a lot more trouble for me. I wished it wouldn't have happened, but I felt like I didn't really have any choice. I couldn't stand the thought of him hurting LaFay again. And I sure wasn't going to let that happen, not when I could do something to stop it.

CHAPTER 19

At school on Monday a lot of students, including some I didn't even know, asked me about the fight with Tony Moran. Word had already spread that I had broken his arm in a fight. I just shook my head and kept silent. I didn't want to get more trouble stirred up.

I couldn't keep quiet, though, when Mick and Andre Grier started in on me about LaFay.

"You got LaFay now," Mick said. "She's yours. You won her fair and square."

"What are you talking about?"

"You whipped Moran's ass, man. Fool has been asking for it, too. Not only that, you beat him while you were taking up for her. That makes you the man—you got to claim what's yours."

"LaFay is just a friend. I don't have any claim on her. Besides, if it wasn't for Terra, Moran would have pounded my face into jelly. He had me where I couldn't move."

"That don't matter now," said Mick. "I hear Moran looks a little ragged. Two black eyes and a swelled-up nose. Right arm in a sling. He ain't going to be doing his rooster act around Pottstown anytime soon."

"I'd just like to move past the whole thing. And I don't want to see LaFay hurt any more. She's been through enough."

Andre said, "You ain't scared to ride that pony, are you?"

"Watch your mouth, Andre."

"Take it easy, Jesse, just trying to help."

"Don't need your damn help."

I walked off, angry and embarrassed by all of this talk about LaFay. I was amazed that Mick and Andre would think that my fight with Tony Moran would give me any claim to her. LaFay Roux was her own person. She could make up her own mind about who she wanted to be with—and whoever that person was, it would surely be somebody with more to offer her than me. I remembered that time she loaned me money out of her little change purse. Hell, I couldn't even afford to buy a piece of pie at the Nick's Café, let alone take a girl out on a date. Some boyfriend I'd make—an ex-jailbird with no money, driving a rusty Dodge truck spattered with peacock shit and trailing blue smoke.

After school that afternoon, I headed out to the buses in the parking lot on the west side of the school. I was surprised to see G.T. waiting for me in the lot. He was leaning against his truck. He didn't look happy.

"Hi, G.T.," I said. "What are you doing here?"

"Get in," he said.

I got in the truck and G.T. pulled off into the stream of traffic leaving the school. He turned right onto Okisko Road, the street that ran in front of Washington High.

"What's up? How come you're not working?"

He just scowled and didn't answer. He had gone to see his doctor recently for a physical. I wondered if he had received some bad news. He turned off Okisko onto Bryce Street. He was heading east towards Pottstown. I tried to get him in a better mood by telling about a conversation I had with my algebra teacher that day. "She said I'm doing better and I can raise my grade to a B if I work hard."

G.T. didn't answer.

I fell silent, then, figuring I would find out what was bothering him soon enough.

When he turned onto Oleander, he said, "How come you didn't tell me you got into a fight?"

"Damn. That's all I been hearing about today."

"Jesse, you ain't nothing but trouble, you know that?"

I wondered why G.T. was so upset about a fight. It wasn't like he hadn't gotten into plenty of them when he was my age. How did he even find out about it? What had got him so riled up?

"I didn't have any choice. Fool had already beat the shit out of a friend of mine—a girl! And he was fixing to do it again. I couldn't let that happen. Besides, no cops saw it."

"It ain't the cops I'm worried about."

"I'm sure not scared of Tony Moran."

"Tony himself isn't the problem, Jesse. It's his old man, Ike Moran."

"What, the guy who owns the Shanghai Bar?"

"That's right. Ike Moran used to ride with the Satan's Apostles, a biker gang that controlled most of the drug trade around here. They were into extortion and prostitution, too. Moran was one of their leaders, probably the main honcho. Cops finally broke the gang up—sent some of the members to prison and ran most of the others out of town. They tried Moran on murder charges a couple of times, never could get a conviction. He's laid low since then, got married and had that no-count son, but he's not someone you want to piss off."

I remembered hearing G.T. and Buddy talk about the time when the Satan's Apostles had been the most feared gang in the city. I was just a little kid back then. It never seemed like something that would touch me.

"How'd you know I got in a fight?"

"Some friends of mine told me about it—*warned* me about it is more like it. The kid is a punk and a bully, but Moran is like a python that drops on you out of a tree—you don't see it until the damn thing is around your neck. You broke his son's arm. Ike's reputation is on the line now."

"What's an old guy who owns a bar worried about his reputation for? Just because his kid got in a fight? Tony Moran is a lot bigger than me, and he's got to be at least five years older. Three witnesses saw him come at me with a knife. Plus he beat up a girl, G.T. Looks to me like his dad would be mad at *him*."

"Ike Moran ain't going to look at it that way. Let me give you a little more of his history. Back in the late seventies there was a black guy in this city named Deon Packer. Real bad ass. Packer was going out with a woman Moran was involved with. Packer and Moran ran into each other in a restaurant. Words were exchanged, and they both started swinging. Some off-duty cops broke it up before anyone got hurt. A week later, Deon Packer turned up in the trunk of a car parked right down the street from his house in Little Haiti. His face and head beaten to a pulp. Cops charged Moran with murder. When the case went to trial, Moran's lawyer argued that plenty of other people had a motive to kill him, which was probably true. Trouble is, most drug dealers just unload a nine-millimeter into their rivals. They don't kill them like that. Moran was acquitted, but the jury was out three days, which tells you it was a close call. Most people on the street thought Deon Packer's murder had Moran's fingerprints all over it."

Listening to this was like seeing something rise up, all spines and teeth, from the bottom of the sea. I didn't know who I was worried most about, myself or G.T., who I could see was caught up in this looming trouble.

"What do you want me to do?"

"I'm going to take you home. And I want you to stay there. Don't go out of the house. Don't answer the door. Just stay there until I get back, you hear?"

"All right, sure. I'll do that. Where are you going?"

"Never mind where I'm going. Just do what I say. You've caused enough trouble already for one lifetime."

Before G.T. dropped me off at the house, he told me to go inside, lock the doors and wait for him. "Don't turn the lights on and don't answer that door."

He sat in the truck until I got inside.

I did what he said, pacing the floor, throwing darts, watching TV. I opened a can of soup for supper. I got my .22 Magnum out of the closet, loaded it, along with two spare magazines, which I slipped into my pocket. I drew back the bolt, placing a round into the chamber, flipped on the safety, and leaned the rifle against the wall by my bed. After the sun went down I lit a candle in my bedroom. I got out my algebra book and tried to do my homework by candlelight, but studying was out of the question. I was too worried about G.T., where he might be going, and what might happen when he got there. The candle flickered in a little draft, casting a tall shadow on the wall. The shadow took the shape of Deon Packer, curled up in the trunk of a car—so near, and yet so far, from home.

I saw headlights coming down the driveway. Sounded like G.T.'s truck, but I had my rifle in my hands as I looked out the front window to make sure. When I saw it was him, I put down the gun and went out to the kitchen. I turned on the light over the stove and sat at the kitchen table.

He came in the back door. He got a beer out of the refrigerator and sat down at the table. The light from the stove left most of his face in shadow. I guessed it was all right to turn the lights on now, but I didn't want to do anything without his permission. I felt too bad about all the trouble and worry I had caused him.

I asked him where he had been.

"Went to see Ike Moran."

"You go alone?"

"I had some friends with me—Buddy McBane and a couple of other guys. Buddy's older brother used to ride with the Satan's Apostles, so Buddy knows Ike."

"What did Mr. Ike Moran say?"

"It's what he didn't say that was important. He wasn't going to show his hand anyway, not with us there."

"Was he pissed?"

"What do you think?"

"You see Tony?"

"No." G.T. took another swallow of beer. "I'm hoping we came to an understanding. Let's just leave it at that."

"How long do I still have to stay in the house?"

"You got to go to school, Jesse. You got to go on living your life. But don't be hanging out on the street. Don't be a target. And stay the hell away from Tony Moran. If he says anything to you, ignore him. He tries to provoke you into a fight, just walk away."

"That's going to be hard, G.T. What if he jumps me? You telling me not to even defend myself?"

"Listen to me, Jesse. I've done what I could to get this situation under control. Now you stay away from Moran. Don't talk to him, don't even look at him. You see him coming, go the other way. You hear me?"

"Sure, G.T. I'll do my best. And thanks for looking out for me."

My mind was swirling with questions but I knew there would be no answer for them tonight. I went back to my room and lay down on my bed. I looked back on that night when we were leaving Nick's Café, the way Tony Moran had followed us, followed LaFay, in his car. I went over the events in my mind, trying to see if I could have done anything different. I kept coming back to one basic point: Moran was determined to get LaFay in his car, which would have placed her at risk of being beaten up again—or worse. Sometimes you are presented with a choice, and you have to do what seems right at the time, just to go on living with your own sorry self. If I was living back during the time of miracles, maybe God would have split open the ground and let Tony Moran fall into a crack in the street or struck him down with a plague of boils, but this was Pottstown, USA, and I figured I was the only person standing between Tony Moran and LaFay Roux getting beat up, raped, or maybe murdered.

Although I didn't see how I had any choice but to do what I had done, I was sick at heart for having involved G.T. in my troubles. I couldn't help feeling that I had taken a wrong turn and I was now moving fast down a road I never wanted to be on.

Chapter 20

I followed G.T.'s order to keep a low profile around Pottstown, staying in my house when I was not in school or at Havenwood Guardian Care. I was careful not to say anything about Tony Moran. I didn't want my words to get back to him.

On Thursday, Mick told me Tony was back in his video game parlor, flirting with the girls who came in there with their boyfriends, acting like his old cocky self, even though his arm was in a cast. Mick said he had overheard someone ask Moran about his injuries, and Moran claimed to have gotten "jumped by a gang." Mick added, "What a pufferfish, huh?" Mick said he figured this trouble would all die down in time and that Moran might even learn a lesson from it and stop being such an asshole and a bully, but I wasn't so sure. Noting that Moran was being so tight-lipped about what happened, I was reminded what my daddy used to say about snakes in the swamp. He said that the best way to go through the brush was to make a lot of noise, hit the bushes ahead of you with a stick, and that most snakes, even poisonous ones, would move out of the way. He said that the most dangerous snakes were the silent ones you don't see. I could see how this advice could be relevant to a two-legged snake like Tony Moran. On the other hand, I figured I couldn't go through life being scared of my own shadow and jumping every time I heard a loud noise, so by Friday I decided to try to put Tony Moran and his ex-biker dad out of my mind and go on about my business. If I saw Tony I resolved to take G.T.'s advice and try to walk away from him.

I was touched that G.T. and his friends had gone to the Shanghai Bar to talk to Ike Moran on my behalf. I hoped Ike would figure I was not worth the trouble it would take to kill me. I didn't know what he and G.T. had talked about but I figured he wouldn't be particularly eager to tangle with G.T. and Buddy McBane, no matter how bad he was.

Saturday morning I went into the kitchen and saw Rosalita sitting at the table, drinking coffee. A ray of sunlight from the window fell across her face, lighting up the fine hairs on her cheek. She gave me a chilly smile but didn't speak.

I poured a cup of coffee from the pot on the counter and sat across from her, trying to survey the situation from her point of view. She knew G.T. was a good man. If she could marry him she would have gained for herself a steady provider, a stepdad for her kids, not to mention G.T.'s faithful companionship. But his main liability was a hell-raising nephew that couldn't stay out of trouble.

I said, "Good morning, Rosalita."

"How are you feeling today, Jesse?"

"Low down and no good."

Rosalita said something in Spanish. I recognized one of the words, "*El Diablo*."

"I guess you're mad at me, too."

"Not angry. No. But I pray for you. I pray for your soul every morning and every night."

I kept my lip zipped shut. I didn't want to get Rosalita started. It was too early in the morning. The Devil already knew my name and there was nothing I could do about that. And anyway, I figured I was too far gone for words.

Carrying a plastic bag of biscuits, I walked down the hall toward Mr. Ebban's room. I had bought the biscuits in the bakery section of the supermarket when I was in there yesterday buying ham hocks for some collards I was planning to cook for supper, along with sausage, black-eyed peas, and cornbread. G.T. had given me the money since he was too busy to go to the store. I brought the old man these biscuits because the last time I had been here I had heard him say he was having trouble getting muffins to feed the ducks. According to Varden, Ms. Lynch had been tightening the screws on the kitchen help in an effort to cut expenses.

These biscuits were a little past their prime but I figured the ducks wouldn't mind.

"Hello, Mr. Ebban," I said, as I entered his room. "Look what I brought you—biscuits!"

I expected him to smile, maybe even thank me for thinking about his ducks, but instead he frowned and crossed his arms in the form of an X. "No. Take those out of my room, please. Right now!"

"But these are for the ducks. You said you've been having trouble getting muffins for them."

"No *chametz*," he said, waving his arms. "Get them out of here!"

I backed out of the room, wondering if Mr. Ebban was getting ready to go off again. Maybe he had another nightmare and thought the biscuits were German grenades.

I went up to the end of the hall, toting my bag of useless biscuits. Damn, I thought. Look what happens when you try to help someone. Look at the thanks you get.

I figured Varden would be able to explain what had gone wrong. But where was he? I asked the attendant at the front desk if she had seen him. She said he should be somewhere on the wing. I went back down Mr. Ebban's hall and saw Varden coming out of one of the rooms.

"What's up, Terrill? Look like somebody stole all your baby candy."

"I tried to give Mr. Ebban these biscuits for his ducks. He acted like I was trying to give him stolen merchandise."

"You can't take those in to him. It's Passover."

"What's that?"

"It's a time of remembrance for the Jews' exodus from Egypt. Jews don't eat any grain products during that time. Can't even have them in the house. They can only eat a special unleavened bread."

"Why is that?"

"They had to leave Egypt in a hurry, when the bread was still in the oven. Didn't have time to let it rise."

"How the hell was I supposed to know that? I was just trying to help him feed the ducks. Didn't know I was going to get fussed out. He's a prisoner of his history. Looks to me like he could lighten up on some of that stuff once in a while."

"Seems like you having a bad day, Terrill. Face all marked up like you been involved in fisticuffs. Tomorrow might be better, but don't count on it."

I shook my head, thinking he was the one person in the world who could be more aggravating than the old man. "Look, where can I throw these?"

"Give them to me. I got some other patients that like to feed the ducks."

I gave Varden the biscuits. "Is he able to have company today or should I leave?"

"I think he can have company. Just don't be waving no more cornbread in his face."

I went down to the room, knocked on the door, saw the old man sitting in his wheelchair, gazing out the window, listening to his record player. A choir was singing in Hebrew, with accordions and drums in the background. His eyes were closed, his lips moving—he was singing along with the record.

I sat in the windowsill, waiting for him to finish. When the record went off, he rolled his wheelchair over to the phonograph and took the stylus off the record, replacing it in its stand.

"I can only eat *matzah* during this time," he said. "No *chametz*."

"I was just trying to help you feed the ducks."

"Have you not been paying attention to the words that you read to me? Do you read them to me like a parrot, reciting words that have no meaning to you?"

"How can you expect me to remember every little detail? Besides, I'm not a Jew. I'm not even a real Christian. I don't believe in anything."

He told me to get his Bible and read some verses from Exodus.

I sat in the windowsill and read the passages—about how the Jews had left Egypt in such a hurry they didn't have time to make their bread, but had to take it with them as unleavened dough. Afterwards, God told Moses to eat unleavened bread for seven days, as a way of remembering the Jews' freedom from bondage. God said that fathers should pass this practice along to their sons.

"OK. My bad," I said, after I had finished reading.

"I see you are angry, Jesse. But you are angry at much more than me. You must let the past go. Put it in God's hands for safekeeping."

You got a lot of nerve, I thought, telling me to let the past go, when you can't even eat a biscuit somebody brought you because of something that may or may not have happened in Egypt five thousand years ago. Still, I couldn't help but admire Mr. Ebban for having survived the horrors of that concentration camp. He had somehow been able to move past his suffering to a state of grace. I wished I could take his advice and do the same thing for myself. But I didn't know how. Maybe I could forgive a lot of things, even try to forget them, but I had no idea how to let one thing go—that the creep who left my daddy bleeding and freezing in an alley was still walking around free. Meanwhile, my daddy was shuffling around zombie-eyed in that cuckoo's nest, frozen somewhere in dream time and unable to care for himself. Couldn't even remember a peacock he had raised. My eyes teared up at this memory, and I looked away fast so the old man wouldn't see.

When I stepped outside of the nursing home, the sun had already gone down. There was just an orange glow in the sky beyond the medical complex across the road. I walked out to the bus stop at the corner and sat down on the bench to wait for the bus. It ran every thirty minutes until seven o'clock, and every hour after that. I thought it was around 8:50, which meant the bus should be by in ten minutes or so. I remembered the way Mr. Ebban had fussed at me for not paying attention to the words I had been reading to him. This made me see something I had been missing—that the old man wanted to teach me about his religion. I wondered why he was doing this, what his true motives were. Did he think he could convert me into a Jew? If so, he was just dreaming. If all those times Mama had taken me to the Assembly of God church—and all of the prayers I had heard from my grandma—didn't give me a faithful heart, why would reading some old stories from his Torah be able to accomplish it? Maybe he just wanted to make me a better person. Or then again he could just be trying to mess with my mind, the way he did with Ray Thorne. Who could tell with him?

Although I had resented reading to him at first, I didn't mind it now. I liked the way he would put his head back in the chair and listen, the way my voice reading these ancient words would cause his breathing to change, to become slower and deeper. I enjoyed doing something for him that he was unable to do for himself. I liked the idea that I was helping him in this small way after all of the suffering he had experienced. I had even begun to concentrate more on how I was reading—trying to put feeling into the words, and pausing at appropriate places. I still stumbled over certain words, however, like "Abimelech" or "Naphtalites." This was another way the old man amazed me, for if I came across a word again that he had pronounced for me before, he always remembered he had already told me how to pronounce it. This was amazing to me, considering that he must have been close to eighty years old. His patience with me at these times showed the teacher in him. Varden had told me Mr. Ebban had taught history at a community college in Savannah and at colleges in the Carolinas, too. I remembered Varden saying Mr. Ebban had been married for many years to a nurse who worked in a hospital. His wife had died a few years earlier. I wondered why they never had any kids. And I thought how lonesome it must be for Mr. Ebban to live alone the way he did in that room, with photographs of his dead loved ones on the shelf. I saw he must appreciate my visits more than I thought, even though he liked to give me a hard time. Maybe he thought that it was for my own good. I wondered if he realized I had begun to spend more time with him than the six hours a week Judge Simms required—seven and eight hours sometimes.

The sun had set. I realized I had either missed the bus or it had broken down somewhere. I didn't know what time it was but I was tired of sitting on that bench. If I had missed the nine o'clock bus, the next one wouldn't come until ten, which would place me out past my curfew. So I decided to jog home. I could get there in less than an hour, and it would be a good workout. I knew I should call G.T., should have called him before I left Havenwood. But I didn't feel like going back into the nursing home, even to use their phone.

I should be able to get home within an hour anyway. Maybe G.T. would be late, too, or be watching TV and not notice how late I was. If he fusses I'll just tell him the truth, I thought, that I had stayed late reading to the old man and missed the earlier bus.

Halfway home, on Isley Street, I took a shortcut through an alley that ran between Isley and Mercer. Jogging down the alley I heard an engine behind me. I looked over my shoulder and saw headlights bearing down on me fast. I sprinted forward, trying to make it to Mercer, but a vehicle pulled into the alley ahead, the headlights shining in my eyes. The driver stopped the vehicle, leaving the headlights on.

I turned around and saw that the other vehicle had stopped, too. A bright light appeared to the right of the headlights.

"Hold it right there," a voice said, from behind the light.

"Who are you?"

"Shut up and don't move."

I turned around and headed back toward Mercer, figuring if he had a gun he wouldn't risk shooting whoever was on the other side. All I could see were the two headlights and the third light, which was moving towards me.

I feinted to the left, and when I saw the light moving that way I darted to the right, trying to get around him. I made it all the way past him before something slammed into the back of my left leg, knocking it out from under me. I went down fast, pain shooting up my thigh like an electric shock.

The light was shining directly in my eyes now, above me. I could hear him breathing.

"How's it feel, slugger?"

Pain shot up my side. Another blow to my left thigh.

"These boots are made for stomping," the voice said. He kicked me in the left shoulder.

Suddenly, there were two lights shining down at me.

"Schoolboy, you do your homework today?" This was the same voice I had heard earlier, flat and toneless, the voice of a hypnotist. "Did you read to the old altar kacker? Did you wipe his ass?" Another blow to my body—my leg this time. "Jew boy. Jew lover."

A blow crashed into my jaw so hard I saw a cascade of bright lights, like a fireworks display. I put my arms over my head as more blows rained down on me, from every direction and in what seemed like a dozen different places at once: my ears, my forehead, my chest, and my back. I heard that one hateful voice the whole time: *Jew lover, Jew lover.*

My face was a mass of pain. Pain shot up and down my body like lightning. I blacked out for a while and when I came to they were no longer hitting me. I tasted blood.

A light was blinding me.

"How you doing, Terrill?"

I tried to speak, but I couldn't.

"What's the matter, cat got your tongue?"

Another blow to my face but I couldn't dodge it because of the light. I had no idea when or where the blows were coming from.

"He's a hateful boy not to talk to us," said a second voice, higher than the first. I didn't recognize it.

"I think he needs to be taught a lesson."

"A lesson."

One of the lights had gone out. I just saw the one. It moved in an arc above me, then stopped.

"Now Jesse, you have something that belongs to someone we know—where is it?"

"It's a knife, Jesse. You stole a knife."

"He's a bad boy. A thief."

"Not only a thief. A vandal."

"Is that right?"

"Yes. He's been in the newspaper. Isn't that right, Jesse? Haven't you been in the newspaper?"

I tried to speak, but my mouth was full of blood. I turned over, spit the blood out.

"Oh, my, look at our boy. He's making a big mess."

Someone lifted me up with his foot, turned me over on my back. I felt a knee in my chest, a fist in my throat. I couldn't get my breath. "Now about that knife, Jesse. We want it. We want you to return the stolen property. Do you have it on you, about your person?"

They felt all around my pockets, taking things out.

"Here's a wallet, a key, a—what's this? A good luck charm."

"Looks like his charm isn't working," the other voice said. And then the light drew near to my face, like a sun. The voice close to my ear now. "Your daddy had some bad luck, too, didn't he? And it was in an alley, just like this!"

I struggled to sit up but I suddenly felt like the side of a building had tumbled down on my head. There was a brilliant flash of light, and then it shattered into what seemed like thousands of pinpoints of light that slowly faded into a sea of darkness.

Chapter 21

I was crawling through a dark tunnel, trying to find the end. I heard a faint voice in the distance. The voice grew stronger, then weaker, then stronger again. The tunnel opened up suddenly and I saw a shimmering patch of light, which became a section of brilliant blue sky. I closed my eyes against its brightness. When I opened them I saw the outline of a face. And I heard the voice again:

"Lord have mercy, Jesse. What kind of trouble have you got yourself into?"

For a while after that, I was in a kind of dream state. I vaguely remember being pulled up out of the tunnel, Varden holding a water bottle to my mouth, then easing me back to the ground, where I lay there with my left arm up over my face to block out the sun. My whole body throbbed and ached. I had lumps on my head and face, a split lip, a long gash on my cheek, a missing tooth, and it hurt every time I breathed. I remember feeling sick to my stomach from the smell of garbage and aggravated by the big green flies buzzing all around me. While I lay on the ground, I drifted in and out of consciousness. During this time Varden, who had climbed over the fence at the landfill, was trying to figure out how to get the lock off the gate. He called a cousin who lived nearby, and his cousin soon showed up with a hacksaw. They cut the lock off the gate, opened it up, and then helped me into the back of the Havenwood van. From there, Varden set out for the hospital, the van rattling and bumping on the rutted road. Every bump shot jolts of pain through my body. I was grateful when the van turned onto the road.

I kept trying to piece together what had happened. I remembered being in the alley between Isley and Mercer, remembered the blinding lights, the terrifying experience of being hit from all sides when I couldn't defend myself. But I couldn't recall anything after that—not until I had the sensation of crawling in the tunnel and then seeing Varden's face. I didn't understand how he had entered the picture. How did I get in the county dump?

Varden had gospel music playing on the van's tape player. A man sang,

> When the trumpet of the Lord shall sound,
> And time shall be no more,
> And the morning breaks, eternal, bright and fair;
> When the saved of earth shall gather over on the other shore,
> And the roll is called up yonder, I'll be there.

Listening to this music I slipped back into the dream state. I imagined I was riding on the strong back of an angel, flying high above the land below, on my way to a better place.

At the ER doctors examined me, cleaned out my wounds, stitched up two gashes in my head and one in my cheek, gave me pain meds, and sent me to X-ray. G.T. was there, looking red-eyed and haggard. I talked to him about what happened in the examination room while I was waiting to go to X-ray. I just told him the basics—that I had gotten jumped jogging home from Havenwood, and that I didn't remember anything after that until I woke up in the dump and saw Varden looking down at me.

"Jogging? Why the hell didn't you take the bus?"

"Missed it."

"I told you to be careful, dammit."

"Wish I'd listened better now."

"You get a look at them?"

"Too dark. They had bright lights in my eyes."

"How many were there?"

"Two, I think."

"They say anything, anything at all that would help you identify them?"

"Asked me for the knife I took off Moran."

"There it is then, all laid out," G.T. said. "Where is the knife?"

"I gave it to someone."

Before G.T. could ask me any more questions, two attendants came into the examination room with a gurney to take me to be X-rayed.

"Don't leave, G.T.," I said, as they were wheeling me out. My heart was beating too fast.

"I'm not going anywhere," he said.

After I got back down to the ER from X-ray, a uniformed cop showed up and questioned me about the attack. I told him the location, that there had been at least two attackers, and that they had shined lights in my eyes while they beat me. He wanted to know what I was doing there, and I explained that I was walking home from Havenwood, where I had done my community service. By then, however, a fog was rolling into my mind from the pain medicines and I drifted off to sleep while the officer was still questioning me. I vaguely remember him telling G.T. that a detective would want to talk to me. I woke up a while later with G.T. and the ER doctor in the room, the doctor telling G.T. that I had "a severe concussion, numerous cuts, abrasions and bruises, at least three cracked ribs." He said they were going to keep me overnight for observation.

Sometime later, I was in a private room, with G.T. sitting by the bed.

"You tell the cop about the knife?" I asked.

"I filed it away for right now." G.T.'s voice had a soft, deadly tone I didn't hear very often.

"G.T.," I said, "how did Varden Story know to find me in the dump."

"I asked him that. He said the old man, Mr. Ebban, told him to look there. He said the old man stayed on him about it until he drove out there, just to get him to quit pestering him. He almost missed you, too. You were covered up under some trash, but he saw your hand sticking out."

"Mr. Ebban? He told him to look there?"

"That's what he said."

"How did he know where I was?"

"I've got no idea, Jesse."

I pictured Mr. Ebban's face, his deep-set black eyes, his bushy eye-brows, the tufts of white hair. How could he have known?

I was almost asleep when I remembered something that jerked me awake again: the last thing I had heard before it seemed like a Mack truck had slammed into me. Those hateful words, spoken by the man with the Devil's voice: *Your daddy had some bad luck, too, didn't he? And it was in an alley, just like this!*

After breakfast the next morning, a nurse came in my room and told me I had "a visitor who needed to ask me some questions." The nurse left and a minute later, a huge black man entered the room. He was bigger than Buddy McBane. Looked to be at least six five. He wore a gray suit, white shirt, and blue tie.

"Good morning, Jesse," he said. "How you feeling?"

"Like I fell out of an airplane," I said. No matter how I shifted on the bed, I couldn't get away from pain somewhere—my ribs, my head, my legs, even my feet.

"Well, I see you still got your sense of humor."

He stood at the foot of my bed, smiling down at me.

"I'm Detective J. W. Applewhite, from the Second Precinct," he said, showing me a gold badge. He had a deep, silky-smooth voice. "I'd like to talk to you a little while if you feel up to it."

"I already talked to the police."

"I know. I've read the report. I stopped by to see if I could fill in some missing details, learn a little more about your case."

I shrugged, made a mental note to watch what I said.

"Do you mind if I sit down?"

"No, sir."

He pulled up the chair G.T. had been using and sat down near the head of my bed. I caught the spicy scent of his aftershave. He asked me what school I attended and when I told him "Washington High," he told me he had graduated from there eighteen years earlier. He said he had been a lineman on the team the last two years he was there. I could tell he was trying to put me at ease, but it wasn't working. Cops made me nervous.

When he finally began asking his official questions, I noticed he had a small notebook in one hand and a pen in the other. He started out by asking me what time I had left Havenwood. I told him how I missed the bus and decided to jog home, then decided to take a shortcut down the alley between Mercer and Isley and how the men caught me in the alley between two vehicles. He asked me a lot of questions about that, if I had noticed any vehicles before I ran into the alley, about the sound of their voices, about any identifying marks like tattoos I could have seen on them, names I heard mentioned. He was very patient, seemed like he had all the time in the world.

I described the attack, but I left out a lot of key details, the references to Mr. Ebban, the way they were looking for the knife I had taken from Tony Moran, and the man's comment about my daddy. I didn't mention Mr. Ebban because I didn't want to involve him in my personal trouble. He had suffered enough already. I didn't mention the knife because then I would have had to explain who the knife belonged to—information that would reveal I had broken Tony Moran's arm in a fight. I figured that would put me in Sheridan. I didn't tell him about the man's hateful reference to my daddy because it was something I felt like I had to take care of myself. I had no confidence in the police.

While the detective took notes, I told him about the way the men had gone through my pockets, and their comments about my four-leafed clover charm. He asked me to describe my charm. He said he would check the alley to see if he could find any evidence. I figured he would be able to find my blood there, if nothing else.

Detective Applewhite asked me if I knew why the men had attacked me.

"No, sir."

"So you have no idea at all why these men would want to jump you, a young person just minding his own business? Beat you up and stomp you and leave you for dead in the back of a dump way out in the county?"

"No sir."

He gazed at me until I looked away. I could see he didn't believe me.

"Jesse, you know anything about police work?"

"Not a lot."

"One thing we try to do when we are trying to catch the perpetrator of a crime, is to meditate on a little thing called a motive. If we can establish a motive, that can be very helpful to us. It can help us narrow our list of suspects, for one thing, often to the main suspect. But without a motive and without any eyewitnesses, physical evidence or a confession, finding the perpetrators of a crime can be like hunting doves in the dark. This is where I need your help. Can you recall any comment your attackers said that might shed some light on a motive?"

"No, sir. They just beat me and kicked me."

Mr. J. W. Applewhite seemed like a genuine person. Suddenly, a part of me wanted to open up and tell him everything, the whole story, and let him catch the thugs. I could almost feel myself giving in to this impulse—until fear took over. If I told this detective everything, he'd find out I broke Tony Moran's arm, and that would be all Dopodja needed to haul me back into court, with a one-way ticket to Sheridan. As much as I wanted to trust Detective Applewhite, I felt trapped by my past decisions and behavior. What choice did I really have except to take care of this problem myself?

"Let's try this from another angle," the detective said. "Word on the street is you had an altercation with an individual about a week ago and that he got the worst of the fight. That might be the missing piece that would tie all of this together. Would you care to comment on that?"

I shook my head. I had a sick feeling, unrelated to the beating I had taken.

When he saw I wasn't going to comment, Mr. Applewhite nodded, sighed, and looked thoughtful. He put his notebook in his pocket and stood up. "You take care of yourself, Jesse Terrill. I'm going to leave you my card, and I want you to call me if you have anything you want to tell me, if you can remember anything that might help us find these criminals. OK?"

"Yes, sir."

He put his card on the stand by my bed. "I'll be seeing you."

"Mr. Applewhite."

"Yes?"

"I'm on probation. I've got to stay out of trouble."

"I understand that. I'm not looking to get you in more trouble. I want to find the men who attacked you, get them off the street. Now you give me a call anytime if you can think of anything at all that might help."

He went out then and shut the door behind him.

The stress of talking to him had worn me slam out. I closed my eyes and tried to sleep. But I kept remembering that bright light in my face and that flat, hypnotic voice that seemed to be coming from all directions at once, like the Devil had transformed himself into a bunch of ventriloquists, all speaking in the same voice.

The next morning G.T. drove me home from the hospital. He stopped by a drugstore to fill prescriptions for painkillers and an antibiotic. At home the first thing I did was look at my face in the bathroom mirror. I was a wreck. Both eyes swollen and discolored, stitches in my cheek and head, patches of hair shaved. A huge lump in the center of my forehead like I was on my way to being a unicorn. It hurt to breathe and it hurt to walk. I wondered how I could go to school like that.

I took a nap and when I woke up, G.T. had lunch ready. Soup and sandwiches. I asked him if he was going to work today and he said no, that Carlos and Ricardo had everything under control. I figured that made one more day of work he had missed on account of me. As my legal guardian G.T. received a Social Security check for me every month, but I knew for a fact that it didn't cover all of my expenses. Every penny he spent on me after that was out of the generosity of his heart. And all I seemed to be able to bring him was trouble.

After lunch, he said, "You talked to a detective named Applewhite."

"That's right. I forgot to tell you about it. How'd you find out?"

"He came by here this morning while you were asleep. Had your four-leafed clover charm with him. Wanted me to ID it as yours."

"You tell him it was mine?"

"Yes. You tell him anything that could tie the Morans to this?"

"No."

G.T. nodded once. I could see his mind was working, but I couldn't tell in what direction.

"That OK?"

He sighed and ran his scarred hand through his hair. "I don't know what's OK and what's not, Jesse. Just trying to take it one day at a time."

"What did you tell him?"

"Told him I was worried about you."

I looked up at a stain on the ceiling, one that G.T. had been meaning to fix. It seemed to take the shadowy shape of a man, curled up in the trunk of a car.

I took another pain pill and went back to my bedroom to lie down.

Saturday morning Rosalita brought me breakfast in bed: tortillas, orange juice, and milk. There was a get-well card on the tray, too, signed *Love, Rosalita*.

"I forgot to pray for you last week," she said. "Carmen was sick. I had trouble at work. Too much distraction. I should have prayed for you."

"That's OK, Rosalita. You don't owe me anything. I was just in the wrong place at the wrong time."

But she frowned and shook her head. I was mystified by her guilt. She had already made up her mind that she was to blame because she had forgotten to pray for me. "Jesus and Mother Mary will look after you now. I pray every night and every day."

I looked away from her then, nearly moved to tears by her concern. I could see that her faith was a kind of blessing, even though it had somehow passed me by.

G.T. appeared in the doorway to my room. "How come I never got breakfast in bed?"

"You are a big strong man, Mr. G.T. You can walk out to the kitchen where the table is, no?"

"Jesse can walk too, last I looked."

Rosalita smiled at me. "I believe your uncle is jealous."

"Aggravated is more like it. You're going to spoil him, Rosalita. Next thing you know he'll be wanting breakfast in bed every morning. Hell, he's liable to be expecting me to bring it to him."

Rosalita blew me a kiss and shut the door.

After I finished the breakfast she had brought me, I tried to rest but my mind was revved up like an engine stuck in neutral. I knew the Morans had sent those thugs to beat me up. That in itself would have called for revenge on my part. But what kept eating at me now was my memory of what the man with the hissing voice said about my daddy. How did he know about a crime that had happened three years ago? He was the man I wanted, the one I had to find. But first I would have to get my strength back and give myself time to heal. Then I would begin my quest to track him down.

CHAPTER 22

Sunday morning, I was in even more pain than I had been the day before. I took a pain pill and drifted off to sleep. I woke up with G.T. in my room. He said I had some visitors and I asked him who they were. "Some of these Pottstown kids you hang out with. Want me to tell them to come back later?"

"No, I'll see them."

Mick, Bone, Skeeter, LaFay, Terra, Andre, and Snookie were all sitting around the living room when I made my gimp-legged, bruised, and stitched-up entrance. I registered the shock and concern in their eyes with a weird mixture of satisfaction and self-disgust.

Terra and Snookie asked me a lot of questions about the attack. I told them what had happened, leaving out the references to the knife and my daddy. Snookie asked me if I got a look at them, and I told her no, that it was too dark and anyway they had lights shining in my eyes most of the time.

No one mentioned the Morans by name but they were all thinking the same thing.

"Assholes think they run Pottstown," Terra said. "Act like they think they are the Mafia. I'd love to see them brought down."

They were all staring at me. I smiled at them, showing more of my damage, the missing tooth, and the gash in my lower lip. A snake uncoiled itself in my heart. My blood hissed in my veins. I felt like a freak in a sideshow. A thought flopped around in my mind like a wounded bat: *I'll only feel better when I can kill him.*

Mornings the sky was full of a cool, pink light as G.T. drove me to school. G.T., who had hardly ever been a talker, was even more quiet in the morning. He usually had the radio tuned to a classic country music station, the ones that play songs by George Jones, Conway Twitty, Hank Williams, and Loretta Lynn. G.T. hardly ever listened to the modern singers—he said most of them had gone commercial and lost their connections to the working man. He complained about the outfits they wore, too.

"Ever seen a real cowboy's hat?" he said once. "It's covered with dust and beat to shit. It's a tool of his job, keeps the sun off his head. No genuine cowboy would be caught dead in some of those hats those Nashville Romeos wear today. Only thing they ride is a four-wheeler or an RV."

One morning while I was waiting for him in his truck, I opened his glove compartment looking for a tissue and I saw his Colt .45 in there. I pulled out the clip and saw that it was loaded. He had two spare magazines in a leather case. I didn't know what G.T. had in mind, but he was not a man who bluffed. I figured if G.T. was carrying a loaded .45 in his glove compartment, he was ready to use it, and this thought was one more scary thing rising up out of the deep. I would have liked to talk to him about this, but I had no idea how to even bring the subject up.

All the next week, G.T. wouldn't let me ride the bus home after school. He said either he or his friend Buddy McBane would be taking me home. The first time Buddy picked me up, Wednesday, he was driving his truck. But on Friday, Buddy picked me up on his Harley, which attracted a lot of attention from the other kids. Buddy had on a denim vest over a black T-shirt, shades, tattoos all over his powerful arms. He looked bad all right up on that black and silver Harley. I rode out of there on the back seat, my arms around his thick chest. It was a smooth-riding machine, but the ride still hurt my ribs and my back; and by the time I got home I was so sore I had to take two pain pills and lie down a while before I could get up to eat supper.

"Jesse, what you getting jumped in an alley for?" Clarence asked. I was sitting across from his desk, in his office in the basement of the courthouse on Main Street.

"I guess somebody didn't like my looks."

"Don't try to run your games on me. You and me both know that's not the reason. You're copping a foolish attitude here, considering your general predicament."

"Sorry, Clarence. I've had a bad week."

"I can see that. Look like you went a few rounds with the wrong end of a mule. I don't know what you did to piss somebody off, but you did something. What was it?"

"I never saw them before in my life, and that's the truth."

"I already read the police report. Didn't figure you'd have anything new to offer. But if you do want to talk, I'm ready to listen."

"I got nothing else to say about that. I did want to tell you I missed my community service this week. I got a doctor's note." I put the note on his desk.

"You got plenty of time to do your service. Mr. Ebban ain't going anywhere. But you know I think the gentleman has been worried about you. So you might want to give him a call, just to let him know you're all right."

"What makes you think he's been worried?"

"Process of induction. Know what that is?"

"Not really."

"That's where you look at a set of facts and draw an obvious conclusion. Now in this case, when you turned up missing, the old man got to cogitating about it. Ruminated about it all night long. Seems he somehow got the idea he knew where you were. Maybe it come to him in a vision. Could be he's got some kind of special powers. I don't know how he knew it but he somehow did. And he was able to convince Varden Story to go out to that dump and find you."

"How do you know all this?"

"It's my job to know things. When one of my clients is in trouble, I make it my business to find out what the problem is. In this case, I went to talk to Varden. He's a very smart man. And he had enough sense to listen to the old man and believe him. If he hadn't have done that you might still be out in that dump—what would have been left of you, that is, on account of all the ravenous creatures that tend to hang around a dump like that. Snakes and rats and such."

"But how did Mr. Ebban know?"

Clarence leaned back in his chair, put his hands behind his head. "That's a good question. You might want to take that up with him."

"I'm going to try to see him this Sunday."

"Let me know what he says. I'm kind of interested in how he knew myself."

A dark thought took hold of me.

"Maybe he knows the ones that did it. Those Jews are probably still mad at me for what I did."

"Jesse, when you going to learn to see out of your eyes?"

"How come you giving me such a hard time?"

"Looks to me like somebody else has already given you a hard time. I'm just trying to help you." Clarence drummed his fingers on the desk. "In fact, if you'd stop and think for a minute you'd see there's a lot of folks trying to help you. Mr. Ebban, Varden, your uncle, me, Judge Simms. But what are you doing? Tearing all around here with your bull-headed self, hoping someone will knock that big chip off your shoulder."

A cold black wind was howling deep in my brain. I felt like I had been possessed by one of those evil spirits Mr. Ebban told me about. A dybbuk, he had called it. "How did the judge get the idea of sending me out to Havenwood anyway? How'd she even know about Mr. Ebban?"

"Probably heard about him from Varden."

"Varden?"

"His mama's her sister. Judge Simms is Varden's aunt."

I looked up at the ceiling, trying to digest this disturbing revelation. *That means she knows everything he knows.* This image came back to me: Varden looking down at me, his head surrounded by a ring of light, like those old paintings you see of saints.

"You need to get some rest, Jesse," Clarence said.

I was in the hall on the way to health class when this fat kid with a greasy face came up and walked beside me. "You the one that broke Tony Moran's arm, ain't you?"

"I got nothing to say about that."

"I'm surprised you're still alive."

"Why don't you just mind your own business?"

"Watch your mouth."

"Maybe you know something I don't," I told him. "Maybe you got some information for me."

"Maybe I do."

"Let's hear it." We had both stopped walking and were facing each other. This kid was big—taller than me and heavier, but he looked slow and clumsy. The problem with fighting him lay with the overall condition of my body—cracked ribs, bruised muscles and joints, and the cuts and gashes in my face, which had not yet healed.

The boy was scowling now, his face turning red.

"Could be you don't have anything for me," I said. "Could be you're just a big fat-assed fool, huh?"

He puffed out his chest, like he was getting ready to do something foolish.

That was when Mick stepped between us, facing this kid, and said, "How would you like me to snatch your head off and use it for a football?"

"You wouldn't do that," the boy said, but he took a step back.

"Yes I would. Your head going to look like a watermelon that fell out of a airplane."

"I ain't going to fight both of you." This fat kid began walking backwards, like he was afraid to turn his back on us. He disappeared around the corner.

"Thanks, Mick," I said. "Who is he?"

"Dumb-ass that hangs around Moran's video game parlor. One of his monkeys."

"I'm glad you came along. Things were moving in the wrong direction for me. Can't afford a fight right now. Too many injuries for one thing."

"Pottstown rats stick together, Jesse."

We walked down the hall together. Mick would have fought that kid for you, right there in the hall, I thought, and risked getting thrown out of school. But I would have had to jump in, too, I thought. Wouldn't feel right, letting him do that.

I had a sudden sensation of dizziness, like I was about to fall down. I stopped and put my hand against the wall.

"Hey," Mick said, "you O.K.?"

"Sure," I said. "Just a little lightheaded is all."

Mick touched my shoulder. We stood there like that, Mick's hand on my shoulder, waiting for my sense of balance to return.

Mr. Ebban had a shaving cut on his chin. There was a small spot of blood on his collar. I noticed these things when I visited him on Sunday. Sitting in his wheelchair by the window, he peered at my face, as if he was memorizing each one of the lumps, cuts, and bruises that still lingered there. Embarrassed, I asked him what he wanted me to read. He directed me to a section of Psalms in one of his Bibles. I found the place and read to him from my spot on his windowsill.

"*My voice shalt thou hear in the morning, O Lord; in the morning will I direct my prayer unto thee, and will look up. For thou art not a God that hath pleasure in wickedness; neither shall evil dwell with thee . . .*"

When I finished, I sat there, waiting for Mr. Ebban to ask me to read again, but he was silent a long while, his eyes closed like he was meditating. I saw his lips forming the last of the words in the psalm: *For thou, Lord, wilt bless the righteous; with favour wilt thou compass him as with a shield.*

I felt small and worthless in the presence of Mr. Mendel Ebban, whose faith I had mocked and belittled. I had planned to question him about how he knew where I was, but I couldn't even summon the will to do this. I considered all the horrors he had endured in that Nazi concentration camp. The drunk Ukrainians marching him at gunpoint to the open grave, Mr. Ebban standing there, waiting, then hearing the crashing shots, seeing the others fall, their bodies shattered by bullets, then feeling the shock of the bullet grazing his skull and falling himself, tumbling down amid the bleeding, dying men, everything turning black, then awakening to see starlight overhead, realizing he was still alive, crawling out of the grave and staggering into the forest, to be haunted forever by the hell he had lived through, including the loss of his family, neighbors, and fellow Jews.

He looked up at me suddenly, causing me to flinch.

"What do you have to say for yourself?"

"I don't know where to begin."

"You are staying out of trouble this week?"

"Yes, sir."

He stared at me with an odd expression on his face, as if he knew more than he was saying. He made no mention at all of my injuries. I felt off balance somehow—as if the nursing home floor, the whole world, was slipping out of gear, moving away from its normal mode of operation. I looked around the room, at his ram's horn, the photographs on his dresser, the Star of David over his bed. I am in Mr. Ebban's room, I thought. I am doing my community service. "How did you know where I was?"

"I listen, I watch, I dream. Sometimes the right things come to us in quiet moments, when the heart is open, when the ears are listening. That is what I have been trying to tell you."

I wanted to tell him what I was feeling, how sorry I was that I was an *apikoros*, how much I wished I could have been saved before the Devil learned my name, but I didn't know how to get my feelings out, how to shape them into words. I was angry with myself for this—this failure to tell him what was in my heart. I was still trying to mobilize my will to speak when I saw him lean suddenly forward, his hand on his chest.

"Mr. Ebban, are you all right?"

"A little chest pain is all. Let's get to the park. I want to hear the birds."

I put the Bible on the dresser and followed him out into the hall. He was moving so fast I had to run to catch up with him. And I stumbled over my feet when he went around the corner to the lobby. He rolled by the front desk too fast for me to stop and sign him out. I waved to the attendant as I went by, told her I was going to be with Mr. Ebban in the park. "Sign me out, OK?"

As we were going out the front door, we met Varden coming in pushing old Ms. Zahorski in her wheelchair.

"Welcome back from the dead, Jesse!" he called out.

I would liked to have stopped and talked to Varden, express my gratitude to him, too, but Mr. Ebban was still turning the wheels on his wheelchair. So we went on through the door before I could thank Varden Story for hauling my miserable self out of the trash dump.

At the fountain Mr. Ebban tossed a penny in, closed his eyes. I had a stone in my hand. I threw it into the water.

"Something is bothering you," he said. "What is it?"

"Nothing."

"Don't tell me nothing. You are *farblondjet*. You have much *tumul*."

"What?"

"Trouble in the heart."

"Why do you use those Yiddish words all the time? Nobody understands them but you."

He shut his eyes, like he was in deep thought. What the hell, I thought, leaning on the fountain. He was just trying to help. Why can't I show him a little kindness?

"I was born in Lodz, Poland," he said. "There were three million Jews in Poland when I was born. We had different beliefs and ways of dressing, but the one thing that held us together was the fact that we were Jews. We spoke a common language, Yiddish. It is a beautiful language, very down-to-earth. Part poetry, part music. I learned to be a Jew from the time I was a baby, what was kosher, when to pray, the value of knowledge. My first day at school, the *heder*, the teacher gave us little sweetened letters of the alphabet made out of bread to eat. We were literally eating knowledge—learning that it would sustain us, like food. Most of us lived in *shtetls*, small towns and villages. We were separate communities within Poland and all of eastern Europe, with our own system of government, a council of elders who made decisions. We worked hard all week, and we were poor. But on Shabbat, everything changed. My mother put a white linen table cloth on the table. The night before all the families in the community would prepare a dish, usually a stew of some kind, mostly vegetables because we didn't have much meat, and they would take their stews to the baker's oven, because there is no work to be done on Shabbat, and they would leave them there overnight to be warm and pick them up the next morning. Shabbat was a time when we were together in our faith, a time of peace and rest. Everyone was the same. There was no rich, no poor, we were all part of the creator's design. We shared what we had with each other, with our neighbors. It was a time when the ugliness of the world was gone. A time of peace and family and, above all, a time when we remembered God, that He was the center of our lives, of everything."

"I thought you still celebrate that same day."

"But it is not the same as then. Then, Shabbat was interwoven with the fabric of the community I lived in. And that time, that place, too, is gone forever."

"So you speak Yiddish to remind you of that time."

"That time? Let me tell you about that time. Here in America, I had a house, a job, a wife. But how could I forget my homeland? It was in my bones, my blood. When I was forty-eight years old, I took a vacation from my job, I went back to Poland. I wanted to see the house I was born in. I wanted to see the *heder* I attended, my father's old watchmaker's shop, the stores, the marketplace, and the synagogue.

"When I got to Lodz, I took a taxi to what had been the Jewish quarter. I walked down the street I had lived on but nothing was as I had remembered. Every sign of Jewish life had been stripped from the city. As I walked down the street I remembered the children playing, the cobbler, the watchmaker, the posters on the walls advertising Yiddish theater, the boys selling Jewish newspapers, the vendors selling their vegetables from stands and in wheelbarrows, the water carriers. I stood on the street corner where Sol, the street musician used to stand with his fiddle—sometimes he was joined by an accordion player. I heard their music in my memory. I heard, too, the ringing of the blacksmith's hammer as he worked in his shop, the voices of the children, the squeaking of the peddler's carts, the Yiddish words spoken. I walked past the baker's shop, where Ari used to bake the best bagels, and the smell of baking bread drenched the street in front of the church so that my mouth watered when I went by—there was a Pole looking out at me from the window now, with suspicion in his eyes. Ahead, there was a mark in a doorway, where a *mezuzah* had once been attached, long since torn away, but the discoloration was there, evidence that Jews had once lived there. I saw a house with shutters on it and remembered how the sexton used to come around and rap our shutters with a wooden mallet on Friday night, to remind us that Shabbat was approaching. I remembered the soot-covered chimney sweep, holding his straw broom. And the rabbinical students sitting on benches, in their black hats, silk waistcoats, black shoes and white socks—in fervent discourse about some idea from the Talmud. As I passed by these buildings, that had once housed the cobbler, the weaver, the folk doctor, the *heder* where I learned to read, there were Polish people inside them now, with no memory of who or what had lived there before them. The whole magical world of my childhood now existed only in my memory. I kept walking on this street until I came to the building that once housed the shop where my father made and repaired watches: it was a hair salon. I pressed my face against the glass, saw women sitting in chairs, getting their hair done. A woman turned and saw me, said something to another woman, and they both looked at me, their eyes cool and curious. I was a stranger in my homeland, where I had formed my earliest memories, created my whole picture of the world. You asked about Yiddish. It was as much a song as a language, in that like music itself, it was an expression of our very lives. But the millions of people who spoke it are gone. They died at Treblinka, Birkenau, Dachau, and Auschwitz." Mr. Ebban shook his head. "A whole world, murdered. Gone forever."

He closed his eyes, his lips trembling. A tear slid down one of his wrinkled cheeks.

I didn't know what to say. All the words that came to my mind seemed like cheap little trinkets. I stood there with my hand on his shoulder while he wept. My heart felt like some big useless thing floating in a river, waterlogged and foul.

CHAPTER 23

At the end of the second week in May, G.T. finally told me I could ride the bus home from school, and he and Buddy stopped picking me up. I didn't know what G.T. had worked out with the Morans, but I figured he had a good reason for letting me take the bus again. Even so, the first few times I walked from the bus stop down Rose of Sharon Road to our house, I was edgy and apprehensive. Each day I was reassured to see Mr. Hoagie out in his garden, or sitting on his front porch. The fourth or fifth time I saw Hoagie, it occurred to me it was not a coincidence that he was on his porch or in his garden every afternoon when I was walking home from the bus stop.

My bruises, cuts, and cracked ribs had mostly healed, but the problem was my mind. I had trouble sleeping, for one thing. And when I did sleep, I was troubled by bad dreams. I would be locked up in a car trunk, trying to get out. Or wandering in a cave, trying to find my daddy. In one dream I was in a funeral parlor, trying to buy a casket for someone. I dealt with a backlit man sitting so far back in the shadows that all I could see was his oily hair. Speaking in this flat voice, he said he would have to fit the body. "But I don't have the body with me," I told him. "Yes you do," he replied. Two men appeared and began measuring me with pieces of string. The face of the man in the shadows lit up slowly. His eyes glowed like red-hot coals. Something swished around from behind him: it was his tail. I tried to get away, but the men held me down. I struggled with them until I woke up, my heart hammering, that dream voice still echoing in my memory.

This dream, and others like it, ratcheted up my desire to find the man who hurt my daddy. In time I might have been able to just let the beating those guys gave me go, figuring I was lucky to get off with my life. But I knew I would never forget what that man had said: *Your daddy had some bad luck, too, didn't he? And it was in an alley, just like this.* I was determined to find him. Since my main connection to his identity was the Morans, I decided I had to figure out a way to force them to tell me who he was—either that or lead me to him. I didn't see any way around this, even though I had no idea how I was going to make it happen.

Although I had not seen Tony Moran, he cast a shadow over my whole life. I was also worried that he would hurt LaFay. Someone had been calling her up at night and hanging up when she answered the phone. Sometimes the caller just stayed on the line, not saying anything. Terra was sure it was Moran. So far he had not bothered her any other way, though. And I thought I knew the reason. G.T. told me that J. W. Applewhite, the detective, had visited Moran and spoken to him about his relationship to LaFay and his fight with me—he had apparently learned about this from one of his sources on the street. Although I figured the detective didn't get much information from Tony, his interest in the case might be enough to encourage Moran to back off from causing me any more trouble, at least for now. The possibility of tangling with G.T. and his friend, Buddy McBane, might also have caused the Morans to think twice about another direct attack.

I was hoping my trouble with Moran would blow over and be forgotten. I didn't want to give Dopodja and Rizzo a reason to haul me back into court. Also, when I made my move on Tony Moran and his ex-biker dad, I wanted to catch them by surprise.

The same way that man with the Devil's voice had caught my daddy.

The third Saturday in May, I was in the backyard by the shed feeding Amos when I looked up and saw a sky-blue Mercury coming down the driveway. It was Terra, driving her mom's car, an antique from the sixties, with an eight-cylinder engine that got about eight miles a gallon.

LaFay Roux was in the passenger's seat.

Terra revved up the engine, then turned it off. They both got out of the car as I walked over to meet them. Terra had on tight, low-riding jeans and a black T-shirt, no bra, turquoise rings on her fingers, her mom's cellphone clipped to her belt. LaFay wore a white sundress and sandals. The bruises on her face had all healed, and her skin looked tanned and beautiful against the white dress.

Terra was holding a box wrapped in blue paper, with a red bow around it. "Hear you had a birthday, Jesse," she said.

"That's right. It was yesterday."

LaFay put one hand on her hip. "How come you don't tell any of your friends?"

"Didn't know anyone would be interested."

"Snookie would have thrown you a party," Terra said.

"Right."

"Well, anyway, we brought you something."

"Thanks."

Amos fanned out his tail feathers, showing off for them.

"What's your bird's name?" Terra asked.

"He's a peacock. His name is Amos."

"Nice spread that you got there, Amos," Terra said.

"*Aaaaaaaiiiooo,*" Amos said.

Terra and LaFay laughed. LaFay squatted down and Amos came over to her. She rubbed his back, talked to him in French.

"What's she saying?"

"Damned if I know. Terra nudged LaFay's back with her knee. "Speak English, girl."

"I told him he's handsome. Told him I hope he lives a long life and has lots of little peacocks."

"He'd like to have a lady friend," I said.

"How come he doesn't?" Terra asked.

"G.T. says it would be too much trouble."

"Love ain't no trouble for a peacock," Terra said. "No trick mirrors, no masks, no lies. Everything straight up and simple."

"Raising a family is trouble. You got to worry about the peahens. Keep them warm in the winter, protect them from snakes and hawks and dogs. It's a hassle. G.T. doesn't want to mess with it."

"What else has your uncle got to worry about besides making sure people's roofs don't leak?"

"Everybody's got worries, Terra."

"What are you doing now?" LaFay asked. "You got to be anywhere?"

"Not really."

"Terra and I were thinking about going to the ice cream shop on Willow Street. Want to come with us? We'll treat you to a banana split for your birthday."

"O.K., sure. Let me leave G.T. a note."

I went into the house, looked around to see if G.T. had left any change lying around, but I couldn't find a dime. Then it occurred to me that I didn't need any money because LaFay had said they would treat me. I felt a little bad about this, especially where LaFay was concerned, because it seemed like I was always broke when I was around her. Her mom had a job at the county hospital, doing something in medical records. She couldn't make all that much money, and LaFay didn't have a regular job either, other than baby-sitting for a few families in Pottstown.

I found a pencil and left G.T. a note on the kitchen table, telling him I was going for a ride with LaFay and Terra. I figured he might be a little worried, so I told him I wouldn't be gone very long.

In the bathroom I looked at my face in the mirror. The damage the thugs had done to my face still showed—bruises, a shaved place on my head, a red scar on my cheek. I was not a pretty sight.

When I got back outside, LaFay was standing there with Amos. Terra had left in her car.

"Where's our ride?"

"Terra's mom called her on her cell phone. Said she needed her car back right away. I think she had to take one of her neighbors somewhere. Terra's going to try to come back as soon as she does whatever it is her mom wants. She said she'd try to meet us at the ice cream shop."

"How come you didn't go with her?"

"Terra didn't give you your present." She held up the box.

"Thanks. I didn't need a banana split anyway."

"We can still get one."

"We lost our ride, remember?"

"How about that truck?"

I looked at the Dodge, wishing I'd thought to clean it up a little. "I guess we could go in that—if you don't mind being seen in it."

"I like old trucks." LaFay said.

I went back into the house to get the key.

At the ice cream shop on Willow Street, LaFay bought us both jumbo banana splits, and we sat in a booth at the back to eat them. In the booth behind LaFay, a man in a sailor's uniform was sitting beside a woman in a blue dress. They were eating ice cream cones and laughing together.

"How long have you had Amos?" LaFay asked

"I raised him from a baby. He's from another time, really—when I used to live out in the county."

"When was that?"

"Four years ago. We had lots of peacocks then. The others wandered off or got killed. Amos is the only one left."

"I'd like to have a peacock. They're so pretty, with all those feathers."

"G.T. won't let us raise any more."

"Maybe he'll change his mind."

"I doubt it."

"Why is he part of another time?"

"Amos?" I looked at the sailor, trying to think of a simple way to explain it. "It's a long story."

"I've got time."

"It was when my parents were still together. I guess that's the best way to put it."

"And before your brother died."

"How'd you know about that?"

"Terra told me."

"Yeah, it was before he died, too."

"Where did you live back then?"

"A house out in the country."

"You have whipped cream on your nose."

I rubbed my nose, wiped the whipped cream on my shirt.

"Why'd you wipe it off?"

"Look kind of silly with whipped cream on my nose."

She picked up some whipped cream on the end of her finger and put it on her nose. "Do I look silly?"

"What do you want me to say?"

"Well, do I? Be honest." She took some more whipped cream and put it on her ears. "Whipped cream earrings."

"You're kind of crazy, LaFay."

"Why, because I like whipped cream earrings?"

I just shook my head, smiled. I was more and more mystified by what she would see in a guy like Tony Moran. I had thought it was his money and his car. But seeing the way she didn't mind riding with me in the old Dodge—now I didn't know for sure.

"So when are you going to let me see this place, where you used to live?"

"You really want to see it?"

"Sure."

I tried to remember how much gas I had in the gas tank. The fuel gauge didn't work, but I remembered G.T. saying he had put some gas in the tank last month. I hadn't driven it much since then. I wasn't sure how much he had put in, but he usually filled the tank. It ought to have enough gas. "I guess we could drive out there, if you really want to go."

"I do." She still had that whipped cream on her nose and ears. "I really want to."

The sun was setting by the time we got to our old house on Cotton Gin Road. The front windows, facing the sunset, were so red they created the illusion that the house was on fire. I turned into the driveway, not knowing who lived there now. Although the grass had been cut fairly recently, there were no curtains in the windows and no vehicles parked outside. We got out of the truck, walked around to the back door, and looked inside. I saw a teething ring on the floor of the kitchen, an empty baby bottle on the stove. I could tell nobody lived there now. I tried the door but it was locked. I wondered who had lived here since we had moved out, what their lives were like.

LaFay was standing in the backyard, looking at the grove of peach trees. The air was sweet with that old familiar scent of pink blossoms. The grape arbor on the other side of the yard was thick with green leaves, although the grapes wouldn't be ready until fall.

"You had lots of things to eat, I see," LaFay said.

"Yes. Grapes and peaches. Daddy made wine out of them, too."

LaFay closed her eyes and inhaled through her nose. "Mmmm. Those blossoms smell good."

"I don't even know who owns it now. A farmer who lives on out the road owned it when we lived here. I heard he sold it after we moved, and the new owner later moved to Florida."

"How far back does the land go?"

"The lot goes all the way back to a creek."

I stood up and we walked back to the peach trees. Some of the leaves were purple and misshapen. "That's peach leaf curl," I said. "Nobody has been tending to the trees."

LaFay pulled a limb down, smelled one of the pink blossoms.

"Where did you keep the peacocks?"

"We had a pen at the back, and my daddy built a shelter. It's gone now. Someone must have torn it down."

LaFay looked at the woods behind the house. Locusts were singing back there in the trees.

"We used to have a tree house in that oak." I pointed it out for her, and we walked back to look at it. There were only a few boards left. A frayed section of the old rope we used to climb up there was still hanging down.

LaFay touched the rotting rope. "Is that how you got up?"

"Yes."

"And I'll bet after you got up there you pulled it up after you so no one else could come up."

"That's right. How did you know?"

"Just a guess."

I looked up, remembering Lee and me, lying on our backs in that old treehouse, gazing at the stars. I felt a tightness around my heart.

"You must have had a lot of fun up there," LaFay said.

"Yeah."

"I always wanted a tree house. I found a perfect tree for it once, too. But I was too little to build one, and my mama sure couldn't do it."

And your daddy wasn't around to do it, I thought, remembering her story about why she got that tattoo on her shoulder.

LaFay said she would like to see the creek.

We walked on through the trees, scaring up a covey of quail. When we came to the creek, the ferns and tall grass growing there seemed to glow with a light all their own, although I knew the light was coming from the sun.

LaFay sat down on the bank, took off her sneakers, and put her bare feet in the water. Sitting down beside her, I could see the reflection of the trees in the slow-moving water. A locust cranked up his song. LaFay lay down on the bank, and I did, too, looking at the branches arching overhead, the eggshell moon, the clouds tinted red and orange by the setting sun.

"This water that's flowing here now could have come from anywhere," she said. "Anywhere in the whole world."

I closed my eyes. The air smelled of ferns and water and trees. I could feel her shoulder and thigh touching mine.

"Jesse, did you ever wonder why so many people like to live close to the water? They will tell you different reasons, that they like to fish, or swim, or just watch the water. But I think there's another reason—the sea casts a spell on our bodies, the part of us that's water."

I opened my eyes and saw the whipped cream on LaFay's ear.

I reached out to wipe it away and she caught my hand in hers. Her dark eyes had a hint of gold in them, a reflection of the day's last light lingering in the water.

"You didn't open your birthday present," she said, still holding my hand.

"The one from you and Terra? It's still in the truck."

"That one is really from Terra."

"I thought it was from both of you."

LaFay's face was so close to mine I could feel her breath on my lips. I wondered if she could tell how fast my heart was beating. "I haven't given you mine yet," she whispered, and she traced her finger along the side of my face as if she were writing a message on my skin.

— Part III —

CHAPTER 24

A heat wave descended on the city like a plague out of the old man's Torah. Day after day a fierce, merciless sun, with no rain. Hoagie's vegetables shriveled up, turned yellow. In the afternoons as you left the air-conditioned school for the buses, the hot air hit you like your first blast of hell. I wondered how G.T. could stand it up on those roofs all day. He came home sunburned, soaked with sweat, and too beat to do much more than drop in his recliner and drink iced tea.

By now most everyone at school knew about LaFay and me. This created some tension at our lunch table, especially with Snookie, who would hardly talk to either one of us. Even Mick and the boys seemed different around us, quiet and withdrawn.

My new relationship with LaFay was like a whirlwind that turned everything upside down, especially my plans for revenge. At night when I lay in bed thinking of possible ways to force the Morans to tell me the name of the man who had attacked me in the alley, my mind would often drift to her—the way she would look at me with a little half smile, causing me to wonder what she was thinking. I recalled her body, naked and warm against mine, and my heart would beat fast as a bird's. I fretted about how I could see her again and what we could do together. I tried to figure out how I could see her and still have time to meet all of my other obligations, especially studying for final exams. I meditated about that tattoo on her arm, the way she was looking for her daddy. Sometimes I fantasized about us driving cross-country after school was out, stopping in every town and city along the way, to see if we could find him. We could visit the place in New Mexico where my mom was living the last time she called me. In my rambling reverie of LaFay and me traveling around together, I didn't factor in my probation, the money it would cost, or even if she would really want to go; it was just a daydream that distracted me from my work and obligations.

Rosalita, who had been to Mexico to visit her parents, came to see G.T. the last Saturday in May. During lunch, I caught her staring at me.

"Jesse, do you have a girlfriend?"

"What makes you say that?"

"There's something different about you."

"That's all in your mind."

"G.T., do you sense a change in Jesse?"

"Seems a little less ornery, maybe."

"Well, I think he has a special friend."

"He's got no time for a girlfriend. A girlfriend would just get him in trouble."

"May is a fine time for romance, G.T."

"It's a fine time for schoolwork. Final exams are coming up."

"Oh, look at the bird feeder outside the window. Two hummingbirds. That's a good omen."

I turned to look. A hummingbird hovered in the air by the window as if it had been painted there. "I only see one."

"No, there were two. The other one just moved out of sight."

"G.T., you see another bird?"

"Wipe your face, Jesse," he said. "You got salsa on your chin."

Later that afternoon, after I finished studying, Terra, LaFay, and I went for a ride in Terra's mom's Mercury. The AC was broken, so we rolled the windows down to feel the air and get some relief from the heat. We sat in the front seat, LaFay in the middle, and listened to LaFay's tape of Blackie Forestier and the Cajun Aces. I recognized two songs that my daddy used to play, "Pistol Packin' Mama" and "Cypress Island Stomp." I told them this, and we talked for a while about Cajun music. LaFay had grown up listening to it, on the radio when she was little and later in bars and honky tonks. A cousin on her mother's side used to play fiddle in another band I listened to, The Wild Boys of the Bayou. She said she had an accordion in junior high school, and she could play some Cajun tunes on it. I was thrilled by this shared connection between us. I had never met anyone outside of my immediate family who listened to Cajun music.

This music from the Louisiana bayou put LaFay in a good mood. She wiggled her shoulders to the beat and sang along with the French verses: her timing was perfect, the words rolled off her lips like incantations. Hearing her sing in French set my whole body a-tingle, like somebody was running one of Amos's tail feathers along my spine.

Terra stopped at a light on Tull Street, near Tony Moran's video game parlor. I looked out the window and saw the greasy-faced kid I'd had words with at school standing in front of a pizza parlor. He stared at us the whole time we were at the light.

I was wishing we hadn't come down this street, wishing this fool hadn't seen us. He was too connected to things I didn't want to think about today.

"Take a picture, asshole," Terra said, as the light changed.

I didn't tell them about my run-in with this thug wannabee who hung out at Tony Moran's video game parlor. I didn't want this information to cast a shadow on the good time we were having, cruising the streets of Pottstown, listening to music and waving at people we knew.

LaFay said she had to get ready to go to a babysitting job, which started at six o'clock. Terra dropped her off at her house on McAlester Street at 5:30. She lived in a two-bedroom house around the corner from Snookie. Terra looked the other way while LaFay and I told each other goodbye. LaFay squeezed my hand, kissed my lips, and told me she would see me soon. I watched the easy sway of her hips as she walked up to the house, and my body temperature felt like it was rising ten degrees.

As she pulled off in the car, Terra turned off the tape player. "I've had about all of that Cajun music I can stand." She turned the radio to a country music station.

She asked me if I had to be back home and I told her not right now. She drove out Oleander to the bypass, heading south. She took the Herring Road exit leading out to Cotton Gin Road. The fields were dry and the crops withered-looking, everything covered with a layer of dust.

"So what do you think of LaFay?" Terra asked after a while. We were just past the railroad tracks. I could smell the creosote on the oak crossties.

"Seems like a straight up girl," I said, knowing that everything I said would get back to LaFay. No way would I tell her how much of a spell she had put me under. "Still can't figure what she saw in Tony Moran."

"Animal attraction. Makes the little birds and fishes, Jesse. Makes the whole fucking world go round."

Moran was older than LaFay, twenty-three or twenty-four. Maybe she thought he would be a good man to settle down with, since he could have provided her with financial security. I thought Moran's money might have had a special appeal for her, because she had grown up hard and fast, without even knowing who her daddy was.

I wished I had a fine car like Tony Moran, wished I had a business of my own. Although I knew I would treat LaFay better than he ever would, I wondered what I really had to offer her. I wouldn't even be able to work steady until next summer and I sure wouldn't be able to afford a car before then—not until after I had paid for the damage to the

B'nai Shalom Temple. I thought how complicated a relationship with a girl was, the way money always entered the picture. Any time I took LaFay out, she would have to ride in an old Dodge with spiderweb cracks in the windshield. And I would always be just this side of broke. I couldn't help bringing my worry up with Terra. I told her I felt bad about not having any money to spend on LaFay, about having nothing to drive her around in but a rusty Dodge truck that left a trail of blue smoke. "Looks like she'd miss riding in that Lexus, with a guy who has a steady supply of cash."

"Love is a hall of mirrors," Terra said. "Just like at the carnival."

Terra sails high and cool above the storm of love, I thought. I wondered if she ever got broke up in little pieces by anyone. She didn't seem like the type. Although Mick claimed she gave him the clap, I had never heard of her giving it up on a casual basis, like a lot of other girls in Pottstown. She went with a line boss at the mill for a while, but they broke up last spring. She had that fling with Mick last summer. Since then I hadn't heard of her even going out with anyone. Mostly she just hung out with her friends. On weekends and after school, she had a job working as a waitress at Roma's, the Italian restaurant. She was cute enough that plenty of guys must hit on her, ask her out. I wondered why she didn't date more. I figured she was either very picky or else she didn't trust guys. Probably a little of both.

Maybe she didn't give Mick gonorrhea, I thought. Could be he gave it to her. That would make more sense.

Terra said, "Where did you live out here?"

"Just around that next curve. First house on the right." I wondered if LaFay had told Terra about us coming out here.

When she neared my old house, Terra slowed down. At first I thought she was going to pull into the driveway, but she stopped on the roadside and slid over to look at the house. She was so close to me I could smell her female scent and feel her breasts on my shoulder. I was wearing the blue T-shirt she had given me for my birthday. On the radio Hank Williams was singing about Kalijah the wooden Indian that falls in love with a real Indian maiden. She can't love him back, though, because he is made of wood with a heart of knotty pine.

Terra took the wheel again, checked to make sure there was no traffic, and pulled back onto the road, driving fast now. She said something that was almost drowned out by the radio and the air rushing in through the windows. It sounded like "I'd like to live in a house like that someday so I can have a garden." I wondered if she really said that. I thought maybe I didn't hear her right. I had never known Terra to be interested in growing things.

She took a curve at sixty, the heavy car careening on the road, the speedometer still climbing on the straightaway. I wanted her to keep driving forever. I didn't even care where she went, just as long as I could hear the roar of the engine and feel the wind against my skin.

The low-lying sun was a bloody bullet hole in the sky.

All afternoon the sky was a dark metallic gray, with bruise-colored clouds low on the horizon. The hot, still air seemed charged with electricity. At dusk, lightning pulsed behind the clouds.

"Looks like we're finally going to get some rain," G.T. said.

After supper, he went off somewhere with Rosalita. I went back to my room and tried to study for my algebra exam, but I had trouble concentrating on the problems. There was always a single right answer for a math problem in a textbook; even if you couldn't figure it out, you knew it existed. Too bad other problems couldn't be that simple—Ike Moran, for instance. All week long I had been trying to think of a way to force him to tell me where I could find the creeps who had attacked me in the alley.

I have to do something, I thought, the numbers and letters on the page blurring before my eyes. I can't put it off forever.

I gave up on studying, went outside, and cranked up the Dodge. I drove down Decatur Street, past Ike Moran's bar. A broad-shouldered bouncer stood by the door, beneath the Shanghai's neon sign—the bar's name accompanied by a rust-colored image of a schooner. No way could I get in through the front without being seen. I remembered hearing G.T. say Ike Moran had an office in back. I was going to have to figure out a way to get back to his office and catch him by surprise before he could call anyone or go for a gun. Then, after I got him alone, I would have to think of a way to force him to tell me who he had hired to beat me up. He wouldn't want to talk, but maybe G.T.'s .45 would convince him to tell me what I wanted to know. I pictured all of this as if it was a film running in my mind: me slipping into the bar after it had closed, walking back to the office, opening the door to see Ike Moran sitting at his desk, Ike looking up, his eyes cold and hard. I would already have the pistol out. I would tell him to keep his hands where I could see them.

"Who the hell are you?"

"Jesse Terrill."

"G.T.'s nephew?"

"That's right."

"What do you want?"

"I want you to pick up that phone and call somebody you know, and ask him to come over here right away." I rack the slide on the .45. "That's the only way you're going to get out of this room alive."

"Who do you want me to call?"

"I want the man who jumped my daddy in the alley down from the Flamingo and left him a burned-out shell of the person he used to be."

"How am I supposed to know who that is?"

"You know who he is. He is the man with the Devil's voice, the man who floats up out of your nightmares and turns your blood to ice."

"Look, kid, I don't know what the fuck you're talking about."

"Does the name Marc Steigner jerk a chain in your memory?"

He flinches, his tongue darts out like a snake's.

"Call him up. Right now. Tell him you want to see him here."

In my reverie, I see him squint, lick his lips, look around the room. A businessman, he is considering his options, he is figuring the odds.

"A forty-five makes a big hole," I tell him. "It will let the light shine all the way through."

Ever so slowly, keeping his eyes on me, he reaches for the telephone on his desk. . . .

That's the way it should play out all right, I thought.

But I immediately saw cracks appearing in my bold plan, like the spiderweb fractures in the windshield of the Dodge truck. What if he wouldn't talk? What if he denied having anything to do with the attack on me?

What if he goes for a gun and I have to shoot him?

I don't really want to kill him. It's the one with the Devil's voice I want.

I parked the truck down the block and walked back to the Shanghai's parking lot beside the bar. There was a metal security door in the side of the building, a security camera above it. No way could I get in that way without breaking down the door, plus I would be captured on videotape.

There was a whip-crack of thunder in the sky. A flash of lightning revealed a bony dog in the weed-strewn vacant lot next to the bar. I heard a woman's shrill laughter. The dry air smelled of rotting food, stale beer, and piss. The strobe-like lightning flashes made the dog disappear in one location and reappear in another.

A car pulled into the parking lot, catching me in its headlights. I turned around and walked away fast, hoping no one in the car had seen my face. I didn't want anyone to be able to identify me later.

I returned to the truck and drove on around the block.

I'm crazy to be thinking like this, I thought. Even if I can get Steigner, what will I do afterwards? How can I keep from getting caught?

If I followed through on this plan I would go to prison for years, maybe even for the rest of my life. I would never see LaFay, Terra, or any of my other friends again, unless it was through a Plexiglas window. Not only that, I would hurt G.T.—the one person who had always stood by me—even risk drawing him deeper into the conflict, placing him in danger, too.

Maybe there was a way to do it so I wouldn't get caught. A way to get revenge on the thug who hurt my daddy without all the risks and danger. Something I hadn't thought of yet. I had a sudden recollection of Mr. Ebban holding up the spirit level by the fountain in the park that day. *"Imagine that the whole world is like this level—poised in perfect balance between good and evil, between love and hate. One side is the world when it has a heart of stone and the other side is the opposite—the ears that hear the cry of the wounded, the eyes open to the light of God. Imagine that what you do or say every moment of your life influences this fragile balance . . ."* I wanted to let Mr. Ebban's words guide me, to trust that God would somehow make things right, but I couldn't muster up the necessary faith. Trusting in his God, or "Adonai," as He was often called in the Torah, seemed like walking across a frozen pond, without knowing how solid the ice was.

I felt there was a dangerous vacuum outside the truck, a force that could pull me into some black hole in distant space. I had broken into a cold sweat. Suddenly I had a powerful urge to see LaFay, to be with her for awhile, maybe even find a place where I could hold her close and feel her heartbeat, her body warm against mine. I remembered her telling me she would be babysitting tonight, but where?

Terra was working tonight. She would probably know. I drove to Roma's. It was an upscale restaurant, one of the few really nice places you could find to eat in Pottstown, although the neighborhood itself wasn't much to speak of. The southern end of McAlester was mostly pawn shops and tattoo parlors. But Roma's had been operated by the same family since the 1950s, Sicilians who knew how to prepare real Italian food.

As I stepped inside and caught the tangy scent of Italian food cooking, I realized how hungry I was. I had not eaten supper. I would like to have sat down in one of the booths or at the tables and ordered a plate of spaghetti, but I didn't have any money. I looked around for Terra, saw her talking to a couple in a booth against the far wall.

A woman in a black dress appeared, smiling, and asked me if I would be dining alone.

"I—just need to see someone."

The hostess' painted smile faded. "Who do you need to see?"

"Terra."

"I'll tell her."

The woman went over to Terra and said something to her. Terra turned to look at me. She held up a finger, indicating I should wait a minute, then disappeared through some swinging doors into the kitchen.

Although it may have only been my imagination, I felt as if the restaurant's patrons were watching me coldly. I remembered Mr. Ebban's story of going back to Poland, wandering the streets of his childhood. "A whole world murdered. Gone forever."

I felt a dull throbbing in my forehead. Closing my eyes, I rubbed my temples and pictured him sitting in his wheelchair, looking out the window. I wondered what he was doing just then. Maybe listening to his Hebrew hymns on his antique record player or struggling to read one of his books.

"Look what the wind blew in," Terra said. Her mascara had run a little bit around her eyes. She smelled of tomato sauce and fresh baked bread.

"Hi Terra. Sorry to bother you at work, but I'm looking for LaFay. Do you know where she is babysitting tonight?"

"Kind of late for a last-minute date, isn't it?"

"I just want to talk to her."

"LaFay babysits for three or four different families. I'm not sure which place she's at tonight. You could call her mom."

"That's all right. Maybe I'll see her tomorrow."

"You look a little ragged, Jesse. Final exams are just about here. How come you're not home studying?"

"Restless, I guess."

"I'm getting off at ten. But I guess I wouldn't do, huh?"

"I got a curfew."

"I know all about your curfew. I got to get back to work."

I watched her walk away, remembering the way she pressed her body against mine when she slid over to look at the house on Cotton Gin Road. If it weren't for LaFay, I realize I would have wanted to wait for Terra, maybe even hold her close for a while. Terra, who kept so much of herself hidden, made me feel like she had these locked doors leading to places no one had ever been before. But LaFay was who I wanted now, and she was nowhere to be found.

Leaving the restaurant, I looked at the clock on the wall by the entrance: 9:51. In ten minutes I would be a curfew violator, and any cop in the city could bust me.

As I stepped outside, it began to rain. A few drops at first, then a torrent. The rain was cold and hard and felt like it was coming from way up in the sky.

I was soaked by the time I got to the truck. I drove home, the rain pounding the truck like a hail of bullets. Lightning flashed and I saw the old man's image in the cracked, rain-streaked glass.

CHAPTER 25

An item on the evening news entered my brain like shrapnel: a steve-dore was going home Friday night, his cashed paycheck in his wallet. Some lowlife slunk out of the shadows, stabbed him in the back, and stole his wallet. Man left a wife and three kids behind. A picture of the victim's face appeared on the screen, only I saw my daddy's face there instead.

The reporter interviewed a neighbor who said the dockworker was a good, hard-working man who put his family first. I thought about the man's kids—pictured them crying and saying, "I want my daddy." Only Daddy wasn't ever coming home again. Daddy was in heaven, maybe. Or maybe he was just a spirit riding the wind.

All the rest of the evening I was cat-jumpy and full of torment. I kept remembering the voice of that man in the alley.

I've got to do something, I thought. I can't keep walking around like this. I'll go crazy.

That's when I got the idea of kidnapping Tony Moran. I could slip into his video game parlor, get the drop on him, and then let him call his daddy and tell him what I wanted. That way we could have a fair trade—Tony Moran for Steigner. I was counting on the fact that the Morans weren't the kind of citizens who would call the cops. They would want to take care of the problem themselves. After I dealt with Steigner, I would have to pull a major vanishing act, in order to avoid the Morans' wrath and also to protect G.T., keep him from being drawn into any more trouble on my account. I could go out West—to New Mexico, where Mama was. If I could find her, at least I'd have a place to stay until I could figure out what to do next. This plan would require major sacri-fices. I would be giving up my friends, my education, my close relation-ship with G.T., and the opportunity to see my daddy on a regular basis. But I would have gotten revenge on Steigner, and, as long as the Morans didn't go to the cops, the only official charge the police would have on me would be violating probation. I would have to make a new life for myself somewhere else. I could always work as a roofer. I'd helped G.T. enough over the years to have the basic skills and knowledge, but I would need to learn a lot more, especially about the business end of roofing—procuring materials and handling the money. Maybe I could even come back in a few years, after the heat had died down, and open my business, like G.T. I didn't like the idea of leaving Pottstown forever.

It might work. I might be able to do it. Even though my plan was a minefield of risks and dangers, the main problem I kept coming back to was LaFay. She was the one piece of the whole crazy puzzle I couldn't make fit.

After G.T. went to bed, I lay in my bed, waiting for him to go to sleep. When I heard him snoring, I got dressed and went into the kitchen. I found the keys to his truck hanging on the peg by the door. I eased out the back door, down the steps. The truck was parked in the driveway, close to the house. I heard Amos cooing up in the branches of the oak he roosted in at night. I unlocked the door on the passenger's side, looked in the glove compartment for G.T.'s Colt .45, but it wasn't there. I looked under both seats, too, but no luck.

Must be in his bedroom, I thought.

Besides the Colt, G.T. had a .22 target pistol, a Mark II Ruger, and an old lever-action thirty-thirty. I didn't know where the .22 was, but I figured it must be somewhere in his room—if he still had it, that is. He could have loaned it to somebody, or sold it, or it could be at his office.

I shut the truck door and sat on the front porch, looking across the road at Gladstone and Company. The tin roof on their warehouse shone like a sheet of ice in the light of the frost-white moon. Too wired to sleep, I rocked back and forth on the porch, listening to the wind high in the trees.

All day Monday every step I took made me feel like I was trying to walk through molasses. How was I going to get revenge on the man with the Devil's voice? How could I let him get away with what he did? His crime against my daddy knocked the whole world cockeyed, and I felt like I had to put it back in order. I walked LaFay down the hall to her class, sunk down into the black swamp of myself, unable to think of any words to say to this girl I loved.

"What is it, Jesse?" she asked. "You all right?"

"I'm O.K."

I squeezed her hand outside of her class, told her I would see her later. Being around her made me see how crazy I was to be thinking about taking on the Morans. If I followed through with my half-assed plans for revenge, I would be risking my chance of ever seeing LaFay again—unless it was from behind a Plexiglas window in the state prison. I've got to put this crazy idea out of my head, I thought, if I am ever going to have a chance of living a normal life.

Tuesday afternoon, when I got to Mr. Ebban's room, he was in the bathroom. I got out his Bible and sat in the windowsill waiting for him to come out.

But when he came out, he wanted me to read from Psalms. I began reading the passages he asked for. He moved around from chapter to chapter but I saw a pattern in the themes. They were about death terrors, the suffering of body and spirit, being surrounded or pursued by enemies—and prayers to God for mercy. He stopped me once and asked me to reread these lines: "*Kings are not delivered by a large force; warriors are not saved by great strength; horses are a false hope for deliverance; for all their great power they provide no escape. Truly the eye of the Lord is on those who fear him, who wait for His faithful care . . .*"

All the while I was reading Mr. Ebban was in his wheelchair, his eyes closed, his lips forming the words I read. I never stopped being amazed at his faith in these words.

After I finished reading, he asked, "What do you think of Psalms?"

"They're OK," I said. "Just words."

"Words."

I nodded. *Sounds, floating on the air like dandelion fluff.*

"Don't underestimate the power of words, Jesse. Words are tools for bringing about either good or evil in the world, depending on how they are used. The Holocaust didn't begin with the crematories but with evil words—of defamation and belittlement. Words must be chosen very carefully. They hold the power of life and death."

I was thinking that if I was facing Marc Steigner, I'd much rather have a gun in my hand than a bunch of words telling him how evil I thought he was. What good could words do? How could words punish him for his sins?

Mr. Ebban was watching me shrewdly now, in his preaching mode.

"We must listen to words carefully, too. Do you remember reading in Genesis, when God asks Cain what he has done with his brother, and Cain says, 'I do not know. Am I my brother's keeper?' What does God say in response?"

"I don't remember."

"He says, 'What have you done? Your brother's blood is crying to me from out of the earth.' The Hebrew word for blood, *d'mei*, is in the plural.

That means God is saying the *brother's bloods* are crying out. What does that tell you?"

I shook my head, regretting my decision to step into his personal briar patch.

"Not just his brother's blood, but all of his descendents," Mr. Ebban said, his shoulders slumped now, his eyes turned inward, looking at who knows what horror. He said this next sentence in a low voice, almost a whisper, as if he was speaking more to himself than to me. "When you take a life, you take not only that life, but all the lives that would have been."

What difference does it make when it's a thug? I wanted to say. A snake who strikes from the shadows, who leaves his victims lying helpless on the ground, who laughs at their misery? Why should you have to worry about his blood calling from the ground?

But the old man's aggrieved expression lingered in my mind, and I left his presence with a troubled heart.

On Thursday, after lunch, Snookie grabbed my arm as I was leaving the cafeteria. "Yo, Jesse. I got something you been wanting."

"What's that?"

"A name and an address."

"You kidding me?"

"No. That person you been looking for—Steigner. I know where that sucker lives."

Snookie told me how she had gotten her information. Her mom was getting her hair done at the beauty parlor, and a woman there talked about one of her old boyfriends who beat her up.

"The woman mentioned his name, and Mama remembered hearing me say I was trying to find this man, only she doesn't tell the woman that. She just played it sly, asked her if he's the Marc Steigner who lives on Camille Street, and the woman, she says, 'No, he lives on Tilden Avenue,' even calls out the number of his place. Says she sure as hell remembers it because of all the times she called the cops to the address when they used to be together. She said he lives alone now—he's too mean for anyone to put up with him."

"Tilden Avenue. He's not listed in the phone book."

"You won't find his name in the phone book. He doesn't go by 'Marc Steigner' these days. He's got an alias, Jesse. I got the phony name he's been using, too."

"That's great, Snookie. You're a sweetheart. What does he call himself?"

"Not so fast. You still going to give me fifty dollars?"

"Sure. I'll give it to you."

"When?"

"I don't have it on me. Can I owe it to you?"

"So this is going to be an IOU situation, huh? I thought we was talking cash."

Two girls walking by turned to look at us. I moved close to Snookie, lowering my voice: "I really need that name and number. I promise I'll give you the money."

"Yeah, like when?"

"Soon—as soon as I can."

"You get the money, I'll give you the number." Snookie tossed her head like a horse and walked off.

I could see her hard-assed attitude about giving me the name and address was her way of punishing me for being with LaFay. What the hell, it was her choice to spend the night with Ric Farina, not mine. Why couldn't she just let the past go? Why did she have to keep holding on to what was not meant to be?

I went on to my health class, wondering how in the hell I was going to get hold of fifty dollars.

That afternoon, after I got home from school, I sat on my bed, looking at the items in my box of keepsakes—the pictures of Lee, the picture of my mom, the old man's brass spirit level, the pencil Angela Salazar had given me. I looked at the twelve silver dollars I had left from the canvas bag of dollars Lee and I had found in the landfill. We had been poking through the trash with broomsticks when I saw the bag. I just pushed it aside, but when I felt the resistance on the stick I realized it had something in it. I picked it up and loosened the string around the top. "This is money!" I could still see the way Lee's face lit up when I poured those silver dollars out into his cupped hands.

There were twenty-four of them in there.

We took them to the coin man to see how much they were worth— that was back before he had his Rottweiler. He said he'd give us sixty bucks. Lee sold his share of our find, twelve silver dollars, for thirty dollars; he wanted the money for a date he was planning with a girl he liked a lot. I kept my share, though. I figured if the coin man was willing to pay us sixty bucks for them they were probably worth more. Also, I didn't really want to sell them. Later, I had thought about selling them plenty of times, but I never could bring myself to do it. For one thing, I liked the idea of something that rare and valuable turning up in a landfill full of trash. They seemed lucky somehow, a reminder that hope was always possible, even in a bad situation. Then, too, I had found them with Lee; they were a way of feeling connected to him.

I didn't know how much they were worth now, but I was thinking they would bring at least fifty dollars. I hated to sell them, but I had to get that name and address, and the coins were about the only thing I had of value that I could sell easily—except for my .22 Magnum, and I figured I might need my rifle more than the money.

I called the coin man at his shop, and asked him what he would pay for twelve silver dollars. He said he'd have to see them first.

"Can you just give me a range? I'm trying to decide whether I should sell them or not."

"Could be three, four bucks apiece. Like I say, I'd have to see them."

I told him I might bring them in and thanked him for his information. He hung up without saying goodbye. The coin man was all business. Him and his Rottweiler.

I figured if he was willing to pay four bucks apiece for them, they were bound to be worth more than that. I decided to offer them to Snookie, to see if she would just take them for the fifty dollars. Maybe that way I could buy them back from her someday—if she didn't sell them, that is.

I dialed her number and her mom answered. Her voice turned a little chilly when she heard who it was. "I'll see if she's here," she said.

After a minute Snookie picked up the phone. "Yeah."

"I got your money."

"That's nice."

"But it's—uh—not regular money."

"What do you mean, 'not regular money?' What kind of shit you trying to pull, Jesse?"

"It's silver dollars. Uncirculated silver dollars in mint condition. Probably worth five or six bucks apiece, maybe more. I got a dozen of them. I'll give you all twelve for that name and address."

"I don't know, Jesse. What am I going to do with silver dollars—sell them to the coin man?"

"Yeah, you could do that."

"How about you taking them to that creepy dude? He's the kind of guy who looks at your boobs the whole time he talks to you. Besides, that Rottweiler is liable to eat me up."

"Snookie, these coins are kind of special to me. I was hoping you could just hold them for me—until I get the money. That way I wouldn't really be giving them up for good."

"I ain't a pawn shop."

"Come on, Snookie," I said, hating to have to beg her like this. "Help me out."

She was quiet a moment. I heard her mama say something in the background.

"I'll think about it. Look, I have to go now."

I asked her when she was going to let me know something. She said to meet her tomorrow at Nick's Café at five.

After we hung up, I picked up my darts and threw them at the dartboard, missing the bull's eye all three times. I felt like there was a couple of Gila monsters fighting in my brain.

I got to Nick's at ten minutes till five. Snookie wasn't there. I ordered a Coke from Mimi, took a seat in a back booth, and got my U.S. history book out of my book bag. I had my coins stored in there, in a navy blue sock, tied in a knot at the top.

While I waited for Snookie I opened my history book and tried to concentrate on preparing for a possible essay question on Futrell's final—why the South lost the Civil War. I considered some of the more obvious points: the North had more people, a stronger economy, and a better industrial base. Because of the South's obsession with states' rights, it lacked a strong central government, and, unlike Lincoln, Jefferson Davis hadn't been able to build a base of popular support. Still another textbook argument was that the South's early military strategy could be viewed as being too aggressive. Lee's losses at Antietam and Gettysburg cost him many more of his own men, relatively speaking, than the opposing forces. If he would have fought a more defensive strategy, he could have dragged the war out longer, possibly long enough to force a political settlement.

I kept looking at the clock on the wall over the counter. It was ten after five. Snookie was late. I got up, walked to the window, looked down the street for her, returned to my seat, and drummed my fingers on the counter. I looked at my book again, tried to think of some other reason why the South might have lost the war, a less obvious one. The history teacher, Mr. Futrell, liked students to look beyond the facts; he liked personal interpretation, as evidence of "critical thinking." It was OK to go out on a limb in his class on an essay question, as long as you didn't go too far. I figured the South was too hung up on slavery and the "Southern way of life," and who did that system benefit really besides the rich plantation owners—the mint julep set? Most of the men and boys who died at Vicksburg, Gettysburg, Bull Run, and Antietam probably didn't have much more than a pot to piss in, and yet there they were, sleeping in the rain and cold, eating bad food and shedding their blood in a struggle to give rich folks the right to sit out on their verandas and watch their darkies picking cotton. I figure you could make a case that the South lost the war because too many Southerners were locked into a rigid system of thought, a bull-headed way of looking at the world. If Southerners could have been more flexible, more willing to think of ways to solve their problems creatively, the Confederate government could have done something really bold and daring, like set the slaves free themselves. Jefferson Davis could have issued his own Emancipation Proclamation long before Sherman stormed through Georgia and the Carolinas, burning and plundering the countryside. With the slaves set free, the Confederacy would have undercut the North's moral edge, undermined its morale, and maybe even encouraged Europe, especially England, to intercede on the South's behalf. What did the South have to lose really, with its economy in ruins, so many of its citizens dead and wounded? The South had determination, sure, and bravery beyond belief, but its problems were a rigid mindset and failure of vision.

I was considering the validity of an argument like this, and wondering if Futrell would go for it, when I looked up and saw Terra pull up to the curb in the Mercury. Snookie was in the passenger's seat by the window. She got out and they walked down the sidewalk toward the front steps. Both of them were in tank tops and jeans. Snookie had on her big, gold hoop earrings. She saw me in the window and gave me a little nod.

They both came into the café and slid into the booth across from me.

"You reading that book?" Snookie said. "Or just looking at the pictures."

"Been reading it. Studying for Futrell's final."

"You'll probably ace it, Jesse," Terra said. "You always were a brain."

"If I had any brains I wouldn't be here."

Snookie asked, "What's that supposed to mean?"

"Never mind." I took out the sock full of silver dollars, put them on the table. "Here's my money."

"Is that sock clean?" Terra asked.

"Fresh out of my sock drawer." I untied the knot at the top, poured out some of the dollars onto the table.

Snookie held one up for inspection. "These ain't hot, are they? I don't want the po-pos knocking on my door."

I didn't want to tell her where these dollars had come from—but I also didn't want her to think they were stolen. I figured I could have make up some dumb lie, but instead I just told her the truth—that Lee and I had found them in the landfill. "I think they're worth more than fifty dollars, and you can sell them if you want to, but I'd appreciate it if you'd keep them a while. I'll buy them back from you for fifty dollars."

"Told you I ain't no pawn shop."

Terra rolled her eyes. "Jesus Christ."

"This is business, girl," Snookie said.

Terra put her hand down into her tank top, took some folded money out of her bra. She peeled off two twenties and a ten and laid them on the table in front of Snookie. "Here's the fifty. I'll keep the silver dollars."

"Terra, I didn't mean for you to—"

"I always wanted some silver dollars," Terra said, putting the other bills back down into her bra. "Maybe I'll have them made into a belt or something."

I put the silver dollars back in the sock and handed it to her. "Thanks, Terra."

She picked up the coin-filled sock. "These would make a good black-jack," she said, hefting them in her hand.

Terra's generosity was like a balm to my sore heart, but now wasn't the time to show my gratitude.

Snookie frowned, but she picked up the money and put it in her pocketbook. She took a folded up piece of paper out of her wallet. "Here's your name and address."

I opened it up and read: *Leon Delgado, 1331B Tilden Ave.*

I had a sudden sensation of dizziness. Like I was standing on top of a tall building, looking down. I folded up the paper and put it in my pocket.

"Why do you want this guy so bad, Jesse?" Snookie asked. "You think he was one of the thugs who jumped you?"

"Never mind about that. Look, you got to promise to keep this quiet. Don't tell anyone, you hear?"

"No problem."

"I want you to promise."

"OK, I promise."

"Terra?"

"You be careful, Jesse," Terra said.

"I'm always careful."

"Right," Terra said. And she rolled her eyes.

When I got home, I saw a note from G.T. on the table.

Jesse,
Beef stew in the fridge.
Working late with Carlos to finish up a job on East Carlyle.
Hit those books.
G.T.

I was too jumpy to study. And I didn't feel like eating. I got the keys to the Dodge and cranked it up, drove across town to Tilden Avenue. It was just off the bypass near Mercer Hospital and Memorial Gardens, where Lee was buried. A neighborhood of dilapidated old houses, the kind with couches and washing machines on the front porch, junk cars in the yards. Not all of the houses had numbers on them, and some of the numbers were missing. I finally found 1331. A white frame duplex, storm doors with the glass knocked out. Whole place needed a coat of paint. I saw "B" on the second door. I would like to have parked in front of the duplex and watched it for a while, but I was afraid someone would be able to ID my truck later, so I just kept driving. I circled the block and drove by the place again. I thought about how I could park the truck on another street and walk here, after dark. That way I could walk up the steps, and knock on his door.

I was already trying to figure out what I would say to him to get him to talk—to open up and confess. I had to hear him say something, to prove beyond a doubt he was the same man who had beat and taunted me in the alley. I was sure I would know that hateful, hissing voice when I heard it again. *Schoolboy, did you do your homework today? Did you read to the old Jew? Did you wipe his ass? Jewboy. Jew lover.*

I got back to our house at sundown. I walked in and heard the phone ringing. It was G.T. calling to see if I had been studying, but I knew he was really checking up on me, making sure I was all right.

"I got my book right here," I told him. I had my hand on it, which made my words seem like less of a lie.

"You eat the beef stew?"

"Not yet, but I'm fixing to eat it soon."

"All right. I'm going to pick up a burger for Carlos and me. Be home in about an hour."

After I hung up, I went into G.T.'s room, looked around for his Colt. I looked under his mattress, in the drawer by his dresser, where there were bills and magazines: *Field and Stream*, *Sports Illustrated*, and *Modern Roofing*. No gun. I walked around the room, thinking he must have taken it with him. His Winchester rifle was in the closet, but I needed something I could hide.

I wondered if he still had the target pistol—maybe he had sold it or loaned it to someone. If I could find the .22 it would be a better choice than the .45, which boomed like a cannon. I looked in his footlocker and his dresser drawer, feeling guilty for violating his personal space like this. I got a chair and climbed up to look in the shelf of his closet, where he kept some of his business records and cancelled checks. No gun there, either.

I was about to give up when I noticed the panel in the ceiling that led up to the attic. Standing on my tiptoes on the chair, I pushed the panel out and felt around, hoping I wouldn't disturb an ill-tempered spider or rat. I didn't feel anything but dusty floor. I got the flashlight G.T. kept by his bed and pulled myself halfway up into the attic. A couple of feet away from the edge, I saw a dusty gray case. Using the flashlight, I pulled it towards me, then I eased myself back down onto the chair. I already knew what it was.

It was G.T.'s Ruger.

Along with the gun there were two empty magazines and a box of .22 hollow-points.

I took the gun, magazines, and box of shells back to my room and locked my door. Sitting on my bed, I racked the slide and pointed the pistol at the wall, squeezing the trigger to make sure it worked. I opened the box of shells and put ten of them into the magazine. I inserted the fully loaded magazine into the handle of the gun, felt it lock in place.

As I held the pistol in my hand, I thought of that flat, hateful voice in my ear. I pictured my daddy's scarred head, the blank look in his eyes, my own face bruised and swollen in the mirror.

I have something for you, Mr. Marc Steigner, AKA Leon Delgado, I thought.

A one-way ticket to hell.

CHAPTER 26

On Tuesday, after I finished my service hours with Mr. Ebban, I drove to the duplex inhabited by "Leon Delgado." I left the Havenwood parking lot just after dusk, and by the time I got to the duplex, night had fallen. There was a navy blue Chevy van parked in front of his side of the duplex and a light on in the front window. I had a feeling the van was the same one that had hauled me out to the landfill. This thought brought back painful memories: the light in my eyes, the taste of my own blood, that hateful, hissing voice in my ear.

I circled the block and pulled up behind the van. I tried to read the license number, but the plates were covered with a layer of mud, and I couldn't make out the numbers. Where had he been to get them so dirty? I wondered what he did for a living, if he even worked a regular job, or just did the Morans' dirty work for them. I wondered what he looked like, if I had ever seen him before. On the street perhaps. Or going into the Flamingo. Various suspects I had seen from the third floor window of the Magnolia Hotel flowed through my mind—a weasel-faced man who wore a red jacket, a burly man in a fedora, a skinhead wearing high black boots.

Looked like no one was at home in 1331A. Maybe the occupant worked second shift. There weren't many people out on Tilden. The ones I did see walked fast and didn't take much interest in vehicles going by. Must be a neighborhood where people stay inside at night. The .22 shouldn't make enough noise to attract anybody's attention—unless it would be someone in 1331A; and if luck was on my side, whoever lived there wouldn't be at home when I returned here Thursday night.

Driving home, I planned what I would say to him when he opened the door and saw me with the .22 aimed at his face. *Put your hands up and back into the room, Marc. You and I are going to have a little talk . . .*

My heart was booming like crazy. Jesus, I thought. I've got to get myself under control if I'm going to pull this off.

I am in a dungeon, my wrists chained to a wall. There are red-eyed rats in here. I see them moving around. I scream and shout, pull against the chain, but it's no use. I am trapped. Suddenly a slat in the dungeon door opens and a bright, blinding light hits my eyes. The door swings open and guards unlock my shackles, drag me down a long hall. Their voices are like echoes. They take me down another corridor, up a stairway, into a wide, sunlit room with a polished floor. A trumpet sounds. A curtain opens and I see Judge Simms sitting on a throne, flanked by two winged warriors on either side. She has on a white robe, and she is wearing a crown of thorns. The guards throw me to the floor in front of her. I am filthy and soiled from having spent long days and nights in the dungeon without bathing. Repulsed by my own foul smell, I have cobwebs on my clothes and fingers. The backs of my hands have weird tattoos—images of demons and spiders. Judge Simms gazes down at me with disgust. There is no mercy in her eyes.

All day Thursday, the last official day of school, I tried to make sure everyone saw me being my bad-assed fool self. I kissed LaFay outside of her math class and got into a food fight with Skeeter and Andre in the caf. I held up my hand and volunteered the answer to a question in Mr. Futrell's history class. I wanted everyone to remember I was here at school, and not acting quiet or withdrawn, just in case the cops got the idea I was involved in a murder on Tilden Avenue and started asking questions. I reminded myself to act relaxed and natural tonight when I visited Mr. Ebban's room, in case the cops talked to him or someone at the nursing home, too.

Sharp-eyed Terra was the only one of my friends who seemed to notice something was different.

"You asked what time it was three times this morning, Jesse," she said, at lunch. "Got a doctor's appointment or something?"

"Just like to keep up with the time," I told her.

She was studying me with her dark eyes. "Right," she said.

Suddenly, I wanted to talk to her—to unburden my heart, tell her my crazy plan and get her to talk me out of it. Terra had more common sense than almost anyone I knew, and I trusted her more than most people, too. *Why not take her into your confidence?* I thought. *Tell her you want to talk to her later.*

I might have done it too, only at that moment the bell rang, and everyone got up and left, leaving me alone at the lunch table, staring at my half-eaten hamburger, my untouched fries.

That afternoon, G.T. came home with a bucket of fried chicken, hush puppies and potato salad. We ate on paper plates in the kitchen, washing the food down with iced tea. G.T.'s face was leathery and bronze from all the hours he had been spending out in the sun. His hair was sun-streaked and his eyelashes were turning gold. He said Ricardo had fallen off a roof and broken his arm. G.T. had taken him to Mercer Hospital, but the hospital wouldn't admit him without insurance. So G.T had taken him to the "doc in a box," a Pakistani doctor who provided care for cash up front, out in the Northside Mall. He was the one most of the pill freaks went to around here—he would give you a prescription for just about anything as long as you had the cash. Remembering the way Ricardo had showed me the photos of his wife and kids back in Mexico, I asked G.T. how Ricardo was going to earn a living with a broken arm. G.T. said, "He won't be able to do any roofing work, not until his arm heals up."

I was pretty sure G.T. would help Ricardo out until his arm got better, although he wouldn't want to tell you about it. That was G.T.

After supper, he dozed off in the recliner in front of the TV.

I went back to my room, locked the door, took the Ruger out from under my mattress, and slid the loaded clip into the handle.

I put on my black sweatshirt with the hood and slipped the Ruger into my belt. I left a note for G.T. on the table, telling him I was going to do my community service with Mr. Ebban and that I would be back before ten o'clock.

Driving out of the driveway, I had to wait for a line of cars leaving Gladstone's across the road. A funeral procession for somebody's pet on the way to the pet cemetery for the burial. These grievers had money, judging by the cars: Cadillacs, a Porsche, a Lexus, and a Mercedes Benz. Some of them had tinted windows so you couldn't see the occupants, but I saw a child's face in one window. A little boy with headphones on—lis-tening to music maybe or playing with a Game Boy.

I shut my eyes and counted to ten. My T-shirt was already sticking to my body in this heat.

When I opened my eyes, the cars were moving on down Rose of Sharon Road, leaving a big cloud of dust. I pulled onto the road and fol-lowed the dust cloud to Jessup.

At Havenwood I sat in the windowsill and read from the Book of Jonah while Mr. Ebban peeled and ate an orange. The loaded Ruger was under my sweatshirt, held in place by my belt. I hadn't wanted to leave it in the Dodge in the parking lot, since neither of the doors would lock. I couldn't risk somebody finding it.

While I read this chapter for Mr. Ebban, my mind kept drifting to the duplex at 1331 Tilden Avenue. I saw myself parking on the next block, slipping up the hood of my sweatshirt, and walking around the corner to the duplex. No need for anyone to see my truck parked outside. I would leave the duplex through the back door, run through the yards to the next block, and get back into my truck. The whole thing shouldn't take more than ten minutes. I would have to hear his voice to know for sure he is the one, though, before I could shoot him.

My chest felt hot and tight, and I had a nervous tic in my left eye.

"Why is your community service person dressed all in black?"

I looked up and saw Ray Thorne, slouching in the doorway. I was at that part of the story when Jonah has fled from God, and the sailors on the ship are casting lots to see who among them has angered God so much that he has sent the storm upon them.

Ray said, "He looks like a thug in that sweatshirt."

Mr. Ebban gave me the sign to keep reading. I continued, but I was irritated with Ray Thorne—his rude willingness to intrude on my time with Mr. Ebban.

By the end of the third chapter in Jonah, God had decided not to destroy the city of Ninevah, since the people had heeded Jonah's warning, put on sackcloth and ashes, and turned from their wicked ways. This angered Jonah so much that he no longer wanted to live. He was sitting outside the city waiting to see what would happen to it and God caused a plant to grow out of the ground to give him shade. Then God let a worm eat the plant so that it withered, and afterwards, the wind and sun beat down on Jonah so much that he fainted, and again, he wished that he would die. Then God asked Jonah why he had cared about the plant but not about the people of Nineveh, and he shamed Jonah for not having pity upon them.

"That make any sense to you, boy?" Ray asked, after I had finished reading the chapter.

I glanced at Mr. Ebban. He nodded and beckoned with his open palm, indicating he would like me to answer.

"Sounds like Jonah had a negative attitude." Kind of like you, fool.

"Why is that?"

"He was depressed because God didn't destroy the city."

"You are only commenting on the surface of the story," Mr. Ebban said, "not what's underneath."

Ray said, "Anybody can see what the point of this story is. They teach it in Sunday school, to little kids. Why do you have to make everything so complicated, Mendel?"

The old man was still looking at me, his eyes bright and shrewd beneath his tangled eyebrows.

I looked at Ray Thorne. "What do you think the point is?"

"The point is when God tells you to do something, you better do it. He controls the thunder, the lightning, and the seas, not to mention all the animals, including the finny creatures of the deep. Sharks and such. Piss him off and you're liable to end up as fish food. Some of these drug dealers, hooligans, and gangsters would reap beaucoup benefit from meditating on this little Bible story. And then they need to get down on their knees and accept Jesus into their hearts. Might save them a passel of grief later on—ain't that right, Mendel?"

Mr. Ebban ignored Ray, as if he was a wind blowing by outside the window. "Jesse."

I said, "The point is more about God's mercy, and about people's power to change their fate by living right. It's about the way you can get another chance."

The old man was nodding now. I saw a light come into his eyes. This gave me a little glow inside and for a moment I forgot the wickedness in my heart—the murderous mission I would have completed before the sun had risen in the morning.

"The Bible says good works alone won't save you," Ray said, waving a knotty finger back and forth. "It's all about getting right with Jesus. But you can't just talk the talk, you got to walk the walk, too. You got to be righteous unto the Lord . . ." Ray was off his chain again, but neither the old man or I was really listening to him.

"Jesse, put up the Bible, please. I want to hear the water in the fountain."

I eased off the windowsill and set his Bible on the shelf.

As I pushed Mr. Ebban out of the room, Ray was still running off at the mouth. He followed us out into the hall. "Take these Sodomites clamoring to get married in the church. They can sing hosannas and talk about God until the old red rooster crows, but if they are poking around in each other's nether regions, they got about as much chance to enter the kingdom of heaven as Lot's wife has to change back from the pillar of salt . . ."

We went down the hall, passing Varden, who stopped in mid-whistle. "See Mr. Ray Thorne blessed you all with a visit," he said. "Believe I still hear him. Who's he beating up on now?"

"Everybody on the planet who's the slightest bit different from him," I said.

"Lot of that mess going around. You all have a lovely time in the park."

In the lobby, I pushed Mr. Ebban past the row of old people in their wheelchairs. I nodded at Rhonda, the second-shift receptionist, as we went by the front desk.

Outside, the sun was sinking below the pines, and the heat had eased up some. Mr. Ebban's white hair flew up in the breeze as I pushed him down the hill to the fountain.

I was thinking about the way the sailors cast lots to figure out who among them had angered God. I looked up at the empty sky and thought, what if there's no God on duty? What if the power that created the whole universe is removed from the everyday lives of people? It's funny how all of the miracles were in the distant past. Moses striking a rock in the desert and causing water to pour out, Jesus healing the lepers and raising the dead—what proof does anyone have that these things really happened? You can read anything in a book. You can read that Superman flew up into the sky and smashed an asteroid hurtling toward earth, or that a man traveled back to the Middle Ages in a time machine, but that doesn't make these claims true.

We came to the fountain, and I leaned against it, staring into the water. I pictured my brother's face there, in the swirling water, and I wished I could somehow communicate to him on the other side, tell him that I was about to get the man who hurt our daddy.

A voice broke into my dreamy thoughts:

"Jesse, I want you to give me that gun."

I turned to look at Mr. Ebban, thinking that I had only imagined this statement. I could hear the sound of the water falling in the fountain, the distant murmur of children's voices.

"Sir?"

"Give me the gun."

"What are you talking about?"

"I am talking about a request. I want the gun."

"Gun? What makes you think I have a gun?"

"I saw it. Under your sweatshirt, when you put the Torah on the shelf."

"I can't believe this."

"Believe it." He was holding his hand out. "The gun, please."

I turned away from him. "What the hell is it with you?"

"Jesse, put it in my hand."

"No." I was backing away from him now.

"Jesse, you must give me that gun!"

I turned my back on him and walked away. But I stopped after I had taken a few steps. I couldn't leave him here alone. I had to return him to the nursing home.

I whirled around. He was just sitting there by the fountain, his face red and bronze in the sundown light. His lips were moving, and I knew he was speaking to me, but I couldn't hear his words. There was a roaring now in my ears. I thought maybe it was from my pounding heart.

I looked at his outstretched hand, thinking of him using it to separate bodies in the Nazi death camp—and to pick berries in the forest after he escaped. I walked toward him, intending to push him up the path in the wheelchair, up to the building. But he whirled around in the chair, facing me, his hand out, telling me again that I must give him the gun.

I backed away from him again, shaking my head. And then, suddenly, I was reaching in my shirt, taking out the gun. His hand was still out, he was speaking, but I had no idea what he was saying; I only heard the sound of his voice, pouring over me like one of Rosalita's prayers. As if in a dream I took the pistol out of my belt. Handle first I held it out to him, placed it into his open hand.

Then the spell was broken.

"Damn you to hell!" I shouted, and then I was running, up the hill, away from him, running to my truck, the angry curse I had hurled at him still ringing in my ears, burning my tongue like acid.

I got into my truck and pulled out of the parking lot, furious at myself for being so careless as to think I could hide the gun from him. The old man was too smart. He knew something was up when he saw me in that sweatshirt and hood. I was angry, too, for my willingness to give him the gun, and I felt guilty for leaving him by the fountain. He would have to push himself up the path now.

I pulled off the road beside a phone booth and called the main number to Havenwood. Rhonda, the secretary, answered on the third ring.

I told her who I was, and that I had to leave suddenly, on an emergency, that Mr. Ebban was still in the park.

"Mr. Ebban is still in the park?"

"That's right."

"Where is he in the park?"

"By the fountain."

"He's by the fountain?"

"Yes. Please tell Varden Story. Varden needs to go get him."

Before she could say anything else, I hung up. My hands were shaking. I felt off balance, out of sync with the whole world. I'll have to use another gun, I thought, as I got back into the truck. I felt like Mr. Ebban had robbed me of my chance to bring the whole cockeyed planet back into balance—without giving me an alternate plan. Next time I will make sure I go straight there, instead of stopping off to see him.

Then it occurred to me that I may not even go back to see Mr. Ebban. That it may be the last time I even see him. Didn't I leave him in the park? Didn't Ms. Lynch tell me I was to "stay with our patient at all times?"

I pulled up to a red light and struck the dashboard with my fist. A man and woman in a shiny black Mercedes Benz were in the next lane. The man looked over at my truck with his lip curled, like the very sight of my old Dodge was offensive.

"What the hell are you looking at?" I shouted, and I revved up the engine.

The light changed and the Mercedes shot forward, the man looking back at me through the window. He looked like he was saying something to the woman with him.

Driving home on Oleander I saw a blue light whirling in my rearview mirror. The light was on the dash—an unmarked car. I glanced at my speedometer, remembered it was broken. What the hell, I wasn't speeding. I slowed down, looking for a place to pull over.

I pulled off the road just up from Nick's Cafe. I put my hands on the steering wheel and waited for the cop.

It was Dopodja.

"Step out of the truck, Terrill. And keep your hands where I can see them."

I got out of the truck. Saw Rizzo standing to the right of Dopodja; he had a black pistol aimed at my chest.

"What's with the gun, Mr. Rizzo?" I asked.

"Turn around and put your hands on the truck!"

I put my hands on the truck, and Dopodja patted me down. Then he put the cuffs on me, pushed me to the car. I remembered the man I shouted at outside the window. Did he call the cops? "What's this all about? I haven't done anything."

"Is that right?"

"I'm not breaking curfew."

"No, but you been carrying a deadly weapon," Dopodja said. "That ought to be enough to convince the most liberal, soft-headed judge in the world that your sorry ass belongs in Sheridan."

"What are you talking about?"

"Officer Nolan is on his way to the nursing home to pick it up."

I froze. I was stunned that the old man would drop a dime on me like that. Why in the hell was I so stupid to give him the gun? Why?

"We got a report there was a kid with a gun at Havenwood nursing home. I knew who it was. Didn't even have to hear your name. Now get in the back of the car if you want to avoid another cracked head and a charge of resisting arrest."

I got in the back of the car. Through the wire mesh that separated the front and back seats, I saw Dopodja get in the front, Rizzo beside him. Dodopja was talking on his radio, telling the dispatcher he had the "suspect in custody."

I pictured Mr. Ebban, sitting there by the fountain, holding that pistol. I felt like a rat was chewing on my heart.

Why did he betray me like that? Why?

And why was I so stupid as to give him the gun?

Now I had not only let everyone down—G.T., my daddy, LaFay—I had also blown my chance for revenge. All because I trusted that diabolical old Jew.

I put my head back and howled—a wild cry from the slimy bottom of my doomed soul. Rizzo slammed the Plexiglas window shut between the front and back seats.

I continued howling.

Chapter 27

I was dreaming of flesh-eating zombies. They had stiletto fangs and snakes for tongues. The zombies lived on the other side of mirrors. They could reach through the mirror and pull you through, into their zombie world, where they would take their sweet time eating you piece by piece.

As if from a great distance I heard someone call my name. I woke up. My eyes focused on the ceiling, where former inmates had written their names with fire. I heard keys jingling and a voice. It was my old pal, the fat, bald jailer, wearing the same camouflage pants and grease-stained T-shirt.

"Let's go, Terrill. I ain't got all day."

I was so exhausted I didn't even want to get up from the mattress, where I had spent much of the night sleepless. I drifted off sometime around daylight after the trustee delivered a bowl of cold oatmeal and a cup of warm black coffee.

I swung down off the bunk, slipped into my shoes, and stood by the barred door, waiting for the jailer to unlock it.

My cellmate, a dark-skinned black guy named "Milk," was snoring on the lower bunk. On the floor beside him was the deck of cards I had made up just after midnight. In my anger I had torn pages from the Gideon Bible and made them into a deck of cards, identifying each card with a broken piece of pencil I had found on the floor. It had taken me all of Matthew and most of Mark to create a 52-card deck. One more sin I will have to answer for when I get to the other side, I thought.

Milk and I had played cards into the night, using my makeshift deck. He said he had been arrested for DUI. He was twenty-four now, but he had turned eighteen in Sheridan, a place he said he hoped he would never lay eyes on again. I remember him telling me he had gotten so depressed there he had once thought about cutting off a finger while working with a saw, because he knew it would get him out of that hell-hole for a few weeks—to get physical therapy.

Milk opened one eye. "We in heaven yet?"

"Still down below, man."

"Damn. Dreamed I was in heaven."

"What was it like?"

"Had three beautiful wives. A money tree in my front yard. A BMW that could fly like a plane. A river of whiskey flowed right by my back door. Nothing but blue skies and sunshine all day long."

"You need to go back to sleep." I was thinking his dream was sure better than mine.

"Let's go, Terrill." The jailer swung the door open, and I stepped out into the corridor.

"Where you taking me?"

"You got a visitor."

"Who is it?" I asked, although I knew it was G.T.

"Your lawyer."

I walked ahead of him down the long corridor, wondering why he didn't put the cuffs on me.

We went down the stairs, to the front room on the first floor. Jake Quittlebaum was sitting at a card table by the wall. He had on a yellow shirt and bright green pants, the kind of colors you'd expect to see on a parrot. I blinked my eyes. I was so drained of energy I felt like I was moving in a dream.

"Good morning, Jesse," he said. "How you feeling today?"

"Not so good."

"Misfortune just seems to dog you, doesn't it?"

"Yes, sir, I got—"

"Hold on, son. Before you say anything else, I have to advise you to wait until we can have ourselves a confidential attorney-client discussion."

"I'm just leaving," the jailer said, holding up his pudgy hands. He went into his office and shut the door behind him.

Jake fixed his hound dog eyes on me.

"Sit down, Jesse."

I sat down across from him. "I wish I was dead."

Jake studied me thoughtfully a while before he spoke.

"You know when we're young, we always think we got a corner on the misery market, but that isn't necessarily true. You ought to spend a day with me sometime, meet some of my other clients. This afternoon, I've got to see what I can do to help out a single mom I represent. Her baby daddy paid her a visit in the middle of the night. He was high on crack and had romance on his mind. She wasn't in the mood to let him in, so he kicked the door in. She was behind the door with an iron skillet—one of those big, black things. She gave him a little love tap with it, only she hit him a little harder than she intended to—at least that's what she said. He died on the operating table, and now she's facing a murder charge. She's mighty depressed, too, cause she can't make bond. And she wonders who's going to take care of her little girl. Child's in a foster home now. Mama wants to get out of jail so she can take care of her."

"He was breaking into her house. Couldn't that be seen as self-defense?"

"You could look at it that way, sure. Man had a history of using her for a punching bag. But the DA says it's murder. I guess he thinks she should have scooped up her baby and run out the back door."

I put my head down in my arms, identifying with the morbid hopelessness of this woman's plight. But when I closed my eyes, the zombies came back. A hand reached for me from behind a mirror, and I raised up fast. "G.T. called you, huh?"

"I've spoken with G.T., yes."

"I'll bet he's pissed right now."

"He's right concerned about you—as well he should be."

"Where is he?"

"Imagine he's at work, son. Putting a roof on somebody's house. Man's a hell of a fine roofer. Best one in the whole city. And he's got the fairest prices, too."

"I made a dumb mistake, Mr. Quittlebaum."

"Sounds like someone else made the mistake. At least that's what the facts say at this juncture."

"They got me for carrying a gun—a concealed weapon."

"You were accused of being in possession of a firearm."

"What kind of defense do I have?"

"The issue before us now is what kind of case do they have. At this point it's looking mighty pitiful. In fact, you might say it's nonexistent."

I wondered what he was talking about. Did he have me mixed up with someone else?

He took a small notebook out of his pocket, opened it, and studied it a minute. "A witness claimed that he saw you take a gun out from under your sweatshirt and hand it to Mr. Mendel Ebban. Witness's name was Mr. Ray Thorne. Trouble is, no one could find the gun. And Mr. Ebban claims he never even saw a gun. Says Mr. Ray Thorne must be confusing him with somebody else."

Mr. Quittlebaum returned the notebook to his pocket.

"This witness said he saw the gun in Mr. Ebban's possession. Mr. Ebban disputed this claim and invited the officers to search him and his room, which they did. And after a thorough search, guess what—no gun."

I shook my head, the significance of Mr. Quittlebaum's statement slowly sinking in. I wondered how Mr. Ebban had gotten rid of the gun so fast.

"If there was a gun, young Mr. Jesse, I certainly hope you realize that you have made a fortuitous escape from a burning ship—let me amend that to a *miraculous* escape. Because there's nothing I or anyone else could do for you, if you were to be caught carrying a concealed gun while performing your community service out there at Havenwood." Jake raised his eyebrows. "Am I making myself clear?"

"Yes, sir."

"Now, I'm going to holler for that jailer in a minute, and after we do a little paperwork and visit the magistrate, he's going to let me take you home. And when you get there you might want to get yourself cleaned up, 'cause, frankly, Jesse, you are carrying a little odor."

"They're going to let me go home?"

"That's right."

"What about Dopodja?"

"Man doesn't have a case. If he was hoping to have one, ain't nothing he can do now but scratch his little mad place." Jake stood up. "Now let's get you released and let me get back to the golf course, see if I can get at least nine holes in before lunchtime. This was supposed to have been my morning off."

I followed him to the door, feeling like Lazarus right after Jesus raised him from the dead.

G.T. came home for lunch.

I was half-asleep on my bed when I heard him come in. He came down the hall and threw my door open.

"Where's the Goddamned gun?"

"I don't know."

"You don't know?"

"No. I gave it to the old man."

"So that witness wasn't lying, huh?"

"No. He wasn't lying."

"Are you crazy? Are you out of your mind? What the hell were you going to do with that gun?"

I just shook my head, looked down at my hands.

"What the hell's going on? I want to know. And no bullshit, you hear me?"

"I found that guy—Steigner."

"Steigner? Christ, Jesus. How'd you do that?"

"Friend of mine gave me his name and address."

"Oh, and you were going to go take care of him, huh? Just like that? And use my gun. You've decided he's guilty, and you're going to go smoke him. You know something, Jesse, I'm sick of you. I hate to say it, but it's true. I'm just sick of you. From the top of my head to the bottom of my feet. I got half a notion to send you up to Lynette's to live. Get you the fuck away from these Pottstown sleazes you can't seem to stay away from."

"I'm sorry, G.T. I—"

"Shut up! I don't even want to hear it." He paced the floor, clenching and unclenching his hands. "I got to get out of here. I got to get back to work. I want you here when I come back, you hear me? Don't you leave this house. I mean it. Not in the yard, not even on the front porch. You stay in this house, you hear me?"

"I won't leave."

He walked out of my room. When he left he slammed the front door so hard I could feel the vibrations in the walls. I lay back down on my bed but sleep was out of the question. The worst thing about making G.T. that mad was I knew he was justified in everything he'd said. I hated myself for letting him down the way I had—stealing his gun, being so hell-bent on getting revenge I'd never really stopped to seriously consider him. I wondered if G.T. would ever trust me again. It occurred to me that even though Dopodja hasn't been able to connect me to the pistol, Mr. Ebban wouldn't want me to come back to Havenwood again. And Varden—the judge's nephew—was bound to know everything that was going on. As soon as he told his aunt, Judge Simms, my probation would be revoked quicker than you could say, "the Sheridan express."

I could see I ought to just take off, go out West, and try to find my mom. LaFay was the only thing really holding me here, but what did I really have to offer her? I was on probation, with no money, no job. I couldn't even take her out to eat.

That's what I ought to do all right. As soon as I could get some money together, I needed to take off from Pottstown. I was just a stone around G.T.'s neck. I needed to leave this whole state and start a new life somewhere else. If I stayed here, sooner or later, I would get busted for being a probation violator and end up in Sheridan. And anyway, G.T. would be better off without me in his life.

I heard a rapping at my window. I opened the blinds.

It was Amos.

"I can't come out, Amos," I told him. "G.T. told me to stay in." I slid open the window and pushed out the screen. The breeze stirred my best peacock feathers in the vase by my window. Amos pushed his head through so I could rub his neck the way he liked. He closed his eyes, made a cooing sound down in his throat. I rested my forehead against the window frame, grateful for the opportunity to do something right for a change, even such a small, insignificant thing as this.

CHAPTER 28

The first day of my summer vacation G.T. woke me up at dawn. I was out of that bed like a fireman, not wanting to give him another reason to be mad at me. I was to help Carlos put a new roof on a house in a neighborhood near Washington High School. G.T. would have given me a summer job anyway, but I knew my help was even more critical since Ricardo's arm was broken. G.T. had Ricardo helping him in his office, answering the phone mostly, although he had an answering machine. He was also supposed to take messages from any potential clients who stopped by.

I was grateful for the opportunity for a job, even a hard grueling job like roofing in the heat of summer. G.T. hadn't said how much he would pay me. I wasn't sure if I would get paid, since I still had to reimburse him for the monthly payments he had been making to the B'nai Shalom Temple.

Being ever mindful of his threat to send me up to the mountains to live with my Aunt Lynette, I was on extra good behavior with G.T. Damned if I was going to go up there and live with her and her snake-handling friends. I would pull a major disappearing act first. I also felt ashamed and guilty for taking his gun.

When I had devised my plan, I figured I'd throw the gun away after I had used it on Steigner—no sense in leaving it around for evidence. I didn't factor in G.T.'s reaction to my losing it, didn't think that far ahead. So much for my skill as an assassin, I thought. I couldn't even get to see my intended victim before I lost my weapon. On top of that, I got thrown in jail.

Before we left, G.T. gave me a tube of sunscreen, a pack of salt pills, work gloves, and a gallon thermos of ice water. He said Carlos would have more water if I needed it. "Coat yourself with that sunscreen and be sure to stay hydrated," he said.

On the way to the house, G.T. went over the job with me. He said we would be working on a low-pitched roof with a lot of curled and broken shingles. First Carlos and I would have to tear them off with shingle scrapers and pitchforks. We would dump the shingles into a utility trailer, which G.T. would bring to the site later today. When it was full we would haul it to a nearby Dumpster. After we finished with that job, we'd clean the roof up, pulling out the exposed roofing nails, or else pound them down good and clean. Next we would install the edge iron along the eve, put down the roofing felt, and lay the new shingles. G.T. said he would be ordering materials and meeting with potential customers today, but he would stop back by later.

The house was near the high school, in a neighborhood of brick ranch houses built in the 1950s. Carlos was already there, up on the roof tearing off the shingles. I got a shingle scraper out of the back of his truck, and climbed up the ladder and got to work. I used the scraper to pry up the top layer of shingles. After I got them up, I took them to the edge of the roof and dropped them in a pile below. As usual, Carlos worked much faster than me, regardless of how hard I tried to keep up, and by mid-morning he had cleared the top layer of shingles off an area nearly twice as big as mine—basically, most of the other half of the house. By then we were both drenched with sweat.

I took salt pills and drank water, but the heat still beat me like a whip. Not only that, although I was wearing work gloves, I was already developing some blisters. We got all the shingles off after lunch, but there were still lots of little pieces stuck to the wood, and dozens of roofing nails that needed to be pulled up or pounded down. Carlos and I used a rip-claw hammer to yank out the nails, and we pulled up the remaining debris by hand. Then we used 8-penny nails to secure the roof sheathing boards to the rafters. We put the tar paper down to prevent leaks and we installed the edge iron along the eave. We nailed it down with galvanized roofing nails. Then we carried the new shingles up to the roof.

By the time Carlos dropped me off at home, I was flat-out exhausted from working all day in the sun. I felt too tired to even eat the supper G.T. had fixed. But I did eat it, anyway, then collapsed on my bed and took a two-hour nap.

After I woke up, I called LaFay, but her mom said she wasn't home. "Just tell her Jesse called," I said.

I was hoping LaFay would call me back when she got in. But I didn't hear from her. I wondered where she was, what she was doing.

The next day, Carlos and I finished up the house near the high school and started on another house, on Sonora Street, in the same neighborhood. Although Thursday was my regular day to do my community service, I didn't go to Havenwood. I didn't even call in to say I was not coming in. I was not ready to face Mr. Ebban again, not after the way I had cursed him and left him by the fountain. I didn't even know if he would want me back.

After supper, I got a phone call from Varden Story. I took the phone into my room to talk to him.

"Yo, Terrill," he said. "Where you been?"

"Working for my uncle—up on roofs in the blazing sun."

"What about your community service? Mr. Ebban ain't got nobody to read to him. You want him to find somebody else?"

"No. Didn't know if he wanted me to come back or not."

"He needs somebody to read to him. Either it's got to be you, or the judge will send somebody else over here. On that subject, seems like you got a bit of an obligation to come out here on a regular basis, don't you?"

"That's right, but like I said, I didn't know if he wanted me to come."

"He wants you to come. Durned if I know why. But he does. I'm just delivering the message."

"I'll be there Tuesday evening." I figured I would get G.T. to let me off early. Surely he would want me to do my community service.

"One more thing, Terrill."

"What's that?"

"The next time you get the urge to tote a piece in here, I want you to remember something Jesus said when he was way out there in the desert. He said, 'Get thee behind me Satan.' You need to practice those words. Cause if that shit happens again on my watch, I'm going to make a phone call and you'll be in the penitentiary so fast you'll feel like the human flash. You hear me?"

"I hear you."

"And don't be looking to get your piece back, either. I threw it way out in Indian Lake, down where that snapper lives."

"Varden . . ."

"What?"

"Thanks."

"See you Tuesday, and don't be late."

I hung up and sat on my bed. Ray Thorne must have followed Mr. Ebban and me down to the fountain and been watching us from behind the trees. He had evidently run inside and called the cops after he saw me give the gun to Mr. Ebban. But the old man had outfoxed him somehow—slipped the gun to Varden before the cops got there. I was touched and amazed by the way they had protected me. And ashamed of myself for thinking the old man had dropped a dime on me. One more way he was forever staying one step ahead of me. I could see now how much he cared about me—and I couldn't forgive myself for cursing him by the fountain.

Friday afternoon, when I got home from work, I called LaFay's number again. Her mom answered and said she wasn't in.

Ms. Roux said she would tell her I called. I thanked her politely and hung up, concerned that LaFay hadn't tried to call me back. I resisted my desire to call Terra or Snookie to find out where she was. I didn't want them or LaFay to think I was trying to hawk her, the way Tony Moran had done.

Ms. Roux will tell her I am trying to get in touch with her, I thought. And LaFay will call me back.

But LaFay didn't call me back.

The longer I went without hearing from her, the more worried I became. I tried to call her several times Saturday afternoon, but got no answer. I finally gave in and tried to call both Terra and Snookie, but they weren't home, either. G.T. had gone over to Rosalita's. I paced the floor in my bedroom, hurling darts at the target on the back of the door. Where the hell was LaFay? Why didn't she call?

I heard a car coming down the driveway. I looked out the window and saw Terra driving the blue Mercury. There was someone with her. LaFay! Now I would find out where she had been, why she hadn't returned my calls.

But when I went to the porch I saw that Snookie was in the passenger's seat. No sign of LaFay. Terra was wearing a Stetson, a big white thing with a fake rattlesnake band around it.

I figured they would have some news about LaFay, and it was all I could do to keep from asking them about her, but I didn't want them to know how worried I was, so I just kept silent on the subject, hoping they would mention her.

"Yo, Jesse, nice tan," Snookie said. "You 'bout brown as a Mexican."

"I'm burned, mostly."

"Looks nice to me. What's been going on? Heard you got busted."

"How'd you hear that?"

"Andre's brother saw Dopodja and Rizzo bust you from the window of the pizza parlor. We went by the next day and saw the Dodge still parked there. It was gone that night. We figured your uncle got it."

"Yeah, he got it."

"When did you get out?"

"Been out."

"I know that. Seen you over by the high school working up on the roof with your uncle."

"G.T. has got me on a ball and chain. Got to earn my keep."

"Sure beats the jailhouse. We heard you were going to pull some serious time."

"For what? I didn't do anything. They only held me one night."

"Heard you got caught with a gun."

"Who told you that?"

"Bone's mom has a cousin that works out at Havenwood. Cousin told Ms. Selig and she told Bone. Funny how news gets around, huh?"

"Yeah, but you know it was a case of mistaken identity."

Terra said, "Is that right?"

"Do I look like a gunslinger?"

"You don't need to be caught with a gun, Jesse."

"It was just a big mix-up. Everything is cool now. You all want something cold to drink?"

They both declined my offer. Said they just finished drinking lemonade.

Just then Amos came strutting around the corner of the house. He hopped up on the porch and spread out his tail. The girls cooed at him. Terra scratched his head. I couldn't stand it anymore, so I asked Terra if she had seen LaFay. She shook her head, avoiding my eyes.

I said, "What's going on with her?"

"LaFay is gone," Snookie said.

"Gone? Where?"

"On her way to St. Thomas."

"St. Thomas?" I glanced at Terra. She was still looking at Amos.

"Yeah, down in the Caribbean."

"What's she going there for?"

"Does she need a reason? What the hell she's got going for her here, in Pottstown?"

"When is she coming back?" I asked, ignoring Snookie's diss.

She shrugged, then dropped an envelope in my lap. "Your sweetheart left you this."

It was a sealed envelope with my name on the front. I didn't open it. I was trying to maintain some kind of dignity, being that I knew the girls would analyze how I reacted and discuss it later. I gave them both a little smile, but I felt like a man in one of those crazy paintings where nothing is the right proportion to anything else. The nose cockeyed, the eyes too small, the mouth in the wrong place, the face in the shape of an egg. Why did LaFay leave? Why didn't she tell me goodbye? Terra scratched Amos's head a minute longer, then she said she had to be going. "What's your hurry?" I asked, still trying to put on a show of nonchalance.

"We'll let you read your letter," she said.

"So long, Jesse," Snookie said. She gave me a little smile over her shoulder.

I waited until the car turned onto Rose of Sharon Road before I opened the letter.

> *Dear Jesse,*
>
> *I am sorry I didn't get a chance to tell you goodbye, but it was just easier this way for me. I hate to leave you right now. I don't expect you to agree with my reasons, but I hope you can understand why.*
>
> *My Aunt Annette (my mother's sister) is a travel agent, and she has gotten me a job for the summer and fall on a cruise ship. The job pays very well, but, even more important, it will give me the chance to look for my father. The ship will not only have lots of different passengers from all over the country, it will also stop at places all through the Caribbean and in Mexico. If I keep this job through the fall and winter, I will lose a year in school. I thought about this a lot, and decided that it was worth it to me, at least at this time in my life. I can always make up the year later.*
>
> *I don't know if I will come back to Pottstown or not, but if I do and you are still around, I would like for you to keep the door open for us, but I will understand if you don't.*
>
> *You are a fine and decent person, Jesse, and I already miss you—your eyes, your voice, and the way you make me feel when you touch me. Please try to understand how and why I need to take this step at this time in my life. (Even if I don't find him, I won't have to look back years later and say I never tried.)*
>
> *I am enclosing an address where you can write me. It's a PO Box in New Orleans.*
>
> *All my love, LaFay*

I had a sudden urge to cry, but I held the tears in. What good would they do? I was angry at myself for not seeing this coming. I sat on the porch a while, in a kind of daze, rereading her letter a couple of times. Then I went into the house to see if I could find the whiskey bottle G.T. broke out sometimes when Buddy McBane came over.

G.T. would be pissed if he caught me drinking his whiskey, but I was knocked down too far to care. Maybe he would just decide to send me up to Aunt Lynette's to live—and I could just leave this city and everything in it in a big, fat cloud of dust.

Chapter 29

LaFay is standing at the prow of a ship out on the sea, her head back, the wind blowing her hair away from her face. I move through the crowded ship, trying to get to her, but by the time I reach the bow, she is gone. I wander the ship's decks and passages, searching for her, describing her to strangers and asking if they have seen her. A man laughs and says, "No, and I'm not looking for her, either." As he turns away I see a tattoo on his arm—an image of a black cat with ruby-colored eyes. I chase him and try to grab him, but he slips away and dives into the sea. "Man overboard!" someone cries. But he is no longer a man. He has changed into a dolphin.

Early Monday morning, Carlos and I began working on the roof of the house on Sonora Street. We installed the new edge iron along the eaves, finished the flashing around the roof penetrations, and stapled down the tarpaper. All morning I worked at a frenzied pace, without talking much. After I passed up the opportunity for a snack, Carlos asked me what was wrong.

"Just thinking about a dream," I said.

He smiled, flashing his gold tooth. "*Un sueno de la muchacha?*"

"How did you know?"

He shrugged, smiled.

"She is gone, no?"

I nodded, and he said something in Spanish. I asked him to translate. He meditated awhile and then said, "Sometimes you have to lose your love in order to find it."

I puzzled over this comment the rest of the morning. What the hell did he mean? How could I find LaFay again after losing her? Was he even talking about her? I finally decided I was spending too much time worrying over Carlos's comment. Should have just told him not to look for a bright future in dream interpretation.

By noon, we had all the tarpaper down. After a one-hour siesta in the shade of a magnolia tree in the yard, we began installing the shingles, fixing them to the roof with hand-driven roofing nails. Doing it this way takes a lot longer than when you use a pneumatic nailer, but G.T. says you do a better job nailing them by hand. With the pneumatic nailer the nails can enter the roof at an angle and damage the shingles.

The sun blazed overhead, burning my face, arms, and neck. Although I was soaked with sweat and my hands were blistered and torn, I was glad to have this hard physical work to do. It helped take my mind off LaFay.

A couple of hours before quitting time, G.T. came by the job site and told me he wanted me to knock off early. I gathered up my things and got into his truck. G.T. talked to Carlos a few minutes, then he returned to the truck and started up the engine. I saw Carlos going back up the ladder to the roof, a pack of shingles under his arm.

"Carlos still on the clock, huh?"

"Yes."

"How come you want me to quit and not him?"

"We're going to go talk to someone. I'm taking you home first so you can get cleaned up."

"Who we going to see?"

"J. W. Applewhite."

"The detective?"

"That's right. He wants to talk to us."

"What for?"

"I guess we'll find out when we get there."

G.T. had said "us" but I figured he really meant me. Why did that big detective want to see me? And why all the mystery? I didn't ask G.T. any more about it, though, mostly because I could tell it wouldn't do any good. He was still pissed at me about his gun. And who could blame him for that?

As I meditated on this issue, an ugly little hobgoblin of a thought paid me a visit: what if G.T. had told the cops about the missing gun and my thwarted plan to kill Steigner? My heart raced like the engine of a car floored in neutral. I had a sudden urge to jump out of his truck at the first stoplight. In an effort to calm myself down, I told myself that G.T. wouldn't betray me like that. We're blood kin, I thought. No way would he turn me into the law.

But I still couldn't shake my fear. I had developed this thing about cops. To me they were bogeymen who lurk in the shadows outside your window on those nights you are crazy with dread, when everything you see and hear is a prophecy of doom.

Back at our house, I took a shower and put on a clean, white shirt and khaki slacks. I came out of my room and saw G.T. in the recliner, jingling his truck keys.

"They going to bust me, G.T.?"

"What for? You done something wrong?"

"Cops make me nervous."

"I reckon they do." He raised his eyebrows and fixed me with a meaningful look. "Come on, we got to be there in twenty minutes."

"Where's 'there'?"

G.T. didn't answer.

I followed him out to his truck, my left eye twitching like I was a psycho in a slasher flick.

Mr. Applewhite worked out of the city's Second Precinct, a two-story brick building on East Main, several blocks west of the courthouse. He talked to G.T. and me in a room with *Criminal Investigations* in bold, black letters on the glass section of the door. There was a map of the city on the wall behind him. On his desk there was a computer, manila folders, a Carolina Panthers coffee mug full of pens and pencils, and a framed photo of a pretty woman standing between a boy and a girl. The woman had an arm around each child.

Although there were several other desks in the room, the only other occupant was a ruddy-faced man, seated at a desk directly across from us. Like Mr. Applewhite, he had a gold badge pinned to his belt.

I was relieved to find that Mr. Applewhite only wanted to talk to me about the men who had beat me up in the alley and dumped me in the landfill. He said they had "two suspects in custody."

When I asked him who they are, he said, "I'll get to that in a minute." He took a plastic bag out of his desk drawer and held it up to show me what was inside. "Do you recognize this?"

"Yes, sir. Looks like my good luck charm."

"I found it in the alley between Mercer and Isley, the day after you were attacked. It had a legible fingerprint on it. We were able to identify an individual through the print—a local ex-con named Marc K. Steigner with a long rap sheet. He's in custody now. We got the other assailant, too. Gerard L. Rudd. You recognize either one of these names?"

"No, sir."

"Are you sure?"

Realizing I had answered too quickly, I pretended to be turning these names over in my mind. My first thought was that I wouldn't be able to get to Steigner now. If he was in jail, how would I be able to kill him?

"Yes, sir, I'm sure," I said, trying my best to look sincere. "Did they confess?"

"Steigner stonewalled it at first. Came up with lie after lie, even after we confronted him with the evidence we had—the fingerprint on the charm left at the crime scene, the bloodstains in the van—A negative, which is your blood type—and a couple of your prints in there, too. After he got to thinking about it, and talked to his lawyer awhile, he finally decided he wanted to deal. He gave us Rudd, but he wouldn't give up the person who hired him, claimed it was somebody named 'Victor' he'd met in the bowling alley."

"Did you find out who it was?"

"We got the individual's name from Rudd. He said Antonio Moran paid them both a thousand dollars apiece for their night's dirty work. We picked Antonio up yesterday morning." Mr. Applewhite shook his head. "Two thousand dollars to get a young person kidnapped, beaten, and left for dead in a landfill."

"You could get it done for less than that," G.T. said.

"But then you get what you pay for. The real pros are in and out of town like a night wind. They don't leave a trace."

"Did Tony Moran want them to kill me?"

"He wanted them to hurt you bad, cripple you up. I don't think they were given a specific order to kill you, though. Boys must have gotten a little carried away with themselves. Hard to find good help these days."

I was beginning to like Mr. J. W. Applewhite. I looked at the photo of the woman and kids, figuring they were his family. I pictured all of them in their backyard, Mr. Applewhite barbecuing on the grill. He seemed like he was a decent man, even though he was a cop.

"You've done some good work," G.T. said. "We appreciate it."

"No need to thank me. I'm just doing my job. By the way, while you are here, there's another matter we need to discuss."

Uh oh, I thought. Here it is. I looked down at my palm, peeled away the skin around a broken blister.

Mr. Applewhite called to the man at the other desk. "Mr. Cotes, could you come over here, please."

The man got up and came over to Mr. Applewhite's desk. He pulled up a chair and sat down beside G.T.

G.T. and the detective shook hands, addressing each other by their first names. Seeing that they knew each other made me nervous—revived this crazy fear I had that G.T. was ratting me out.

Mr. Applewhite said, "Jesse, this is Detective Woody Cotes. He's our cold case specialist. He has some information for you and your uncle."

Although I nodded at Mr. Cotes, he gave me the same kind of heebie-jeebies I got around strange cops. I couldn't shake this idea that he had something on me.

But Detective Cotes wanted to talk to us about something else—his investigation of the attack on my daddy three years earlier. He said a witness had recently come forward with new information related to the case.

"We had a prime suspect early on. I wish we could have charged him with the crime, but the evidence just wasn't there."

"But you knew who did it?"

"We had a suspect is all. You can't convict someone on suspicion, though. We needed evidence."

"Who was your suspect?"

"The same one the witnesses implicated—Wallace Rankin. That was his type of crime and his territory, only he'd never hurt anybody that bad. But Rankin had a grudge against Mr. Terrill. Rankin was a part-time house painter and he had done some work for a friend of your father's, a man named Harlan. Harlan accused Rankin of stealing some money out of his house. Rankin swore he never set foot in the house. When the case went to trial, your dad testified on behalf of Harlan, said he'd seen Rankin in the house the day the money went missing. A month or so before your father was hurt, he and Rankin had words over his testimony, an argument in a restaurant that nearly ended in a fight. The way we figure it, Rankin had a clear motive to hurt your father. He knew Glenn Terrill, knew his habits. He waited until he saw his opportunity, and he struck."

Wallace Rankin—where had I heard that name? Suddenly, I remembered: the woman at Wolf Creek Properties had said the house on South Rhodes Street had been rented to Wallace Rankin. He skipped out owing them rent. Steigner and Wallace Rankin must have shared the house.

"How do you know it was him? How can you be so sure? Did he confess?"

"He's not going to confess now."

"Why not?" I can make him confess, I thought.

"Wallace Rankin was in a head-on collision out on the bypass earlier this year. His first week out of prison. He suffered brain damage, and he's been in a coma ever since. Doctors don't expect him to live much longer."

I looked at Mr. Cotes, trying to take all of this new information in, trying to make sense out of it.

"How do you know he's the man that mugged my daddy? How can you be sure?"

"Luanne Jarvis, his girlfriend at the time, told us that Rankin had Glenn Terrill's wallet the night your father was attacked. She swears she saw Mr. Terrill's driver's license in the wallet, and she saw Rankin throw the wallet in a dumpster."

"Couldn't he have gotten the wallet from someone else?"

"Yes, but Rankin had blood on his clothes that night. His girlfriend remembers that clearly. He had the wallet. He had the motive. He had committed similar crimes in that same neighborhood. That's strong, incriminating evidence, Jesse."

"Why is his ex-girlfriend coming forward just now with this information?"

"She's trying to turn her life around. I believe she just wants to clear her conscience and get right with God. All things considered, that's not such a bad idea."

"Amen," said J. W. Applewhite.

I was having trouble accepting this—that the mugger who had caused my daddy and me such grief wasn't the backlit devil man in my dream with his face in shadow. Still, I had to admit the story made sense. I remembered my daddy taking some time off from work once to testify in a trial involving one of his friends. "How do you know it wasn't somebody else—this Steigner, for instance?"

"We already checked into that possibility, since the two men knew each other. Steigner was in jail down in Lurie the night your daddy was mugged. DUI."

I looked down at the gold triangles in the tile floor. The full meaning of what they were saying hit me like a piano falling out of a clear blue sky: *I was going to kill the wrong man.*

"Jesse, I wish I could tell you that we arrested him and prosecuted him for that crime," Mr. Cotes said, "but we didn't. That happens sometimes. It's one of the toughest challenges we have to face in this job—seeing the guilty either walk or escape justice. But I did want you and your family to know about this new evidence, in the hope it could bring you some degree of closure."

"Thanks for letting us know, Woody," G.T. said. "This sure will ease our minds some."

But my mind was not eased exactly. I felt like I had been lost in a hall of mirrors. I believed I had all of the facts I needed to get revenge on the man who hurt my daddy. How could I have been so wrong?

G.T. was telling Mr. Applewhite about my daddy, how we visited him in St. Aubin Hospital, but I had slipped down into the dark well of myself, and I was not paying attention. Steigner must have learned about the mugging from Rankin, and he wanted to use that information to hurt me more when he was stomping me in the alley. I was amazed by how close that act of cruelty had come to costing him his life. For I surely would have killed him if Mr. Mendel Ebban hadn't taken the gun from me. I recalled the expression on Mr. Ebban's face when I cursed him by the fountain. Not hurt exactly; it was more a look of calm determination, like he was willing to take whatever meanness I could throw at him as long as he could get that gun away from me. He was trying to save my miserable soul. One more way that he had always been one jump ahead of me, ever since the first day I met him.

Mr. Applewhite told me I would have to be ready to testify in court.

"How about Moran—did he confess?"

"Not yet. So far he's refused to talk at all. But considering the evidence against Mr. Moran, he's not holding a very good hand."

Detective Cotes said, "Ike Moran will pull every string he can to keep his son out of prison. He'll have the best lawyers available."

"And we're going to apply ourselves faithfully and diligently to the task of seeing that he is sent there." Mr. Applewhite held up the evidence bag containing my four-leafed clover charm. "Your lucky charm worked pretty good, Jesse. Like to have one like this myself."

As G.T. and the detective discussed a time for us to meet again, I marveled at how much good fortune Mr. Ebban had brought me. First, he had kept me from going to Sheridan, since Judge Simms had decided being around him would benefit me more than making license plates for the state. Then he had saved my life by sending Varden out to find me in that landfill. And, finally, he had prevented me from killing the wrong man—a murder that would have surely damned my soul. I wondered how I could ever thank Mr. Mendel Ebban.

I didn't even know how to begin.

I would like to have taken him a gift, but I knew I had nothing of value to give him. I hadn't even gotten my first paycheck from G.T. yet. After meditating on this dilemma awhile, I finally decided to take him my best three peacock feathers. I figured they would brighten up his room. I didn't know whether he would want them or not, but they were the only thing I could think of that he might like. I guess I was thinking of his story about the birds and the time he lived in the forest.

I got to Havenwood late Tuesday afternoon. Rhonda, the front desk attendant, was talking on the phone and filing her nails, a sure sign Ms. Lynch wasn't around. She didn't pay me any attention as I signed in—she was talking about a new guy she was dating. I went on through the front lobby. The attendants were pushing their metal carts through the wings, picking up the trays and dishes from the rooms of the residents who had eaten there instead of the dining room.

I had Amos's tail feathers wrapped up in newspaper, to protect them from damage. Although I was flat-out beat from working all day in the hot sun, I was looking forward to giving these feathers to Mr. Ebban. I still didn't have a clear idea of what I would say to him.

As I walked down the hall toward his room, I saw Varden talking to a woman in a wheelchair at the end of the hall.

No sign of Ray Thorne yet. I was thankful for that.

Mr. Ebban's door was partially open. I knocked once, then went in.

He was not in the room, but the bathroom door was shut. I guessed he was in there. The late day's sunlight coming through the window lit up a rectangular section of the wall above his bed. Dust motes whirled in the light. His prayer shawl was folded up neatly at the foot of his bed. I sat in the windowsill and waited for him to come out of the bathroom. I didn't know how I was going to thank him. G.T. said I was good with words, but I was worried they would fail me now. All I had to give Mr. Ebban were these peacock feathers. I figured that was a beginning. I hoped the right words would come to me when I saw him and gave him the feathers.

I would like to take him for a ride one day, out to my old house on Cotton Gin Road. I wanted to show him the house, the grape arbor, and the tree house Lee and I used to sleep in. He would probably like that. I could ask Ms. Lynch for permission to take him there. She might allow it, if Varden came along, too.

Varden appeared in the doorway, as if he had been conjured up by my dreamy thoughts. He didn't look well.

"Yo, Terrill. What you got all rolled up in that newspaper?"

"Feathers."

"What you got feathers for?"

I opened up the newspaper, showed him the peacock feathers. "They're for Mr. Ebban. A gift. You got something I can put them in?"

"You can't give him those feathers now."

"Why, you all got some kind of rule against feathers?"

Varden flinched, like something had just flown by his face. "He's gone."

"Gone? Where?"

"Mr. Ebban died last night."

"What?" Everything went out of focus except Varden's face.

"They found him this morning. He was right there on his bed, eyes closed, hands folded. Like he was waiting for the angels to come. Heart must have gave out on him sometime during the night."

A sudden pressure filled my chest. I was having trouble getting my breath. "I—I wanted to tell him I'm sorry."

"Too late for that."

I remembered the way he looked at me the last time I saw him by the fountain, after I had cursed him. "He looked up at the sky," I said, not even realizing Varden wouldn't know what I was talking about. "Just for a second or two. Then he looked back at me." I looked down at the peacock feathers in my lap. "I wanted to thank him. I just wanted to say 'thank you.'"

"You know that old man loved you, Jesse," Varden said.

I put my face in my hands. The noises of the nursing home—the squeaking of the wheels on an attendant's food cart, the rattling walkers, the distant voices—all sounded muffled, as if I was under water. I felt as if the whole world had been disassembled and been put back together all wrong, with missing pieces and edges that didn't line up right.

When I looked up, Varden was gone.

I stood up and placed the peacock feathers on the stand beside Mr. Ebban's bed. I looked at a slice of orange peel on the stand. His Star of David on the wall. His ram's horn hanging by the leather strap on the bedpost. His record player on the stand in the corner. His leather boxes and Bibles on the bookshelf, along with the faded, yellowed photographs of his lost family members. His presence was so strong in this room that it was as if he was still here.

I picked up his Torah and sat in my regular place in the window-sill, drawing comfort from the book's familiar scent of leather and old paper. I pictured his face, his tangled eyebrows, his shrewd black eyes, the satellite dish ears full of white hair. I remembered the way he would

sometimes pray in Hebrew, the words sounding more like an incanta-
tion than a prayer. I wanted to pretend for a while that he was still here.
I closed my eyes and imagined that he was taking a nap in his wheelchair
and that he would wake up soon and ask me to read to him again—from
Devarin, Vayikra, or Shemot. I gazed out the window awhile. The sun
was setting and the swirl of red-tinted clouds reminded me of the design
of a peacock's feather. Resting my head against the ledge, I drifted off
somewhere and when I looked again the three-quarter moon was up, and
the stars were shining. And then, half-asleep, I was back in the tree house,
listening to my brother tell me how old-time sailors used the stars to find
their way when they were lost at sea. He was pointing out Pegasus when
I felt a hand on my shoulder. For a brief, dreamed moment, I thought it
was my daddy, but then I saw it was Varden, who had come to tell me it
was time to go home.

Chapter 30

I was nearly to my truck in the parking lot, moving in a kind of daze, when I turned around and went back into Havenwood to find Varden.

I met him coming around the corner from the east wing.

"Getting past your curfew, ain't it?" he said.

"Where did they take him?"

"What you want to know that for?"

"I've got to know where he is, Varden."

"Ain't but one Jewish funeral home in the city. That's where he'll be. It's west of the Catholic Hospital, corner of Vessy and Dexter."

"Would it still be open?"

"Don't know about that. They'll get him buried quick, though. Jews don't believe in embalming and drawn-out funerals. They have certain rituals about washing and preparing the body."

"It's probably closed by now."

"No, somebody will be there."

"How do you know?"

"'Cause they don't ever leave a dead person alone, not until the burial. Somebody's got to be sitting up with the person till his time comes round to go back to the earth. There will be at least one person there, 'a guardian' I think he's called. Reads him psalms and keeps him company. What you got to be busting your curfew to go out there for?"

"I got to tell Mr. Ebban something. Look, if G.T. calls out here, don't tell him where I went, OK? Just tell him I said I'd be home late and not to worry."

Varden nodded. He held his hand out to me, and I took it, put my other hand over his, too, and he brought his other hand up so that both of our hands were touching. "You best stay under the speed limit, Jesse."

Varden had a tired, hurt look in his eyes, and I could tell he was grieving, too.

The Jewish funeral parlor was on the corner of Vessy and Dexter, like Varden had said. There was a light on in one of the front rooms. I could see it through the window to the left of the door. I parked the Dodge in the street and went up on the porch. I looked through the window. I could see a man with his back to me, sitting in a chair beside a coffin.

I went to the front door and knocked. The front door had these words printed on them:

Chevra Kadisha Mortuary
Tahara performed with reverence,
care and respect for the dead.

I knocked again. When no one answered, I opened the door and stepped into a hallway. I turned left toward the lighted room. The floorboards creaked as I entered

The man sitting in the chair by the coffin looked up at me. He had on a black skullcap and wire-rimmed reading glasses on a chain around his neck. He had a prayer book in his lap, and there was a long-necked floor lamp beside him, but it was turned off. He gave me a long, questioning look, like he was trying to place me. His eyes were wide and solemn.

"I'm Jesse," I said. "Mr. Ebban's assistant at the nursing home. I wanted to sit here with him for a while, if you don't mind."

He nodded and pointed to several chairs against the far wall. I got one and set it down near Mr. Ebban's head, so that I was on the opposite side of the coffin from the guardian.

Mr. Ebban lay in the coffin with his arms at his sides, the palms turned up. He had a linen shroud over his head, his prayer shawl around his shoulders. His few tufts of hair, along with his eyebrows, had been neatly combed. His face, so still and colorless, looked like a mask made from his real face.

I could smell the pine coffin and the fresh, clean scent of the linen.

The man turned on the reading lamp, put on his glasses, and began reading psalms in Hebrew. Sometimes he chanted them, other times he seemed to sing them. He continued for fifteen minutes or so and then stopped. I knew I couldn't say what I wanted to say to Mr. Ebban with anyone else around, so I decided to wait until the man went to the bathroom or took a break. I figured he would have to do that sometime before the night was over.

But he didn't leave the room. Not once. Not once the whole night. He just read and chanted the psalms every so often. After a while I could tell he was doing this at regular intervals.

During the times he was silent, I was conscious of every move he made, every sound, every cough; but from the beginning of our shared vigil until the sun came up neither of us said another word to the other.

It didn't really bother me that we weren't speaking; I didn't have anything to say to him, and anyway, I was glad he let me have that time with Mr. Ebban. I spent awhile remembering things about him—like the first time I met him, the way he had been listening to that ghost music on his antique phonograph. He told me everything in the earth came from dead stars and that they had only been here since time began. I thought of the way he used to offer me pennies to make a wish in the fountain in the park, and I thought about him as a child in that lost world he had known in Poland, where he had learned to be a Jew, where his beliefs and his faith had become a part of his whole being. I thought of the way he had sent me out to rescue the snapping turtle that day on Mauphin Road. And the way he would bless rainbows and thunder. And that time he gave me the spirit level by the fountain. I must have dozed off half a dozen times during the night, but I woke up every time the guardian began chanting the psalms. When the sun came up, he looked at me and said, "I need to use the bathroom. You will wait here until I return?"

"Yes," I said.

He stood up then, and, taking his prayer book with him, he left the room. I could hear his footsteps in the hallway. I heard a door open, close.

A bar of sunlight from the window lay across Mr. Ebban's coffin, turning the section it touched gold. I could hear the birds singing outside.

I stood up and leaned over the coffin, and I told Mr. Ebban I was sorry for what I had said to him by the fountain. "I want to thank you for caring about me and trying to straighten out my life," I said. I was trying to tell him goodbye and that I would miss him, when the tears started falling. I couldn't stop them. And that was the way the guardian found me when he came back—standing over Mr. Ebban's coffin, wiping the tears and snot from my face with my sleeve.

He took a handkerchief from his pocket and offered it to me. I shook my head, but he continued holding it out to me—long enough for it to become a test of wills. I finally took the handkerchief, and as I touched it I felt my hand brush his. I wondered if he had gone to the B'nai Shalom Temple with Mr. Ebban and if he knew who I was.

I wiped my tears away with his handkerchief. The man sat down and began chanting another prayer in Hebrew. I closed my eyes and listened. I remembered Varden saying Mr. Ebban had loved me. I wondered what he possibly could have seen in me that was worthy of love. My eyes were still closed. Perhaps that is why I fell under the spell of the guardian's chant. I realized I was humming the simple melody, in perfect time with him. As our voices blended together, I began to feel the spirit of that ancient psalm, although the words themselves remained a pure mystery.